STROKE OF OBSESSION

LILAH LANCE

TITAN SECURITY BOOK V

To finding your voice in a sea of doubt

AUTHORS NOTE

Welcome to the fifth installment of the *Titan Security* series.

Each book in the series has its own standalone HEA (Happily Ever After), but they're all connected by a *larger* mystery.

The stories in Titan occur simultaneously, with Easter eggs and clues scattered throughout to help you uncover the full picture.

While this book can be enjoyed on its own, it is recommended starting with the earlier books to avoid spoilers or to gain a deeper understanding of the evolving mysteries within Titan.

This book is split into two timelines.

The first part happens **before** the events of Stroke of Luck Book I.

Gemma and Nathan's journey continues in Part II, expanding during the events of all of the other *four* books before them.

As always on your assignment, remember that appearances can be deceiving, and things are not always what they seem on the surface.

MISSION BRIEFING

Welcome to Titan

You are now a part of a team of security professionals working on saving face, saving lives, and sometimes saving their enemies.

Your objective, if you choose to accept it, is a **reckoning with your past.**

Your team consists of:

Agent Nathan Wyatt & Miss Gemma Marchand

This will be your last mission with a team.

Pay attention.

Don't get too obsessed with Nate and Gemma.

PART I

SEVEN YEARS AGO

ONE
GEMMA

"His name is Nathan Wyatt. He is your chaperone for the summer."

Those were the first words out of Nigel's mouth.

Nigel had been the family butler for years.

And the wheels of our private jet hadn't even scraped the concrete when he admitted I would have a chaperone for my holiday.

"Nigel, why did I need a chaperone? I'm not a child."

Nigel's lips curved into a smile, his blue eyes glinting with a mix of fondness and amusement behind his wire-rimmed glasses.

"Miss Gemma," he began, his British accent crisp. "While you may not be a child, you are still the daughter of the Marchand family. And as such, certain...precautions are necessary."

At nineteen, I had just graduated from high school.

This summer in Capri was meant to be my reward.

A chance to relax before plunging into the demands of university life. A chance to just breathe.

Not suffocate under the watchful eye of a chaperone out of all things.

I resisted the urge to growl frustrated by Nathan Wyatt, and I hadn't even met him yet.

Breathe. Perhaps he's halfway decent.

"Nigel, you know as well as I do that I have earned this time to

1

myself. I have worked hard for years. And now, when I finally have a moment to breathe, to *enjoy* my gap year, I am saddled with a babysitter?"

I sighed, thinking of my father. *What was he thinking?*

Gerard Marchand, businessman and a *Lord*.

Well, *former*.

My father had left his entire world behind when he'd met *Maman*, Jacqueline, a model and artist of all sorts and they'd had this whirlwind romance having me.

It hadn't worked out when I was young and I spent much of my life back and forth with *Maman* and Papa trading until *the incident* when I had been a child had stopped her from seeing me.

I hadn't really been in touch with her save for holidays and lots of presents from her. Like she felt guilty.

Like she wanted to see me but couldn't deal with Papa's overbearing family.

Neither had ever remarried until recently when Papa got engaged to a woman named Camilla Delacroix.

Papa shared the news of missing my graduation. And while I was happy for him, I didn't know Camilla at all.

"Your father may feel a bit guilty for leaving you alone while he travels the world with his—"

"Have you met Camilla, Nigel?"

Nigel's gaze flickered away. "Yes, I have, Miss Gemma."

"And?"

I'd known Nigel most of my life, and even with our occasional separations, I could always tell when he was hiding something from me.

He couldn't keep secrets for long.

"I would rather you form your own opinion on such matters, Miss Gemma," he replied diplomatically.

So Camilla was awful.

I didn't say anything else, knowing Nigel wasn't one to gossip.

Instead, I returned to the pressing matter at hand—Mr. Nathan Wyatt.

"But isn't staying at our family villa enough? Must I also have a shadow following my every move? This is supposed to be my summer of freedom, Nigel. How can I experience that with someone constantly watching over me?"

"Between you and me, I think your father worries more than he lets on. Can't say I blame him, given how headstrong you are."

Realizing I was stuck with my chaperone whether I liked it or not? I asked Nigel. "Is Bonnie here?" And immediately grinned at his squirming.

Nigel's not-so-secret crush on Bonnie was evident to anyone who observed them together.

"Ah, yes," Nigel replied, clearing his throat flushing two shades of red deeper. "Miss Bonnie arrived earlier this week. She's been busy getting your room ready and preparing a rather spectacular feast. I'm sure Bonnie will be delighted to see you."

Bonnie and Nigel were a duo made in Heaven.

While she looked out for the household affairs, Nigel often took care of everything else.

And the two of them had been more familiar to me sometimes than Papa.

I smoothed my hand over my custom-made Davina&Co dress in a shade of lilac so pale, I felt like a goddess, as the sun beat down on my legs.

The scent of grapefruits and lemons filled the air, a nostalgic aroma I had missed during my time at school across the States and Europe. I loved being out here.

It reminded me of better days. Capri was my favorite place in the world.

Summers spent here when Maman would visit, when Papa's family wasn't around—just the three of us.

It was pure bliss.

Before I was aware of the ninety nuances of being a Marchand.

Before I knew the pressure of being my father's daughter.

Before I had ninety social calls to make, designer gowns to try, and my senses bombarded with fake people.

I missed my normal life with Maman and Papa running around Capri.

I hated any other aspect of my life.

School had been a nightmare in study since I didn't exactly fit in. I had friends—sure—but I didn't connect with anyone.

Girls in my school were competitive. Who was prettier, nicer dressed, better hair, the latest salon, the latest manicure, and so on and so forth.

It became exhausting to *compete* when I didn't understand *what* women were competing for.

Was there an enormous unicorn at the other end of the tunnel with barrels of lip gloss and endless amounts of chocolate waiting for me if I beat every single woman in the competition of life?

Did I win a prize for being nasty?

What was that prize?

The affections of a man who looked like a toad?

What did I get as a woman if I was fake?

Besides a headache?

It felt like everything in my class was a competition.

Every. Single. Thing.

It felt like a lie.

This existence feels like a lie. A lie sold to me...like a really bad piece of furniture. Low quality.

Or someone in school was trying to weasel their way into my life and hurt me for that invisible competition we were in.

I didn't understand what everyone was competing for.

Wasn't there enough to go around?

Why were people trying to hoard it all?

And I didn't want to exist around it.

I had just wanted to go to school.

Not...whatever the heck women believed in doing to each other.

Exhausting.

It was soul sucking.

Being the perfect marionette doll waiting to be retired into the chest I came out of.

I wore my mask and pretended to be Gemma *Marchand.*

Smiling for people who didn't care.

Participating in things I didn't want to boost my own resume for life. It was just what was done—and I was beginning to crave something else.

But I just wanted to be Gemma.

Without a Marchand attached to the name.

When I came here?

I fell back in love with myself.

I liked who I was here on an island where despite people who did know me? I calmed down.

I didn't have to surround myself around anyone else but the people I loved and I felt at home on this island.

Not trying to size down to a corset I didn't fit in but able to just breathe.

Maybe meet someone and have a summer fling.

That would be nice.

A cute boy. On the beach?

Wow.

Romantic notions of love were not the Marchand way. Most of us married for duty or obligation to another family.

My cousins and I had always known this, but that didn't mean I wasn't allowed to have some fun.

Nathan Wyatt, you better watch out.

"I shall pay Miss Bonnie a visit once you meet Mr. Wyatt."

"Ah, yes, the dashing Mr. Wyatt. Have you met him already?"

"Indeed, Miss Gemma, I interviewed him after your father heard good things about him…"

As Nigel began listing all of Nathan Wyatt's accomplishments and his former military background, my mind drifted, taking in the familiar surroundings of Capri.

"Besides, someone needs to keep you out of trouble."

"Don't think for a moment that I shall make it easy for Mr. Wyatt."

"I wouldn't dream of it, Miss Gemma." Nigel motioned to a man who stood up to face us from his chair. "This is Mr. Nathan Wyatt."

My heart sputtered in my chest as I saw who Mr. Nathan Wyatt was.

His eyes met mine first, a striking navy blue, deeper than the ocean at twilight. His features were rugged, his jawline sharp, and his golden hair tousled by the breeze.

Mon. Dieu.

This is Nathan Wyatt?

This must be a joke.

5

He had to be in his mid-twenties standing at a solid six-two, maybe three. I didn't know, I just knew he was taller than me and I was five-eight.

How much of a difference was that?

His smile was easy as he looked at me, his eyebrows rising in a way that made my stomach not just flip but gallop like I had just run a mile. Or two. Or several.

He was attractive. Downright attractive.

He held out his hand. "Name's Nate Wyatt. I'll be your guard this summer. A pleasure to meet you."

Non, no the pleasure is all mine, I assure you.

Mon Dieu.

American.

From the south. That *voice...*

"Right," I took his hand, and I caught the faint hint of a smirk on Nathan Wyatt's features, which I bristled at a tiny bit.

Who did he think he was? Showing up like this?

Like some attractive sun God looking ravishing—

Focus.

"Pleasure to meet you, Mr. Wyatt."

I was not imagining his smirk growing. "How was your flight?"

Acutely aware now that I looked a mess, likely wrinkled dress from my flight I looked at Nigel.

I cleared my throat. "Nigel, might I have a word—"

"Naturally, Miss Gemma," Nigel hid his smile. But I caught it. I ignored the amused smirk on Nathan Wyatt's face. Or how handsome he looked with that disheveled blonde.

"Oh mon Dieu, Nigel."

"I'm afraid so, Miss Gemma—"

"This cannot be—"

"Yes, Miss Gemma—"

"Where is he from again?"

"Texas." The deep baritone voice from behind me sent a chill down my spine and I froze. I just stopped moving.

Nigel stopped breathing next to me.

Oh.

I turned over my shoulder to find the curtains blowing in and still standing there with an easy smile on his face that would qualify as a smirk—Nathan grinned at us.

No man should ever be that attractive.

He needs to be illegal.

Jailed.

Guilty for being handsome.

Straight back to America with him.

This was my chaperone?

"Apologies, with the windows open, the breeze carries your voice," Nathan tapped a finger to his ear. "I've got solid hearing."

"Mr. Wyatt was in the service, Miss Gemma," Nigel added. "He is rather competent at his job."

I didn't doubt that.

Is he competent with women?

I volunteer—

"Miss Marchand, would you like a moment to speak with Mr. Wyatt about your security measures while I grab you both refreshments?"

Yes. I'll take some rum. On the rocks.

Never mind. Just bring the entire bottle of rum.

I looked at the other man taking me in his navy blues absorbing all of me. Blonde. Beautiful. Handsome in a way that shouldn't be allowed in reality.

Mon.

Dieu.

I'm in trouble.

"Yes, Nigel. That sounds lovely. Mr. Wyatt, shall we?"

TWO
NATE

Security gigs were shit.

They weren't a cakewalk.

Most of the time, some spoiled rich kid with daddy's money?

I knew the drill. I got it. Trouble. *Disaster*.

Tanking daddy's yacht because you took in too much cocaine? Done.

Begging him for money in Paris because you couldn't afford to pay your dates dinner for forty grand plus tip? Done.

Catching one of them with his pants down and his soon-to-be sister-in-law going down on him? With her sister?

Done.

I had seen it all.

After four years in the service and bouncing between contracting gigs for various three-letter agencies, I figured this one was just another just.

I'd gotten out thanks to the shit pay, the fake sons of a bitches trying to ruin my life every step of the way, and the fact that what I thought it was going to be?

Wasn't it at all.

And now? I was cruising.

Easy money for a last-minute job, protecting a nineteen-year-old at her parents' vacation home for the summer.

8

How hard could it be?

Gerard Marchand, some big shot businessman, was worried about his daughter's safety over some attempted break in at his ex-wife's apartment in Paris.

Now, with Gemma in Capri after high school, he didn't want anything to happen to her.

With him remarrying and going on his honeymoon, he wanted extra security for his precious daughter.

That's where I came in, recommended by a friend of a friend.

Another contracting gig, but I was damn good at what I did.

On a fucking vacation island, guarding another princess.

Just my luck.

I waited in the villa's living area with Nigel, the family's long-time driver and head of household staff.

He'd filled me in on some of the details while we waited for Miss Marchand to arrive from the airport in her private jet.

Because, of course, they had a butler. In a villa worth millions.

The royal purple Marchand logo with a fleur-de-lis behind it was a mark of them being descended from fucking royalty once.

The Marchand's now had two sons. One was a Duke.

And the other? Was *Gerard* Marchand—which technically made Gemma related to *royalty*.

Technically.

Gerard I was sure got married to some American actress and as a French national—it had caused an uproar. Gemma had been the only good thing to come out of it.

But they no longer had a title. Her mother was somewhere in Paris. Gemma lived with her father. Sort of.

So yeah, it was a big gig. Now? I was in her villa.

One of maybe twenty-seven they owned. Twenty-fucking-seven properties.

For shits and giggles.

The entire family was loaded, drowning in the kind of old money that could make anything happen.

Drowning in it.

Something I wasn't.

Old money, my boss called it. The kind of wealth that could move mountains and bend reality to its will. Gemma could snap her fucking manicured fingers and I'd go right back to bumfuck, Texas.

It was completely over my head and this was something totally different for me.

This client was just one of many members of the Marchand family, but I knew enough about her from the photos and intel I'd been given.

Private schools, polo matches, equestrian on the side, and a part-time modeling gig for jewelry brands and swimwear—copy pasted straight from every rich girl's bible.

Right?

Wrong.

Gemma Aurelia Valois Marchand.

Was.

Gorgeous.

I waited quietly, scrolling through my phone, all too aware that I was in over my head. If anything happened to Gemma, my career would be on the line.

She might've been the highest profile gig I'd had at this age.

And I intended on sticking to my rules about this.

When I'd arrived, Nigel had parked in an enormous garage housing multiple million-dollar cars. On an island.

Gerard, Gemma's father, had them shipped for fun if he wanted to visit Monaco, and he'd buy new ones on a whim.

His words, not mine.

Nigel, had filled me in on everyone in the house.

I had met Bonnie, a petite middle-aged brunette woman with warm eyes who insisted on feeding me the moment I walked in.

This place was a dream, a far cry from anything I'd ever experienced.

No, my parents raised me in a double wide trailer in bumfuck, Texas.

This?

This was the kind of home my Mama talked about from her magazines. Not reality for me. Never for me.

And if I wasn't already out of place enough?

She walked into the room, and I felt my heart do a backflip.

A vision, at about five-eight, all long, sun-kissed legs and curves in all the right places.

Golden hair cascaded over her shoulders, framing a face that had clearly graced the pages of magazines.

Gemma Marchand was a Renaissance painting come to life.

The kind you saw at expensive museums where artwork had guards around it.

Except I was the one that was supposed to guard said artwork.

High cheekbones where the light cut into it like crystal, eyes shifting between blue and gray into opal. Opal, like the prettiest of sea glass. She looked like a regal mermaid queen come to life. Cupids bow lips. Lashes fanning out over her cheeks.

Lilac dress. A fucking vision.

Easy, Wyatt. She's your new job.

Just another princess on an island full of millionaires and billionaires.

I stood up, plastering on my best professional smile and hoping my voice wouldn't betray the effect she had on me.

But there was no mistaking the way she fidgeted under my gaze, a pretty blush creeping up her neck.

She's a job.

Breathe.

Prim and proper Gemma Marchand, affected by my presence?

I didn't doubt it for a second.

But this was my charge. Dangerous territory, Wyatt.

Keep it professional.

"Shall we?" Nigel cleared his throat, breaking the charged silence.

"Yes. Miss Marchand."

As she moved closer, I caught a hint of her perfume, something expensive but subtle. Grapefruit. Lemons. Something light.

Effervescent.

Chill the fuck out, Shakespeare. We can't be waxing poetry two seconds after meeting her? Can you relax?

"I'll be here for your protection and safety, Miss Marchand. I made a list of things for us to go over…" I said casually as she walked over to the couch, motioning for us to sit.

11

Nigel left, but not before casting a watchful glance in my direction.

I hadn't done anything out of the ordinary, but it was his job to be vigilant.

"I see," she said, her accent unmistakably upper class, with a hint of attitude that sent a bolt of lust straight to my dick. "And what exactly am I to be protected from, Mr. Wyatt?"

Me.

You're fucking gorgeous.

The thought flashed through my mind before I could stop it.

I swallowed hard, trying to regain my professional composure in the face of a literal goddess.

This job was going to be a lot harder than I'd anticipated, and not for any of the reasons I'd expected.

Keeping my tone neutral took more effort than I'd like to admit.

"Miss Marchand, I'm here to make sure you can enjoy your summer without any...unwanted interruptions. Your father mentioned some concerns about your safety."

She raised an eyebrow. Something in her eyes lit with fire.

And I knew she was going to be a handful.

It all spoke of a woman who knew her own mind and wasn't afraid to speak it.

And I liked that.

"Did he now? How thoughtful of him."

The sarcasm in her voice was as clear as the Mediterranean waters outside.

"Is this because of the one time in Paris?"

"I do believe it's simply out of my father's concern." But I saw how it rattled her.

Gemma had almost been kidnapped, and as much as she'd passed it off as a freak accident with her friends?

I could tell this was going to be more challenging than I'd anticipated.

Not just because of her looks, which was proving to be a distraction I hadn't counted on, but because she clearly wasn't thrilled about having a babysitter for the summer.

And if there was anything worse than a teenager, or enough of one?

It was a rebellious one.

And I wasn't about to fuck this up.

"What are your plans for the summer?" My eyes involuntarily traced the curve of her neck as she tilted her head, considering my words. "We could start there."

THREE
GEMMA

THE FIRST FEW WEEKS WITH NATHAN WERE...AN *ADJUSTMENT*.

Initially, his constant presence felt like an intrusion on my long-awaited freedom. I bristled feeling nothing but irritation at every bit of his presence.

I wanted to fight back. I *tried*.

Valiantly.

And failed in every single attempt to thwart him.

Because Nate must've been a fortune teller. The man knew when I was doing anything.

He knew if I was sneaking out.

He knew if I was on the balcony of my room when I shouldn't have been.

Somehow he knew when I woke up and how late I stayed up.

And he was *everywhere*.

"Are you determined to get on my nerves, Mr. Wyatt?"

"That depends, Miss Marchand."

"On what?" I raised what I hope was a regal brow.

His smirk was grating. "If you plan on running away again."

"I wasn't running."

"Right." Somehow he didn't sound like he believed me.

We were both sitting at the breakfast nook with my eggs and toast in front of me untouched as Nate quietly ate his food, eyes averted from me letting me in take in his handsome features.

When I really thought about it? Nate wasn't unattractive.

The more I looked at him the more impossible it was to not find him attractive.

Rugged masculine features, that rough stubble on his jawline, his golden and dirty-blonde hair worn a tad too long.

Nate looked almost like a modern day outlaw with a romantic edge to him. Like a former norse god who traded in his helmet, spear, and golden wings in Valhalla for the highways.

The kind girls in my school was swoon over on television. Beauty with edge. Masculine with soft lips.

I bet he even owned a leather jacket.

The kind that smelled like musk and spice and—

STOP IT. HE IS YOUR CAPTOR.

AND YOU NEED TO FIND A CUTE BOY.

On the beach. Anywhere but with Nathan Wyatt. Near him.

Inside me—Oh.

I need to relax.

"You don't sound like you believe me."

"That's because I don't," he muttered.

"What?"

"Nothing."

He was infuriating. I despised him.

And he was determined to drive me insane.

One afternoon at the beach, a local began flirting with me.

I could feel Nathan's eyes on me like a physical weight, and he stayed close the entire time.

The other man's smile faltered as he glanced at the six-foot-plus behemoth behind me intent on glaring down every man who approached me on this beach. "Your boyfriend?"

"No."

"Yes," came the gruff response next to me. I sighed and scowled at Nathan who I couldn't see his expression through his glasses.

Just another rugged heathen next to me.

"Well, it seems like your boyfriend does not approve of me lingering."

"He isn't—"

"No, he does not."

Nate's dark voice cut through the air. In my head?

I was going to murder him.

"Oh, would you—" I turned sharply to Nate who smirked at the local leaving me alone. I growled a little. "I don't understand why you had to do that."

I just want to be normal.

Nathan wasn't mine in any way.

But it shouldn't have felt good to hear it even if a part of me was annoyed. An annoying flutter began in my stomach

"He could've had bad intentions."

"Maybe I'd like a man to have bad intentions with me," I growled under my breath. "Did you ever think that I'd be all right with that?"

As soon as the words left my mouth, Nate's expression went blank.

I felt something unfamiliar churn in my stomach at that and I tried to be nonchalant as I said. "You don't have to keep me safe from attractive men."

"His hair had more gel in it than a dolled up poodle, I did you a favor."

I covered my mouth to hide the snort but Nate let out a huff of breath that sounded like laughter.

"Did you think that maybe I *might* be into him?"

"Could've fooled me."

"And why is that?"

"Because I've seen you more interested in Bonnie's lemon pasta than that motherfucker."

I tried not to bristle. I really did. And I failed.

Because I liked that Nate cursed around me. I liked how easily he spoke to me. How casual he was. Like I was another person.

A normal person.

But.

Damn, his superb hearing.

Nate caught everything anyone said.

Despite the distance and the ambient noises?

He had his super sense turned on, attuned to his surroundings and specifically to me.

"Why is your hearing so good?" I dared to ask him one day.

His lips turned down in that brooding frown again I was sure was permanently etched onto his face. "Military."

"What did you do?"

He hesitated for a moment. I got the feeling he might not tell me. Because why would he?

"Just another grunt," he murmured. "No big deal."

But he was lying. It was a big deal.

That's why he wouldn't talk about it.

"What does that mean?" I asked softly, almost afraid of the answer.

"Means you need good hearing, Miss Marchand." His tone was clipped, his gaze distant.

I frowned at his evasion, sensing he was deflecting.

For the first time, I really looked at Nathan—not as my bodyguard, but as a person.

Nigel's offhand comment about Nathan having been to war echoed in my mind, and I realized there was so much about him I didn't know.

He knew every detail of my life, my habits, my preferences—it was his job, after all.

"You know so much about me, but I can't ask about you?"

"It's my job. Not yours."

"*Pourquoi es-tu si distant?*" I frowned deeper. "Why are you so distant?"

"Why are you so curious?"

I didn't know how to answer that. Maybe it felt like if I got to know him, then maybe I'd understand him a little better.

"Pardon me for wanting to get to know the man that polices the air I breathe—"

"I haven't even *started* doing that."

I narrowed my eyes on him. "Don't you dare."

"Don't give me a reason to," his eyes met mine with an equal fight in them.

I wanted to growl in frustration.

Tu me rends folle.

You drive me crazy.

Oh, I despised Nathan Wyatt.

~

LATER THAT WEEK, SEEKING A MOMENT OF SOLITUDE, I SNUCK OUT TO the pool.

I dipped my feet into the cool water and submerged myself, muffling the world and my thoughts.

For a brief moment, I could almost forget the weight of my name and the expectations that came with it.

How much I hated it.

When I surfaced, I took a deep breath, trying to clear my mind. The last few weeks I'd spent around Nathan I kept noticing things about him.

Like how his shirt always stretched tight over his pecs. Or his biceps bulged when he lifted things up for Bonnie. Or how

When I was around Nathan I felt things I hadn't felt before. This want. This need.

I wished sometimes I was like the other normal women around me. With nothing to their name.

Being a Marchand meant living with certain expectations and limitations.

A Marchand did not simply date the help.

A Marchand did not step a toe out of line.

A Marchand was not lusting after her bodyguard.

No. I was not.

But lately, it also meant having Nathan by my side, and that was becoming increasingly complicated.

If I was another woman, would Nathan want me?

If I was another woman without all the strict schedules, the constant scrutiny, the pressure to be perfect in every way, would he see me differently?

I loved Nigel and Bonnie, but they couldn't shield me from the suffocating expectations that came with being a Marchand.

The galas, the forced smiles, the whispers behind cupped hands—it all left me feeling hollow.

Even my future felt...predetermined.

University loomed, but I wasn't even sure I wanted to go—I didn't know what I wanted.

But I don't want to be this girl.

What was the point when my path had been laid out for me since birth?

The freedom to choose, to make mistakes, to live—that's what I craved.

That's what being a Marchand had taken from me. I didn't want to be someone else's wife.

I wanted to do things that filled me and made my soul happy.

This life didn't.

I didn't want to compete with people. I didn't want to wear my mask. I didn't want to tear other women down to win at a game I didn't agree to play.

And I didn't want to play by the rules of men.

Because men were exhausting and I was pretty sure they were the reason why the world was so messed up in the first place.

Maybe not every man…not Nathan.

I wish he was here with me.

I ducked under, letting the silence envelop me. Grateful for a moment of solitude and peace, I sank deeper.

I had always loved the beach. The sand. The water.

Underwater, everything felt different. Muffled. Peaceful.

I closed my eyes, enjoying the sensation of weightlessness, of being cut off from the world and its expectations.

I didn't feel like a butterfly trapped in a cage of her own making here.

A gilded cage with a scenic background.

Here, I felt like a…a girl.

Who could fall in love. *Maybe.*

For once, I wasn't Gemma Marchand, heir to a fortune.

I was just...me.

In this suspended moment, time seemed to crystalize around me.

No responsibilities.

No competition.

No dangers.

No complicated feelings.

Just safety.

Suddenly, a noise erupted in the water around me, violent splashes shattering my silence.

I gasped in shock, panic flowing through me as something caught me wrapping around my waist—someone—*Nate*.

"*Gemma!*" Nathan's voice cut through the night. "*Goddamn, baby. What the fuck—*"

Nathan's powerful strokes having carried us there in seconds.

The moonlight bathed us both, casting everything in a silvery glow. Water streamed from Nathan's hair, his clothes plastered to his body.

I'd never seen him so disheveled, so...human.

"Gemma, you scared the fuck out of me. I thought—*What the fuck were you thinking?*"

"You said my name," I whispered.

No, he called me his baby.

In that moment, I saw his gaze flicker down, then quickly back up to my face. "I...you're..."

"Nathan."

Our faces were mere inches apart, his breath warm against my lips. I could see every detail of his face—the droplets clinging to his eyelashes, the slight stubble on his jaw. Everything.

"We shouldn't," he murmured, but his eyes never left my lips.

"I know..."

Nathan's eyes dropped to my lips.

The world seemed to narrow down to just us. I could almost taste him, we were so close. Centimeters.

Suddenly, the sound of distant laughter shattered the moment. Nathan's eyes widened, and I felt his body stiffen.

Reality came crashing back in an instant.

"*Shit.*" The professional mask slipped back into place, though I could still see the conflict in his eyes. "We need to get you inside. Now."

FOUR

NATE

Being around Gemma Marchand was going to kill me.

Living in the same house? Existing in her space?

Pure, fucking torture.

The fucking mini skirts, the teasing glimpses of smooth skin with every step.

The scraps of fabric that did not qualify as bikinis?

Fuck. My. Life.

Shamelessly, I gripped my dick in the shower feeling out of it as I came to the thought of me ripping that bikini off.

Shoving it into her mouth while she screamed as I pounded that tight little—I groaned feeling less than satisfied at another empty orgasm for her.

I finished my shower and quickly got dressed to go meet her since driving me to the edge of sexual frustration wasn't the only thing Gemma was doing this summer.

No, she was on a mission to drive me insane in every way possible.

To live, to experience, to push every goddamn boundary she could find. And me?

The bastard trying to keep her safe while she did it.

I'd faced down insurgents with less anxiety than I felt watching Gemma plot her next adventure.

Because my career was on the line with this woman.

She wanted to go do *everything* on the island.

The locals who flirted with her wanted to go with her.

And I couldn't have that. Sure, she would date.

Who was I to stop her? Didn't mean I couldn't vet the guys.

This job was going to be the death of me, one way or another.

Nigel had warned me Gemma was "spirited."

That was putting it lightly. I was running around the island with her every day in the damn bikinis she wore.

As I headed downstairs today, I caught sight of Nigel polishing some silverware in the dining room.

He looked up with his warmer blue eyes offering me a smile. "Good morning, Mr. Wyatt. I trust you've slept well?"

"As well as I could." I mumbled and then cleared my throat at his brow rising. "Any idea where Miss Marchand is?"

Nigel's smile grew as his eyes twinkled. "Ah—I do believe she snuck out—I'm only kidding Mr. Wyatt." Nigel chuckled. "You looked ready to chase her down."

I was in more ways than one.

"You damn near gave me a heart attack."

He grinned ear to ear. "I'm rather glad she keeps you on your toes. It's good for her and you, hm?" His tone held nothing but fondness at my expression. "Thought I must admit, Miss Gemma seems...different since you've arrived."

I paused composing myself as he said it. His eyes gave nothing away as he looked back at the silverware setting it down.

"Different." It left my lips unable to stop. Because I was starving for anything...

Nigel paused not looking at me. "Well, I dare say she looks better. It's been a long time since she's been engaged with someone close to her age—"

"I'm twenty-three—"

"Ah yes, the age of a fossil—" He said dryly.

"Nigel—" I broke off with a laugh.

"How could I ever forget how I am withering away—"

"I get it, I get it." My cheeks hurt from laughing.

Nigel's smile was quick. But I felt something in my chest, foreign and unfamiliar tighten with those words. She seemed better…with me? "Maybe it's all the pasta and lemons."

Nigel looked doubtful and I tried not to let it warm my chest anymore as Bonnie hustled in, arms full of greens and groceries. "Oh! Mr. Wyatt! There you are! I was hoping to catch you before you and Miss Gemma left!"

"Everything good?" I asked as I went to help her.

"Quite," she replied. "But I did make a picnic basket for you two—"

"Ah, Bon, you didn't have—"

"I wanted to," she puffed as Nigel grabbed the other basket from her and I didn't miss how he watched her. My man, Nigel, wanted Bonnie badly.

Watching them for a moment as Nigel made a joke and Bonnie laughed loudly about it—I felt a pang of my parents.

I knew this. I knew what Gemma had.

The only people she seemed to really have in her life besides me were them. Her makeshift parents.

"What a strapping fine Mr. Wyatt is to carry more than me. We should keep him." Nigel quipped.

"I told you we should keep him the day he showed up." Bonnie grinned over at me.

I shook my head. "You two are something else."

But I knew they liked me.

Nigel appreciated my straightforward, no-bullshit approach, and I admired his dedication to the household. And to Gemma.

For all his prim and proper ways, I got the feeling Nigel understood the mess of duty and desire better than most.

The way he and Bonnie danced around each other, years of working together creating something…more.

When Bonnie hustled off to grab something I dared to ask him.

"Ever think about asking her out?"

"Oh," he stammered, embarrassment rolling off him as he smoothed his hands down his suit. "I couldn't—"

"I don't know, she seems into you too."

"I rather…I reckon Ms. Bonnie has…other pursuits…"

I grinned at his fumbling. "Don't know until you try."

He looked anywhere but at me. "Mr. Wyatt…I…I understand you're

23

with us for the summer...but there happens to be a nice little eatery on the other side of the island..."

I grinned at Nigel trying to get me to take out Gemma which surprised me. They were friendly to me, protective of Gemma.

And that warmth that filled me up was dangerous because it made me feel a part of something.

I couldn't get that night in the pool out of my head. Gemma. Soaking wet. In my arms. Fitting perfectly on me.

If that laughter hadn't interrupted us...I don't know if I could've stopped myself.

And the worst part was? I didn't even think I wanted to.

And I knew I didn't quite fit into the picture. Not this one.

Even more so when I found Gemma curled up on the balcony with her book.

Honey-blonde hair piled messily on her head, bare feet tucked under her dress. Gemma wanted to dye it black for some reason. She thought it would look better. So I helped

She wasn't an heiress or socialite anymore.

And I wished deep down, Gemma was just another girl I met in normal life.

Not a Marchand.

Just Gemma.

Just for me.

FIVE
GEMMA

I wanted Nathan Wyatt.

I wanted this man, but I didn't even understand why.

There were plenty of strapping fine men on the island, as Nigel would say.

But *this* one was the one my body responded to. The one my body wanted. And it was frustrating.

A Marchand did not crush on her bodyguard.

But I did.

I had a crush on my guard.

Nathan felt different than anything I had ever met.

He watched me with navy eyes and that messy hair on the beach like he knew who I was down to my bones. Nathan

He didn't treat me like everyone else or put me on a pedestal.

Sure, he did his job and challenged me—but it was different. Other men danced around me, with polished lines and even rigid manners. But Nathan...

I felt normal around him.

I was just a girl.

Instead of treating me like I was made of glass, he treated me like...I was capable.

Letting me do things, not babying me, but protecting me.

Everyone else around me had a title and fortune, and for some reason the only one I wanted was a six-feet two strapping Texan with harder eyes that had seen things no man should ever.

When he left me at night, I found myself reaching for my breasts, tugging, imagining him over me.

When I slid my fingers inside of me, I moaned his name.

This was torture.

Another week passed as we learned to be together, and I found myself increasingly aware of Nathan's presence.

Nathan didn't feel like a guard. Nathan felt like...something more.

He was closer in age to me, surprisingly only twenty-three.

But his time in the military, combined with his skills that Nigel boasted about, made him seem older. Experienced. Dangerous in a way that made my heart race but not because I was afraid of him. But no—he made me feel safe.

Protected.

Women certainly stared at Nathan. Eagerly. *Avidly.*

And I couldn't blame them.

Especially when he took his shirt off to do something at the marina. His tattoos caught the sunlight, drawing my eyes to trace the lines across his skin.

His abs were prominent, sculpted in a way that made my fingers itch to touch them.

Unlike the prim and proper gentlemen I'd grown up around with silver spoons in their mouths, Nathan Wyatt was raw masculinity personified.

He inspired fantasies of being utterly taken. *Fucked.* In ways I didn't ever think were...I didn't know I could.

He had a teasing sense of humor that left me both bristling and burning with desire. His smirk came easily, a crooked lift of his lips that never failed to make my stomach flip. But Nate was proper in ways, too.

He was charismatic when talking to everyone, and his easy charm was drawing people in. Especially *women.*

And that...that bothered me more than it should have.

He wasn't mine. He couldn't be.

One afternoon, we were walking along the dock when Mrs. Went-

26

worth, a well-known socialite in her fifties, spotted us—her eyes lit up when she did.

"Why, Miss Gemma, who is this lovely young man with you?"

"This is Mr. Wyatt, he's just visiting."

I was under strict rules not to tell anyone that Nathan was my guard. Nobody knew save for Papa, Nigel, and Bonnie.

For my safety, Nathan was a family friend just visiting with me. And that reality made it ache more.

"How exciting!" Mrs. Wentworth exclaimed, her eyes raking over Nathan appreciatively. "I wasn't aware of the Marchand's having American relatives."

We do. Just none like Nathan.

I watched, a knot forming in my stomach, as Nathan gave her a polite nod. "It's a pleasure to meet you, ma'am."

She leaned in, her voice dropping to a stage whisper. "You know, we simply must have you both over for drinks sometime…"

"I'm afraid Mr. Wyatt won't be staying long," I answered for him, aware of his eyes taking me in. "Will you?"

I caught him fighting a laugh. "No."

"If you'll excuse us—" I began.

"For the short duration he is here, you must come by," Mrs. Wentworth persisted. "With my husband and I recently divorced, company would be a delight. My villa isn't far from the Marchand's."

I want to stab her.

The thought was so violent it surprised me. *Since when did I…*

Before I could respond, Nathan intervened smoothly.

"Actually, Miss Marchand keeps me quite occupied. But I appreciate your offer." His words, though polite, carried a hint of finality. She didn't seem too happy, eyeing us up and down. But she relented.

As we walked away, Nathan leaned in, his voice low near my ear. "You know, that shade of green suits you, Duchess."

I felt heat rise to my cheeks, embarrassment and something less definable—a warmth that spread through my core.

"I don't know what you mean," I replied, striving for nonchalance.

"No?" His tone was light, teasing. "My mistake, then."

"Indeed, Mr. Wyatt." I tried to be cool. I tried. And failed. "Would you truly consider it? Her…that is…"

27

At that, a different look entered his eyes.

The amusement faded, replaced by something more intense. He shook his head, and I felt my heart thundering in my chest at his response.

"What do you—"

"I don't think I should answer that, Miss Marchand."

Well, why not? I wanted to demand, torn between frustration at his evasion and a thrilling anticipation of what his answer might be.

The jealousy that had flared earlier warred with a desperate need for...something more. Something I couldn't quite name but craved nonetheless.

And I didn't know what to do, or why I felt powerless.

Without warning, I reached for the hem of my cover-up, pulling it over my head in one fluid motion.

The fabric whispered as it fell to the deck, and I heard a sharp intake of breath behind me.

Slowly, deliberately, I turned to face Nathan, reveling in the way his eyes widened.

The nude color of my bikini blended seamlessly with my tanned skin, creating the illusion of nakedness.

The top was little more than two triangles of fabric held in place by whisper-thin strings, leaving little to the imagination of the beholder. And Nathan.

"Is something wrong, Mr. Wyatt?" I asked innocently, tilting my head to the side.

Nathan's jaw clenched, his Adam's apple bobbing as he swallowed hard.

"Miss Marchand, I don't think—"

I didn't let him finish.

Turning my back to him, I reached up and untied the strings of my bikini top.

I heard him make a strangled sound as the fabric fell away, leaving my back bare.

"Miss Marchand—"

I lowered myself onto the lounger, lying on my stomach. The sun warmed my skin as I turned my head to look at him, my eyes meeting his.

28

"Yes, Mr. Wyatt?" *I don't even know why he makes me feel like this.*

As I watched him struggle to maintain his composure. Women gawked and stared at him daily.

I'd seen their hungry gazes, their not-so-subtle attempts to catch his attention.

"I'll just...keep watch from over there," he managed, gesturing vaguely toward the other end of the deck.

Take that, Nathan Wyatt.

SIX
NATE

"Going somewhere?"

I caught Gemma by her waist, deftly so.

She'd tried to outmaneuver me, testing the boundaries whenever she could.

When she realized it wouldn't work, sometimes she tried giving me the slip.

I would've sighed had it not been entertaining.

Not that I wasn't a fan of the chase, but damn—she was hot, and she ended up in my arms every single fucking time. Squirming and all hot. Making that tiny noise like she'd been having.

I grinned wide every time I did.

This time, she'd tried when the market got busy with a group of tourists, but my job was to be her blood-hound. I was attuned to everything, Gemma.

And she wasn't slick.

"*Mr. Wyatt, I just needed space—*"

"I can give you space," I'd kept her tight to me for a nanosecond longer than necessary, feeling her curves pressing into my body.

Or that afternoon when she'd attempted to lose me in a garden. I'd spotted her sundress fluttering as she neared an alcove.

Come on, baby. At least make it challenging.

"Admiring the flowers?"

"I was just—"

"Just taking in the sights?" I'd finished for her, my thumb unconsciously tracing circles on her skin. I held her tight to me as tourists moved around her.

How am I supposed to keep you safe from yourself?

Each time I caught her, there was that moment—her body tense in my arms, my heart racing, a heat between us that had nothing to do with the Italian sun.

But as days passed, her escape attempts became less frequent.

Maybe she realized I wasn't just going to let her slip away, or maybe she found that my presence wasn't as stifling as she'd first thought. I didn't know.

I just *stuck* to her side.

"I used to steal from that vendor," she motioned to me. "Well, I thought I was stealing. It turns out he knew the entire time, and Papa had just slipped him some cash. I thought I was a rebel."

I grinned at the idea of little Gemma thinking she was slick. *Just like an older Gemma.*

As we continued walking, Gemma pointed out more landmarks from her childhood—the bakery where she'd hide when she was upset, the church steps where she'd sit and watch tourists, the little cove where she learned to swim.

Her laughter became a sound I craved. Her eyes, when they watched me softly, made my pulse quicken in a way no threat ever had.

Today, along a winding path, the scent of lemon blossoms and sea salt hung heavy in the air.

We'd just left a small restaurant where Gemma had insisted I try octopus and pasta. Everything.

Gemma wanted me to try new things.

"You have to try the lemon cake."

I wasn't big on desserts, but as the tart sweetness hit my taste buds, I found myself savoring every bite. Lemon anything was becoming my favorite. Just like her.

"You're trying to fatten me up so I don't chase after you, aren't you?" I teased, trying to ignore how my heart raced when she smiled at me.

Her laughter rang out as she grinned wide, the sound sending a jolt through me. "I imagine you'd find a way to catch me no matter how fast I ran."

You fucking bet.

The possessiveness of the thought caught me off guard.

I was just her bodyguard. That was it.

But as we walked, I caught myself inhaling deeply, not just the sea air, but the scent of her.

Lemons and something just Gemma.

Trying to shake off these dangerous thoughts, I focused on a question that had been nagging at me since I'd started my research.

"Your father's royalty? Is that why he calls you Duchess?"

Her long blue-black hair, lightened by the Mediterranean sun, cascaded down her back, swaying gently with each step.

She looked like a fucking nymph, something out of those old myths I'd read as a kid.

Unreal, but undeniably present.

Her opal eyes glanced at the water around us, and I found myself wondering how many men had lost themselves in that gaze.

How close I was to becoming one of them.

She nodded, her lips quirking up a little.

"He was the younger brother of a Duke," Gemma explained, her voice carrying a weight I hadn't expected. "He married a commoner though, my mother, out of love. He used to be Lord Gerard Marchand."

I hesitated, knowing I was treading on sensitive ground. "What happened to..."

I trailed off, thinking of Jacqueline Cotillard. She'd been an American-French model who'd captured his heart.

The divorce when Gemma was a pre-teen.

I knew about her only because I had to.

It was part of my job to know every detail of Gemma's life, but that one had been particularly rough.

A royal mingling with a model and actress.

The Marchand's, according to Nigel, did not like *scandal*.

"Mama struggled with the pressure, even after Papa left the royal life," she started, her voice over the distant crash of waves. "I remember them fighting often. The press...they were merciless."

"What do you mean?"

Gemma's gaze fixed on the horizon where sea met sky. Gemma loved coming to the beach. She did it all the time.

"My entire life I've been educated that I exist in a man's world Nate. It controls every aspect of my life. My image. The food I ingest. The way people perceive me. The hatred."

I didn't get it.

"Every single decision in my life is based on the general public will receive me," she continued. "When the press attacked my mother? They only attacked my mother. They—the press and mostly men crafted a narrative about her, painting her as this scheming seductress who'd *ensnared* my father."

She laughed softly without any humor.

"In reality, Papa loved that she didn't care what anyone thought. And Mama...she just thought he was wonderful."

Her smile was tinged with sadness. "My parents didn't think falling in love was a crime. But the world did. And when they both stumbled, only Mama paid the price. Mama made a choice for love and they assumed she had ulterior motives. She was destroyed by a system that built up a woman to be impossible in the first place. Because God forbid women actually have brains."

I noticed her hands trembling slightly as she continued.

"They decimated her career, her reputation. You didn't see her breaking to pieces."

Gemma was quiet as she wiped her eyes. Seeing her crying sent a visceral reaction through me. I didn't like seeing her upset.

I wanted to fundamentally shift my entire life over to make sure she wasn't upset.

"They hurt your Mom?"

She dipped her head chewing her lip and I saw her blinking back emotions. "She was devastated. Suffocated. She lived under judgment and scrutiny for the longest time. Policed by everyone around her. Through Maman I understood the fundamental way society viewed women and controlled women. Every bit of the way they can. She always said she wasn't allowed to be happy."

"Your father made a choice too," I murmured. "He didn't take any of the weight?"

"It doesn't matter what Papa does, society will never hold men

33

accountable for their actions. Papa apologized frequently and said he wishes he had done more for Maman. And then…they turned on me."

As Gemma spoke, a heaviness settled in my gut. And something unfurled in my gut about Gemma's experiences.

How they sounded like she had been an outsider in the public eye.

She's been judged too.

Just like me.

"I was just a child. But they dissected every part of me. It was suffocating, especially since Papa wanted none of it for me."

Her face clouded over, pain etched in every line. I fought the urge to reach out and comfort her, my hand clenching at my side.

"Once, Maman was pregnant with me. They took photos of her with her hand on her belly and called her vain for constantly touching her stomach. Her own body. Another time, she was walking with me when we were suddenly surrounded by paparazzi. I still remember how afraid I was. I was screaming. Maman was crying. She thought she was safe. Their flashes, their shouting…I was terrified. Maman nearly dropped me, trying to shield me from the cameras." She swallowed hard. "The next day, the headlines painted her as an unfit mother."

"Shit," I muttered, my jaw clenching. I didn't know that. The Marchand files had erased all knowledge of Jacqueline Cotillard. They'd only kept the fact that she had been married and then divorced.

And that Gemma was with Gerard. That's it.

"For Papa's family, it was the last straw. They were and are extremely cruel. Controlling. They went ballistic." She hugged herself and her voice broke. "Mama was devastated. I was devastated. I was afraid to go out in public when I had to stay with Papa after. Deal with people. I didn't see the point if they would turn on me in a heartbeat. And even when I see Maman it's not very often. I think it hurts her more to see me."

I didn't even know what to say.

I couldn't imagine not having my parents in my life. At all.

"You like it here though."

"This island is different. I feel safe here."

And she didn't feel safe anywhere else but the beach.

I nodded, thinking of the way she'd flinch at unexpected camera flashes. It all made sense now.

Gemma didn't like to pretend.

She didn't like to be fake.

She wanted to be a real girl.

Just herself.

And the world didn't let her.

"What makes you say it's men?"

Gemma's eyes met mine.

"I'm not disagreeing with you," I told her easily. "I just wanna understand your mindset. I do. I'm a grunt Gem—Miss Marchand. I get where you're coming from. I do. I promise. But I want to hear you say more on it."

Because I didn't disagree with Gemma.

But this was my first time ever having conversations like this with her. Systemic root of gender oppression was not on my bingo card for a beach conversation.

And I fucking loved it.

"The fundamental issue isn't double standards my mother and father faced," Gemma said quietly. "The issue is a deliberate construct of a system of control. Power maintained through systemically, constantly degrading women. Treating women like trash. Devaluing women's rights. Autonomy. Your agency as a woman."

"You don't get to make choices, and every choice you make is judged—"

"And every single woman I have ever met has been on a diet or hated herself at one point in time!" She said louder. "I've never met a truly happy woman! Think about it. Not once."

"You think women are conditioned to internalize this?"

"Yes," she looked at me with surprise and I smirked.

"I understand you, Gem—Miss Marchand. I do."

"But I do think that self doubt is a tool of control. My mother's identity was stripped from her. Systematically. Even awareness of what is wrong does not free her."

"She's in a man-made prison where she can't make choices—"

"Or else they will torture her."

And Jacqueline Cotillard had passed that trauma and torch down to her daughter.

Not teaching Gemma to navigate a hostile system.

But expecting Gemma to play along.

Watching Gemma…

"I don't want to be destroyed by a system that destroyed my mother. My family," Gemma whispered. "It's not bad press. It's general sexism. It's not my mother fell out of love, she was tormented. It's not my father isn't trying—the game was already in his favor. Every mistake. Every normal experience a female has, that I have, becomes gossip fodder. It made me doubt everything. Am I dressed right? Am I saying the right things? Will this be twisted into some scandalous story? Would they blame Mama…"

Because naturally to gossip rags, Jacqueline was the only bad influence in Gemma's life when she would have been the best.

I felt a surge of protectiveness, my hands curling into fists at my sides. I forced them to relax, reminding myself of my role.

The ugliest part of what Gemma was saying?

I couldn't even deny it wasn't the truth.

In the military women were ripped and torn apart to pieces.

I opened my stupid mouth. "In the military there was a girl I knew, she was sexually assaulted by a supervisor. They punished her for it. She was the best at her job. The fucking best. And once she said she was assaulted by her boss, everything she ever did was questioned. He was promoted…they accused her of sleeping her way to the top or trying to. And I saw so many men fucking their troops…sorry…their…"

"Juniors."

"Yeah," I nodded. "Same playbook. Different world—"

"Different genders—"

"To tear down any woman who threatened the system and then make an example out of her to keep others in line."

That's why Reed had gotten out. One of my buddies. He had been done with the games and bullshit. He fucking hated being in the military as much as me.

Both of us saw it as a means to an end.

"I'm sorry," Gemma wiped her eyes.

I shook my head. "No, listening to you talk about it, I realized what you said wasn't just true—"

"It's normalized for women and men to hate on women."

I nodded. It's not about morality.

It's not about tradition.

Hurting women was a method of control.

And it was so normalized to constantly hurt women and girls that if you stepped up and said—I want you to stop hurting them—you were labeled as radical.

Radical.

She looked at me, taking a deep breath. "Whenever I did something right, it was all my father's doing. When I messed up, it was my mother's influence. Do you see?"

I nodded, understanding the impossible situation she'd been in.

"Its not double standards—"

"No—"

"It's a system of oppression designed to control at the root."

"Exactly."

"It's not just the impossiblity of meeting these contradictory standards—"

"No, it's about who and why made them exist in the first place!"

I stopped speaking watching Gemma's opal eyes flash, blonde hair whipping around her in the wind.

"You ever think about being something other than a Marchand?" I heard myself say.

"Every single day."

Every single day.

"Mama found peace away from all this..." The weight of her words hung in the air between us. "Sometimes I wonder if I would too. Sometimes...I wonder if I'd be happier if I was like Mama. Not a Marchand. No pressure. Nothing..."

She told me about the night in the pool, where she'd felt for a moment like another girl.

"Just someone else," she whispered. "Not me. Not this. Not playing pretend in a world that doesn't care about me."

"You don't think you have value?"

"I think an authentic woman in the world does not have any value. The system is designed so we don't. Authentic women are a threat. A threat to everyone. An authentic woman would inspire people to stop doubting themselves. To stop hating themselves. To let women believe they are beautiful."

Gemma smiled softly without any humor.

"Men do not want authentic women. They want things they can contain. Boxes to fit us into. To control us. Constantly questioning our sanity. Our worth."

"I don't ever wanna put you in a box, Gem—Miss Marchand."

"I know, but I think an authentic woman is someone the world will destroy. Communities will come after. I don't want to be a part of this system, Nate. I want to escape it. I want to be me."

I was quiet for a moment.

"You want to be a girl who goes to the beach and travels and has fun?"

Her smile was light. "I want to be a girl that goes to beach. Period."

My heart thudded loudly in my chest at the idea of Gemma being...just Gemma.

A woman you could have.

The woman behind the name, the one I was starting to see more clearly every day.

"I've never said that out loud before," she whispered, glancing around as if someone might overhear. "Even now, my mother receives threats on social media, reminding her how she 'cost' my father everything. As if love could be measured in titles and wealth. As if he wasn't a full-fledged adult who made his own choices. Papa says that all the time. He thinks the media is stupid. He stays away from it. And even then, they blame his silence on Mama."

"Idiots."

I knew the real reason I was here—the attempted kidnapping in Paris had been the final straw for her father.

Gerard was determined to prevent another incident.

But hearing the pain in her voice made me wish I could do more than just physically protect her.

"What does your father think about all this?"

"He says he was fully capable of understanding what it meant to leave it all behind for my mother. I asked him once if he would do it again. He said he would if it meant having me over and over."

I felt my lips tip up in response, a warmth spreading through my chest. "He's good to you?"

"He is. He tries to shield me from the worst of it. But... it's hard.

Sometimes I feel like I'm living someone else's life, playing a role I never auditioned for."

She broke off then and looked at me, her eyes searching mine. "I'm fully aware of my privilege, and I don't want to complain—"

"I don't think you are," I interrupted, surprised by my own vehemence. "I think you're being real."

Something in her expression softened. "In the future I would like to spend my time doing something valuable instead of just being me," Gemma said, her eyes lighting up with a passion I hadn't seen before. "My mother does quite a bit of charity work still with organizations helping women. With girls. She thinks the world isn't fair to them. It isn't. It's an aspect of her I've always admired, and Papa said it was why he fell in love with her. One of the many reasons…Instead of going to university, I want to work with people, set up charities, and organizations to help others. Maman did that. She wanted to pay it forward. Maman says the world has enough hate in it to not contribute to it any more."

"That sounds amazing," I looked at her honey hair and wide eyes. "You know, Miss Marchand. You're not who I thought you'd be."

Her lips were wide. "And what's that? Spoiled heiress?"

I grinned. "Nah, but…not you."

"And as for my feminist tirade?"

I laughed again. "Don't call it a tirade, I like when you're honest and you talk about shit you're passionate about. It's important to you because it's true—"

"It's important to me to not contribute to the hatred against my own sex."

"I gotcha. I promise I do."

And I'd be her backbone temporarily for the summer to make sure I could take care of her through this.

I didn't know how to say it to her right then and there.

Didn't know how to tell her she was full of more heart than a person should have.

Because admitting it would land me in dangerous territory.

Because Gemma Marchand wasn't just another client.

No, she was turning into a breath of fresh air that I took into my lungs after inhaling smoke and ash for my entire life.

39

Someone I cared about.

Someone I could admire.

Someone I could easily fall for, if I wasn't careful enough.

And that wouldn't do.

"Let's sit there," she suggested, her voice soft against the rhythmic crash of waves. She pointed to a lone umbrella stuck in the sand with two seats around it.

"What does your father think of all the things you want?"

Gemma hugged her knees to her chest, her gaze fixed on the horizon where sky met sea in a blur of blue. "I've never told him." Her eyes met mine searching.

"I won't say a word," I kept my voice low.

"He's married now," Gemma said. "To Camilla."

I nodded, recalling what I knew.

Nigel's subtle disapproval, Bonnie's downturned lips at the mention of Camilla's name.

I'd looked her up—widow of a wealthy businessman Fernand Delecroix, now in a relationship with Gemma's father.

"You haven't met her?"

She shook her head. "Nigel doesn't like her." I knew that. I didn't think anyone did. I'd have to dig up a bit more on Camilla myself.

Trying to lighten the mood and distract myself from my thoughts, I asked."So why does he call you *Duchess*?"

"It doesn't fit, but Papa wanted me to feel special growing up," she explained, biting back a wry grin. "It did *not* help my ego. When he called me that, everyone started labeling me with it. It's just a nickname."

"What about you?" she asked, her voice soft, curious.

"I'm not a Duchess."

"I hope not," she laughed, her eyes twinkling with mischief and making my dick and body respond to it. Gemma Marchand was fucking pretty.

The way she looked at me made my pulse quicken. And my dick lose its ever loving mind. Every defense I had was crumbling like a sand castle in the water.

"Miss Marchand—"

"You can call me Gemma," she offered, leaning in slightly.

40

The scent of her perfume, mingled with sea salt, was in my senses. For a moment, I was tempted. *God, was I tempted.*

To close that gap, to let myself believe we could be more than guard and charge.

But reality crashed back in. I shook my head, hating the disappointment that flashed across her face. "I don't think that's a good idea, Miss Marchand."

"Why not?"

Because I'm so blue collar it would make you cry.

Because I'm just a poor kid out of my league.

Because I can't be your man.

I shook my head, my tone turning serious. "I don't have much to my name…"

"I think you have a lot to your name," she said, her eyes meeting mine with an intensity that made my breath catch. "Plenty."

"Oh yeah?" My voice was husky, betraying my attempt at nonchalance.

She nodded slowly, her gaze never leaving mine. "Plenty. I think any woman would be lucky to have you."

"I can't buy her diamonds—"

"She might not want them—"

"Or a *villa*—"

"She might not need that—"

I let out a breath, a huff of laughter escaping me. *This woman is going to fucking kill me.*

I puffed out a breath feeling at a loss for words. I was a good for nothing son-of-a-poor woman and man unable to provide for anything. But myself.

"I can give her a one-bedroom apartment in a city I rarely go back to and make her pasta on our first date at home. *Maybe.*"

"Maybe that's exactly what she likes." Gemma sounded casual as she gave me a smug smile, a gleam in her eyes I rarely saw. My heart was pounding a little harder now at that look.

"Oh yeah?" I dared knowing full well I was walking into a trap. "And why would she ever want any of that?"

I was almost afraid of the answer.

"Because all she might want is you."

41

SEVEN
NATE

It was official. Gemma Marchand was going to kill me.

"How do you know so much about the island?"

Gemma was curious about me. Always.

She sat across from me brushing her hair back in the beach chair. The sea breeze caught it, golden strands dancing in the sunlight as she looked over at me.

There was always a soft look to her eyes as she watched me with those eyes.

A shade of blue that didn't quite have a name. Somewhere between opal and azure, sparkling a little bit brighter.

It wasn't like me to want things like her.

Un-attainable. Untouchable.

Unacceptable.

Every Un-word in the dictionary.

"I've always wanted to come here," I admitted reluctantly not wanting to tell her about my Mama. She was why I was happy being here, but not quite.

"Then why do you look unhappy?"

Her eyes watched me still and I resisted the urge to squirm under it. I had faced down deadlier situations than Gemma, and I could do so here. Right?

Wrong.

For a moment I hesitated if I should answer her.

If I should admit to anything. Gemma Marchand's family had billions. And my family didn't.

I had grown up scraping by and I knew it. A mixture of something foreign crested in my stomach that I didn't know how to identify. I wasn't ashamed of my upbringing by any means. But I was aware that I was lacking things she had.

Even with Gemma—even if I knew my place? It didn't matter.

Because Gemma was the one reaching over the line in the sand pulling me over to her every single time.

Do I tell her?

"My Mama really wanted to come here…once." I started slowly releasing a breath I didn't know I had been holding onto. "She had a magazine…and I remember being a kid and her telling me she wanted to come to Europe, travel the world…"

"My family didn't have much money. Barely had enough to have me. My parents met in high school. Neither of them of them went to college and Mama dropped out when she had me. My pops realized it was easier to make money then doing odd jobs than to go to school. So they did it. To make their ends meet. He didn't make enough. And she never got it."

But I made enough now.

"My contracting gigs got me comfortable enough to get her a few trips out of the small-town we were in. But nothing like this."

I shook my head at the beach, my surroundings. Being in Capri was surreal for me. I told Gemma that.

"All my life I never imagined I would end up anywhere. I thought I'd up in jail or worse. And now…my life is different. So I try to give my parents better."

"That's very noble of you—"

"Not at all, Gem—Miss Marchand." I swallowed correcting myself.

"You can call me Gemma, Nate." I couldn't look at her as she said it.

I couldn't face her. I was a fucking coward sometimes, but if I looked at her? And I saw an ounce of that empathy in her eyes I heard in her voice? I'd kiss her.

I'd kiss her and call her Gemma. Which meant admitting she was something more to be than just a charge.

But I couldn't. For both our sakes, I couldn't. I'd already slipped up too many times, letting my guard down in ways I never had before.

"I don't think that's a good idea, Miss Marchand."

"Why not?"

I shook my head looking down at my hands in my lap. The hands that had killed so many fucking people. I never told Gemma what I did when she asked what I was in the military.

I was a sniper.

And I wasn't proud of anything I did.

None of it. I'd been given awards, decorations, my uniform—I'd burned it all. I changed the subject.

"I don't judge you for anything, Nate," her eyes were warm, her mouth turned down into a pout. "I just wish you'd say my name the way I did yours."

Fuck me. She's so sweet.

But I never break the rules.

Never step out of line.

I took a deeper breath unable to stop myself from looking a there and finding those soft eyes on me. Her pink lips pouted and intent on me.

"They busted their backs to give me a decent life. Never had much, but we never felt like we were missing out either. We had just enough to be free..." I looked away. "My parents were poor, but they gave me everything."

"That sounds really lovely," Gemma said, her smile genuine but trembling slightly. I could see in her eyes she truly meant it.

"It was." Until things changed. "And then my Dad got sick for a bit. Turns out inhaling fumes for hours and hours could make a man really sick."

Gemma straightened and focused on me as I said it.

"I was seventeen at the time. My mom tried to keep it from me. The doctors said it was a combination of things. Years of inhaling fumes had damaged his lungs, making it harder for his heart to pump oxygen. The stress of working long hours didn't help. They called it occupational cardiomyopathy—fancy words for a mechanic's heart giving out after years—"

"I'm so sorry."

I shook my head. "Don't be…I joined the military a few months later. Mama wasn't happy but it was a regular paycheck." I shrugged lightly as I felt her moving closer. "It was enough. I didn't need much. But I also hated every second of it."

"You asked me what it meant for me to be a sniper," I looked away from her. I couldn't look at her for this part. "It means I killed people… and I was good at it."

My throat tightened as it worked. I had hoped I'd never have to say it.

The longer I talked to Gemma, the more it poured out of me.

Maybe I was comfortable. Maybe I trusted her. Talking to Gemma felt like something easier than I had ever had with someone. Wanting to talk to her and be around felt natural as existing, as the fiber of my being —she felt *comfortable*.

And so it slipped out.

"I had a steady hand and good eyes. The best hearing. I was good at it, which almost made it worse. Every time I pulled that trigger, I felt a piece of myself slip away. But I kept doing it, because every shot meant another paycheck for my folks back home. It didn't matter if I was killing someone deemed bad by the government. I felt it every single time."

A trained killer.

A man who did everything for everyone around him. Never truly fitting in. Never truly a part of something anymore. Always on the outside, looking in.

"Do you think it makes you a bad person?"

"I don't feel like a person anymore." I admitted. My eyes locking on hers. "I don't feel like me ever. Feels like I'm just trying to put on my best mask and keep it moving. When I got out, I thought I'd find a hobby. Something to help."

Her brows knit together. "Do you have…"

"Post traumatic stress disorder?"

A wealth of sadness entered her eyes. "I'm sorry."

Me too. I didn't say a word. Because that was the other fact of the matter.

I had done too much wrong. Been through several wars.

I had fucked up beyond measure in so many ways and I didn't

deserve her. I didn't. Because what kind of a woman with her worth? Would ever be with me?

No matter what I did?

Or how I tried?

I'd never be the man she would end up with. I was gutter scum compared to Gemma Marchand.

And that truth burned through me the most.

Gemma was quiet for a moment, her gaze never leaving my face. I could almost see the wheels turning behind her eyes, as if she was struggling with some internal battle.

Finally, she spoke. "I want to go somewhere."

"Right now?" I looked around. "Suns going down."

"No. Tomorrow." Her lips quirked up and her eyes did that shimmering thing again. "To the blue grotto."

EIGHT
GEMMA

Nate's truth broke my heart.

Not just because it hit me square in the chest where I felt my own insecurities.

But because despite our differences...I realized how much I felt for him. Whether he realized it or not we had more in common than he knew.

I didn't know how to tell Nate just how much of an outsider I felt like I was. How the pressure of my name.

Or my society made me feel. It made me want to crawl out of my skin.

While it wasn't the same.

I just saw him as someone struggling to define himself. The same way I did.

Outside of a sniper and an heiress.

A bodyguard and his charge.

As simply Nate and Gemma.

And because I understood how he felt in my own ways. Because I reconciled his emotions and mine?

I understood. On the beach, he dressed like I did.

Nate adapted to me.

If I had somewhere fancier to go, he'd adapt to that too. But as I watched Nate, his eyes sparkling as he talked about his family, I realized something profound.

I had more in common with Nathan than most of the people around me.

Nathan, the man who was there for everyone in the villa.

When the old generator sputtered to a stop, leaving us without power, Nigel had been hunched over it for hours, and Nate had offered to take a look.

Within an hour it was humming steadily and Nigel was looking at Nate with newfound respect.

"I do say, Mr. Wyatt, you're a man of many a talent."

"My dad's a mechanic, Nigel. Hardly a big deal—"

"Nonsense," Nigel had been flustered and began asking Nate plenty of questions.

As for Bonnie, her appreciation grew when she nearly took a nasty fall in the kitchen.

She'd been carrying a tray of glasses when her heel caught on a loose tile. Nate, who'd been passing by, reacted with lightning speed.

He caught Bonnie with one arm and steadied the tray with the other —preventing both a painful tumble and the loss of Papa's favorite crystal.

I watched Bonnie turn into a blushing lady who Nate had deftly sat down and I helped her clean while she fumbled over her words. I bit back all my laughter.

After that, I noticed Bonnie often saving slices of her lemon bars for Nate, and Nigel would occasionally invite him for a nightcap on the terrace.

Their subtle approval only made my growing feelings for Nate harder to ignore. Because Bonnie and Nigel were my family.

And they liked Nate.

I told myself it was because Nate was familiar—*safe*.

I feel seen by him.

Not as Gerard Marchand's daughter, not as the society princess I was expected to be, but as *just* Gemma.

I don't ever want anything other than him.

So I took Nate to see the Blue Grotto, the small rowboat bobbed in the water gently as we approached the narrow entrance to the Blue

Grotto. Late sunlight dancing on the water, casting reflections around us that shimmered against weathered limestone cliffs.

Our guide maneuvered us through the low arch and Nate ducked to my giggles. His broad shoulders cleared the opening and I found myself so close to him I felt his heat as he held me tighter almost.

"Lie back." My hand found his in the darkness.

I ignored the jolt it sent through my body, the way my butterflies fluttered in my stomach and I was grateful we were in the dark.

And then the world erupted in otherworldly blue. So vibrant. It was alive.

Ethereal like light that danced on the walls. And it felt like magic.

"Do you like it?" I asked him?

I found my gaze drawn back to Nate. In the ethereal light, his features seemed softer, yet more defined and his mouth was a little open.

"Gemma," he whispered. "This is insane."

I grinned wide at his expression.

His eyes, usually alert and scanning for threats, were wide with wonder. And for a moment I didn't see the ex-soldier. I saw a man from a small town.

With these big dreams. Of keeping his family together. His life. His mom and dad whom he loved.

For a moment, he wasn't my bodyguard, and I wasn't his charge. We were just two people.

Just Nate and Gemma.

"You like it?"

He turned to me for a moment and I laughed at his expression. "I do."

I tried not to let my heart flutter as I looked away, but it was a losing battle.

The blue light of the grotto enveloped us, and I felt as if we'd stepped into another world—one where the barriers between us didn't exist.

For a moment, I forgot to breathe. In that instant, surrounded by beauty, I realized I was falling for him. Hard.

The intensity of my feelings scared me, but I couldn't look away.

"I can see why my Mama had this place in her dreams," Nate said softly. "She's the best. My father worked his ass off to provide for us.

But you know, I grew up in a small town. It was like a box of crabs...no matter how hard they tried...this is a dream."

Nate's eyes gleamed as he spoke, genuine appreciation coloring his words. The itch to hold his hand was there.

To speak to him freely and tell him the more time I spent with him?

The more I fell for him.

I like this man. More than I liked anyone else. What started out as me being annoyed with him? Transformed into me realizing Nate had been through a lot with his family.

And in turn, I saw a softer side of him and realized why Nate never talked about himself.

I chalked it up to him being everything I secretly wanted but couldn't have.

Every dream of mine I longed for.

Outside of being a Marchand.

Nate grinned at me with boyish charm and easy eyes. "I swear if you'd met me then, you'd hate me..."

I smiled along with him doubting I could ever hate Nathan Wyatt.

I wanted to hold his hand and be there for him through everything.

Go back in time and be with Nate at sixteen running around his town.

Meet him in another world. His world.

Re-introduce myself.

Not be Gemma.

Or a Marchand.

"Maman, she used to say to me, the heart has reasons for everything, that reason does not know. I do not remember how she said it perfectly. But it does."

"Whatcha trying to say, Miss Marchand?"

"I am saying, you are a good man, Nathan."

He smiled slowly and in a way that made my heart clench with no real reason behind it. *Un moment hors du temps.*

A moment out of time.

That's all this was.

"Not so bad yourself, Miss Marchand."

NINE
NATE

I was in trouble. *Big time.*

She was the kind of woman I had no business being with. Not like how I was.

Not like I wanted. And tonight? She was a vision that made my mouth go dry and my heart race.

Where I came from—a small town in Texas—girls like her existed only on TV screens and in impossible dreams.

One night, she told me she had to go out, a party she had to attend because of some family obligation.

"In my circle, you have to mingle," she said softly, her voice carrying a hint of resignation. "I don't want to go."

Neither did I.

She said all that while wearing the tiniest white sundress I had ever seen.

Clinging to her curves like a second skin. Strategic cut-outs teased glimpses of sun-kissed skin, and the see-through bits left little to the imagination.

Her hair cascaded down her back in loose waves, and when she turned, the dress dipped low, revealing the smooth expanse of her back.

A nymph come to life.

That's what she was.

The white shirt she'd gotten me to wear felt constricting, and I resisted the urge to undo another button. I'd walked over the hallway where the royal purple Marchand logo hung. An ever-present reminder of everything I wouldn't be.

I was in over my head.

Not worthy of someone like her.

My outfits felt like a costume, a disguise I had to wear to blend in with her world.

That's all I ever did. Blend in.

Four years in the military and countless missions as a sniper had trained me to become invisible, to adapt to any situation.

But here, next to her, I felt exposed, stripped bare by the intensity of her presence.

Gemma's eyes met mine, and I saw a flicker of something in their depths, a heat that mirrored my own.

She bit her lower lip, a gesture that sent a jolt of electricity through me, igniting a fire I knew I shouldn't let burn.

"You clean up nice," she said, her voice low and husky.

I cleared my throat, trying to maintain some semblance of professionalism. "Thank you, Miss Marchand."

As she moved past me, I caught the scent of grapefruits and lemons. Lemons like I'd never smelled before in my life, it was like perfume on her skin.

I wanted to pull her close, to feel that flimsy dress under my hands, to taste the salt of the sea on her skin.

The thought of sliding deep into her, hearing her moan my name as I hit that sweet spot—*fuck*—*citrus and sunshine and Gemma.*

Soft breasts against my chest, her legs wrapped tight around me, pulling me in deeper.

Don't stop, Nate.

Shit. Shit. Shit. Stop.

"Shall we go?" Gemma asked, her voice pulling me back to reality.

Yes, Duchess.

The drive to the party wasn't too bad, but Gemma insisted on getting gelato beforehand. When we made it there the thump of bass grew louder.

The party in question was at a sprawling enormous villa perched on the cliffs. The sounds of music, laughter spilled out into the night and as we stepped in—I knew we were fucked.

Something was off about this place.

And the moment the doors opened, I got it.

Pure hedonism.

A scantily clad girl was licking salt off another woman's stomach before downing a shot.

Gemma grimaced as we passed a couple making out against the wall, the man's hand disappearing under the woman's skirt as she moaned. A sickly smell of alcohol clung to everyone and I caught the sharp tang of vodka and tequila in the air.

Leaning in close, my lips nearly brushing her ear, I murmured. "Are you sure you want to stay?" I felt Gemma shiver into my side. We don't have to stay, Duchess."

Her hand tightened on my arm. "I went to school with some of these people. It's always like this."

"If you want to leave, just say the word," I insisted, fighting the urge to pull her closer, to shield her from the gazes surrounding us. "I'm all yours."

Gemma nodded, relief washing over her features. "Let me just grab a quick drink, then we can go. I've made an appearance, that's enough."

At the bar, Gemma ordered an apple martini. Just as she turned, drink in hand, a drunk partygoer stumbled into her, spilling his cocktail all over her white dress and the sharp scent of the vodka filled the air.

"Oh, shit! Sorry, babe," he slurred, his hands reaching out to "help," fingers grazing the now-transparent fabric of her dress.

In that instant, something inside me *snapped*.

My vision narrowed, focusing solely on the threat to Gemma.

Without conscious thought, I was between them in a heartbeat, my hand clamped firmly around the drunk's wrist. *"Back off."*

The drunk's friends stepped forward, faces twisted in anger. "Who the hell do you think you are?"

"Stay behind me," I murmured, my eyes never leaving the potential threats. "If I say run, you run. Understand?" She nodded, her body pressed close to mine.

One of the guys, a lanky blond with a face contorted in drunken rage, took a wild swing at me. Time seemed to slow.

I moved with practiced efficiency, each motion precise and controlled.

A quick jab to one attacker's solar plexus, an elbow to another's jaw. I wasn't fighting to hurt, just to create space and escape. My mind raced with a single thought. *Gemma.*

I reached for her turning around and hauling her into my arms.

"Don't let go."

We moved as one unit, me clearing a path while Gemma stayed close, her trust in me absolute. A large guy charged towards us.

Around us partygoers erupted in screams and shouts. People scrambled to move out of my way.

Without breaking stride, I used his momentum against him, pushing Gemma behind him. redirecting him into a table. He went down hard.

Pandemonium broke out and glass shattered. Furniture toppled. And the pounding of the music was getting on my nerves as Gemma's hand slipped into mine.

"Nate—"

"Almost there," I muttered, seeing the exit ahead. With a final push, I burst through the doors and into the cool night air.

Gemma stumbled, and I caught her, steadying her against me. She was clutching the torn pieces of her dress together, her hair disheveled, eyes wide with shock.

"Come here, baby." I hauled her into my arms.

As her eyes welled up with tears, and she began sobbing, her whole body shaking against mine, I held her tighter.

"I'm sorry," she choked out between gasps. "I'm so sorry..."

"Shh, it's okay," I murmured, stroking her hair.

I pressed my lips to her forehead, no longer caring about maintaining professional distance. In that moment, all that mattered was Gemma in my arms, safe and sound.

"Hold onto me," I murmured into her hair, pushing aside the ache in my ribs where I'd taken a hit.

I noticed my shirt was torn and bloodied. In one swift motion, I shrugged it off, leaving me in just my undershirt. I draped the linen shirt over her shoulders, covering her torn, wet dress.

Gemma looked up at me, her tear-stained face illuminated by the moonlight. Her eyes widened as they focused on something above my eye.

"Nate, you're bleeding."

I caught her hand gently, bringing it down. "It's nothing," I assured her, even as I felt the warm trickle of blood down my temple. "I've had worse."

"This is because of me," she whispered, fresh tears forming in her eyes. I cupped her face in my hands, forcing her to meet my gaze.

"No," I said firmly, my voice low and intense. "This is because some entitled jackasses don't know how to behave. You did nothing wrong."

Without warning, I scooped her up into my arms, cradling her against my chest.

Gemma nestled her face into the crook of my neck, her breath warm against my skin.

"Let's go home, baby."

TEN
GEMMA

"I GOT YOU, BABY."

Nate's lips brushed over my ear.

He hadn't let me go since he'd left the party. No, he'd parked the car in the garage and then came over to the other side to hold me to him.

The house was dark and silent—Nigel and Bonnie must have been asleep, thankfully.

He carried me up the stairs and straight to my room.

Despite the lingering fear, I felt a new, urgent need building. I wanted him to take me, to bury himself so deep inside me that I'd forget everything but his name.

I want to be his baby.

The way he had moved through the brawl, shielding me from harm, his movements precise and powerful—Nate made every polo-playing swim team captain I had ever dated look like a boy in comparison.

And I liked it.

I found myself hyper-aware of his hands on me, the heat of his body against mine, and I craved more.

Craved *Nate*.

He set me down gently on the edge of my bed, his touch tender for someone who had just fought off a room full of people. I caught his hand, marveling at how small mine looked in his.

"Stay." My voice was hoarse.

Nate hesitated for a moment, his navy eyes searching mine.He nodded, looking around my room as I felt the rush of relief.

"Let me get the first aid kit."

His face, bruised, a cut above his eyebrow still oozing slightly. His knuckles raw.

The beginnings of bruises forming on his arms.

Without hesitation, I wrapped my arms around him, pulling him close. I clutched at his back, burying my face in his neck.

I didn't cry, but I held onto him as if he were my lifeline.

"I'm so sorry you got hurt."

"I'm just glad we got you out, Duchess," he murmured, his deep voice rumbling through his chest.

He held me tightly, one hand stroking my hair while the other rubbed soothing circles on my back.

But beneath the comfort, a different kind of heat began to build within me.

"If you hadn't been there..." I started, my voice muffled against his skin.

"But I was there. I'll always be there."

"You're the one who's hurt," I said, my voice husky as I reached for the first aid kit. "Let me help you."

"Gemma," his voice was a velvety growl as he said my name.

His eyes dropped to my lips, then to the torn neckline of my dress, before snapping back up to meet mine.

Just as his lips were a breath away from mine, he hesitated. "I *can't.*"

"It's one summer...that's it," I said, the words painful but necessary. "I'll never see you again after this, will I?"

Nate's internal struggle was visible—I arched slightly, unconsciously offering myself to him, my body aching for his touch.

"Please...Nate." I spread my legs wider. His eyes dropped to my legs, my inner thighs, higher. "Please...I need you." So bad.

With that he snapped. His eyes were dark as he looked up at me. When his lips came down on mine, I wanted to scream.

I melted into him, my arms wrapping around his neck, pulling him closer.

At that moment, nothing else mattered—not my family, not his job, not the uncertain future.

There was only Nathan Wyatt.

Moving over me, bending me to the bed until he was between my legs and kissing me hungrily. So hungrily.

My entire body was thrumming with energy. This felt like a dream. And I was in love. My breasts ached.

My entire body *needed* him.

"Nate—" I gasped in between hot hungry kisses. "Nate—" I tore at our clothing.

Until I felt the length of him, harder than iron between my legs despite his pants being on. I gasped looking into his darker eyes.

"Gemma," he whispered over my lips. "Tell me to stop."

"No." I answered without hesitation. "Take me."

I'm yours.

I have been yours for a long time.

"Take me."

His mouth stamped down on mine and hard as he thrust his tongue in. He tasted like mint and something else purely him, as his tongue tangled with mine. I moaned around it as I sucked.

A growl left Nate's lips. "Baby, baby—we gotta stop—"

"No, don't you dare—"

"Gemma—"

"Nate," I met his eyes. "I want you. I want you so—" I broke off as his eyes widened at the panic in my voice.

I didn't know who reached for what but he was all over me in seconds.

My hands roamed his back as he tugged his shirt off me. The moment his tongue and lips worked down my throat, my collar—and sealed around my nipple—I almost came off the bed.

Finally.

Finally.

I pressed my lips together as soft moans escaped me. Nate sucked and played with the other while tugging with his teeth.

"Nate."

"Lay back."

His tongue darted out, switching sides, licking to my nipple until I covered my mouth to stop the noises from escaping.

58

Get inside me. Nate.

But he had other plans. His tongue drawing lower and lower. His breath over the part of me that ached for me.

The moment his tongue darted out over my clit, I felt my back bend. And then he did something sinful as he sank lower, and shoved it into me.

My scream was muffled at Nate ate at me like a starved man. The growls coming from him were animal as he did. And I writhed under him as his mouth worked.

The moment his tongue flicked back up to my clit, white hot sensations coursed through me. The orgasm that was building was going to make me scream.

I could feel it. Muffled cries left me as I grabbed a pillow and screamed into it.

Dimly I felt his fingers at my entrance.

One of them sliding deep as he sucked on my clit again. And again.

I was shaking, my thighs almost clenching around his head, had he not been so strong. That finger in me curled and rubbed somewhere sweet as Nate sucked and I felt my orgasm crest—right there.

I bucked up into his mouth and Nate growled holding me down—I exploded. Just like that.

I was crying into the pillow hoping the sounds were muffled as he growled louder, the sensation on my clit exquisite.

S'il te plaît, s'il te plaît.

I was beginning and I didn't know if I said it out loud or in my head.

Wave after wave crested through me and it felt like it lasted forever as he lapped it up between my legs. I screamed a little as I pushed at his head.

When Nate let me go, I hauled him up to me, holding him closer.

"Nate—"

I was pushing him back to the bed myself and rising up over him, my fingers going to his shorts.

"Duchess—"

"No, let me." I wanted him. I was starving for Nate. "I want to—I need to."

I had his shorts down and briefs uncovering his length.

59

My eyes widened a little as I gripped the hot, hard length of him in my fist. My fingers not touching as I gripped the thick stalk.

My mouth watered as I licked the tip swirling my tongue around him.

My lips stretching wide as I took him into my mouth. His groan of pleasure sinking straight to my pussy as I clenched wanting him.

It coursing through my veins—the hot need—to get him inside of me.

"Nate," I whispered. "Fuck me." I took his length in my mouth again, tonguing it down and taking him deeper and deeper each time my head bobbed.

"Baby—I c-can't—oh. Fuccck. Just like that…"

"Why not?" I took him deeper.

"Condoms…" he panted, as his hand reached for my hair, his mouth open as he looked at me with narrowed eyes filled with dark heat and lust. "I don't—fuck, Gemma."

I moaned around his cock as I kept going. He didn't have condoms and neither did I. That didn't mean we couldn't try something else. I couldn't fit all of him down my throat, but I tried, pausing until it was easier.

Bobbing my head until Nate growled nearly yanking me off.

"No, let me—" I whispered. "Let me taste you." I swallowed him again this time taking his deeper and Nate groaned giving up as I did it over and again. Faster until I felt him swell.

When he finally came I took him deep in my throat and relaxed it to let him finish. His orgasm shooting into my mouth, the salty taste of him becoming a part of me as I swallowed. Nate was losing it.

"Baby, fuckfuckfuck…" he bucked up deeper and I whimpered at the intensity of it—loving this. I'd never been with anyone like Nate.

As I slowly licked him clean and raised my head up, Nate dragged me up until his mouth stamped over mine.

"Shit—" he whispered. "*Shitshitshit*—"

I giggled. "Was that—"

"Fantastic? Yeah."

Our chuckles filled the air. My eyes met his. "Stay with me, tonight. Here."

To my surprise, Nate didn't argue. And I felt something new

blossom in my heart for him. Something I'd never felt for anyone else before.

But I didn't dare say it out loud or let myself wonder what it was.

Even though deep down I knew.

I knew I liked Nate more than I should've.

ELEVEN
NATE

I KISSED HER.

No. I ate her pussy like a starving man and then she sucked me off like a wild woman.

My charge.

I never broke a rule before in my life until last night.

Until her.

And now, I was crossing every damn line for Gemma Marchand.

And the worst part was? I wanted to do it again and again and again. I couldn't get those little whimpers and moans out of my mind.

I wanted to *keep* hearing them.

Fuck. My. Life.

Last night Gemma and I had barely gotten any sleep.

It didn't matter if I didn't have condoms with Gemma's mouth wandering all over me.

Both of seemed to want to explore each other with an ardent need that encompassed weeks of sexual frustration.

Tasting each other over and over until Gemma lay panting under me, over me and in every position possible.

Part of me cursed myself for not having condoms and another part of me knew it was probably best we didn't.

I'd tasted that soft wet center of hers, fucked with my fingers, let her come around my tongue.

When morning came, I slipped out while she slept, my body aching all over—part from the fight, part from holding myself back all night. Shower. Change.

Try to get my head straight. Cleaning up and laying in bed processing what the fuck I'd done.

Nothing prepared me for the way Gemma burst into my room rushing to me and kissing me with those eyes of hers.

One summer. One fucking summer.

That's all we had, all we could have.

Her hands on my chest sent sparks through me, even where the bruises were tender, a reminder of the fight that had brought us to this moment.

My fingers dug into her waist, probably too hard, but I couldn't help it, couldn't control the need that surged through me.

This girls making me lose my mind.

"Stay with me today?"

"Anything you want, baby."

I would give this woman anything.

We holed up in her room all day, Gemma curled up against me, her head on my chest.

Every now and then, she'd touch one of the bandages she'd put on me last night, her fingers gentle—but now it wasn't just the bruises making my skin feel on fire.

I wanted her. *Bad.* But I held back, clinging to the last shreds of my self-control with this woman.

One summer.

That's all we had.

But lying there with Gemma, feeling her warmth against me, hearing her laugh...I knew I was in deep. Too deep.

"What are you thinking about?" Her soft voice crested over me as I watched her. I tucked a lock of her hair back.

That you're out of my league.

"I can't believe I kissed you."

She smiled. "I can." She straddled me, climbing over me with bright eyes and eager kisses all over my face. "I can do it again."

She giggled as I rolled her over and made out with her.

Slow, languid kisses that set my blood on fire. Passionate, heated kisses that left us both gasping for air. Playful, teasing kisses that had Gemma giggling and me grinning like a fool.

"You want me, baby?"

"I do."

I memorized the taste of her, the feel of her body against mine, the little sounds she made when I kissed that spot just below her ear. I settled over her, clothes still on, moving in a way that left nothing to the imagination and driving both of us to the edge of madness.

"Nate," she whispered, her voice a breathless plea. "I want you...please..."

"I don't have condoms," I admitted, gritting my teeth against the urge to just take her, to lose myself in the heat of her body.

"Get some," she panted, her hips arching up to meet mine. "Please."

As the day wore on, our kisses became more heated, more urgent, the need building between us until it was almost unbearable.

"I feel like I belong when I'm with you," she whispered over my lips. "I feel the most like I'm with someone whose like me."

I felt my lips quirk. "Duchess, I got nothing on you."

"But you do," she insisted. "You have more in common with me than anyone." No. I didn't.

But I ignored all my thoughts to focus on her.

She kissed me quietly after that. I didn't go any further with her even though I wanted to.

Wanted to haul her tiny nightie up and sink my dick into her.

We made our way down to the kitchen, my arm around her waist, unable to keep from touching her, needing the constant reassurance of her presence.

The moment we entered, Bonnie and Nigel were there, preparing dinner.

Nigel's eyes swept over us, a knowing glance that made me want to explain but Bonnie beat him to it.

"Good lord, Nate!" Bonnie exclaimed, rushing over, her eyes widening at the sight of my bruised and battered face. "What happened to you?"

"It's nothing," I started, but Gemma cut in, her hand tightening on my waist.

"There was an incident at a party last night," she explained, her

64

voice steady, a hint of steel beneath the calm. "Nate helped me." Nate. Not Mr. Wyatt. Nigel caught it even if Bonnie didn't.

Nigel's gaze hadn't left me. His eyes curious. "You did well, Mr. Wyatt."

I tipped my head to him unable to even speak.

"Dinner will be ready shortly." His eyes drifted to Gemma's arm at my waist.

I knew what we were doing was wrong, complicated, potentially disastrous.

But as I watched Gemma move around the kitchen, catching her secret smiles and heated glances, I couldn't bring myself to regret it.

Just one summer.

One summer to have something I never thought possible.

One summer to love her, to hold her, to make her mine in every way that mattered.

Until I couldn't anymore.

TWELVE
NATE

NIGEL WANTED TO SPEAK TO ME.

I found him tinkering with his beloved car.

The familiar smell of motor oil and grease hit me, reminding me of countless hours spent in my dad's makeshift garage back in Texas.

For a moment, I was that kid again, learning to fix engines because we couldn't afford to take our beat-up truck to a mechanic.

Nigel looked up as I approached, his expression unreadable. "Ah, Mr. Wyatt. I was hoping we might have a word."

I nodded, bracing myself. My heart raced, but years of military training kept my face neutral. I'd faced down enemy fire, but somehow, this conversation felt more daunting.

Because you like this girl.

And she might ruin your life if you're not careful.

He wiped his hands on a rag, then leaned against the car.

"I think you know what this is about."

"Miss Marchand."

Gemma. My girl.

Nigel sighed looking uneasily at his car. "Indeed. Mr. Wyatt...You're a wonderful addition to the summer home. I like you. Bonnie likes you. And it's clear that Miss Gemma is...*fond* of you." Nigel was polite. Tactful.

A warmth spread through my chest at his words, quickly followed by a cold dread. I'd never belonged in Gemma's world. Hell, I'd spent most of my life fighting just to belong anywhere.

"Nigel, nothing is going on between us." I felt the need to protect Gemma as much as myself. She couldn't be seen sinking as low as me.

Nigel held out his hand. "It wouldn't matter to me if there was, Mr. Wyatt. Miss Gemma deserves to live and experience her life as any blossoming adult sees fit." As shocked as I was by what he said, I sensed a but coming.

"But," Nigel continued looking regretful. "You must understand the complexities of Miss Gemma's situation—"Nigel smoothed himself down. "Her father has certain expectations. The Marchand family...after Miss Jacqueline...Miss Gemma's mother, nothing was the same again. He wouldn't allow himself to tarnish the name his family built."

I knew about Gemma's mother. Enough to know Jacquline Cotillard was a famous actress and model who'd gotten married in a whirlwind affair to Gemma's father.

It hadn't ended well. To say the least.

I felt my jaw clench, a familiar tightness settling in my chest.

"I'm aware about his ex-wife, Nigel."

He nodded. "That being said, after that Gerard is protective of Miss Gemma. He doesn't like outside influences in her life and keeps her... grounded to the Marchand values." His eyes were soft and contemplative. "Something Miss Gemma does not always appreciate."

No, she didn't.

"Miss Gemma would rather pretend she isn't a Marchand. But she is. And because of that alone, she cannot defy her father." I swallowed as Nigel continued. "It is not my place to judge her or you." His eyes met mine with kindness. "I can imagine being young and in love—" As he said it my heart leapt in my chest. "And relishing every moment. I just don't want to see her get hurt."

Gemma Marchand was out of my league.

Old money.

I was shit.

Memories flashed through my mind—patched clothes, free school lunches, the shame of not being able to afford class trips.

My parents' love had been abundant, but love didn't put food on the table or pay for college.

I'd fought tooth and nail for everything I had, and still, it never seemed enough. Because no matter how much I fought for Gemma—she would never truly be mine.

He held up a hand. "I don't agree with it, mind you. But I've seen how this world works. I don't want to see you get hurt, Mr. Wyatt. The Marchand's are not...forgiving nor kind. To you or to Miss Gemma. And I fear when the wrong people find out—something even worse could happen."

I frowned as he said it. And I didn't give us up. Not once.

"There's something else." Nigel lowered his voice like someone could hear us, but nobody could. "Mr. Marchand has remarried recently. His new wife, Camilla...well, let's just say I haven't heard the best things about her. She seems to have very particular ideas about Miss Gemma's future."

"What kind of ideas?"

"The kind that likely don't include a relationship with her body-guard, no matter how worthy that man might be," Nigel said gently. When Nigel's eyes met mine, the weight of his words settling into my chest like stone.

"I see." My voice was hoarse.

"You are a good man. Your background doesn't change that."

His kindness only made it worse, twisting the knife deeper. Because it didn't matter how good a man I was, did it? In this world—Gemma's world—good wasn't enough.

Gemma would end up with someone...not me.

"Bonnie agrees. We just...we want you both to be prepared for what you might face. Should it come to it, Bonnie and I believe you should be ready."

"What are you saying, Nigel?"

He straightened his tie, a small smile playing at his lips. "That is...we will not stop Miss Gemma from living her summer before university. I do not see the problem with..." he trailed off, motioning to the garage and outside.

"With me...and her..."

"With the two of you continuing your lives. I do not know what happens." Nigel had a face of mock innocence on and my lips tugged upwards even as my heart bled. "All I ask is you keep your discretion and watch your back."

I swallowed. "You got my six, Nigel?"

"I beg your pardon, Mr. Wyatt?"

I smiled reluctantly. "Means watching my back."

"Ah," he smiled easily. "In that case I do believe I have your six, Mr. Wyatt."

I grinned even if my heart cut open with knowing that while I could temporarily have Gemma.

Eventually—this would all end.

But Nigel was telling me to enjoy it before it did. When it did.

As though the inevitable was on the horizon and I didn't have much time left.

~

"WHERE DID YOU GET THIS SCAR?" GEMMA MURMURED KISSING HER way on my spine. "Or this one? You're covered in them?"

We were in bed and this time I was cuddling her after dinner.

Her lips traced another jagged line near my shoulder blades.

I felt my shoulders and back stiffen at the mention of it. Because I knew exactly where I got them. The whole host of them.

Each scar was another reminder of things I did—I wasn't proud of. Ever. I hated my time in the military. And I didn't care to talk about it.

"Work hazards, Duchess."

"Hmm, I smell a lie. Mr. Wyatt." She nipped my ear and I growled rolling her over. Gemma squealed as I tackled her playfully kissing her. "Must've been...dangerous work?" She laughed as I tickled her.

She wouldn't let up. No, she didn't usually.

But she had no idea. "Sometimes." I felt my smile drop a little.

"Nate," she cupped my face. "You can talk to me, you know?"

And I stared into her opal depths I imagined I could. I could tell Gemma I killed people. And I didn't know or understand why. I could tell her I thought I was serving my country and fighting for something I thought...mattered. Only to find out it was a crock of shit and spun up fairytale to line politicians pockets. I could tell Gemma the truth.

"Nate?"

69

I swallowed watching those soft eyes on me. "It's complicated, Duchess."

She smiled softly, leaning in to kiss me. "We've got time."

I let out a breath, sinking into her chest loving the way her fingers threaded through my hair.

Did I tell her?

How?

"You asked me back at the beach why my hearing is good..." I swallowed. "I was a sniper. Special Forces. We go for what the military considers high-value targets...intel. We kill people." I paused feeling Gemma's heartbeat under my ears. I took a breath. "And I hated every minute of it."

"That's why you left?" She whispered.

I nodded into her chest. "I can't do that anymore. A buddy of mine went into contracting and told me the money was better and I really didn't have to do half of what I used to...so I took it."

Gemma was quiet as she rubbed my hair, the sensation relaxing even as I talked about the heavier things.

"And now here I am."

"With me." Her voice was low but bright. "It led you to me."

That it did, baby.

I smiled into her body. "It did." I let out a breath. "But even after it, I feel...out of place everywhere I go. Not in the military. Not out of it. Like I'm wandering through my life."

"You feel lost," she whispered. "You don't want to be yourself?"

I shook my head. "I just wanna be fixed—"

"There's nothing wrong with you." Her voice was firm. "I think you're wonderful..."

I raised my head up to finally look at her. "You like me, Duchess?"

Her eyes softened. "I more than like you, Nathan Wyatt."

"What if I do something? What if I mess up with you—"

"Not possible," she pulled me up and kissed me soundly. "I'm sorry for what you went through. I can't imagine it's easy. But I am proud of you for being self-aware enough to admit it. Maybe life isn't about finding yourself—but creating a better you. Would you say you're doing that?"

I considered it listening to her. "A better me?"

She nodded. "Someone you're proud of. Someone you're happy with. Someone whose company you'd enjoy?" She smiled up at me. "Do you like yourself?"

I think so…nobody had ever asked me that. "I think so."

Her smile widened. "You just don't like how the world thinks of you?" In her eyes held a wealth of emotion. Like she knew the feeling.

I shook my head. And I was right. That look in her eyes was back.

"Fuck them." At that I grinned. I rarely heard Gemma curse but when she did it was funny. Her laughter was radiant. "Fuck what the world thinks, Nate. You are defined by you. If you like yourself why should the world make you hate yourself? Why? Hm?"

I let out a breath my smile not stopping for nothing. "Duchess—"

"I'm serious, Nate—"

"I know—"

"Fuck those people!" She was giggling at my expression. "I think you're fantastic, Nate. I think your past sins do not equate to your current goodness. And I think it's possible to heal. I do. It just takes time."

Her eyes watched me process it as I let out a breath. "Where have you been all my life?"

She look mock surprised. "Oh me?" I grinned down at her kissing her soundly.

"Gemma…" I swallowed. "I don't know we're doing…" I watched her carefully as I said it. "But I don't wanna fuck it up. Don't want you to hate me."

Ever.

Her smile was soft as opal eyes bat up at me. "I could never hate you Nathan Wyatt. I more than like you."

THIRTEEN
GEMMA

IN PUBLIC NATE WAS PROFESSIONAL.

My guard. Attentive and alert, his blonde hair neat and tidy, navy eyes sharp on the world making sure I didn't get hurt.

Nathan was a wolf in his semi-designer clothing now. All ripped muscles, lines carved from marble, and calculated down to his carefully control mannerisms.

In private? He was all over me. That toned body over mine, sculpted muscles rippling as he moved over me now.

That mouth closing over my nipples and tugging enough that I came off the bed again.

Nate had gotten us a bottle of limoncello. And had poured some of it all over me.

I was going to lose my mind if he kept swirling his tongue everywhere but inside of me.

And I think that was his point.

His hips still clothed in his shorts moved between my body in a way that left nothing to the imagination.

"Nate," I panted. "Nate. Please." He'd finally gotten condoms on this godforsaken island and I wanted him. My hips lifted to push him closer to me—anything—but Nate chuckled taking his time.

"Greedy for me, baby?"

I was shameless. "Yes."

Nate grinned as he eased off me, his eyes dark on my naked body.

"Stay there for me." His voice was two octaves deeper and gruff. He set the bottle down and grabbed a condom or two. I felt so drugged up on him, out of it—I couldn't even think.

The length of him was long and thick, daunting as he rolled the condom on and by the time he was in bed I was panting for him.

"Nate—"

"I know, baby." He settled over me rubbing the head of his cock along my pussy and I shivered with anticipation.

"You're trying to kill me."

A gruff laugh left him looking less than delighted at that. "Maybe with orgasms, baby." The tip of him pressed into me then and I stopped thinking. Only nonsense leaving my mouth as Nate lifted one of my legs onto his shoulders and I almost screamed as he thrust into me.

He sank down on me with a groan. "I think you can let me in a little more, can't you, baby?"

I nodded whimpering. I couldn't even think anymore. I could only feel Nate, his dark whispers over me.

"Arch your hips...there you go...a little more..." Nate groaned and then a soft sigh left him as he stretched and filled me. Until I was certain I couldn't fit any more of him. And only then did he stop.

A low chuckle left him. "You did so good, baby. Is that too much?"

It was. Entirely too much, but I couldn't even think as Nate rocked in little circles until I was a mess under him.

"Such a good girl," he crooned over my lips. "You take me so well. I'd say you were greedy for me, weren't you?"

"Yes," I sobbed shamelessly. I was.

"You gonna be a good girl and take my dick tonight?"

YES.

I wanted to scream as he moved his hips, grinding into my clit. He didn't thrust, just rocked in a way that was driving me mad as he slowly put my other leg on his shoulders. It changed the angle so much I was shaking and ready to come with electric hot sensations.

Nate's forehead dropped to mine as his eyes met mine, low-lidded and filled with dark pleasure.

"Gemma," he whispered over my lips, doing that thing with his hips I knew was going to kill me. "I want something from you, baby."

"A-*anything*." I couldn't speak.

"I want you to come for me…" he sighed. "Just like this…"

I clenched tighter as he said the words feeling my orgasm drawing so close so fast, I couldn't stop it. "*Nate.*"

"I know," he growled. "Be a good girl and come for your man."

And just like that—I obeyed. It coasted over my body on Nate's voice and his quiet urging and I thought I was going to pass out from the delicious sensations alone.

"Nate…" I breathed his name as wave after wave rocked through me and his smile was pained as he kept it up.

"Shiiit," he groaned. "That's incredible, baby…I can feel you losing it around me."

I felt like screaming, holding onto the bedsheets so tight as I came down. Swearing a little.

When I opened my eyes Nate was watching me, his hips still as I pulsed around the length of him. He brushed my hair back despite having me folded in half. His lips moved over mine. "That was so good, baby. Now I want you to hold on…"

I licked my lips at the glint in his eyes.

"…that got you so wet. I think you're ready for me."

Imgoingtodie.

Nate drew his hips back and the first thrust in felt like white-hot fireworks burst in my body.

My orgasm made me hyper sensitive to him in this position.

He hit somewhere so deep every single time, I thought I might shriek but his mouth came down on mine as he worked and he swallowed my screams.

Nate didn't have sex. He destroyed me.

Pounding it out. Savage. Rough.

Almost vicious in his intensity and I died.

I lost count of how many times I came just like that. I was a sobbing mess under him in that position feeling my orgasm hit me time and time again.

"God, you're so fucking good," Nate panted working on me like a savage god as he took me. "Come for me one more time, baby."

I was helpless as he plunged into me with a brutal thrust, pounding mercilessly. Reduced to nothing but a wreck I gave in. It was mind-numbing. And I reveled in it as I felt him slow, shudder as he swelled in me.

When I felt his heat, I came down slowly and settled. Nate slowly let my legs down as he dropped his mouth over mine.

"You all right, baby?"

I could only mumble unintelligible noises as he kissed me. All over my face. Wiping my eyes.

"I'm gonna clean us up—"

"Don't go—"

His laugh was low. "I'm not going anywhere, baby."

"Don't leave me." I whispered.

His smile dipped as his lips brushed over mine. "I'm not leaving you. Ever."

And he sealed that promise over my body with a kiss.

FOURTEEN
GEMMA

"I think I want to get a tattoo."

Nate sat on my terrace with my feet in his lap as he had some lemonade. Half of it almost ended up on the floor as he choked.

"Duchess—"

Laughter bubbled up in my throat at his reaction. Without his shirt on, his tattoos scattered all over him, across his muscular chest and back, made him all the more enticing. I handed him a towel as I closed the distance between kissing his cheek softly.

"I want to get one," I whispered, my lips moving over Nate's lips. "Would you go with me—"

"To get a tattoo?" His eyes widened. "Duchess—"

"It'll be small." I batted my eyes at him, a coy smile playing on my lips. "One tiny tattoo, just for us."

"Duchess—"

"Please—" I licked his lips. He let out a breath and closed his eyes.

"I can't—" he groaned as I licked his lips again. "I can't think when you do that. How tiny?"

"Let's go find out what my options are."

Nate groaned and kissed me hungrily.

Grinning mischievously, I took his hand and led him down to a nearby tattoo shop.

Once inside, I pointed to a dainty purple bow design displayed on the wall. "That one."

"Duchess, please tell me you're getting that on your wrist."

I shook my head and pointed to my bikini line. His eyes went hard. Dark. "*Duchess*."

An hour later, I found myself lying on the tattoo table.

Nate hovering protectively nearby. A skilled *female* artist worked on inking the delicate bow just above my bikini line on one side.

The pain wasn't as bad as I had anticipated, more of a slight burning sensation that was easily manageable.

Nate held my hand throughout the process, his thumb rubbing soothing circles on my skin. He shook his head at me promising retribution for the torture I'd inflicted on him.

And I knew I'd love every minute of it.

One warmer evening, Nate surprised me by appearing at my door. He was dressed in a crisp white shirt and tailored pants, a far cry from his usual casual attire.

"I'm taking you out, Duchess."

"Out?" I echoed, a smile tugging at my lips as I turned to him dropping my book. "As in, a date? A surprise?"

"A surprise." Nate's smile was warm on me as he stepped into my room. I was in his arms a second later.

The restaurant was a small, family-owned trattoria tucked away from the main tourist areas and Nate had to duck his head to enter.

"Relax," I said softly, reaching across the table to touch his hand after we'd sat down. "It's all right. Tonight we are just ourselves. Just Nate and Gemma."

"Just Nate and Gemma," he repeated, as if testing out the words with an easy grin. "I like the sound of that."

"Me too." And I felt like my happiness was exploding in my chest. I thought Nate was the love of my life. And nothing could take this moment away from me ever. Throughout the night, Nate and I split bowls of pasta with wine and he told me stories of his childhood and I told him mine—minus the details about my wealth.

I never brought up my money around Nate. I didn't see why I should or how I could. But I could tell Nate knew.

While he had been running around with his friends, I'd been in ballet.

Nate went to a small high school with less than five hundred people and I had been in the most prestigious academy in Switzerland. Nate had played football in high school. I'd landed my first magazine cover.

Our lives were so different and yet. The theme was always there.

The longing for more.

The wanting something else.

Nate wanted to escape his town.

I wanted to escape my life.

And I got the feeling sometimes we were doing it with each other.

"Do you think…" I tried to form the words properly. "Do you think we give each other a taste of something different?"

Nate paused considering my words, the emotion in his eyes evident as he nodded. "I do." He shook his head then. "But not like…something fancy like…"

"Like a breath of fresh air."

His smile was wide as he watched me across the table. "You feel like a breath of fresh air."

I swallowed unsure of what to do with myself. "I'm eating so much with you," I said it out loud taking more bread. "You're one of the few people in my life that doesn't tell me to eat less. I think that is something that I liked the most."

He frowned. "Who the fuck is telling you not to eat?"

Everyone. It was a thing in our world.

I was five-eight, but I'd had to maintain being under a size five.

This summer, with Nate eating with him, I'd become a size eight in the span of a few weeks and Nate loved me either way.

"*People* tell you to eat less?" Nate looked stunned as he processed that. "Duchess, you get any thinner you'll vanish."

I shook my head with a light laugh. Nate was refreshing. In many ways. I seem to forget so much of myself and who I was as a Marchand. I felt like I was discovering myself as *Gemma*.

Is this why Maman wanted a normal life?

"I used to model and it was quite literally awful. I watched everything I ate, obsessed with counting every single calorie for so long." I told Nate about what it was like. The girls I went to school with eating disorders. "I feel like I have never met a woman who wasn't on a diet."

78

"Duchess, you don't have to make yourself smaller for me ever. I like your body." His eyes heated dropping to my breasts and I wanted him to take me right there. "You do whatever you want. As long as you're safe."

And my heart clenched a little. A lot. The butterflies in my stomach felt like they'd lost their mind around this man and the way he made me feel. Warm. Loved. Safe.

"What do you want to do? In life? I never asked, but I never thought you'd want to do this forever?" I didn't know what Nate wanted to do if he wasn't a guard.

"Honestly?" Navy eyes looked brighter as he looked at me, as if gathering his thoughts, his blonde hair glinting in the candlelight. "You're gonna judge me, but I don't want any of this. I think..." his eyes looked uneasy as he shifted, a flush on his cheek. "In my mind I want...I want to build my future wife our home. Have kids. Settle down. Be normal. And just be a father and a good husband."

His eyes met mine. "I shit you not, that's all I want. My parents taught me the value of not wanting too much and I think the gratitude made me better as a whole. I am grateful for my life. But I'm aware that the simplistic life is for me. It is."

As he said it, my heart sank. "That's it? A simple life?" I breathed the words because if I said anymore? Any more of the picture he painted? So pure, so raw and everything I could've ever wanted?

I wanted to cry.

The ache in my chest expanded.

"That's it. That's all I want. I'd work to save up enough but with the money I make, we could retire comfortably. I want a home with a family."

And just like that for first time in my life, I felt something else.

Despair. The kind that made my heart swell and shatter.

In that moment, there was nothing else I wanted more than to tell Nathan to marry me. To be with me. I didn't know him well. I didn't need to. Because I felt like I knew his heart.

And I would die for Nathan I loved him so much. I hadn't said the words but my emotions threatened to overwelhm me. The life hd described was so idyllic so peaceful.

In that moment, an irrational, burning jealousy consumed me. Jealousy for this nameless, faceless woman in Nate's future.

That woman would be Mrs. Nathan Wyatt, who would help design their perfect home, who would bear his children while he...no doubt massaged her feet when she said they were sore.

He'd come home after a long day and she'd have her stupid pitcher of stupid lemonade and his smile would light up their house while she talked about how their five year old son failed his math test.

Nate would laugh about it.

Nate would be there for her.

All throughout.

I wanted to be her.

Not Gemma Marchand, with her vacation homes and inheritance, her life mapped out by duty and expectation.

I remembered Mama and my father fighting all the time as a child, their raised voices echoing through the halls of our too-big house. But not with Nate.

No, Nate would kiss his wife firmly if she tried to fight him, his strong hands cupping her face, his navy eyes filled with a love that promised forever.

I could see it all so clearly—Nate, strong and steady, building a home filled with laughter and love.

Children with his hair and eyes running through a yard, a life measured not in wealth or status—but with moments of joy and connection that had nothing to do with...me.

Gemma. Marchand.

"And you?" Nate asked, his navy eyes curious. "What do you think you'll do?"

Because...we were one summer. Not forever.

And just like that I wanted to cry.

"I haven't given it much thought, to be honest." *Until now, I didn't know I wanted you.*

Later that night, back at the villa, I couldn't shake the longing that had taken root in my heart.

Nate cupped my face in his strong, calloused hands, his touch gentle yet electrifying, sending shivers down my spine.

"We can stop anytime," he murmured, his voice rough with desire, his navy eyes darkened to a midnight hue. "Just say the word."

The moment Nate finally slid into me, I struggled for a bit, my body stretching to accommodate his size.

"I got you, baby." His mouth opened over my neck, sucking on the sensitive spots he'd discovered, marking me as his.

His fingers found my clit, circling, teasing, driving me higher. I moaned, taking him deeper, further, desperate to feel every inch of him.

"Tell me you're good," his voice was gruff, strained with the effort of holding back. "You're so fucking tight, so perfect." I could only nod.

He swore, his voice filled with awe. "Goddamn. I haven't even done anything, and you're losing it around me—"

"Nate, I think I'm falling in love with you," I whispered desperately. I wanted to cry. I couldn't lie to Nate like this. Not when he was inside of me.

He paused over me. Navy eyes widening as he took me in.

I rushed despite not being able to think straight.

"This—*us*—it feels right," I said, cupping his face in my hands, traced the strong lines of his jaw. "I'm not being rash. Or stupid. I just want to love you. Nate, *please* love me." As I said I felt the hot tears I'd been holding back all night crest over me.

"I will." His eyes met mine as his expression broke. "I want to."

Everything else disappeared, the world narrowing down to the feeling of him inside me, stretching me, filling me so completely that I couldn't tell where I ended and he began.

He wasn't gentle, wasn't holding back, and I reveled in rough fucking.

Nate sealed his mouth over mine, swallowing my cries as he pounded into me. He groaned as my inner walls clenched around him, the deep, guttural sound vibrating through me and pushing me higher.

In that moment, as he filled me with his heat, I wanted nothing between us.

No barriers, no titles, no responsibilities.

There was no Marchand legacy, no class divide, no uncertain future.

I felt my identity slipping away, replaced by something new, something pure and untainted by the world outside our haven.

Just Gemma. *His* girl.

Not anyone else's. And I only wanted to be *his*.

I wanted to belong to Nathan Wyatt.

FIFTEEN
NATE

NATE, I THINK I'M FALLING IN LOVE WITH YOU.

I didn't know how to tell her I was too. I was.

When Gemma asked me what I wanted, I didn't know how to tell her my ideal life only happened with her.

But Gemma fucking Marchand wasn't the kind of woman to wear summer dresses and run around a meadow with my kids.

That was for my dreams.

No. The faceless woman in my life wouldn't be Gemma.

She'd marry royalty. And I'd end up with…who the fuck knew.

While I took her like a man possessed. All over the villa.

I snuck into her room every night.

Gemma buried her screams into her pillows as I took her from behind. And when she turned the tables, her curious mouth exploring my body with tentative licks and teasing sucks, I nearly lost my mind.

"There you go, baby. Take it deeper," I encouraged, my voice a low growl as she swallowed around my cock. "You looked so fucking hot out there by the pool, wanted to drag you in and fuck that sweet mouth of yours."

On her yacht, Gemma straddled my lap, her hips rolling as she rode me. I sucked marks into her skin, worshipping her breasts as she came apart from just my cock buried deep inside her.

In the shower, I muffled her cries with my palm, my other hand gripping her hip hard enough to bruise as I fucked her with abandon.

"Deeper. Please." I flipped us over, positioning a pillow beneath her hips and throwing her legs over my shoulders.

With a single, powerful thrust, I buried myself to the hilt, hitting that spot deep inside her that made her eyes roll back.

"Nate!" Her walls fluttering around me like a velvet vice. Hot and wet and soaked for me.

"Fuck, you feel incredible." I groaned into her neck, inhaling her scent, grounding my body deeper.

"YesyesyesyesNatedon'tstop."

I set a punishing pace, each stroke designed to drive her higher.

"You'd like my dick like this all the time, wouldn't you, Duchess? Buried so fucking deep you can't think straight."

"Yesyesyesyesdontstopdontstop."

Gemma I was learning, was a little kinkier than me and she pushed herself back with every slam until I knew she'd be sore after. But she came harder every single time screaming around my dick.

I was in love with Gemma Marchand. Irrevocably, *irresponsibly* in love. I felt the words unable to stop them.

"All those days of you breaking my rules, I wanted to tear those tiny bikinis off you and do this to you."

At that she clenched rapidly, her eyes taking me in, her throat working. But I had the upper hand. Her ankles near her ears.

"This is your lesson, Duchess. I'm going to fucking destroy this pussy." I smirked. "And you are not allowed to come."

A helpless noise left her.

"*Ahhh*," Gemma didn't look happy about that in the slightest. I resisted the urge to grin when I was balls deep in her. "Nate!"

"Say my fucking name, Duchess." I held on tight to the headboard slamming myself into her over and over. Animal screams left her throat. Spurring me on.

"One day, I'm going to take you somewhere and fuck you just like this where you can scream all you want."

And then I held onto her ankles slamming myself into her with every thrust, leveraging the bed to keep her pinned.

And when I knew she liked that, I drew up on her more, on my toes, dropping myself down on her as she shrieked into my mouth.

Her muffled screams were music to my ears as I drove deeper and deeper on her hitting that spot in every single thrust.

"*Natepleasepleaseplease.*"

Goddamn, that was good.

"Please, what, Duchess?"

"Please let me come!" I could see her holding back or trying to and I saw her neck straining.

Her screams grew louder and wilder as she came.

I drove her insane that night as I fucked her in that position as it unleashed something in me.

And the next morning Gemma couldn't walk.

I tried not to feel the satisfaction as she winced and I held her during the day.

Licking at her until she felt better. Sliding my tongue in to taste where it ached, loving the way she arched into my mouth pleading for more.

"Does it ache now, Duchess?"

"No," she moaned as I fucked her with my tongue. "*Nate.*"

When she felt better, one night I took her from behind on her balcony overlooking the ocean.

She straightened her chest to my back, both of us slightly bent over as I drove deep into her.

"Hold onto the rails." My voice was gruff. "Feel me." Her gasps taking up the night sky.

A soft sob left her as I drove deep into her long strokes to drive her crazy, her mouth opening in a soft O.

"I do, Nate." My throat worked looking at how beautiful she was then. "I do."

Something shifted. A moment of clarity in the haze of passion. "You want me, baby?"

"*I do.*"

The sound of that...something slipped past my lips that shouldn't have as my cock tunneled into her. "You love me, Duchess." Not a question. A truth I needed to hear.

"I do." No hesitation.

I couldn't stop. Didn't want to. "You want to be with me, Duchess."

"I do." Her voice was a quiet sob. *"Oh, God. I do."*

I buried deep in her then not moving too far gone in the moment taking in my girl. Time stood still.

My heart was pounding for another reason. "You want to be mine?"

My heart thundered.

Be my wife?

She bit her lip, tears streaming down her eyes as she whispered. "I do." I pulled out of her, turning her around searching her eyes, pools of darkness, as she said. *"Yes. I do."*

"I promise I'll always protect you, Gemma." I whispered, unsure of what the fuck I was even saying. "Always. I'll cherish every moment with you. I'll be faithful to you, only you." The words poured out of me. "I'll stand by you, no matter what comes our way. You're my girl."

She was crying. *"I love you, Nate."*

"I love you, Gemma. With everything I am."

I kissed her harder than I ever had wrapping her legs around me sliding deep into her holding her there.

"Make me yours, Nathan." She whispered as I fucked her deep. My heart raced and sputtered as she said the words. "I want to be *yours*. I want to belong to you."

All I want is you.

"You are mine. You'll always be mine, Gemma."

My heart was racing. Because I knew what she was saying.

I knew her. She was my whole entire heart. And she couldn't be.

My wife.

That night, sex took on a new dimension. Heated, passionate, but with an undercurrent of desperation.

Gemma moved with an urgency I'd never felt before, as if trying to imprint herself on me forever.

You're mine, I'm yours, always.

Consequences be damned.

SIXTEEN
GEMMA

NATE WAS BEGINNING TO DISCOVER I DIDN'T LIKE SEX.

I loved it.

Especially with him. I felt comfortable and safe. Uninhibited, to say the least.

And I wanted him all the time. His mouth ghosted over my sensitive clit, making me shudder with anticipation.

And then, finally—*mercifully*—he sealed his lips around it.

I buried my face in the pillow, muffling the scream that tore from my throat as Nate's tongue licked and sucked.

Just when I thought I couldn't take anymore, he slid his fingers into me, curling them, rubbing somewhere so sweet—I shattered with a silent scream. He peppered soft kisses along my inner thighs, soothing as I slowly floated.

I thought back to the boys I'd known in school—entitled, self-absorbed, more concerned with their own status than anyone else's wellbeing.

Not a single one of them had ever looked out for me the way Nate did, with his chiseled features set in lines of genuine care and concern.

They saw my name and my family's wealth. Nate saw me. I belonged with him.

And Nate listened, really listened, his handsome face softening with comfort and understanding, free of judgment.

"I think we're both outsiders, in a way," I whispered to him while lying on his chest. "You don't feel like you fit into your world. I feel like I don't fit in mine." Nate's eyes met mine. "We look perfect on the outside for the world we exist in, but we both hate it."

"You hate being you, Duchess?"

I didn't even hesitate as I blinked back emotion. "I do."

His throat worked as he held my face. "I don't like you hating being you."

I worked up the courage to say the words to him I'd been fumbling with. "I don't hate who I am when I'm with you."

"And who's that?"

"Just Gemma." I kissed him. "You make me feel like I am just me. And that, me, is enough." He kissed me harder.

By the end of July, my relationship with Nate had transformed into something I couldn't quite define.

One evening, as we strolled home beneath a painted sunset sky, I found myself stealing glances at Nate.

Suddenly, the roar of an approaching scooter shattered the moment.

Before I could react, Nate's arm snaked around my waist, pulling me against him. The scooter clipped his shoulder with a sickening thud, and Nate grunted in pain.

"Nate! Are you alright?"

He winced, rolling his shoulder. "I'm fine. Are you okay?"

"You're hurt," I insisted, my voice breaking. "We need to get you checked out. Please, Nate."

"It's nothing, really, baby. I'm solid."

But he wasn't.

Inside the cool, herb-scented shop, I practically begged the shop-keeper to examine Nate.

"Baby, this really isn't necessary."

"Hush," I replied, surprising myself with my boldness. "You're hurt."

And the shopkeeper, an older Italian woman, examined Nate. A nasty bruise had formed on his shoulder.

And my heart began racing seeing him injured.

After, we went straight home, where I just put him into the bath and curled into him. I couldn't stop kissing Nate. He felt like mine, and I had to protect him, too.

I told him this, and he smiled down at me.

"Baby, you don't have to do anything."

"Shh, I'm pampering you," I rubbed shampoo into his hair as he grinned adorably at me. For some reason, it made me want to cry.

As July unfolded like a sun-drenched dream, Nate and I fell into a comfortable rhythm.

Every inch of the island felt like ours, and I dared to take him onto the yacht for some time with him.

I felt him behind me, his fingertips brushing over my skin as he pulled a towel over my bikini.

"Gemma," his breath was husky. I clenched at the sound of my name on his lips. "Arch your hips for me."

I lifted my hips a little higher for him, unsure of what he was doing. I felt his fingers trailing higher until it rested on my hip. "Higher."

I obeyed. The last thing I saw coming was him sinking two of his fingers into me. I felt a noise leave me in pleasure. Unable to think about anything else as he filled me.

He groaned. "You're so fucking wet for me. Were you lying there thinking about me?"

I whimpered as he worked deeper, and I panted right there. "Should I take you right here? There's no one else around."I wanted to say yes, but I knew better. I did.

"Take me downstairs."

And he slid those fingers out of me and did. We didn't even make it into the private room. Nate plunged into me with a savagery that left me breathless. He'd push me into the cushions of the bottom deck and rip my bikini bottoms before fucking me. I moaned in heat and need as he fucked into me with a savage desperation.

He'd grip my hair in his fist, hauling my head back and licking my throat as he sank so deep I saw stars.

"Did you like being a little cock tease, Duchess?"

Yesyesyesyesllovedit.

I felt it in every plunge. "Harder."

I needed something more.

The length of him driving into me felt delicious. I wanted it forever.

And he obliged. Pounding into me with a fervor that had me convulsing in pleasure quickly. Nate groaned behind me, folding over me, his lips at my nape while he ground deep.

Later, at the villa, I lingered at the kitchen doorway, watching Nate perched on a stool at the island.

His plate was half-empty, forgotten as he regaled Bonnie with a story.

Her cheeks were flushed, eyes bright with interest.

Meanwhile, my body was reacting to the sheer proximity of him, memories of his mouth working at my pulse while he pounded deep, filling me.

His grin was easy at Bonnie, who blushed. "Your mum sounds like a wise woman, Mr. Wyatt."

"You can call me Nate, Miss Bonnie. No need for—"

"It's not proper," Bonnie interrupted, ever the stickler for protocol. "Miss Marchand refers to you as Mr. Wyatt—"

"I call you Bonnie—"

Bonnie paused. "Well, I suppose that is fair. Mr— I mean, Nathan."

Nate grinned, his eyes finding me, and something in them made the butterflies go wild. He popped a grape into his mouth as he watched me with a smile on his face. I returned.

Love you. Bonnie had turned around as I mouthed it.

Love you. I wanted to cry when he said it back.

Because out of all the nice things I had in my life, Nate felt like the nicest thing I'd ever had. Ever wanted.

The only thing I needed. Everyone was sitting there in my kitchen, smiling at me. I loved him so much.

Later, I found Nate and Nigel in the garage, hunched over Nigel's prized vintage car.

I perched on a nearby workbench, content to watch Nate's hands move expertly over the engine. The easy camaraderie between them was a balm to my soul.

"Mr. Wyatt," Nigel said, his voice enthusiastic. "you're a man of many talents. Cars, cooking...Is there anything you can't do?"

As summer unfolded, Nate became an integral part of our world at the villa.

He'd won over Nigel with his mechanical skills, charmed Bonnie with his Southern manners, and as for me...I was finding it harder to remember life before him.

Nigel's approving glances didn't escape my notice. One evening, as Nate and I returned from a sunset boat ride, cheeks flushed and eyes bright, Nigel pulled me aside.

"I daresay Mr. Wyatt has proven to be more than just a capable bodyguard."

"Nigel...why do you...approve of Nate?"

Nigel's eyes softened as he turned back to me. "Miss Gemma, I've known you since you were a little girl. I've seen the toll your father's...business has taken on you. Mr. Wyatt, he's different. He cares about you, truly cares. Not just as a bodyguard but as a person. I've seen how he looks at you when he thinks no one's watching. And I've seen how you've blossomed..." Nigel paused, his words hitting me like a physical blow. "He is good for you..."

I hugged myself tightly, suddenly feeling exposed. "But my father..."

Nigel gently cut me off. "Your father hired a guard. I dare say Mr. Wyatt is doing a fine job at that. I may be overstepping, but I believe Mr. Wyatt could be good for you. He brings out a light in you I haven't seen in years. And if I may be so bold, I think you bring out something in him too..."

Tears pricked at the corners of my eyes. "I think I'm falling in love with him. And I don't want to let him go."

He let out a breath, and suddenly, his arms were around me as he hugged me. Since *Maman* had been absent, Nigel and Bonnie filled that space well.

He rubbed my back. "I know, Miss Gemma. And that's not a bad thing. You deserve happiness, real happiness. And if Mr. Wyatt is the way to it, I am not one to stop you."

And for that alone, I cried harder.

"I want to be his everything," I admitted. "I love him so much, Nigel."

"I understand."

I leaned back as his throat worked. "I need to tell you... I'm sorry,

Miss Gemma...your father called me." Nigel looked uneasy. "He's coming here in a week."

And just like that, my heart sank.

SEVENTEEN
NATE

GERARD MARCHAND'S ARRIVAL HIT ME LIKE A BUCKET OF ICE WATER during a good dream.

Even if Gemma had warned me.

Almost my height, he strode in with the confidence of a man who owned the world. Because he might as well have.

His new wife Camilla Delacroix followed, her smile made of ice and her eyes even harder.

This is Gemma's stepmother?

The moment I laid eyes on her, every instinct I had honed over years in Special Forces screamed danger. It was her eyes.

"Mr. Wyatt," Gerard boomed, his handshake firm, all crinkly-eyed smiles. *I'm sleeping with this man's daughter.* "I trust you've been taking good care of my little girl?"

If he knew how I'd taken care of her, he'd have me killed.

I swallowed hard. "Yes, sir. Miss Marchand has been perfectly safe."

Camilla's piercing blue eyes raked over me, sharp and calculating. I felt stripped bare, certain she could see right through me.

"And you're...the *bodyguard*?" Camilla asked cautiously. Like she didn't believe I was.

"Yes, ma'am." I didn't offer her my hand in front of her husband.

The honeymoon's over, in every sense.

"Let's have dinner tonight, Gemma." Gerard looked at me. "Mr.

93

Wyatt, I hope you don't have any plans. We'd love to have you with us to tell us all about your time with my girl."

"Not at all, sir. I'd be more than happy."

Gerard looked like an older movie star with how styled he was. And Camilla like his step-daughter instead of his new wife.

I barely tasted my food through dinner as Gemma and I concocted the most PG versions of the summer with Gemma remarkably more composed than me.

"I'm afraid I was quite cross with you when I first arrived, Papa," she said, her eyes sparkling with mischief. "But I must admit, I've grown rather fond of Mr. Wyatt. I dare say I couldn't shake him if I tried!" She mock rolled her eyes in my direction, and I smirked back, playing along even as I felt the weight of Camilla's stare.

Why the fuck was she watching me so much? Her diamond bracelet glittered under the lights. I caught a few pieces of jewelry on her that would fund a small country.

"He's been good to you, then?" Gerard asked Gemma.

"Too good, I'd say," Gemma replied with a smile.

"Well, good on you, Mr. Wyatt," Gerard said, raising his champagne in a toast. "Gemma here is a handful, as I'm sure you've discovered. But you seem to be adjusting admirably."

"Thank you, sir," I managed, my heart pounding. "Just doing my best job to serve your family." I swallowed around the knot in my throat as Gemma's hand reached for my thigh. I couldn't even look at her as she ate quietly with one hand.

All the while Camilla watched us with a small smile on her face. *Shit. Gemma. Not now.*

"Speaking of service, darling," Camilla purred, turning to Gerard. "Have you considered inviting the Vanderbilts over for dinner soon. It's been ages since we've had them at the estate."

"Oh, Gemma...you remember Petunia and Harold...they have a son..." And just like that my night soured.

I swallowed around the alcohol burning down my throat as Gerard and Camilla talked about how Harold or whoever his son was attending a private school and how Gemma might like him.

And I felt the food in my stomach turn.

Gemma's smile never faltered but I saw the way her shoulders tightened. She dropped her hand from my thigh.

"Papa, I am more focused on my gap year than I am on a man."

Gemma could've been an actress like her mother with how good she was at lying to her father's face. That was where her thrill-seeker came from, wasn't it? Jacqueline's side of the family.

Gerard smiled at her. "It wouldn't hurt you to try and date a normal young man—"

"Papa—"

"I got it." He held up a hand. "Just like your mother, always seeking adventure…" As Gerard laughed I caught the way Camilla stiffened at the mention of Jacqueline.

I looked away quickly ignoring it.

"Maman is doing well," Gemma murmured. "The last time I'd checked in with her was before I got here and she's displayed her art in her own gallery."

Gerard's blue eyes softened. "That's good of her, finally brave enough to do so." He still had love for Jacqueline. I didn't need to be a rocket scientist to know that much.

My eyes moved over to Camilla and I stilled for a second.

I wasn't imagining it. Camilla did stiffen. I didn't know why. She was married to the man for fucks sake.

"Mr. Wyatt," I was cut off by Gerard's voice. "Gemma speaks so highly of you, and with her gap year coming up, I've considered someone to keep an eye on her while she gallivants around the globe. What do you say?"

What did I say? Holy. Shit.

Yes.

A thousand times.

But I didn't even dare open my fucking mouth then because I was afraid to say something stupid. My eyes were already as wide as the dinner plates.

"Surprised?" The hint of amusement in his voice shouldn't have made me happy.

"Not at all," I managed looking down at the scallops in front of me. "I'm sure you know someone much more qualified—"

"Nonsense, Gemma has been having a great time here with you,"

Gerard continued. "Gemma, do you think Mr. Wyatt is a good candidate?"

I couldn't look at her or anyone. I felt like if I did, they'd know I was dying to burst out of my seat and kiss her. Kiss her and tell her I would. I would follow her everywhere if she wanted me to.

"Papa, it isn't pleasant being pressured on our first dinner. Can we at least wait until the second before answering?" Gemma's tone was teasing. "Mr. Wyatt is wonderful. I'd be delighted if he as you say, gallivanted around the globe."

My heart was pounding, fluttering hard as I stole a glance at Gemma who grinned at me lightly.

I quickly looked away biting my cheeks to not smile.

I was terrified if I looked at her too long they might see how fucking much, I was hopelessly, irrevocably in love with Gemma Marchand, and that I would follow her to the ends of the Earth if she asked me to.

"Well, that's settled then," Gerard said with a glint of amusement in his eyes. "Come prepared for battle tomorrow, Mr. Wyatt."

LATER THAT NIGHT I WENT OUTSIDE FOR A BREATH OF FRESH AIR. Desperate for a moment alone with my thoughts. For some clarity.

Gerard was…out of touch with reality to say the least. He forgot where his wallet was all the time. He accidentally spilled wine on himself and his Rolex. And he didn't have a clue what his daughter liked or wanted. He didn't know her.

And his wife was an icicle.

Camilla had been tense during dinner and I didn't know how to process it all so I just made polite conversation. Her smiles had been brittle at best and her eyes sharp. Eyeing Gemma. And it was my job to protect my girl so I found myself leaning closer to Gemma as though I could shield her.

"Did you have a good dinner?"

I nearly jumped out of my skin. "Jesus Christ, Nigel." My heart was pounding in my chest as I swore again.

The other man was working on his car and he'd been so quiet I hadn't even seen him. And I usually did. My mind so caught up on everything else I didn't hear him.

"Sorry, Mr. Wyatt," Nigel looked amused. "I didn't think I could frighten you."

"Trust me Nigel, me either." I rubbed my chest with my hand. "Quite a change, huh? Having the entire family here…"

Nigel's heavy sigh spoke volumes. "Indeed, Mr. Wyatt. Indeed."

I hesitated, then plunged ahead. "Camilla seems…interesting." I searched his eyes. And they were shuttered.

"It's not my place to speak ill of anyone," Nigel said carefully. "But Mrs. Marchand and Miss Gemma have...different perspectives on life."

"And Mr. Marchand?"

"A good man," Nigel said quickly. "Perhaps...disconnected at times, but well-meaning." Disconnected was an understatement.

His disregard to get to know his daughter, like Gemma was another part of the villa, his current wife looking like she didn't even want to be here. And Gemma…Gemma was…my girl.

Nobody but Nigel and Bonnie knew that though.

"How disconnected, Nigel?"

Nigel looked at me, his eyes full of a sympathy that confirmed my fears. Gerard was gullible to Camilla. Or to anything really.

"Mr. Marchand tries to fight the good fight. But I'm afraid he has always seen what the world wants him to see. And right now…he wants to see a happy family." He looked away and I could see it all over his face.

"Even if that wife is her?"

He didn't say a word. "Mr. Wyatt. If I may. Change is constant. I'm sure you've heard still-water eventually becomes poisonous?"

I nodded. "But that principle doesn't apply to people, Mr. Wyatt. In this case, Mr. Marchand has not changed for years. He has stayed the same and I do not see he intends to change. And myself and Miss Bonnie…" Nigel looked like he was carefully choosing his words. "We would do anything for Miss Gemma."

He paused. And then he looked around as his eyes met mine. "Miss Jackie is the one who brought us into Miss Gemma's life. Before she left. She knew Miss Bonnie as her housekeeper. She made us promise to take care of Miss Gemma. We haven't left her side ever since."

"I didn't know that—"

"Miss Gemma does not remember," Nigel was quiet. "But we do our best to honor Miss Jackie."

"She and Gemma get on well?"

"Sometimes," Nigel murmured. "Sometimes I think Miss Jackie is aware of her distance being an ally for Miss Gemma growing up to inherit what is hers."

What was he—At my confusion Nigel explained. "Miss Jackie gave Miss Gemma to Gerard and his family so that she would have everything wonderful in the world. Not a struggle. She knew if she took Gemma her entire world would be constantly under scrutiny and torn apart because of the divorce."

I had heard a lot of ugly things about that divorce.

"So Miss Jackie gave Miss Gemma over and the rest is history. Now, Miss Gemma has the world at her fingertips. Something Gerard worked very hard to ensure she has."

Except there was one problem. I could see it in Nigel's eyes.

I didn't even flinch as I said. "And Gemma doesn't want a single bit of it."

Nigel looked down at his shoes. There was a long moment of silence after that at the clusterfuck around me.

"You and Bonnie...you've never changed for Gemma."

"We would do a lot for Miss Gemma...as we did for Miss Jacqueline," he paused, his eyes sad. "We will try to extend the same courtesy to you. Be careful, Mr. Wyatt. This isn't the same game anymore."

EIGHTEEN
GEMMA

"Good morning, Papa."

Papa peered over his newspaper, his familiar warm smile crinkling the corners of his eyes.

Instead of the usual comfort his presence brought, a wave of unease went over me.

The morning sun streamed in through the expansive windows of our breakfast nook.

I saw the fresh croissants that were made by Bonnie.

Along with coffee and pastries and pancakes...my mouth was watering. As I kissed my father's cheek and sat down though I was guilty of a few things.

One, Nate had snuck into my room and cuddled me last night, kissing me quiet. Two, I didn't want my father here.

I just wanted Nate.

The summer I had with him and just him. I hated how it was coming to an end, and I wanted Nathan to go with me everywhere. To the gap year. To university.

I wanted him to follow me everywhere.

I talked to Nate about it last night and he admitted he just didn't want them to know what we were, but he wanted to go on my gap year with me. Stay with me everywhere I went.

And in turn I kissed him and quietly had him make love to me. Now, feeling the soreness between my legs as I sat there I was aware of one thought drifting into my head.

He was mine.

And then Camilla walked in.

She sat beside him, a vision of polished perfection in white.

Her gaze swept the room before settling on me, making my skin prickle. "Gemma, darling. How lovely to see you this morning. I hope you don't mind us crashing your little slice of paradise."

"Not at all," I forced a tiny smile. I thought I was losing it a bit but I swore last night she was staring at Nate, his biceps, his arms as he conversed with my father. "How is your stay going?"

As Camilla spoke lightly I smiled and nodded unsure of what to feel about her. How to process her as a 'step-mother.'

"Papa, I was going to eat with Nigel and Bonnie," I remarked. "Bonnie is quite funny when she does impressions."

My father looked at me with mock reproach in his eyes. "I thought you'd be happy to have me back."

Oh no. "I am, Papa. I'm just saying——"

"Gemma seems to have gotten used to Bonnie's company, Gerard." Camilla said smoothly over me. "While we were gone for quite some time, it makes sense."

I smiled at her for defending me. That was nice of her.

But it did strike me as odd now eating with Bonnie and Nigel...and Nate, the stiffness I felt at the table now with the two of them.

"Sleep well?" Camilla asked me.

"Yes, thank you."

"I hope Mr. Wyatt will be joining us," Camilla said, her tone casual, but her eyes watched me. "He seems like such a dedicated employee by what your father has told me."

"He is."

I wasn't imagining the way Camilla watched Nathan. It wasn't new to me. I'd seen that look from countless women before, but coming from my stepmother, it felt strange. No. She couldn't possibly want Nate. Maybe she was just appreciative of his...physique.

After all, she had been nice to me. She was a nice lady, even if her smile never reached her eyes. It was probably just Botox.

Nate appeared in the doorway, as if summoned by our conversation.

Our eyes met briefly before I looked away, distancing myself.

"Ah, Mr. Wyatt!" Papa gestured. "Join us for breakfast, won't you?"

He wasn't seeing Nate, the man I'd grown to love over the summer, but Mr. Wyatt, the hired bodyguard.

A contractor and I was the client. That was it. I reached for the syrup, desperate for something to do with my hands. Camilla's eyes flickered to my plate.

"Oh, Gemma darling," Camilla said, her voice dripping with false concern. "How do you eat that stuff? I could never eat pancakes. They go straight to my hips." She sipped her black coffee delicately. "But you're young, I suppose you can get away with it."

What?

"Actually, Mrs. Marchand, Miss Gemma's quite active. I've had trouble keeping up with her on our morning runs." He reached across the table, passing me the butter and syrup. "My Mama always said you don't need to deserve food."

I didn't dare look at him, afraid all my love would show all over my face.

Papa chuckled, oblivious to the underlying tension. "That's my girl," he beamed. "She used to play polo in school, you know Camilla."

"How could I forget?" Camilla said softly something in her eyes as she looked over at me. "You speak of her so often."

Papa launched into yet another story about my school days, his booming laugh filling the room.

His salt-and-pepper hair was artfully tousled, his casual designer clothes speaking of effortless wealth. Irritation surged through me, over-whelming in its intensity.

He seemed oblivious to the tension at the table, to the changes that had occurred in his absence. *How could he not know?*

As I cut into my pancakes, I thought about how different this was from our breakfasts just days ago.

I looked at Papa, laughing at his own joke, and a pang of guilt nearly took my breath away. He had given me everything. Maybe I was just being...resentful at not having Nate and my Summer? Maybe I was being immature?

"Nigel!" Papa said suddenly. "Get the boat ready today, will you? I want to take my beautiful wife out on the sea."

"Oh, Nigel, that sounds lovely."

Just like that, Camilla transformed into someone I didn't recognize. Something else.

For a moment, I saw how she'd ensnared my father. It was frightening.

I glanced over at Nathan, wondering if he saw it too, the wrongness of it all.

But his face was carefully blank, his eyes fixed on his plate.

He was playing his part, just like I was, just like we all were in this twisted little charade.

And as Papa and Camilla chattered on about their plans for the day, as Nigel hurried off to prepare the boat, I felt a sinking feeling in the pit of my stomach as I watched Camilla.

NINETEEN
NATE

That evening, as I stood in front of the mirror in Gemma's room, I barely recognized myself.

Gemma had insisted on getting me a suit—deep navy blue, tailored to fit like a second skin.

The fabric felt foreign against my skin, a constant reminder of how out of place I was in this world. I fucking hated suits.

The Marchand's were holding a get-together.

A family reunion mixed with a high-society soirée.

Gerard had made it clear he wanted me there, not just as security, but as a guest.

The idea made my palms sweat. I didn't have anything fancy to wear, but Gemma solved that problem.

The door to the closet opened and Gemma stepped out and I lost all rational thought. "Baby…"

She wore an ankle-length baby blue dress that shimmered in the low light, making her look like she'd stepped out of a fairy tale.

The bust was tight around her breasts making them overflow a little at the top and she looked at me with tendrils of hair around her face making her look…*gorgeous*.

"Do you like it?" she asked, giving a little twirl. "Pretty?"

I was stumped. "You look incredible, Duchess." Gemma smiled, a faint blush coloring her cheeks. "You look like a princess."

She stepped closer, reaching up to adjust my tie. "You look rather dashing. I may have to beat off my cousins with a stick."

I laughed low taking her in my arms. "I only got eyes for you, baby. You know that." I sealed my lips over hers.

She flushed, those opal eyes batting up at me. "And I, you. Tonight you'll meet the rest of my family. Do not let them scare you. My cousin Max and his brother Bastian are coming. They have a younger sister, Cecily. They're extremely protective of her, but for the most part, they're wonderful."

"I've faced down armed insurgents, remember? I think I can handle a few trust fund kids."

Her eyes sparkled up at me. "Just be careful, okay? And this time around, should you need anything, I'll be there for you."

"You're my protective detail tonight, Duchess?" I smirked down at her looking all pretty in that dress.

She smiled, her opal eyes tracking me. "We can be partners, what do you say?"

"A team?"

"Mhmm."

"Sounds like a plan."

"*Now*," Gemma narrowed her eyes at me. "I order you to kiss me."

I laughed as I bent down. "Doors locked?"

"*Mhm.*"

I went in for a quick peck, but Gemma had other ideas.

Her hands guided mine under her dress. "I thought after the party, we might step away for a bit..." I felt something—

"What is that?"

She lifted her dress to reveal the black stockings and garters. And my dick throbbed.

"Duchess, you can't be out there wearing that, and I can't—"

She kissed me again, her lips lingering. "After the party..."

"I can make it quick—"

"It's never quick with you," she teased, her breath warm against my skin. I slid my hands under her dress.

"Bend over, Duchess," I whispered, my voice low and urgent. I was already working at my pants, desperate to feel her. "Let your man fuck."

I discovered the filthier I was, the more Gemma liked me. And so I didn't disappoint.

She turned in my arms, pressing her back against my chest. I bunched her dress up around her waist, exposing her lace-clad ass. I groaned.

"We have to be quiet." But she was scrambling to get off my pants as much as I was.

The moment the tip of my cock slipped in, we both groaned low. I hauled Gemma up to my chest as I bent my knees thrusting deep, burying myself into her heat, working my way in.

"I know you can take more, baby," I licked at the column of her throat. "Come on, let me feel it."

And then the knock came at the door. I stopped.

We both just froze. Me pulsing inside of her heat as she adjusted to me, her voice shaking with lust held back.

"Y-yes!"

"Gemma, are you dressed yet? I was going down and bumped into Cecily…"

Holy. Fucking. Shit.

Gerard.

And I was balls deep in his daughter.

The door knob jiggled and I thanked *fuck* Gemma locked it.

"…she was asking for you. She seems to be having a bit of a fashion disaster as she says, and she requires your aid."

"I'm changing, P-papa!" She stammered. "I-I'll be right there."

"Have you seen Mr. Wyatt? He isn't in his room."

That's because I'm inside of her.

Her entire body quivered around me and I held fast to her my hands gripping her hips.

"No, I haven't seen him," as she gushed all around my dick.

"Such a little liar, Duchess." I whispered unable to fucking resist. "That's because he's stretching out this *tiny* little pussy of yours—"

Gemma squirmed, making a little noise in my arms and I resisted the urge to laugh despite the situation.

I was insane for tempting it. But she was clamping down on me wildly. I hid my groan in her neck. My hands move reaching for her nipples. My girl *loved* almost getting caught.

"Well when you see Mr. Wyatt, let him know I'd like to speak to him."

"I will!"

I hid my grin in her neck as Gemma's pussy fluttered around me then the moment I pinched both of her nipples, drawing my dick out slowly.

I felt her desperation.

"I'll see you at dinner!"

I waited until she all but growled at me.

But it was a little risky. I wrapped my arms around her waist, picking her up easily hauling us both into the closet without slipping out of her.

I shut the door and Gemma moaned, quivering around my length. I had her over the little island in the walk in space in seconds.

"N-nate...that was...c-close."

It was.

But I was too far gone to focus on anything else, but her. I slammed back into her as she clapped her hand over her mouth.

"Did you like that?" I was merciless in the way I worked in her.

I didn't care about anything other than fucking her until my name was the only one on her lips.

"Did you like almost getting caught, baby?"

She nodded, sobbing in pleasure as I fucked deep.

My eyes landed on the mirrors lining the walls to my left and how I could see Gemma's legs shaking as I slammed into her over and over again.

I hauled her up and walked us over to the mirrors without missing a fucking beat.

Her breasts had jiggled out and now looked obscene over her dress, like a freshly fucked princess, being taken like a whore.

And Gemma moaned at the sight of her getting destroyed by me.

"Do you like that?" I wrapped my hand around her throat as I fucked into her body, arching her back to hit that angle. "Watching yourself getting demolished like a slut? My slut?"

She nodded as her palms slapped onto the mirror to hold herself upright while I fucked. *"Yesyesyesdontstop."*

I had no intention of stopping.

"You like being my whore, don't you?" I growled squeezing down on her throat.

Gemma squealed as I felt her clamping tighter and tighter. Any moment now she was gonna blow.

"I feel like taking you downstairs like this and showing everyone who you belong to," I growled in her ear drawing my dick back out. "Would you like that? Letting the world see you getting spread open with my cock over and over?"

She shattered. And I groaned as she gushed all over me, warmth spilling around me as I held onto her hips and pounded into her like some animal.

"Is that what you need? My cock in you all night. Want me to keep you here instead buried so deep you can't think of anything else?"

"Yes," she cried out. "Yes! Fuck me harder." And fucking Gemma pushed back on me using the mirror as leverage.

"What do you need from me?"

"Y-you," Gemma was struggling to take me. "I want to belong to you."

She was crying so fucking pretty. Makeup ruined. Tits bouncing. And didn't she look even more beautiful like this.

Something in me melted at those words.

"You already do, baby."

But she didn't and wasn't that the truth.

I buried deep feeling my orgasm in her, filling her up, wishing to God there wasn't a stupid condom between us. I stamped my mouth over hers as I did.

I was losing my shit.

"Nate," she whispered. "I want you inside of me all night. Just like this. Let's skip dinner."

And I groaned because fuck the Marchand's and their dinner.

I just wanted this tonight. This woman.

Her body. Her heart.

"I can't, baby. But I can fuck you all night after."

"I'd love that."

I drew my dick back out of her heat. Tugging on her nipples again both of them, making her mewl. We turned to look at her in the mirror as she let out a light laugh.

107

"Well…I won't be ready anytime soon."

I watched her breasts heaving as I reached for them. "I thought being late was fashionable?"

I loved the sound of Gemma's laughter filling the closet space. "You're learning."

"Am I?" I turned her around and dipped my head to her lips. "I have a great teacher."

She giggled. "Nate…"

"Yes?" I trailed my lips lower.

"We just finished…"

"Did we?"

Her laughter turned into a louder moan as I went lower.

TWENTY
NATE

THE MARCHAND CLAN WAS OUT IN FULL FORCE TONIGHT.

A display of wealth and power in the expertly decorated space—downstairs in the fucking ballroom area in the villa.

I would never get used to this level of money. The kind that gave no fucks about anything. I stood at the edge feeling out of place and over-whelmed.

Gemma glanced up at me after fixing her makeup and hair so she wouldn't looked like someone had demolished her.

Even now I could feel the ripples of her pussy as she'd orgasmed so hard it left *me* breathless.

"Ready?"

I wasn't. But I nodded taking her hand in my arm.

I wanted to take her back and feel her come on my dick again and again until we were both limp. And at the end of the night I could have her again in my bed.

I took a deep breath, squaring my shoulders. "As I'll ever be," I replied, trying to sound more confident than I felt. "Are you going to be okay?"

She shot me a rueful look. "You didn't care about how sore I'd be when you did that?"

No. I didn't. I'd fucked her so hard it was obscene.

And she'd reveled in it.

I may have slammed myself into her the hardest I ever had out, after walking us to the closet and locking us both in there so nobody could hear the sound of my balls hitting her wet pussy over and over.

Gemma had screamed the closet down but I knew those walls were quiet. Pushing back on me even harder.

She'd winced the moment I'd stopped.

And even if I'd checked in on her, Gemma had kissed me reassuring me that she was fine. She loved it.

I'd kissed her back desperately knowing we were out of time.

We stepped into the room, and I felt a rush of possessiveness and fear as eyes darted over me and Gemma.

I tried to keep track of all the names Gemma kept whispering to me, but the sheer scale of the Marchand clan was overwhelming.

Cousins, second cousins, and close family friends all mingled together, their interactions marked by a sense of familiarity and shared history.

Finally, we reached a small group of younger guests near the bar.

Two tall, handsome men turned to greet us, their chiseled features and striking opal eyes marking them unmistakably as Gemma's family members.

The taller of the two, Max, stepped forward with a warm smile.

"Gemma, you look radiant," he said, embracing her affectionately before turning to me. "And you must be Nathan."

"Nate, this is my cousin Max and his brother Bastian." Gemma introduced them. "They're the Spencers. The much less eloquent side of the family since they're fully American. Currently I believe these two idiots are going to All Saints Academy."

"Pleasure to meet you," I grinned at them rolling their eyes at Gemma.

Bastian, the younger brother, grinned as he clapped me on the shoulder. "So, you're the one who's been jet-setting around the world with our Gemma?"

"I wouldn't say that," I told him lightly. "We haven't even left the island."

"No?" Bastian's eyes went wide. "Why not? Cousin Gemma—"

Max cut in. "They're allowed to relax, idiot. Not everyone has to go racing for fun." He looked at me. "Bas and Teo believe in living life to their limits."

Gemma shook her head mock-rolling her eyes. "And a little too much apparently. Didn't you two almost get into trouble?"

"When are Teo and Bas not in trouble?" Max looked at me. "You'll have to excuse my brother, he's got a penchant for riling people up when he shouldn't."

Teo? Who were these people?

"I do not," Bastian cut in with a mock frown.

Max argued. "Like you wouldn't rather be in Monaco with Teo—"

"I would if you and Andrei hadn't stepped in—" Bas shot back.

Max rolled his eyes as Gemma ruefully smiled at them.

"Say Gemma, has your new..." Max eyed Camilla and Gerard. "Has she mentioned anything about her friend's the Nash's? Are they going to bring their daughter out?"

Gemma shook her head with a frown. "What?"

Another woman with strawberry blonde hair stepped into our little circle and Max looked over at her. "Cecily, I thought you'd be late—" he broke off at the sight of her dress.

All of us did. It was a little too puffy for her and she frowned at us as it looked overwelhming for her tiny frame.

"Don't you dare, Bas." She started her voice lacking conviction.

"Who dressed you? Mum?" Bas did in fact start. His voice was teasing as he eyed her. "You look like—"

"Don't—"

"...a bloody strawberry—"

"Bas!" She looked at Gemma. "Gem, I need your help!"

Gemma's eyes softened on the younger woman who looked all of twelve.

"Bas, quit it." Max snapped at his younger brother and then his eyes softened on Cecily. "Where's Mum? Come on, I'll talk to her...Gemma can you help Cecily while I find our mother?"

Gemma looked at me. "I'll be good, just taking her to the ladies room. See what I can do about this..." She motioned to...the fluff.

Max looked grateful as he stepped off to his mother.

"Do you need me to come with you?" I had to ask her.

Her family members were the only people here.

She wasn't in any danger from them.

Was she? I didn't know but the back of my neck prickled as Gemma's eyes met mine.

"No, I promise it'll be fine." Her smile was warm and our eyes locked. I nodded resisting the urge to kiss her as she left.

Gemma took Cecily's hand and the other girl looked grateful. She hadn't been gone for two seconds when I heard Bas open his mouth.

"So...Nate...how long have you been sleeping with my cousin?"

TWENTY-ONE
GEMMA

"Cousin Gemma, I'm hideous."

In the privacy of the bathroom, Cecily sobbed quietly in her dress.

"I'm a hideous strawberry."

She plucked at the fabric of the god-awful dress her mother had her in.

She was all gangly limbs and uncertain smiles at this age drowning in pink ruffles.

I bit back my own laughter. "You are not. Why does Aunt Catherine insist on putting you in these outfits? I don't understand..." I muttered smoothing it down a bit, but it seemed...I thought about what to do.

"She says it isn't proper for a young lady...but I look like a cake topper." I couldn't hold back my giggles as Cecily wiped her eyes. "I'm fourteen, Gem, but she treats me like I'm eight."

"Hmm," I wondered out loud. "I mean..." my eyes met Cecily's. I liked her side of the family a lot. "If something happened to this dress... I mean I would say you had to change into a new one, wouldn't you?"

Her eyes once sad now twinkled. "Cousin Gemma, you're wicked."

I smiled feeling the surge of affection for my cousin.

"I try. Come on, let's go to my room. I believe I have something there that's more appropriate. Aunt Catherine can blame me for spilling..."I looked around the bathroom. "Here's some sparkling water." I held up the bottle to Cecily.

Just as we were about to make our escape, the bathroom door swung open. Camilla entered, her dark green gown shimmering a little under the lights. I don't know why my heart began thundering in my chest as my smile dipped.

"Gemma, darling. Enjoying yourself tonight?"

I don't know why Cecily stiffened behind me, her small hand gripped my dress.

Camilla's tone was honey-sweet, but unlike Nate's there was an undercurrent of steel in her voice.

"Yes, of course. I was just helping Cecily over here with her hair." I fibbed it after years of navigating family politics.

"Help how?" Camilla raised a perfectly shaped brow. "It looks perfectly fine to me."

She turned to look at me. "I heard Catherine speaking about how much she loved the way Cecily looked tonight," she said not too lightly.

"I understand," I said. I had known Aunt Catherine on and off for years. "But I also think Cecily's happiness is important."

"While I appreciate the notion of you trying to help little Cecily with her hair, I do think we should let her get that help from someone…" her eyes wandered over my own locks. I had switched from the updo to putting it down until it fell in waves Nate loved over my back. "With perhaps better skills?"

And then she turned her smile to Cecily.

"I beg your pardon?" I managed my voice tight as a wave of embarrassment went through me.

Camilla's smile was wide. "I mean, I'm not trying to be rude Gemma, but was it appropriate of you to come to our family gathering with your hair down like…like we were…commoners? I thought I made the dress code clear?" She hadn't had a dress-code.

"I don't recall—"

"I know you've been a part of this family and I'm new to this and all, but we can't have people thinking we're losing our standards." She laughed a little, the sound grating on my nerves, and Cecily shrunk into me a bit.

"I don't understand what you're saying—" I broke off frustration building in my chest.

What the hell was happening right now?

I just wanted to do Cecily's hair.

"I'm confused as to what me choosing to put my hair down has anything to do with standards?"

I wasn't confused. But I wouldn't be bullied by my own step-mother. No. She was my father's current wife. She wasn't anything to me.

"Well, I just think it better if I were to help Cecily with her hair. I might be more fitting for it anyway and I'm sure Catherine won't mind since we were good friends. Isn't that right, Cecily? Come now. Let's go to back to the party."

Behind me I looked as Cecily came out from my skirts and gave me a scared look. She was afraid, but she was going to do what Camilla said. Because…she was a child.

And Camilla was an adult.

Hot rage burned inside of me as Camilla extended her hand to Cecily with a smile. Her eyes glittered under the bathroom lights like she had won something.

"Such a sweet girl, Cecily. Your mother was so happy tonight seeing you like this, you wouldn't want to be a bad girl tonight and make her upset now would you?"

"She isn't making Aunt Catherine upset," I muttered. "She's her own person—"

Camilla cut me off. "Come on, Cecily. Let's give Gemma a breather in the bathroom while she calms down—"

"I am calm—"

What the Hell was happening?

Camilla gave Cecily a mock look of disbelief and to my horror Cecily smiled up at her. What the bloody hell was happening?

As she led Cecily who didn't look entirely happy out I was standing there with disbelief on my face.

"I want you to know that you can always come to me, Gemma. I may not be your mother, but I do care about you. Deeply."

"What—"

"I don't have children of my own, as you know," Camilla continued, her voice dripping with false sympathy. "I just hope we can be on good terms. Tell each other everything. This world can be so big and scary, especially for a young woman like yourself. You know, I had a friend

115

once, when I was your age," Camilla mused, her fingers trailing along the marble countertop. "She got involved with the wrong sort of man. Someone in a position of authority, not unlike your Mr. Wyatt."

Her lips curved into a smile that didn't quite reach her eyes. "It didn't end well for her."

What? Why was she? Nate was still my guard.

I swallowed hard, my heart pounding against my ribs.

"Why bring up Mr. Wyatt?" I tried to keep my voice steady, but the rapid thrumming of my pulse threatened to drown out my words. "Why would you say something like that?"

"I wasn't implying anything untoward, Gemma," Camilla continued, her tone honeyed but laced with something sharper. "I simply noticed your closeness with him."

"Mr. Wyatt is my guard, Camilla. Nothing more. He's fulfilling his duties, I assure you."

"Right." Camilla's gaze flickered over my dress, a faint frown tugging at her lips. "That dress is...interesting. It's meant to be that snug, I presume? At your age, I could wear anything," she continued, a wistful edge to her voice. "Of course, I was a bit more...proportional, shall we say?"

The dress that had made me feel beautiful and confident mere moments ago now felt like a second skin, tight and constricting.

"Are you saying I should change?"

"Oh, darling," she said, her voice suddenly gentle. "Don't be silly. The dress is lovely on you. I was just remembering my own youth. You know, confidence is everything. If you believe you look good, others will too. It's all about how you carry yourself, dear. I'm sure you'll grow into that...eventually. I just want what's best for you."

I felt confused.

"Gemma, darling," Camilla said, her voice dripping with false concern. "Don't you remember? At breakfast this morning, when I told you not to eat so much...that might be one reason why the dress looks a bit off."

I blinked, trying to recall. "Oh..." What? I was disoriented. Confused. And I felt something in me frustrated.

Like my body was at war with my mind at what I was going through.

116

What was that sensation?

Camilla laughed lightly, patting my cheek. "Oh, you! You were so focused on your father, you didn't even notice me there. It's understandable, really. You've always been a bit...distracted."

Nate gave me pancakes...

"Let's not dwell on these little things. You look...adequate. And that's what matters, isn't it? We can't all be stunning, but we can certainly try our best. Why don't you polish up while I take Cecily back to her mother?"

As she shut the door I stood there reeling processing what just happened. And why I didn't understand any of it.

TWENTY-TWO
NATE

"WHAT?"

I turned to Bas who grinned at me. "I'm just kidding." He laughed it off but my heart was racing. "But I know you want my cousin even if you'd be a fool to sleep with her."

My heart was racing right now, throat dry as Bas chuckled.

He chuckled at my expression. "I know when a man wants a woman, Nate. Trust me, I've had my eye on one for a long time and she doesn't want me."

I didn't even know how to fucking formulate words around Bastian Spencer the IV or whatever the fuck he was. He was perceptive as fuck so I played dumb.

"Who's the girl?" I asked to distract him from the fact that I didn't want to sleep with Gemma, I already was.

As Bas told me about some girl he liked who he knew didn't want him back, my eyes drifted across the room to find Max talking to a woman right next to Camilla. Who was listening intently.

"Bas," I began. "Is that Max talking to your mother?"

"Yes, it is. I think that's Uncle Gerard's new wife, isn't it?" His tone was casual but his eyes were sharp.

I tipped my head. "Camilla. Come to think of it, what was her last name?"

Bastian swirled his ice in his drink as he spoke. "I think she was married to Jacques Arnoult. Wealthy art-dealer in Paris before Uncle Gerard. She worked in antiquities. Mid-century stuff. Not too sure, I'm not art savvy."

"What happened to him?" I was piqued.

This was the most I'd learned about Camilla.

His voice was quiet. "Heart attack about a year ago. A bit sudden but given his eating and drinking habits, it wasn't a surprise to anyone."

He turned to me fully. "But Camilla inherited everything from him and used that to continue his legacy. She wasn't really with anyone, but she's good friend's with the Nash family."

He took a sip of his drink.

I didn't know that name. "Should I know who the Nash's are?"

"If you want to be around Gemma," Bas winked conspiratorially at me. "They've been around for ages. Winston Nash is the equivalent of God around their world for art and all things security. Art insurance, transportation, they've got a team like an arsenal of people to help build their empire."

Bas looked at me with seriousness. "They not only offer private security for art collectors, but recover services for all things that are stolen. Nobody steals from the Nash's. Part of why they're so popular."

"I've never heard of them." I worked in security and granted I was young but shouldn't I have?

Bas was gleeful as he laughed. "That's the point. If they were well known they wouldn't be good at what they do. They're discreet. The family has been around for ages. The youngest son of Winston, Malcolm, he just took over the family business after his older brother Harry died."

Bas looked over at the bartender motioning for another drink.

"And Malcolm Nash happens to be very close to Camilla Arnoult."

Something about the way Bas spoke told me he knew something more.

"You think…" I drifted off. "He and…"

His eyes gleamed wickedly as the bartender topped him off. "I always know when a man wants to sleep with a woman."

His lips curled in a smirk. "Camilla and Malcolm Nash are thick as thieves. He's got a daughter a little older than Gemma though. I believe she was once married to my friend Teo's older brother. But you didn't

119

hear that one from me. I'm sure the Nash's won't be happy if they heard me repeating that little bit."

This was almost too much information. "Why wouldn't they be happy?"

Bas smirked with mirth in his eyes but a hint of steel. "Because the Nash's make the Marchand's look *polite*. Like I said. Security folk. Malcolm Nash isn't fond of gutter scum. Apparently Malcolm didn't like the idea of his daughter being with a DuPont of any kind. Not good enough for the Nash's. He ended that the moment he found out. Or so I heard…" he drifted off looking at his glass again. "Teo wouldn't tell me but there were whispers. Just a rumor by the way…lucky for you, Uncle Gerard isn't that horrible." He winked at me. "Uncle Gerard would never try and kill you because you're with my cousin."

My heart began racing again. "I'm not with Gemma."

"Yet." Bas grinned. "Fear not. It goes nowhere. I'm only here giving you the information."

He wasn't even older than Gemma and here he was talking to me like some operative.

"Odd, Camilla likes Uncle Gerard. Doesn't seem like his type other than she's blonde but then again, Aunt Jackie is an artist now."

So then why was Camilla with Gerard?

I turned back to Camilla. Or I tried to. She was gone and now Gerard was talking to Catherine and Max who stood there looking a little red in the face.

I frowned. Where had she gone? Gemma…

"You should know, Nate," Bas cut off my thoughts. "If you want to pursue my cousin at all, you should be aware of the connections around us." His eyes gleamed as he grinned at me. "Ever thought about taking her to Monaco? It's fun."

"No," my eyes scanned for Camilla and Gemma. Where did she— *the bathroom.* "Bas…I need to find Gemma."

I couldn't even focus on Bas's assumptions.

I needed to get my girl. Something about Camilla rubbed me the wrong way. And it wasn't her connections with art.

As I got to the bathroom I saw Camilla walking out with Cecily in hand still in her puffy pink dress and hair all…fluffy. And then Gemma stepped out looking confused and pale.

120

I was on her in a second ignoring Camilla and Cecily.

"Duchess—"

Her throat worked nervously as she looked at me. "Does this dress look bad on me?"

What?

"What?" I had destroyed her upstairs in that dress because it looked beautiful.

"You don't think it fits weird?"

"No, Duchess. What's going on?"

She shook her head looking confused and a little off. And even as she retuned to the party, I knew something happened between her and Camilla.

"Was Camilla in the bathroom with you?"

Gemma's eyes met mine and she shook her a head a tiny bit.

I read the message loud and clear.

Not now.

TWENTY-THREE
NATE

SOMETHING WAS UP WITH HER.

A shift I couldn't quite put my finger on, but it had me worried as hell the next morning.

It started off small, little things most people might've missed. I caught her poking at a grapefruit instead of digging into her usual spinach mushroom omelette with toast and butter.

"Not feeling it today, Duchess?"

She just shrugged, avoiding my eyes. "Wanted something light, that's all."

Couple days later, I spotted her checking herself out in a shop window, pinching at her waist and frowning.

The second she saw me watching, her hand dropped and she plastered on a smile. But I knew what I'd seen.

"That why you're not eating, Duchess?" I reached for her, wanting to pull her close. "*C'mere.*"

But she pulled back, letting me kiss her but still not meeting my gaze. Shit. When Bonnie brought out her lemon tart for dessert, Gemma waved it off, claiming she was stuffed. Bullshit.

Her plate was nearly untouched and she almost passed out on the way to her room.

I grabbed her, steadying her, and felt my heart drop. She felt so damn fragile in my arms, like she might break.

"You okay?"

"Just tired." But I could see the dark smudges under her eyes, the way her skin had gone all pale. Something was wrong.

"Duchess?"

She gave me a weak smile. "I'm fine, Nate. Just a little dizzy."

"When's the last time you ate a real meal?"

"I'm just...trying to lose a few pounds."

"Bullshit, Duchess. There's not a damn thing wrong with your body," I said, my voice firm. I pulled her onto my lap, rubbing her back, trying to soothe her. "Talk to me, baby. What's going on?"

She felt way too light against my chest, and it only made me more determined. "We're getting some food in you."

Gemma put up a half-hearted fight, but I wasn't having it. I took her to this cozy little restaurant I knew she'd dig.

Tucked away in a quiet corner, I held her close, feeding her bites from my own plate.

She resisted at first, but when I dipped a piece of bread in olive oil and held it to her lips, she finally opened up.

The way she looked at me as she took that bite, the trust in her eyes...it damn near broke me.

"You keep eating for me like this, I'll feed you every meal," I murmured, pressing kisses to her face. "That better, Duchess?"

She nodded, slow and unsure, but it was a start. My heart felt like it might burst. From then on, Gemma only ate what I hand-fed her. Breakfasts were a bitch, but I worked it out with Nigel to have trays sent up to her room.

One night, Gemma was perched on my lap in the kitchen, eyeing a plate of pasta like it might bite her. "Nate, the calories in that..."

"It's good, healthy food, Duchess," I cut her off gently. "Now, open wide."

She pouted, but I just grinned at her. "That's my girl."

Nigel walked in just then, his eyebrows shooting up at the sight of us. I just shrugged, not about to explain myself.

"Miss Gemma," Nigel said, giving me a look that said he knew exactly what was up. "Fancy a lemon tart?"

"No, I shouldn't—" Gemma started, but I wasn't having that.

"She'll take two." I nuzzled into her shoulder, dropping a kiss there. "Go on, baby. Another bite for me?"

Her cheeks went all pink as she let me feed her, and I saw Nigel fighting back a smile. Later, after Gemma went up to bed, he cornered me.

"Quite the deft hand you have with Miss Gemma these days," he observed.

I grinned, savoring a bite of lemon tart. "I speak fluent Gemma."

He smiled, and I felt a surge of gratitude for his silent understanding and support. As I headed upstairs to join Gemma, my heart felt full, knowing I'd do anything to keep her safe.

One evening Gemma was taking a shower washing off the remnants of my come all over her.

I'd fucked her so hard in the walk in closet, she'd come screaming.

And I'd given up on the fucking condom, pulling out of her and painting her skin with me—Gemma had loved it.

Now, the study was quiet as I reviewed security protocols. The soft click of the door opening barely registered until a familiar scent wafted in. My spine stiffened instinctively.

Camilla.

"Mr. Wyatt," she said, her voice light but with an undercurrent I couldn't quite place. "I hope I'm not interrupting."

I looked up, forcing a polite smile. "Not at all, Mrs. Marchand. How can I help you?"

She drifted into the room, her movements graceful yet purposeful. "Oh, I just wanted to discuss some…concerns I have."

Her eyes met mine, a flicker of something passing through them that set my teeth on edge.

"Concerns?" I echoed, my guard up.

"Mm," she hummed, perching on the edge of my desk. Too close. "About Gemma. She seems...different lately. I was hoping you might have noticed something."

I frowned, choosing my words carefully. "I haven't noticed anything unusual, Mrs. Marchand." Because my girl did talk to me and she told me what happened with Cecily. With Camilla. And I was on edge. It wasn't my place to say anything to my employer which Camilla counted as.

"I thought, given how...attentive you are to her, you might have some insight."

"Just doing my job." I kept it professional and curt.

Camilla's laugh was soft, almost intimate. "Of course, of course. I didn't mean to imply otherwise. It's just...well, you're so dedicated. It's admirable, really."

felt the bookshelf press against my back, trapping me between literature and Camilla's predatory gaze.

"In fact," she continued, her eyes never leaving mine. "I was thinking perhaps we could...work together more closely. For Gemma's benefit, of course."

"I'm not sure I understand," I managed. *Pretend like she's shit leadership grilling you. Lie to her face. Look her in the eyes.*

Camilla smiled, a practiced expression that chilled me to the bone. "Oh, I was just trying to be a better mother. You know I don't have any children of my own and Gemma is such a lovely girl—" she broke off her eyes wide. "I was just worried about her. She seems a little thinner than usual—"

Bullshit. She wasn't. I swallowed around my emotions and the words constricted in my throat.

"Mrs. Marchand," I started, trying to keep my voice steady, modulating my tone like I was talking to my subordinates. "I appreciate your...concern. But I assure you, everything is fine."

Her eyes were cold as she looked at me with that creepy smile. I didn't like this woman one bit. "All right then, I'll let you get on with your...what are those?"

Plans with Gemma. None of her business.

"Just day to day work—"

"And my husband pays you for this paperwork portion of your duties as well when you should be with Gemma?"

What the fuck—

"Mrs. Marchand—"

"Please, call me Camilla—"

I'd rather shoot myself in the foot.

"Everything I do is for Miss Gemma. I can assure you she's safe and sound in her room right now." Because I'd fucked her hard enough to know she wasn't going anywhere.

"How dedicated of you," Camilla's eyes searched my face. See, that was the thing about Camilla.

She thought she was slick.

She wasn't. Because I spent a lifetime around cunts like Camilla in the military. They came in every shape and every size and male or female they never got away with it from me.

Because I knew her. She was the kind of person who would stomp on someone's throat in a firefight to get out of it herself. And then she'd cry her crocodile tears up the chain of command.

I knew Camilla.

The Camilla's were the reason I got out of the military.

People who raised Camilla's were just as guilty as the people who were her. And I knew who she was. She wasn't hiding it from me.

"Just doing my job."

"Well, I won't keep you any longer. Do let me know if there's anything I can do to... assist you in your duties."

Right. As she left, she bent to pick up something off the floor and I looked down at my watch seeing a text from Gemma. She was done showering. And I'd cuddle her for the night.

"Sorry, dropped something." I ignored Camilla and focused on the memory of Gemma sleeping in my arms.

Keeping her safe. Going on her gap year with her.

As Camilla straightened a necklace spilled out of her blouse she tucked back into her shirt. I looked down pretending I saw nothing. Like I didn't see the design on them.

Maybe initials? Whose?

Malcolm Nash. A wealthier man who had money equivalent to Gerard. Only she was…with Gerard? I knew it had been a whirlwind marriage. Gerard might've been in love with her. But I didn't get why. I didn't see anything she did.

I waited a few moments before I stepped into the hall and I nearly collided with Nigel. Our eyes met, and I knew instantly that he'd overheard.

"Mr. Wyatt."

"Nigel."

"Pleasant evening."

"Yes."

Right. I need to go to Gemma. This was awkward.

Of course Nigel was here.

The moment I found Gemma in her bed with her towel around her and a smile on her face, I had her in my arms. Trying to calm down my heart racing in my chest.

Because oddly enough, even though we weren't being threatened—I felt like I was counting my days.

~

ONE EVENING, I FOUND MYSELF IN NIGEL'S GARAGE, MINDLESSLY handing him tools as he worked on one of the cars. The familiar clinking of objects did nothing for me.

My thoughts were a storm of guilt all centered around Gemma.

Nigel's voice cut through my internal struggle.

"Mr. Wyatt. You've seemed...preoccupied these past weeks. Is everything alright?"

He knew *something.*

But how much?

After a long pause, I managed. "I'm...I'm fine. Just...a lot on my mind."

He set down his wrench and turned to face me fully, his eyes searching mine. "If you ever need to talk, I'm here. About anything. No matter how difficult some things may be."

I nodded. How could I?

Camilla was our boss.

I didn't know what to say so I kept my mouth shut.

I snuck into Gemma's room and kissed her steadily, falling asleep with her in my arms. Or trying to. My phone went off, the light flashing but thankfully it was on silent.

My phone was silently buzzing and I stepped out to take the call.

The name on the screen surprised me.

Reed Whittaker, an old supervisor from my military days.

Reed was straight good as a leader. Too good.

He never compromised his integrity for profit or popularity, which had made him unpopular with leadership and higher-ups. Reed didn't sell out his team. He got annoyed whenever people tried to fuck with us. And he backed everyone to the death.

And part of the reason why they had fucked him over.

Eventually, Reed had given them the middle finger and left.

So had I.

"Reed. It's been a while. What's up?"

"I've got an offer for you."

As he kept talking, I slowly sat up. *What…what the fuck did he just say? He's starting his own company?*

"A security company?" I asked, my pulse quickening.

"It's called Titan. I wanna make sure I get you on the team if you want," Reed confirmed, then laid out the details. It was a leadership position, with significant responsibilities. "Think it over. It's a lot."

"One hell of thing…"

"Yeah," he sounded amused. "What is it like midnight?"

"Just about." It was in the evening for him in the States.

"You're working security now for some family?"

"Gerard Marchand," I muttered. "Not too bad."

Reed made a noise. "Let me know what you want."

A chance to be my own boss, to build something meaningful, to use my skills in a way that could make a real difference.

And then another thought crept in as I exhaled.

What about Gemma?

What would I do without her?

All I wanted was her. Just Gemma.

She was my heart. And I loved her. As much as I wanted to go? I wondered if Reed would let me bring her.

Would she want to come? What about school?

We wouldn't be far apart since she was going to school in New York. And Reed was stationing up in Greenwich. It wasn't far.

I didn't know what to do.

It was a chance to prove myself, to build *something* stable and solid without fearing the inevitable, losing my actual job.

But leaving Gemma?

Felt like I was thinking about chopping off my own arm.

"Can I think it over?"

"Yeah. Just give me a heads up, I might already have a job I need you on."

Well. That was fast. But life happened fast in that world. A world where I'd be...not a pawn anymore. But a major player. Reed was going to give me a fucking opportunity and...I'd be a fool to not take it.

But Gemma. Her gap year. Her...life.

I hung up and went back to Gemma, I laid there with her feeling wide awake my thoughts churning.

Until Gemma rolled over and cuddled into my chest, instinctively seeking my warmth. I wanted to take her away from everything. From Camilla. From her life.

My chest expanded and contracted painfully.

How could I leave her? *Ever?*

But if I took her with me?

Would I ruin her life? Would she be happy with my simple life?

Gemma might not have wanted to be a Marchand.

But part of me knew Gemma didn't know what it felt like to scrape by. To do her own laundry. To make food herself. Part of me knew deep down even if I was a summer fancy for her, I liked being hers.

I was conflicted.

Young and dumb and making all types of choices I shouldn't have made.

Even if Reed's offer felt like a green light?

I didn't know what to say. Or do. And so I laid there holding my girl wishing something fucking gave me the answer.

TWENTY-FOUR
GEMMA

I was in the kitchen with Bonnie eating some leftover lemon ricotta gnocchi she'd made when Camilla walked in.

"Bonnie, the towels are not pressed the way I asked them to," she snapped, her voice sharp and cold. The words sliced into the peaceful atmosphere ruining the moment. And I frowned when her eyes landed on me.

Her gaze traveled from the pasta bowl in my hand to my hair, assessing every detail.

"Gemma, dear," she said, her voice now dripping with false sweetness. "You look healthy."

I heard Nate's voice in my head telling me not to let her get to me.

Baby, I think Camilla sees you as competition. I've had leadership like that. No matter how fucking old they get, they have to compete with the younger guys. Don't let her get to you.

"Thank you, Camilla," I managed to reply. I tried to sound strong but my voice didn't have it and I didn't know why.

Why did she make me feel like this?

I couldn't put my finger on it.

Camilla's presence seemed to fill the space, pushing out all warmth and ease like a vacuum of cold.

"What are you having?" Camilla said brightly, her smile not quite reaching her eyes.

"Gnocchi. Would you like some? Bonnie made it," I offered, motioning to Bonnie, who had grown unusually quiet.

Camilla's eyes flicked to the bowl, then back to me.

"Pancakes and gnocchi? I wish I was young again," she said with a light laugh that sounded forced.

Without thinking, I replied. "It's my Maman's recipe. Bonnie always makes it for me when I come here in the summer. Papa said it's his favorite thing since it's the only thing Maman doesn't mess up." I grinned easily at the memory of the three of us. Of different times.

The change in Camilla's face was subtle but unmistakable.

Her smile froze, her eyes hardening slightly.

"Is that so?" she said, her voice carefully controlled. "I'm sure your father's tastes have...evolved since then."

I didn't think before responding. "Maybe, but he still prefers classic comforts. And I do too. Maman loved this recipe."

At that, Camilla's eyes became arctic, though her smile remained fixed in place. The temperature in the room seemed to drop several degrees.

"I think I know what my husband likes," she said, her voice tight. "I'm afraid I have to watch my figure."

I was confused again. Why was speaking to her like mental gymnastics? She found flaws in every single thing I said.

My brows furrowed. "Camilla, I wasn't implying—"

"Bonnie, will you be a darling and please get us the proper towels," Camilla interrupted, her voice saccharine sweet but with an edge that brooked no argument. Bonnie hurried off.

"Gemma, dear," Camilla said, her tone patronizing. "I know you mean well, but perhaps it's time to leave the past in the past. Your father and I have a new life now, and it would be...helpful if you could embrace that."

I swallowed hard, confusion and hurt swirling inside me. "I don't understand. I was just talking about a recipe—"

"Of course you don't understand," Camilla cut in smoothly. "You're young. But trust me, constantly bringing up your mother...it's not good for anyone. Especially your father."

Her words hit me like a slap. My cheeks burned with embarrassment and indignation. How had a simple conversation about gnocchi turned into this?

"Camilla, I didn't mean any disrespect. I was simply telling Bonnie—"

"I heard you."

"...that's what my father likes. I did nothing wrong."

Camilla's eyes narrowed. "I think I know what your father likes, don't you? I'm his wife."

But I'm his daughter, I wanted to say. Instead, I took a deep breath. "I know you're his wife. Why would I want to come between you and him? Is that what you think?" I was so confused by this woman? Why did she come across as so toxic? "Why would you ever assume I might be your competition? You're older than me."

But rather than answering I heard.

"Duchess, is everything good?"

Both of our heads turned to Nate who stood in the doorway.

"I was coming to get you for your trip today." He was talking to me. We didn't have a trip today. But he was going to get me out of here. I took it.

"Of course, sorry, I got carried away. The gnocchi was delicious." I made quiet conversation as Camilla's demeanor shifted instantly, her smile returning, though it didn't reach her eyes. And then those eyes drifted over Nate.

I quickly left with him feeling her eyes on us.

And I was aware something had shifted.

TWENTY-FIVE
NATE

"Miss Camilla has been asking about you. She mentioned needing to discuss some...security matters."

I frowned. "The only person I discuss anything related to Gemma with is Mr. Marchand or you."

And as of the last few months it had been Nigel. He nodded looking uncomfortable. "I'm sorry, Mr. Wyatt." He swallowed hard. "She just has questions. I don't know."

I noted Nigel never called her Mrs. Marchand.

I sighed as I walked to her...whatever the fuck it was...study area. She was lingering wherever I was.

"Nathan," she was sitting there with that cold smile on her face as I walked in. "I've been meaning to speak with you about Gemma's security arrangements for her gap year."

Why? She wasn't going to be there? I had considered Reed's offer but I knew I wanted to spend the year with Gemma and then ask Reed if he was still looking.

I hadn't given either Gerard or Reed an answer yet.

"Is there a particular reason why?" I asked. I knew Camilla was the kind of person who took everything the wrong way. "Do you have specific concerns?"

She stood from behind her desk to perch at the edge of it a few feet away from me.

"Please, call me Camilla. We've known each other long enough, haven't we?" Her smile was brittle, almost forced. "I just...I worry about her, you know? She's so young, so naive—"

"I wouldn't say that. She's nineteen."

"And young," Camilla's eyes were on me. "You understand, right?"

I felt a twinge of unease at her words. "Gemma is quite capable, Mrs...Camilla. But rest assured, her safety is my top priority. How can I assist?"

Camilla's eyes hardened for a moment. "Yes, I've noticed how...dedicated you are to her." She paused, studying me. "You know, Mr. Wyatt. Loyalty is an admirable trait. But it can be...limiting."

She's worse than the military.

And she thought I was stupid.

I swallowed hard, feeling the conversation shift into dangerous territory. "I'm not sure I follow."

She leaned in slightly, her perfume subtle but noticeable. "I just mean that there are opportunities for someone with your skills. Opportunities that might be...overlooked if one is too focused on a single client."

"I appreciate your concern, Camilla. But I'm satisfied with my current position."

"There are opportunities here you might not have considered. Opportunities that could benefit us both." As she said it, something crawled down my spine. Unease settling deep into it.

"What exactly are you suggesting?"

"I'm suggesting we could help each other."

"How is that?"

She leaned in, spreading her legs a little. I wanted to vomit a bit. Camilla was a monster.

The walls seemed to close in. I felt cornered, my mind racing for a way out of this impossible situation.

This is worse than the military because Gemma is right there.

Before I could respond, there was a knock at the door.

Camilla stepped back, her demeanor shifting seamlessly as Nigel entered.

"Pardon the interruption," Nigel said, his eyes flicking between us. I felt a surge of relief tinged with panic. How much had he heard?

"Mr. Wyatt, you're needed urgently."

I nodded, grateful for the escape. "On it." I rushed out of there feeling Camilla's eyes on me.

In the hallway, Nigel looked at me with concern. "Are you alright, Mr. Wyatt?"

"Yeah, what's up? Is Gemma all right?"

"Oh, she's perfectly fine." Nigel said quietly his eyes holding a hint of amusement. "Did I do it at the right time?"

And I felt a reluctant grin tug at my lips. "Nigel. You should've been in the military."

"I don't think so Mr. Wyatt. Green isn't my color."

I laughed outright then as we both walked away.

"Are you all right, sir?"

My career, my relationship with Gemma, the precarious balance I'd been maintaining—it all felt like it was about to come crashing down.

"Yeah, I'm...I'm fine. Thanks, Nigel." The lie tasted bitter on my tongue.

He nodded, a look of understanding passing between us.

"If you need anything sir—"

"I got you, Nigel."

"Exactly."

Except I didn't know how well Nigel would do against a pit viper like Camilla.

TWENTY-SIX
GEMMA

ONE DAY, I SEIZED THE OPPORTUNITY TO CONNECT WITH MY FATHER while Camilla was out and about in town.

She rarely left his side, so I knew I had to make the most of this moment.

With Nate in his room, I made my way to Papa's study.

I found him at his desk, engrossed in his work. Knocking gently on the door, I watched as his eyes lit up when he saw me.

"Duchess," he chuckled, his voice warm with affection. "To what do I owe this pleasure?" I hugged him firmly noticing he'd felt like he'd lost some weight.

"I thought I'd come and pester you for a bit," I grinned, pulling back to look at him. "I missed you, Papa. It felt like forever waiting for you to come see me."

"Ah, I suppose I did take quite a long honeymoon, didn't I? I missed you too, darling," he said softly, brushing a strand of hair from my face. "How have you been? Excited for your gap year?"

His eyes crinkled at the corners when he smiled and I launched into an animated description of my plans to explore New York City before starting school. "Be warned, Papa. I might come back with a Yankee accent."

"Your mother was quite good at mimicking a Brooklyn accent. I always found it rather charming."

At the mention of Maman a wistful expression crossed his eyes. I hesitated but I had to ask. "Do you still talk to her sometimes? Has she met Camilla?"

"No," His mouth turned into a pout, a familiar expression he wore when deep in thought. "Not as much as we used to, no. But Camilla had said she'd been in Paris when you were there. I'm surprised you didn't bump into her."

I frowned. "She was in Paris?"

My father nodded. "She had business in Metz and she thought she'd grab me some souvenirs and macarons. She's always thinking about me." *Was she?* I didn't know that.

I didn't quite know how to express my reservations about Camilla without sounding impolite or hurtful.

"Papa, where did you meet Camilla?" As far as I knew, they hadn't known each other long.

He leaned back in his chair, a nostalgic smile playing on his lips.

"It's quite a story, actually. We met at the annual Sotheby's art auction in New York. I was there to bid on a rare Monet, and she was representing a client interested in the same piece. We ended up in a bidding contest against each other."

"That's fascinating." I couldn't care less, but it was the most I got out of him about her.

"She was a good opponent, but in the end, I won. Afterward, we struck up a conversation about our shared love for Impressionist art, and well, the rest is history."

I absorbed this new information, trying to reconcile the Camilla I knew with the charming art connoisseur my father described. It didn't seem like the same person. Maybe my father heard of a different side of her?

"She seems to make you happy," I said carefully, gauging his reaction. "Does she still work in that industry?"

Nate said Bastian told him, Camilla works with a man named Malcolm Nash.

"She does, Duchess. I know it's been an adjustment for all of us, but I'm rather pleased you are trying. Since you're going to New York, maybe you should talk to her about it. She doesn't work in the city anymore, but she still has a client or two that reaches out to her."

"She still works now?" I asked, genuinely curious about Camilla's life beyond our family.

"Yes, she's currently procuring some pieces for Malcolm Nash. Winston Nash's youngest son."

That was the same man. I didn't know who he was. I didn't know who to ask.

But Nate had mentioned Bastian's friend Teo DuPont's brother knew her.

They'd been together apparently.

I didn't know anything about the DuPont's. Just that their father was handsome as the devil and so were both his sons.

I wanted to know what Papa knew.

"Who is Malcolm Nash?" I leaned forward a bit. I was curious.

"Malcolm is his youngest son. He took over after Harry died. But he's got a daughter just a few years older than yourself. She helps run his company too. Not sure what happened to his wife. I doubt it worked out given that man's work ethic. But Camilla is on good terms with him since her late husband and Harry were friends."

I knew most of this from Nate but it was the part about her late husband that rubbed me the wrong way.

"Camilla's previous husband passed away?"

My father nodded. I knew this but I had to ask.

"He wasn't good at taking care of himself and his health was in decline over the years. Harry I think got into a boating accident. Ever the adventurer he was. But Malcolm and Camilla remained close. He's a good friend to her and myself as well. He actually helped set everything up so we could get married."

Had he? He sounded...helpful.

Now I was piqued.

"Malcolm Nash sounds rather wonderful." A little too much so. Especially since Nate had told me he made us look polite.

Or that he controlled his daughter's relationship with Andrei DuPont, Teo's older brother.

I knew things and I was tucking them away mentally collecting the clues.

Nate told me just to listen to people. Take in the information. We could piece it together later.

But he was good to Papa?

"He was…" My father explained how he'd met with Malcolm and Maman and how they'd spent time together before they'd gone on their honeymoon. "Malcolm has a lovely estate in Cape Verde out of all places in Africa, and Camilla and I toured the place. His daughter Talia, she sometimes stays out there running Nash Group or to Europe."

Talia Nash was the woman married to Andrei DuPont.

But her father did not like him. Why? Why was it important?

"And you met Talia?"

He shook his head. "She was in New York on business at the time. Malcolm sometimes sends her to handle his operation. They have a Midtown office they work in—the Nash Group. You can't miss it. It's a massive tower…"

I listened to my father soaking up the information I could because I could tell Nate. I felt like we were detectives collecting clues and Nate and I loved being a team.

But I didn't know what we were trying to solve.

"That sounds lovely. Camilla sounds very gracious."

"She is. Her expertise and network are truly impressive, Gemma. If you ever considered going into art, she might your cup of tea should you choose to go to New York."

I was going to New York. I hesitated for a moment, weighing my next words carefully.

The idea of Camilla being anything to me in any capacity was unsettling—but I didn't want to overtly criticize my father's wife.

"And do you trust her judgment, Papa?" I was hoping to gauge his level of confidence in her. "I don't mean to be forward—"

His brow furrowed, and I instantly regretted my question. "Of course I trust her, Gemma. What made you—"

"I was speaking about her artwork, Papa." I quickly smoothed over. "I was interested that's all."

His expression softened, and he reached out to pat my hand.

"I know it's been an adjustment for you, but I hope you can see how much she means to me. And yes, her taste in art is excellent, she was thinking about redecorating this place…I mentioned Jacqueline had picked out everything and she liked it all, but wanted to revive it a bit."

"I didn't realize there was a problem with *Maman's* art."

That's why this place felt like home.

I forced a smile, swallowing my lingering doubts.

"But I am glad you've found someone who makes you feel that way."

The sharp knock at the door interrupted our conversation.

We both turned to see Camilla standing in the doorway, a smile plastered on her face as she held a tray.

She looked the part of a doting homemaker in white. All polished and prim, the picture of domestic bliss.

"Camilla, lovely to see you." Papa was obvious to the tension in the room as she stepped inside.

I don't know why it rubbed me the wrong way. I didn't want to despise Camilla. Or my father. I don't know why I did.

"Gerard, I thought you might like some of that blend of tea you enjoy so much."

As she stepped into the room, her eyes locked with mine for a brief moment. Icy blue and pitch cold for me.

I didn't miss the way her smile faltered, replaced by a dark, unreadable expression that vanished as quickly as it appeared. A glimpse into the mask she wore.

"Thank you for thinking of me, darling." And I don't know why my father's voice grated on my nerves. What was wrong with me?

Camilla's smile returned, but it didn't quite reach her eyes. "Of course, darling. Anything for you."

As my father turned to take the tea from her, Camilla's gaze met mine once more. This time, there was no mistaking the icy glint in her eyes.

She had heard our entire conversation.

TWENTY-SEVEN
GEMMA

AND CAMILLA BEGAN TO APPEAR EVERYWHERE I WAS WITH NATE.

She was by the pool when Nate was wrapping a towel around me. Her eyes drifted over us, brows arched as Nate stepped back.

"I didn't know Mr. Wyatt was so…helpful," she said, her voice dripping with insinuation. I fought the urge to react.

I stepped back, my cheeks burning. "Nate was just helping me with my towel."

"Just doing my job." Nate said quietly.

"Of course he was," Camilla replied, her eyes never leaving Nate. "Such a…helpful young man. I had no idea pool and errand boy were included in the line-up of job requirements." She smiled and it rattled me. Irked my nerves and I just wanted to claw it off.

Why did she do this to my head?

He tipped his head politely to her, maintaining his professionalism.

The next morning, when Nate passed me some more food, she materialized at breakfast. "I had no idea you two sat together in the mornings. Might I join?"

What could I say? Nate quickly finished eating and made an excuse about the gym before he left.

"Gemma, what do you think about us having a girls' day?" Her eyes fixed on me, calculating. I would rather fling myself out the window.

I smiled, forcing warmth into my voice. "That sounds lovely. I know you must be busy with Papa, so that means a lot."

"What do you mean?" Her brow furrowed, her head tipping comically, as if confused. I thought I'd been clear.

"I meant, you must be busy—"

"So I don't have time for you—"

What?

"No, that isn't what I said—"

"Then what did you mean, Gemma?" Camilla's voice took on an edge. "Are you implying I'm neglecting you?"

"Why is everything an argument with you?" I snapped. I took a deep breath, trying to keep my composure. "I just meant that I appreciate you making time for me. Why do you take everything I say the wrong way?"

"Oh, so now I need to 'make time' for you?" She leaned back, crossing her arms. "I thought we were family. Maybe you don't realize how you speak might be a bit of an issue."

What on Earth was happening?

How was this conversation spiraling so out of control?

The conversation was spiraling, as it often did with Camilla. Every word I said seemed to be twisted, turned into something I never intended. I could feel a headache building behind my eyes.

"We are family," I said softly, trying to diffuse the situation. "I just meant—"

"I know exactly what you meant," Camilla cut in, her smile not reaching her eyes. "You think I'm some sort of wicked stepmother, don't you? That I'm trying to come between you and your father?"

"That's not—" I started, but she waved her hand dismissively.

"It's fine, Gemma. I understand. You're young, you're used to having your father all to yourself. It must be hard to share."

Her words hit a nerve, but I refused to let it show. "I'm sorry if I've given you that impression, Camilla. It wasn't my intention at all."

She sighed dramatically. "Of course not, dear. I'm sure you didn't mean anything by it."

"I just remembered, I promised Bonnie I'd help her with something this morning," I said, standing up. "Thank you for the breakfast, Camilla. We'll plan that girls' day soon, okay?"

Later that evening, Bonnie pulled me aside, her expression

concerned. She brushed my hair back holding my face. "Miss Gemma. I adore you like my own child, but you must be careful. I understand you're young, and Mr. Wyatt is...well, he's a fine young man. But perhaps it would be wise to be more cautious. Mrs. Marchand, she's... observant."

"I'm not doing anything *wrong*, Bonnie."

Not really.

Nate was not something wrong.

"I know. Just...be careful. Mrs. Marchand, she sees things in a certain way. It might be best to give her less to...interpret."

"What do you mean?" My heart was thumping in my chest because I knew what she meant.

Bonnie hesitated, choosing her words carefully. "Mrs. Marchand is...protective of her position in this family. She might see your relationship with Mr. Wyatt as...threatening, somehow."

I felt a surge of frustration as the knot that had been forming in my stomach since Camilla came in grew tighter. "But that's ridiculous! *Nate is just—*"

"I know, darling," Bonnie interrupted gently. "I know he isn't. But she doesn't see it that way. I overheard her on the phone. Just be careful. Okay?"

I swallowed hard and nodded. But I was rattled. I needed to talk to Nate. He would make it better. We could go to Papa together. He might protect us...right?

Even then I had my doubts about my father and his inability to...be aware of anything.

As I was walking out of the kitchen outside, I took the longer route to my side of the house to clear my head.

And it wasn't until I heard the voice of a woman did I realize I ended up near Camilla's door.

"I know Marcus...I know. I am trying. No...he hasn't yet...his daughter is here and that might be one thing stopping me."

I stilled in my tracks my breath catching in my throat. What?

Camilla?

I slowly crept up to the door like it was a monster. Who was Marcus?

"He's an idiot that's what he is...I can't stand another day here.

Natasha was already annoying and now I have another useless annoying daughter. It's just my luck I can't have a son. I would murder Natasha over and over if it meant I could have a son."

My blood ran cold. Who was Natasha? Why did...had Camilla hurt her? Why? Was she talking about me?

I leaned against the wall, my legs suddenly weak. I felt like I had stumbled into a waking nightmare. I couldn't breathe properly.

I knew I needed to get away, to find somewhere safe to process what I had just heard.

Move. Before she hears or sees you.

But even as I forced myself to move, to slip quietly down the hall and out of earshot—I knew I had to tell Nate.

We had to go to Papa. We had to find a solution to something.

I told Nate everything when we got to my room. He listened intently and nodded. Words rushed from my lips about everything I knew.

"Good job, baby. I think I can make some calls, people who can dig deeper. See if anything Camilla is—is real."

I held his hand. "But it won't cause any repercussions to my father? Will he be safe? Camilla doesn't sound the least bit good, Nate."

Nate's eyes softened, his thumb tracing soothing circles on the back of my hand. "They're discreet, I promise. Your father won't know a thing."

Nate leaned in, pressing his forehead against mine. "We'll figure this out, as a team." I kissed him.

That night Nate made love to me a little differently. There was something unspoken between us. Nerves and something else in between the spaces that let me know something was bothering him. I could see it.

"Nate," I whispered, my voice catching as he moved inside me. "What is it? Please..."

"I fucking love you." He groaned into the crook of my neck. "I love you so much."

I felt my eyes watering, my vision blurred as I whispered it back. "Love you too."

He slid deep inside me, fucking me the way he knew drove me insane, but there was an urgency to his movements that hadn't been there before—as if he was trying to make it impossible for the world to come between us.

144

It only edged me closer to my own orgasm. Pleasure that coursed through me as I clung to him.

"There you go, baby," he murmured stamping his lips over mine as I came.

"I'm not going anywhere," I held onto him promising the words against his lips. "Make love to me. Stay with me. I won't leave you." I didn't even know what I was saying, but it felt like I would do anything to keep him by my side.

I would do anything to keep Nate forever.

Even if it meant taking on Camilla.

THE NEXT MORNING NATE WOKE ME UP TO KISSES.

Lots of them.

So many of them I giggled forgetting the day ahead of me. I sighed as he turned me over, this way and that for him.

When he finally slid into me from behind I was sobbing into my pillows as he fucked into me.

It went on for what felt like forever as he fucked into me. The sensations were overwhelming. I came twice, before Nate finished, warmth flooding me.

It felt incredible this time and I held him tight to me kissing him until Nate had to get up. But Nate pulled away too soon, his face etched with concern.

"Sorry, baby, condom—" he broke off, looking down. His expression shifted from worry to outright panic. "Shit—"

I followed his gaze. "Oh, it...did it break...just now? Or..."

"I think I was in you..." He nodded, guilt flooding his features. "I'm sorry—"

"No—it's—" I did the math quickly, trying to quell the rising anxiety in my chest. "I just finished my period, you're fine. We're fine."

Nate's eyes met mine then, and for a moment, I saw a riot of emotions there—fear, love, regret, and something else I couldn't name. He nodded slowly, but the tension didn't leave his body.

"Let me go clean up. And I'll be back."

As Nate left the room, I lay there, the blanket half covering my body, my mind racing. I didn't care. Not even a little bit. I closed my eyes, imagining a future where I didn't go to university, where instead I stayed with Nate. Where I had his babies, where we built a life together.

It was insane. And I wanted it. I did.

I'd build a house for her.

Take care of the kids.

I wanted to cry. I wanted to go find Nate.

I was about to get up, to go find Nate and tell him everything I was feeling, when the sound of the bedroom door opening froze me in place.

Assuming it was Nate, I started to sit up. "That was qui—"

The words died in my throat as I saw Camilla standing in the door-way, her eyes widening as she took in the scene before her.

Time seemed to stop.

"Oh my," Camilla said, her voice unnaturally calm. "Gemma, darling, I didn't realize you were...entertaining."

I clutched the sheet tighter, my cheeks burning with a mixture of shame and defiance.

Do not freak out. You're allowed a life.

"Camilla—"

She waved a dismissive hand, cutting me off. "No need, dear. The situation speaks for itself." Her gaze swept the room, lingering on Nate's discarded shirt. *She knew.*

"Though I must say, I'm surprised by your...choice."

My heart raced. Nate could return any moment. With trembling fingers, I grabbed my phone, hastily typing.

Camilla's in room.

Camilla's heels clicked softly as she entered the room, each step feeling like a countdown to disaster. "I wonder what your father would say about this...dalliance."

Anger flared within me, momentarily overriding my fear. How dare she judge me for my choice?

"You don't know Nate. Or what we have. And I am doing nothing wrong."

Camilla's eyebrow arched, her smile turning predatory. "Is that why Gerard pays him so much money? *To whore himself—*"

"He is not a whore!" It was as much as I could muster with my

146

blanket around me. "You have no right to speak of him in that manner—"

"I suggest you watch your tone, young lady. I have the power in this house not you!" She hissed at me her eyes wild and wide. "I am in control!"

"You have been nothing but a vapid bitch—"

"I am in control!" Her annoying voice rose to a shrill pitch.

"You are not! This is my house! Nathan is mine! And I won't let you hurt him!" I stood with as much respect as I could muster despite being unclothed, I wrapped the sheet around myself. "I know who you are!"

I was lying. I shouldn't have said it.

"I know who you are!" I yelled again as pure unadulterated rage coursed through me as I trembled not in fear but in rage. "I know you're using my father! I know you're sleeping with Malcolm Nash! And I know you hurt that woman named Natasha."

Her entire demeanor shifted and she paled. I had her. I did. I was bluffing. But she didn't know that. Her composure had cracked.

Her eyes turned narrow and calculating. "And what do you think that matters to me?"

"I know my father doesn't know. And all it takes is me telling him—"

"And you think he'll believe you after your little dalliance with the help—"

"Papa will not care. I am his daughter. You are temporary in his life!"

"You vindictive slut—"

"You're a horrible woman! You're evil. I know it. Since the moment you've shown up you've torn this house to pieces. That's all you do!"

Camilla took a step towards me, her eyes flashing dangerously. "You little bitch. I've killed my own for far less than what you'd said to me today. You say one more word—"

"And I fucking shoot you."

Both of us froze.

Nate.

TWENTY-EIGHT
NATE

My heart hammered against my ribs.

"Get away from her."

Get away from my fucking girl.

I heard the raised voices, I felt it in the back of my neck—the fight brewing. I knew.

I had left my gun tucked behind a picture frame and stuffed animal from Gemma's childhood. They didn't hear me.

But I saw them and I grabbed that gun so fucking fast.

Red clouded my vision. I had to move.

"Step away from Gemma!" I was on her.

Gemma went silent and cold at the sight of the gun in my hands. She'd never felt me like this. No.

I was always restrained around my girl.

I had been in the bathroom out of it after the fucking condom broke but the moment I heard voices I moved.

"Here's what's gonna happen. You're gonna leave this room. You're going to stay away from this family—"

Camilla scoffed. And I didn't give a fuck.

"You're going to leave. Or so help me God I will find you and kill you for threatening my—"

"Or you'll do what? Shoot me? In cold blood?" Her lips curled into a sneer. "I don't care what you've done, nobody would actually believe

you if you did. I couldn't have possibly threatened the Former Special Forces service member who was guarding my family? Could I?"

I didn't say a word as my blood ran cold.

I stood there, gun trained on Camilla with Gemma behind me.

She was right.

Who would believe her threat against me?

I was towering over her. My mind raced.

"Besides, you slept with our girl. Do you really think murdering me is the way to keep Gemma forever?"

"Nate—" Gemma whispered. "Please, don't listen to her. Nate. Please, look at me."

But I couldn't. I had to keep my eyes on the target.

Camilla.

"You threatened me in my home, Mr. Wyatt. What do you think this looks like?"

"No, you threatened my girl in front of me—"

"You mean your charge. Mr. Wyatt." She tsked under breath. "You really have forgotten yourself. Put the gun down. Either way this ends in you ruin. Not mine. And now we can discuss this like civilized people in my study."

"Absolutely not," Gemma growled.

"Whatever you have to say, you can say it here."

I felt the same.

I didn't want to leave Gemma or leave her alone.

"Oh, I don't think so," Camilla replied, her tone light but her eyes hard. "Unless, of course, you want Gemma to hear all about your... colorful past? The things you did in the service that didn't quite make it into your official record?"

I felt the blood drain from my face. "Everything about me is on record."

"Including the fact that you've killed over two hundred people. And I would make it two hundred and one, is that correct?" She tipped her head.

Behind me Gemma was quiet.

I promised Gemma would never know the uglier parts of my life. Let alone this one. But now the past I tried to bury so hard was clawing its way up to the surface and threatening to make the situation worse.

Camilla's smile grew and I wanted to shoot her right there but she had driven me into a hole.

Kill her and be known as the man who murdered his charges wife in front of his daughter who he was sleeping with. I was a guilty man or a dead man. Either way.

I swallowed as I put the gun down.

Gemma let out a breath behind me. "*Nate.*"

"Your study." I motioned to Camilla. "You touch her and I don't fucking care about anything. Move."

I was fired either way. I watched Camilla's smile become snake-like as she stepped out and I turned to Gemma whose entire face contorted, not taking my eyes off Camilla out of my peripheral vision.

My stomach was churning with dread as opal eyes, tear-stained and wide in horror watched me.

She knew.

I knew.

I'm sorry, baby.

"*Nonononono*, don't do it. Don't do it—" she was frantic, her words tumbling out as my heart sank. It was over. "*Nate.* No!" She was livid. "No! I won't let you take him from me, you vindictive bitch!"

"Gemma—" I tried to cut in to stop her but she was gone.

"*Nononono,*" Gemma's entire face contorted with desperation. "*Take me with you. We can leave tonight. We can go. Nate come on—*"

"*Gemma—*"

I wanted nothing more than to take her.

Grab her hand and leave and run. But I couldn't. We couldn't.

I had nothing to protect her with. Nothing to my name.

The consequences would follow us.

She's like her Mama. It's gonna destroy her too. If not more.

"*I don't care! Don't do this!*" Gemma was beyond words and I held her face in my hands aware, the butt of my gun was right there.

By her face. This was *my* life.

The one I didn't deserve to ruin her with.

"Baby, breathe for me. Breathe," I inhaled and exhaled. "Breathe, Duchess—"

"*Nate. Do not go. Don't go. If you go I don't know what to do with myself. Stay with me—Please, please. Stay with me.*"

150

Something akin to panic and desperation in Gemma's voice shattered something inside of my heart.

Baby.

Because in that moment I saw the lengths Gemma was willing to go to for me. She would run away.

And she would hate me if she did.

"I love you."

I couldn't even speak.

I felt like my entire world had been broken, and completely blown to pieces and even if I knew it had been coming—it didn't hurt any less.

I kissed her harder than I ever had. Quickly. I didn't trust Camilla.

"Do you understand me, *Gemma*? I love you. Everything I do is for you." I locked eyes with her. "I love you."

"I love you." Opal eyes crumbled with tears as she whimpered. "No matter what?"

"You and me. Always. We're a team."

Or we were.

Gemma nodded and covered her mouth and I saw how she shook. My vision blurred as I looked at Camilla with an edge. "Let's go."

I followed her out of the room grabbing my t-shirt and shorts as I walked tucking my gun into the back of my pants. Every step I took from Gemma?

My entire being ached. It ached. It hurt so bad I didn't know what to do with myself.

The halls felt endless, the silence oppressive, my heartbeat thundering in my ear as I walked with Camilla.

I wanted to kill her. I did. I fucking hated the rage burning in my gut. The way I felt?

I had felt it very few times in my life.

My hands itched to wrap around her throat to make her pay for every single fucking time she tried to do anything to Gemma.

The air thickened as we got to Camilla's study. She opened the door and gestured for me to enter with that fucking look on her face. I didn't move.

But her smile never left.

The moment we stepped inside she said. "You're going to leave.

151

Tonight. No goodbyes, no explanations. You'll resign, citing personal reasons, and you will never contact Gemma again."

It hit me like a freight train. With all the grace of a slap to the face.

I knew it was coming. I should've seen it. And it hurt no matter what.

I swallowed.

"And if I refuse?" I asked, though I already knew the answer. I fucking knew it and I needed to torture myself a bit more.

Camilla's smile widened, those icy eyes of hers glittering with malice. How had I not seen the crazy in them before?

Or maybe I had and ignore it.

"I will paint a picture of you harassing me and raping her. She's nineteen. You're twenty-three and experienced. The world will know your name and hate you. And Gemma? She'll learn to cooperate or everything she loves and values will be stripped away. She's such a spoiled girl. Do you really think the world will believe some idiotic grunt over my family?"

Each and every single word was something out of my nightmare.

My worst nightmares.

Because the thought of what Camilla would do to me?

I didn't have the ability to protect myself or Gemma and it was jarringly clear.

Camilla didn't feel real.

But she was.

She was every single shitty leader I had in the military. Plotting against the youth. Plotting against their troops. Planning out coups and attacks against anyone they felt threatened by.

Camilla was not special.

Camilla was every single spoiled adult who competed with their children.

"Your parents are nobody's. You're a nobody. Nobody will ever believe you, Nathan Wyatt. You're at the stalemate and you lose either way." She wasn't finished. "You really thought you could corrupt a young girl and there wouldn't bet be consequences? I can make the entire world see you as a predator. Nobody will believe her. She's so young." Camilla made a mocking soft noise. "She is so young and you are nothing but a monster."

"That isn't true. I *never* hurt Gemma."

But even in my own ears I knew how it looked.

My mind was already seeing the articles.

Former Soldier assaults Marchand heiress

Former bodyguard now blamed for attack against Marc-
hand family

The way my parents would be devastated. I would have nothing.

Gemma would be humiliated. My career, my life, my everything ruined. Our love meant nothing because—the truth meant nothing.

She had no voice. No power. No title. Nothing. The idea of Gemma now killing herself because of me?

Ripped.

Through.

Me.

"Truth doesn't matter, Nate. Perception does. And I control the narrative." She stood then all regal. "Let me paint the picture for you. Former soldier preys on teenage heiress for inheritance. Your entire record out there. Every mission. Every body you've killed makes you a cold-blooded killer. Your parents will be hounded. Your dad has that heart condition doesn't he?"

I stopped breathing.

"And poor Gemma...she'll have realized then she made the biggest mistake of her life. You'll never work again. No one will hire a man with your reputation. She will never have money. I'd love to see how grateful my daughter is with you, when you provide nothing. And every day, you'll wake up knowing that you destroyed not just your life, but Gemma's too."

That was the nail on the coffin.

Just like Jacqueline.

"You wouldn't go after Gemma."

"Wouldn't I?" Her laughter was all teeth. "She'll recover. You, on the other hand? Won't." Her smile dropped. "Leave my villa. Tonight. Now. Do not speak to Gemma. Do not speak to anyone in this house or I will go after you and your silly little family." She made a disgusted

153

noise. "Gemma will learn from her mistakes from slumming it with your kind."

And just like I shattered.

"I will make sure Gerard gets nothing from this. And nobody will ever know you worked for us. And in turn, you will leave my family alone."

Because I had known the truth the entire time I was with Gemma.

But to have it laid bare. To have been ripped open from my heart and been told it to my face?

That was another level of pain. Entirely.

One that I knew would kill me if I felt too deeply.

Nathan Wyatt, the boy who loved Gemma Marchand died in that room.

And the person who walked out?

I didn't recognize him.

TWENTY-NINE
NATE

WHAT THE FUCK COULD I DO FOR GEMMA?

A nobody.

A nobody.

A nobody.

The words hammered into my head. Each blow causing another migraine. Each one overwhelming and loud.

To my surprise, Nigel was outside the door a few feet away looking pale. Had he heard?

He looked up, his blue eyes rimmed red as he looked at me in concern.

"Mr. Wyatt? Are you alright?"

Do not speak to anybody.

I didn't say a word to him. I looked away moving quickly and on autopilot.

I didn't remember how I got to my room.

Or how I packed with frantic energy, my hands shaking so violently I could barely zip my duffel bag.

A few shirts, some jeans. A life reduced to a single bag.

I never even deserved Gemma. Not a Marchand.

Never her.

Gemma was…beyond me. And if I didn't leave? I got the feeling her entire existence and mind would be worse.

Then I saw it.

The shirt Gemma had given me, hanging in the closet like a goddamn symbol of everything I was about to lose. Her laughter that night as she held onto me kissing me. And my vision blurred. I grabbed my chest as I felt the ache burst open. I had to hurry.

I grabbed it, my fingers lingering on the soft fabric before I shoved it into the bag.

Gemma. My girl. Your wife.

No. She isn't.

The truth ripped through me like shrapnel.

She would never be my wife.

Never be mine at all after this.

I stood in my half-empty room, memories closing in on me like a vise. Gemma's laugh. Her scent.

The feel of her skin against mine. *Stop. Focus.*

Each step towards the door was agony, tearing me further from her, from us. At the threshold, I froze, my hand shaking on the doorknob. Every fiber of my being screamed to turn back, to run to her, to spill everything and face the storm together.

Tell her. Tell Gemma. Take her.

She said she'll go with you. Take her.

Take her with you.

And for a wild, wild, wild second.

I thought about it.

I did.

Because Camilla was good at getting under my skin. But what if Gemma wanted to come with me?

Asking Gemma to leave with me. Tonight. I could take us to Greenwich. She'd be my with. Reed would protect her. And she'd all mine. She'd be a part of my team.

My new life. Not this one where she hated it.

I felt the searing pain in my chest grow. Growing.

Tell her. Tell Gemma.

My vision blurred. *Everything* in me *hurt*.

But Camilla's icy smile flashed in my mind, her veiled threats a noose around not just my neck, but my family's.

I couldn't protect Gemma from this.

Not from the sharks circling her.

Not from her own fucking family.

I was jack shit.

And a fuck up.

Oh. But. Fuck. That.

Hurt.

A bumfuck nobody. From nowhere.

Shit. Shit. Shit.

I yanked the door open, my breath coming in ragged gasps. The hallway stretched before me, an endless void.

A noise left my mouth and I realized I was breaking down. I wanted to go back to her. To my girl. Go to Gerard.

Tell him his wife was a cunt.

And instead I panicked. I panicked so fucking hard. Shit for brains me.

The pain in my chest threatened to bring me to my knees, but I couldn't stop. Couldn't look back.

Leaving was the only way to keep her safe.

With trembling hands, I pulled out my phone and dialed Reed's number.

"Wyatt, it's 2am. This better be good—"

"I'll take the job at Titan."

THIRTY
GEMMA

She did this to me.

Camilla.

In the wake of Nate's departure, I became a ghost of myself, haunting the villa that once felt like home.

The ache in my chest was one I couldn't put into words how painful it was.

I felt like someone had carved out my insides and presented it out to the world for display.

I couldn't stop crying.

Nate's love wasn't just about a love I couldn't have—or a love I dreamed of. But the kind of love that came without a title. A name. A brand.

It was the kind of love that promised of lazy quiet Sunday afternoons and a backyard full of children and laughter. And that thought alone of not having it with him gutted me.

I knew I was young—but it didn't matter because Nate made me feel like a normal girl. Not Gemma Marchand. But his Gemma.

Just Gemma. I was normal. I didn't have anything to my name. And when Nate had made me feel that way?

I no longer wanted the name.

I just wanted his.

I wanted to be Mrs. Wyatt. More than anything else in the wold.

Dimly, I listened to my father wonder what happened to my guard, aware Nate had abruptly quit and he didn't understand why.

But then again, I was beginning to understand my father didn't know anything. He didn't understand anything.

Nor would he ever.

I was shattered.

Broken.

Irrevocably.

I called Nate, each unanswered ring another crack in my already shattered heart.

Nate, come back.

How could you? Nate, please, just call me.

We can fix this.

Nate, I hate you.

I hate you so much. Just...please.

And then came the blow that devastated me more.

The number you have dialed is not in service. As days passed, my grief crystallized into a simmering rage. I watched Camilla at dinner, her perfectly composed facade only fueling my anger. She'd smile at my father, laugh at his jokes, all while I sat there, silently screaming inside. It was during one of these dinners that something in me snapped.

She waited until Papa took a call in the hall.

And she looked at me. "Such a shame isn't it, Mr. Wyatt failing to do his job."

"You shut your mouth." I snapped so fast Bonnie's head snapped up where she was gathering a dinner plate. *"You vile bitch."*

I couldn't stop myself. "What is your problem? Ever since you came into this home–"

"I beg your pardon—"

"I am still speaking!" I shouted rising. *"You took him from me!"*

And then she did something I never imagined would rankle my blood so much. She smiled at me. She fucking *smiled.*

"Really, Gemma darling. How unlady-like of you to raise your voice at your mother—" Her tone was patronizing, laced with false concern.

"You are not my mother! And there is nothing ladylike about you—" I must have lost my mind with how I was speaking.

159

I didn't even see Bonnie moving to stop me as I advanced on Camilla.

"You did this to me! You took him away! This is all your fault!"

"Gemma!" I whipped my head to find my father standing in the doorway, his face a mask of confusion and anger. "Why are you shouting at Camilla? What on Earth is happening?"

"Papa," I started, ready to spill everything, but Camilla beat me to it.

"Oh Gerard," Camilla's smile vanished, replaced by a look of distress so perfect it almost seemed rehearsed. "I was standing here with Bethany—"

"Her name is Bonnie!" I interjected, my frustration mounting.

Camilla continued as if I hadn't spoken, her voice trembling slightly. "And she just came in. Really, I've tried to be a good mother. I don't understand why this is happening—"

"You're insane," I hissed, my hands shaking with rage. "Papa, she's lying. She's been lying since the moment she got here."

"Gemma." My father's voice was hard, his eyes narrowing. "What is the matter with you?" He moved to stand next to Camilla, and I saw Bonnie's eyes widen at me in concern.

I looked at Camilla, who my father was consoling, her face buried in his chest.

"Apologize to Camilla, Gemma. You have no right to attack her—"

"Attack her?"

I couldn't believe what I was hearing.

"She attacked me. She has been doing nothing but attacking me since she arrived!"

I couldn't stop myself, the words tumbling out in a frantic rush.

"She's using you! She's sleeping with another man—"

"Gemma!" My father roared. *"I will have none of this in this house!"*

Camilla lifted her head from my father's chest, her eyes glistening with unshed tears.

"Gerard, I…I don't know what I've done to make her hate me so much. I've only ever wanted to be a family."

I watched in disbelief as my father's arm tightened around Camilla's shoulders.

"Papa! She's lying! She threatened Nathan! Papa, I heard her. She hurt *someone*—" *Natasha. I wasn't imagining it.*

"That's enough, Gemma. I won't stand for this behavior in my house."

"Your house?" I cried, my voice rising. *"This was our home before she came along. Can't you see what she's doing?"*

My father's jaw clenched. *"I said, that's enough. You will apologize to Camilla right now, or—"*

"Or what!"

"Or you can say goodbye to your gap year. I will send you to university directly from here!"

I stood there, stunned into silence. Camilla's eyes met mine over my father's shoulder, and for a split second, I saw it—a flicker of triumph in her gaze before it was quickly masked by false hurt.

"You bitch," I growled feeling like I was slowly going insane. I was losing my mind.

"Gerard, I told you," Camilla said softly, her voice laced with concern. "Gap years are not healthy. I can imagine she's been under a lot of stress and so she's overreacting. She needs to calm down—"

"Because of you," I screamed. At the top of my lungs. *"You did this to me you bitch! You drove me crazy! You did this to me!"*

I couldn't stop myself. Something happened to me.

Something combined with losing Nate. With something of a smile on Camilla's face.

"I see her smiling!" I shrieked. "I see her!" My hands flew to the vase filled with violets before I could stop myself and it shattered to the floor. And when I looked at Camilla, she rolled her eyes infuriating me even more.

"She did this to me!" I screamed at her. *"YOU DID THIS TO ME!"*

"GEMMA!" My father shouted, his face reddening. *"How could you be so rude? I raised you better!"*

"I'm not being rude! The only person who is rude in this house is her!" I couldn't believe how blind he was to her manipulation. *"She's manipulating you! She lied! She did this! She's been doing this to me for weeks now! This is all her fault! She's driving me crazy!"*

Camilla placed a gentle hand on my father's arm, her eyes never leaving mine and I saw her smile. I saw it, I swear.

"Gerard, darling, perhaps Gemma is right. Maybe I've done something to upset her without realizing it."

I blinked, thrown off by her sudden change in tactic. What was she playing at?

My father's expression softened as he looked at Camilla. "No, no, you've been nothing but kind. Gemma is the one who needs to explain herself."

"I've been trying to!" I exclaimed, frustration building in my chest. *"If you would just listen—"*

I feel like I'm going crazy. Nate, I'm going crazy! Something is happening to me. Something bad.

"Enough!" My father's voice boomed, making me flinch. "You will apologize to Camilla right now, or I'm sending you to New York. Your choice, Gemma."

I stood there, trapped and at the same time the rage in me was fiery red. I wanted to throw something. I wanted to scream and growl.

The triumph in Camilla's eyes was unmistakable now.

"So it's me or it's her?" I shouted. I had to. Bonnie looked wide eyed at my father. *"How could you!"*

"Gemma—"

"Papa, you cannot be serious—She's lying! She's been lying! Look at her smiling! Look at her face!"

"Gemma, I mean it!"

"So do I! She's lying to you! I see her! I see her face—"

"That's it. Pack your things. Your break is over."

THIRTY-ONE
GEMMA

SIX WEEKS HAD CRAWLED BY SINCE NATE'S DEPARTURE, AND EACH DAY, there was a fresh wound.

A fresh version of hell.

I would start school in a week.

Gap year forgotten like everything else in my life.

Bonnie and I had come to the townhouse on the Upper East Side my family owned. I was here alone. It felt alien. It was my time-out and punishment for being a bad girl.

And I couldn't stop breaking down. I didn't speak to anyone but Bonnie who was devastated for me.

On that sixth week since leaving Capri, I jolted awake in the dead of night.

A searing pain knifed through my abdomen, stealing my breath. Darkness pressed in, broken only by slivers of moonlight casting eerie shadows across the room.

As I struggled to sit up, I felt it—something warm and wet beneath me. Panic clawed at my throat as I fumbled for the bedside lamp.

There was *blood* between my legs.

Blood. So much blood. It was covering the sheets whole and I felt the scream in my throat tear from me.

Bonnie burst into the room wide eyed. *"Gemma, Good. Lord."*

I couldn't even speak as I motioned to my body. Bonnie's usual composure cracked, a gasp escaping her as she took in the rapidly spreading stain.

Her hands fluttered anxiously before she visibly steeled herself.

"We need to get you to the hospital. Now."

As we made our way to the bathroom, I felt her hands trembling against my skin, her fear as palpable as my own.

"It's going to be okay, love," she murmured, but I could barely hear her over the roaring in my ears.

"What's happening to me?" I was a wreck.

The ride to the hospital was a nightmarish blur of harsh streetlights and wailing sirens.

Bonnie clutched my hand, her grip painfully tight, as she barked directions at the driver.

"It hurts," I whimpered, curling into myself as if I could hold the pieces of my world together. "Bonnie, it hurts so much."

"I know, love, I know," Bonnie's voice cracked like thin ice. "We're almost there. Just hold on."

At the hospital, everything happened in a dizzying rush of doctors, tests, and pitying looks. I couldn't stop crying. Couldn't stop freaking out.

When the doctor approached, her face a mask of practiced sympathy, I braced myself for the worst news possible.

And nothing could compare to what came out of her mouth.

Absolutely.

Nothing.

"I'm so sorry Miss Marchand. But I'm afraid you had a miscarriage."

～

I WAS GHOST.

It was several days after losing my child. Mine. Nathan's.

My world. Bonnie came to me one day.

Her brown hair lacking its usual shine. She'd been crying for me too.

"There's something you need to know." Her entire face was one of steel as she looked at me.

164

I met her gaze, a spark of alertness breaking through my fog. I hadn't spoken or eaten in days, hunger a distant memory.

"It's about...about why he left."

Nathan.

"Nigel talked to me when we were in Capri." Bonnie's voice was low. She hadn't said a word of this to anyone. "He stayed to make sure nothing happened to your father, but I do have some things to tell you."

And she began to. Bit by bit. About Camilla. Nate. His choices. What he'd been threatened with. Everything.

"Wait," I croaked, my voice hoarse from disuse. "Nate left because..."

"Because Camilla told him..." And then Bonnie laid out what Nigel had heard and I felt my heart break for the

I grasped Bonnie's hands, desperation fueling my movements. "We have to find Nathan! We have to go get him! We have to convince him —" I broke off, seeing the pain in Bonnie's eyes.

"Mr. Wyatt's entire existence was threatened," Bonnie said quietly. "She said she'd ruin both your reputations, destroy his life. His parents. He felt he had no choice but to leave."

The ache in my heart flared white-hot and if I went through anymore, I didn't know how to make it.

"Why didn't he tell me?" I whispered, fresh tears spilling down my cheeks. "We could have faced this *together*. I would've done anything to be with him." I was his girl.

I had...had his baby....

Why would he do something like this?

Why not take me with him?

I didn't care about anything the way I cared about him.

"He thought he was protecting you," Bonnie said gently. "He didn't want to ruin your reputation or your relationship with your father. Mr. Wyatt...he loved you too much to let that happen."

"Love me?" I was astounded. "If he loved me? He never would've left without me."

"Gemma," Bonnie held my face oh so much like Nathan had. "Gemma, listen to yourself." I was stunned. She'd never called me by my name like this. Not since I was a child. "You cannot protect him. He cannot protect you. He did the only thing he could've."

"But I loved him." I choked it out of my throat.

Tears blurred my vision hot and stinging.

I looked at her eyes wide on mine and I saw the moment she saw my pain. My desperation to be with him.

"I loved him. I would've done *anything* for him. I don't care if she took everything, I would stand up for him. He's mine—" I broke off feeling myself shattering.

She wiped my eyes as her face contorted in pain.

"Which is why I am telling you, we need to work on a few things together. For your sake."

"What?" My voice was hoarse. "What are you talking about?"

She held me tight to her then, brushing my hair back. "I promised your mother I'd take care of you, darling. Not about to let her down now..."

But even as Bonnie spoke I realized something.

Nathan had never truly loved me.

Because if he had loved me?

He would've taken me with him.

I would have gone with him.

I would have stood by him.

The thought echoed in my mind, growing louder with each repetition.

Consequences be damned.

I would've been his girl.

I would've had his baby.

I would've been his wife.

Not here. Not alone.

Not like this.

And in that moment I broke all my promises to him. I felt like I died a little.

I didn't recognize myself anymore.

The girl who loved Nate was gone.

I hated being Gemma Marchand.

And in my place was a woman who knew one thing—Gemma Marchand hated Nathan Wyatt.

INTERLUDE
THE NEXT SIX YEARS

THIRTY-TWO
NATE

Darkness was my world.

A first two years at Titan Security flew by.

But I still couldn't shake her.

I never could.

She was all I ever fucking thought of and I swear she was haunting me. Her scent. Her hair. I kept seeing her smile.

And it broke me.

Leaving Capri for Greenwich felt like stepping into a different world. The manor here was a far cry from the villa, from the apartment I'd given up.

No, I lived here now with my new team.

I had the Lilac Suite at Greenwich which was mine downstairs. I had a ton of windows in a pattern that Gemma would've loved.

And a space that was mine in a multi-million dollar home.

On paper, I had everything I wanted: respect, responsibility, a shot at building something that mattered. But it all rang hollow, tainted by what I'd left behind.

My boss was Reed.

All coiled intensity, with eyes like chipped ice. But it was the guy standing behind Reed that really set my teeth on edge.

Gabriel fucking Monroe.

Bigger, broader, meaner. Built like a tank and twice as deadly.

There was a chill about him, like someone had drained all the warmth out and replaced it with liquid nitrogen.

Gabriel tolerated me at best, and the feeling was mutual.

But damn if I didn't learn something new every time we sparred.

Where he held nothing back. Like someone running from his demons. I just didn't know what they were.

Or maybe we were too alike in the worst ways—both of us carrying ghosts, both willing to cross lines that would make normal men flinch.

We recognized the darkness in each other, and it made us wary. And then there was Lena. *Selena* Tavares.

A Cuban with a temper that would roast me where I stood. Standing at five-five with long brown hair and a no-nonsense attitude, Lena would've stabbed me in the throat if I ever crossed her.

And fuck me if I didn't love every second of it.

She called me out on my bullshit, pushed me to be better, and had my back in ways I never knew I needed.

She was fire where Gemma had been softness, strength where I needed it most.

When we were in the field, it was like we shared one mind.

I'd kill for her, die for her, and live for her—but not in the way I had with Gemma.

This was different.

Better in some ways, complicated in others.

Gabriel clearly preferred Lena to me, which was fine. I was there to work, to bury myself in missions so deep that maybe, just maybe, I could outrun the haunting memories of Gemma.

Further from the man I was with Gemma.

Evie, Gabriel's little sister, was the heart of our mismatched family at Titan.

The two years she had been there, she'd transformed from a shy fifteen year old clinging to Gabriel to a seventeen year old who was about to be accepted into college.

Today I'd found her playing her board game with Reed who took his breaks with her making sure she ate.

And she was whipping up some vegetarian concoction,

"It's my tofu nuggets," she'd say proudly, while Reed, the most shredded person I knew, would chug his pre-workout to wash down the taste coughing a little. "Is it good, Reed?"

He nodded, red in the face struggling and I bit back a grin. They were *edible*...

Another time, Evie's big brown eyes locked onto me while Reed and I sampled another cookie recipe.

Selena and Gabriel had opted out of Evie's latest cooking adventure citing they had a meeting. Uh-huh.

And I was just here for shits and giggles.

"How is it? It has oatmeal in it," Evie chirped. "I thought it would be good." And then she bat her eyes up at Reed who fucking adored this girl.

"It's great, kid," Reed was chugging coffee.

I looked at her, an idea forming. "You make regular cookies, kid?"

Evie blinked. "...Yeah, I can."

Reed shot me a look that could've melted steel. Evie was turning eighteen soon—a year younger than Gemma had been when...But Evie was a world apart.

I came around the counter, motioning to her tablet on the counter with the recipe. "You heard of pumpkin chocolate chip cookies? You could make them vegan if you wanted to but my Mama makes 'em..." And as I talked to her, she smiled up at me all wide-eyed and soft.

I began, offering her suggestions, ignoring Reed's disapproving glare.

Teaching Evie to make decent cookies might save us from more health food disasters. Plus, it felt good to be the fun older brother for once. Because lord knew Reed and Gabriel weren't.

Reed tried to be. *Tried.* But Gabriel didn't give a fuck. And Evie was surrounded by a bunch of killers masquerading as her family.

Another two years passed and Evie was upset about something. I caught Lena watching her.

"What's the deal?" I asked Lena one day.

"She wants to go to college," Lena said quietly. Her eyes told me the problem. "Gabriel..." She drifted off. She never spoke ill of her boss. We were in teams and Gabriel was over her.

"Big bro won't let her?"

Gabriel put the over in overprotective. He didn't let Evie do anytime without checking it over. Not her bike. Not leave the manor. He was a fucking fire-breathing dragon over Evie all the time.

And I didn't have a younger sibling so I didn't get it, but Lena did and she said she understood. Now, though, even she felt for Evie.

Lena shook her head looking at Evie sitting alone in the glass solarium like a greenhouse princess. The kid was turning twenty and she wanted to do live.

Gabriel got her all those fucking plants to occupy her, but sometimes the kid needed company he couldn't give her.

People her age. She deserved to go and have fun.

"The plants can't keep her company forever."

"He loves her too much," Lena looked at me. Her eyes moved back to Evie with a soft expression. "She's his heart…too much."

I wasn't too bad at reading Lena now. "You wanna go in there and talk to him?"

She nodded. Lena and I talked about everything.

"I will speak to Gabriel, just be with Evie for support. Otherwise, she will cry. She does not like to upset him either."

We both knew that much. Despite her being an adult, and his sister, we both knew better than to bring her up and test him.

So then, we went to Reed instead. Who went to Gabriel.

Who blew up.

"Are you fucking serious right now?"

Gabriel's rage was like an ice dragon in the room as I stood behind Evie, while he and Selena clashed. Reed was caught in the middle, trying to mediate.

"Wait, just fucking breathe," Reed stepped in. "Evie is an adult now. You need to let her live. She's turning twenty soon. She stayed here like you asked for two—"

"I let her live!"

"She doesn't ever get out unless we take her!" Reed shouted back at him.

"And that's the fucking point! I keep her safe! Do you know what kind of danger she could be in—" Gabriel looked ready to tear Reed apart.

Because he wasn't going to go after Lena who was still shouting at both of them.

"Why the fuck should I listen to you three?" Sheesh, he looked ready to kill everyone at the mention of Evie. Gabriel had one button that was an instant trigger. And it was her. "*I'm her fucking parent.*"

"I am too!" Reed stepped in. "Evie's gotta get out at some point, *we all did—*"

"We're operatives!" Gabriel's pale eyes flashed. "She isn't!"

His head swung to her wide eyes, softening. "You aren't trained like we are, shortcake. What if something happens to you?"

And then he turned right back into the dragon he was on Reed. "Don't you fucking dare tell me how to act with my kid."

I mean, technically she was his sister…but I got why Lena called her his kid. It didn't matter how old Evie was. To him? She was his baby. And she was going to stay that way.

Evie blinked slowly and I looked down at the tiny kid for her age. Evie was maybe five feet one. Solid. Maybe.

I patted her hair, the cherry-cola color glinting off Gabriel's massive lights in his library which made him just look scary as all fuck.

"I can train her," Reed stepped in eyes sensible on Gabriel aware he was pushing all the wrong fucking buttons. "I can teach her—"

"Like fuck you will!"

"Evie," Reed started in on Evie softly. "Do you know what we do at Titan?" I'll give it to him. Reed was way more sensible about everything and much more chill than he looked.

She shook her head looking a little terrified. Gabriel turned on Reed so fast. "Don't you fucking dare, Reed—"

"She needs to know—"

"Reed—"

"Cálmate!" Selena shouted for them to calm down. And I mentally translated Lena saying Evie was a baby and they shouldn't be screaming in front of her over stupid things like college.

And Evie just started crying.

Gabriel looked at her then his expression falling. "Sweetheart…" he was on her in another second. Because if there's one thing Gabriel feared more than something happening to Evie, it was a crying Evie.

Reed motioned for Selena and me to leave the room. Leaving Evie with Gabriel who scooped her up the moment she sniffled.

I saw Reed look frustrated and something else in his expression.

As he closed the door I saw him watching Lena. "You were right to bring this to him, but let me handle him."

Lena looked uneasy. "Si, hice algo mal?" *Did I do something wrong?*

Reed responded in English. "You did nothing wrong. He's just protective of her. It's not about us…" but Reed was watching the door. "I get it, he doesn't want to lose her. Since I've known him she's his family. But she wants to live a little. She's a kid. He's gotta hear her out."

We waited outside for a long time.

Eventually Reed just wanted to go in there until Evie stepped out beaming.

"I'm going to college!" She squealed as I hugged her lifting her tiny frame in my arms as Lena clapped her hands.

Reed grinned, but his eyes darted to Gabriel in the office before the door closed.

As he stepped in to talk to Gabriel, I realized how much I'd grown to respect Reed's leadership—neither one of them bullshit us. They were just real people.

Evie squealed. "Reed can teach me how to drive like he taught you Lena, this is going to be so exciting! I know it's only two years…"

"I can help you shop," Lena's smile was gleeful. The girls giggled as Evie laughed clearly delighted.

"She doesn't need to go to college with your outfits, Lena." I shook my head. "That shit is gonna drive Gabriel insane."

Lena's outfits were going to give Gabriel a heart attack. I thought of Gemma, remembering how I once thought she wore next to nothing.

Lena made that look like child's play. And just that quick any mention of Gemma brought in all the thoughts I didn't want to remember.

What do you want in this life?

I want to be a husband and a father.

In a way, I was Lena's work husband. And a sibling to Evie.

It's enough…

"Can I wear your red dress for the first day?" Evie asked Lena, her big eyes sparkling with excitement. "The one with the bows—"

"Si." Lena grinned, already planning the outfit in her head. "And you can wear the how you say—"

"Stockings." Evie's eyes lit up and I groaned.

"Kid," I shook my head ruefully. "That's not a dress. Lena's clothes are a hazard." It was basically some fabric held together with floss.

Lena smacked me upside the head, but I caught a glimpse of amusement in her eyes.

"She can have it. And the black dress you like so much…"

"That's gonna get every man on campus on her," I grumbled. Reed frowned about that and I could already see him planning on giving Evie a bracelet or key chain with a tracking device in secret.

Evie squealed and I laughed with them at her excitement. It was contagious.

I'd watched the kid grow up turning sixteen and now watching her go off to school. Time passed with these guys.

And before I knew it?

As Titan expanded—splitting into specialized teams.

I took charge of security for celebrities—it was familiar, a reminder of my time with Gemma.

Even after all this time, her name still caught in my throat.

It wasn't the life I had originally wanted. The life I craved. The life that would've made me happy.

But maybe I didn't need the old life.

Maybe I didn't need the old me.

The old me fucked up enough and I didn't want to feel anything anymore.

THIRTY-THREE
GEMMA

I DIDN'T WANT TO EXIST ANYMORE.

The world outside continued to spin, but mine had shattered.

I didn't have the energy to talk to anyone.

Bonnie never told my father what happened. Or anyone.

By my twenty-first birthday, Bonnie had already given me lessons for the last two years for me to survive as a normal girl.

"It's up to you, Miss Marchand," she began that day she told me about Nathan years ago, her voice steady. "But, if you'll allow me to say something..."

"Leaving?"

"Darling, I don't want to overstep, but given recent events, I believe it's time for you to make a choice." She laid out everything I needed to do if I ever wanted to stop being a Marchand.

The idea had been a seed in the back of my mind, long before Nathan came along.

Maman had done it; she had left.

But I didn't know how to turn to her. Part of me felt abandoned by her. Part of me felt angry with her for not protecting me. And part of me? Didn't know how to reach out. I also didn't have the skills.

Nathan had only watered that seed, and now...

I need to be a normal girl.

Now it was time to decide whether I'd let that seed grow into some-

175

thing substantial. Bonnie was guiding me through what she said any woman in my position would need to do, given Camilla's influence.

The idea *terrified* me.

"You need resources," she urged me to open a separate bank account from my family. She opened it for me and added me to it.

And I used that to put all my money into it from the jobs I had worked. I invested into stocks and bonds and put my money into assets instead of just the bank so I could have standing of my own.

Nigel stayed with my father and we talked sometimes now.

Not as much as I used to.

Both Nigel and Bonnie adored Nathan. Because both of them believed deep down and I knew Bonnie had openly admitted this—they had known about Nathan.

He never once told anyone they had been complicit.

Both of them felt like they failed him.

Me.

Us.

My child.

Bonnie shared it with me privately that she felt guilty and knew even without her power, she couldn't protect young Nathan. And me?

I despised him.

Every day that built in my own image, I hated Nathan Wyatt. I told myself these stories about him. Stories that I replayed justifying why I lost the love of my life and the potential kids I had wanted.

If he had loved me, he would have stayed.

If he had loved me, he would've taken me with him.

If he had loved me? He would be here with me.

He would find me and stay with me in my home. Be my husband. Make pasta with me…

And I cried.

Because it sounded so stupid.

So bloody stupid to want something so small.

So…inconsequential.

There were people suffering in foreign countries and children who needed food and water and shelter and I needed to go help them.

Not think about…Nathan. Navy eyes. Blonde hair. His smile.

His sense of humor.

The way Nathan made me feel like I was normal.

Just a normal girl.

My stupid dreams had been crushed by him. Even though I knew I felt *stupid* for even thinking it.

Because Nigel and Bonnie deeply loved him. And me?

I was determined to grow into who I was.

"How am I supposed to survive on my own?" I asked Bonnie.

Without Nathan?

"A woman's financial independence is everything. Men have always tried to take that away from girls. And sometimes the worst kinds of women, the ones who absorb every single thing men want—and hurt younger girls try to take it away from them as well." Bonnie told me that when she had been younger her mother had been controlling.

"I didn't know that." It made me wonder what else I didn't know.

Bonnie nodded, her dark curls bouncing a little. "My mum was particularly awful. My father controlled her expenses and so she controlled mine. I learned awfully young, any sensible woman needs access to money. Something even if it's small. To get by. Your finances will set you free. So when Camilla does come after you again? You'll be ready."

"You don't think I'm free of her?"

"No. And I dare say miss, you need to pay attention to everything now. Be smarter. Learn everything you can. And start saving your money."

Because Camilla would come back.

I was already set to go to university.

I needed a way forward.

So while juggling my degree, I learned to be sufficient in all ways around the house. Cleaning. Cooking. Doing everything myself like a normal college girl.

Yes, my parents took care of some things with their money. But unlike my peers? I was plotting. Every single day and night Bonnie and I sat down working *strategically* in between studying sessions on how to financially separate myself from my family.

Stumbling through recipes with a determination that surprised me.

The first time I successfully made pasta from scratch, I felt a surge of pride I hadn't experienced in years.

And as I did, memories of Nate lurched through my body.

Our baby. And I experienced the greatest wave of sorrow I ever had.

What can I offer her besides a one-bedroom apartment and home-made pasta?

You.

And even now…I *wanted.*

I blinked back my emotions as I tackled laundry, cleaning, and all domestic tasks. Bonnie advised me to act as if I were already a Marchand no longer.

Sometimes I broke down. But I kept going.

The days and nights blurred without Nathan but maybe becoming your own woman was more important than being a man's wife.

Maybe there were other things out there in life than love.

"Do you ever think about being in love, Bon?" I asked her one night when we cooked.

A contemplative expression crossed her face. "Sometimes."

"But?"

Bonnie was quiet. "I think every woman I have ever met has always wanted a love story. You know? The kind you and Mr. Wyatt have had—"

"We didn't have a love story, Bon." I quickly looked away. "Love doesn't abandon you."

"But he didn't abandon you," she whispered. "Camilla hurt him. Threatened his existence. Even now I bet she keeps an eye on him. Nigel says he overheard Camilla talking to someone saying how she can't touch Mr. Wyatt anymore now that he works at some security company. Something about a murderous boss."

"What?" I spun around at that. "Where?"

She shrugged lightly a light smile on her face. "Nigel says Camilla won't say, he couldn't hear the rest someone called him away but Mr. Wyatt is protected. My guess is, he ran to someone who would take care of him, much like you. He's just a small town boy. He rarely does anything exciting. He's frugal. He's kind. He loves his mother." I turned away to the pot stirring the sauce as Bonnie talked. "Mr. Wyatt loved you Gemma. Whether you still love him or not."

I was quiet.

"But no, I've never seen myself with someone—"

"Not even Nigel?" I was quiet and I didn't turn around.

I heard her quiet laughter. "I think Nigel and I found love in other things before each other."

Now, I was curious.

"What do you mean?"

Bonnie smiled over her wine glass. "Gemma, you can find love in everything you do. You don't need it from Mr. Wyatt and I know you love him, I do. But he isn't here right now. I imagine in another life or in this one, you might find him again or he might find you and you two can be together. But right now? You must extend love for yourself. Build yourself up. When the time is right? Love will always find you."

"Why are you so determined to help me?" I finally asked facing her and turning the stove off. "You've served the family for..."

"You never know when you might need these skills," Bonnie would say, her knowing look conveying a wealth of meaning. "It's best to practice now. I was with your mum when she...I saw her and your father fight constantly about his inability to help her. He tried—"

"Just not enough."

My father.

The enabler. Bonnie spoke about how she saw my mother, the family now, and the night at the hospital when I felt utterly alone.

I enrolled in Astor University Downtown and moved like a robot throughout school

At twenty-two, I had grown accustomed to the city's anonymity and the joy it brought.

Bonnie was right.

Without Nathan I filled my life with other joys. Classes. Exploring. Making new friends and connections. I filled my cup with love.

I filled my cup with good things.

I didn't stop thinking about Nathan.

No.

I don't think I ever could.

But I thought about things other than him.

At nineteen? Nathan was all-consuming.

As I grew older? Nathan became a part of me. A chapter in my story.

Not the whole book.

And maybe that was a form of love too.

THIRTY-FOUR
GEMMA

MY SECOND YEAR AT ASTOR, I MET ALISHA MALHOTRA.

A young English woman who was attending the same charity gala I was.

We were seated at the same table during a charity gala, one of those stifling events I had come to dread.

I was poking at my plate, counting the minutes until I could escape and get some real food.

"I always come to these events hungry thinking one day, I might survive the singular portion of risotto." I looked at the hazel eyed woman next to me, her doe eyes batting up at me. Dark waves all around her. "I'm going to need a burger after this."

She looked radiant in peach against her olive skin giving off the impression she was almost nude, but it suited her. She smiled at me. "Hi, I'm Alisha."

"Gemma." I extended my hand.

"Do you come to these often?" She motioned to the gala.

She doesn't know who I am. And I felt my smile grow.

"I do. On occasion I even eat at them."

She giggled looking delighted with me. I had always met such competitive women and cutthroat girls who internalized the misogyny by the patriarchy.

I was learning something very important in my life about men and their misogyny.

My evil step-mother was not unique.

No.

Camilla was a victim herself of internalizing all the decades of hatred men, specifically men who associated themselves with patriarchy pushed out.

The nonsense that women were inferior.

The nonsense that women could not do what they could do.

The nonsense that women were emotional and inept when I knew men who assaulted women for saying the word "NO."

If you told a woman no, she moved on. When you told a man no, he set your house on fire, ruined your life, and gutted you.

Camilla had internalized the belief that women should have to "compete" for a man who was not qualified to be with a third of one of them. Women who competed with their daughters.

Women who competed with their sisters for men.

Why?

Most men weren't qualified to be with monkeys. Most men were not providers. Most men could not find a jalapeño in a grocery store.

Most men?

Violently attacked their pregnant spouses. I worked with women's charities on purpose, specifically domestic violence shelters that did not allow men.

Because of how they hurt women and their children at their most vulnerable.

And *yet—women* had been *lied* to for centuries where idiotic men had convinced women that we were not worth anything because THEY SAID SO. As if.

What a fucking lie.

What a scam.

Women have been sold a lie. A con. By men. For centuries.

I'm so fucking exhausted.

And Alisha? She was a breath of fresh air.

Because Alisha was warm, friendly, and kind. Her eyes sparkling with a kindness that was so rare for me in my circle.

I latched on.

"I would *murder* someone for a burger." Her candidness made me happy. "Honestly, with fries and a shake. I think that sounds so good. Or lemon pasta. My gosh what I would do for some pasta."

I laughed lighter. "Lemon pasta?"

"Mhm, my sister Avani, she does this quick recipe with spaghetti and lemon and parmesan and..." Alisha grinned her smile dazzling a little as she spoke with pride. About her family.

She values women.

The women in her life are important to her.

"It's my first time here, but I was so nervous. What if there was a real food, and I ate too much at home? What if the food is delicious and my dress no longer fits. Avani made me promise to send her photos, but I haven't found anything exciting enough."

I could listen to Alisha talk forever about herself and her life.

"I know a diner nearby," I found myself saying, surprising even myself with my boldness. "Would you like to grab some real food afterward?"

"I'd love to, are you sure though? Are you not here with friends of yours?"

What friends? The community I exist in will turn on me and side with Camilla.

"No. I'm free."

Ever since everything happened with Camilla and Nate?

I kept to myself. It felt safer than ever exposing myself to hurt ever again.

The circles my family ran in were connected. But if I never gave them something to talk about?

They never had much ammo. I didn't like competing with women.

I only wanted to stand up for all the women who had been torn down like me.

Even if I was a Marchand.

Even if I had money.

Even if it seemed on paper that my life was perfect?

It was not.

The weight of the Marchand name seemed to lift from my shoulders, if only for a few hours and I loved Alisha in that moment.

She complimented me, offered me her lip gloss, and asked me if I liked mochi donuts. Because they were her favorite dessert for some reason.

Alisha wasn't just refreshing, she was the anti-thesis of a woman who wanted to tear me down. I realized in that moment in my life I was lacking supportive women.

And I needed to surround myself with other women who believed in uplifting girls. Not tearing them down.

Men already did an efficient job of tearing women down.

We did not need to add to their torture.

As we talked late into the night, I found myself opening up in ways I never had before.

Alisha was different than the girls I'd grown up around. She had a warmth about her that I didn't expect.

"Why are you so kind to other girls?" I murmured out of curiosity. "You're not competitive or rude…"

Alisha looked confused. "Why would I be?" She chewed on some curly fries.

Because that's all girls have been taught.

"My entire life, I was brainwashed into thinking I had to be pretty enough, good enough, and cater to men. My entire existence has been solely based off my commodity in relation to others. But you don't base your judgements of yourself and others off that."

"No, why would I?" Alisha looked genuinely confused. "Why would I hurt another woman for a man? Over a man? That's preposterous."

I laughed, I had to because Alisha always made it sound simpler than it was. And I realized I wanted to be friends with her. I did.

"Lish," I asked her quietly. "Do you…do you ever get insecure of yourself when you do your shoots?"

"Of course," Alisha didn't care about which side of her plate the utensils fell on. She didn't care about my name. Or who I was. She liked me for me. And I immediately felt comfortable. The rest of the night we just talked like we'd known each other for years.

"Lish," I started. "You don't care that…I'm me?"

"No?" She looked perturbed. "Why would I?"

"You don't care about my parents?"

"No."

"Or my life?"

"No...are you...pray tell a nudist?"

I burst out laughing so hard the milkshake toppled onto the diner table and Alisha burst into laughter.

"It's all right, I promise, it is—"

Not good enough. Not skinny enough. Not pretty enough. Not kind enough. Too mean. Too nice. Too fat. Too bitchy. Too pretty. Too ugly. Too everything.

And Camilla?

Camilla was the epitome of a woman raised in a man's world.

I promise to be different.

I promise to never hurt a woman ever again.

I promise to be better than those who came before me.

Like Alisha.

Alisha managed her influencer career while caring for her younger sister, who was a bookworm.

Avani became something like my little sister too.

And I wanted to help both of the girls.

Alisha had faced so much—losing her parents, raising a teenager in between building a career from scratch—and yet she remained open to love and new experiences.

The sisters were close and tight knit. And they let me in.

I felt an odd sense of protectiveness toward her, wanting to shield her from any potential hurt, even as I admired her resilience.

And I found...family.

I FOUND MYSELF LEARNING FROM ALISHA NOW. NOT JUST BONNIE.

She didn't care about my family name—in fact, I'm not sure she even knew who the Marchand's were too much—which was really nice for me. Because Alisha didn't understand any of it and she didn't want to.

To Alisha, I was simply Gemma, a twenty-two-year-old girl trying to find her place in the world.

I did my best to support them in any way I could.

Avani spent time with me if Alisha needed to work and sometimes I spent time with the girls. Movie nights. Dinner dates. Shopping trips.

I had found my tribe.

And it was one where I felt a little better in.

For the first time in my life, I felt like I was part of a family I had chosen, rather than one I was born into.

Which was all I had ever wanted.

Avani would run to put on movies and I'd curl up on their couch watching romantic comedies or whatever boy band Avani was crushing on.

I had told Alisha bits and pieces about my life. But it didn't matter because I couldn't talk about Nate without talking about the baby and I couldn't talk about the baby?

Without losing my mind.

So I got help from somewhere else.

I went to therapy in my spare time while struggling through school. I barely comprehended anything related to class. I barely knew what I wanted to do.

I spent the rest of my days with Alisha and Avani for the next few years.

Especially Avani who had my heart since she sometimes reminded me of the memories I didn't get to make with my cousins.

I found her on the comfy white couches Alisha had, her blanket half on her, chestnut hair flowing over the arm of the couch as she sighed at the photos on her phone.

I bit back my laughter.

"Why are you looking at photos of Teo?" I whispered, pouncing on her as she curled into the couch with a book and her phone.

Matteo 'Teo' DuPont was the CEO of Roadsters. His mother was the CEO of EllaBeauty, the brand Alisha worked for.

Avani gasped, hiding her phone from me. "I was *not*."

I giggled, flopping on top of her as she turned a few shades of red. "Gemma!"

"It's all right to admit it," I teased. "He's not ugly."

"I never said he was—"

"I mean he's very handsome—"

"Uhhh."

I laughed harder.

He was too pretty to be real. In the photo Teo's rakish black hair fell over his bright blue eyes rimmed with this black ring around the pupil making them alien bright.

I had seen him in person. And I knew his brother had been married to Malcolm Nash's daughter.

Since leaving my family years ago? I hadn't gone back citing school and other commitments and in that time?

I had forgotten about all the people in Camilla's life.

Until Alisha worked with EllaBeauty and I remembered that Maxine DuPont's son's were Andrei and Teo.

Avani had a photo of him and Alisha together, but I caught her peering at his photos alone.

"Does Alisha know you like him?" I mused out loud as she brushed her hair back, her big mocha eyes looking away like she'd been caught committing a crime.

She bit her lip, not answering.

"Hey," I murmured. "What's wrong?"

"Nothing."

But I caught how quickly she got upset.

"No, tell me." I squeezed her between the arm of the couch and me, hugging her. "What's going on? You look so upset—no, don't cry. I'm sorry, I didn't meant to—"

I moved, shifting until I was at her feet on the floor facing her as she wiped her eyes.

"N-nothing." But *something* was wrong.

Avani was the softest thing in the world, mostly because of who her sister was.

She'd been raised by Alisha for so long and sheltered so much. Even with the exposure Alisha had, it never touched Avani.

She looked at her phone again, quietly wiping her eyes.

"Is it Teo?" I whispered. "Do you like him? Did he hurt you?"

"No. Not at all." She traced circles on the couch and nodded slowly. "He likes Alisha...she's pretty. And I'm just her...sister..."

Poor thing.

Teo liked every woman.

I didn't think he...discriminated in the slightest.

But Avani was so young. She didn't understand that. And I got that she was telling me for another reason.

"Oh, sweetheart, you don't think you're pretty?"

I reached up to hug her then.

"Come here." I held her tight as she sniffled quietly, wiping her eyes. Both her and Alisha cried quietly. But I sensed Avani was upset about more than just Teo.

"Alisha's so pretty and I love her, I'm not angry with her—"

"I don't think that—"

"But I'm nothing like her—"

"You don't have to be—"

"But Teo—"

"*He* is an adult," I reminded her. "Twenty-three. And it's perfectly normal to have a crush on a boy at your age. Even if he's an absolute cad when it comes to flirting with the female population."

I also understood why years ago Cousin Bas liked him.

I didn't know what happened to my family now.

A reluctant smile spread Avani's lips.

"I think he's cute. And I know—" she broke off looking embarrassed. "But then he speaks to me and my brain goes to mush. The other day he said. "Hello Avani' and do you know what I said?" Her horror shouldn't have been funny. "Do you know what came out of my mouth?"

But I covered my mouth to hide my laughter as she looked so embarrassed.

"No. Tell me."

"I made a noise. A NOISE. And then he's all like, 'do you want some water?' And my brain stopped working. It shut down. Nothing was computing anymore."

I squeezed my hand against my mouth as I knew my face was turning red and Avani was crying. I really shouldn't laugh but it was really bloody cute.

"...and I know he has a crush on Lish—"

How did I break this gently?

"Darling, I don't think your sister has a crush on him. Which might matter in the whole situation."

She blinked at me, slowly confused. "No? But she's friendly with him."

I shook my head. I knew Alisha didn't.

187

She was off at a dinner tonight, juggling too much.

"She also works for his mother. I doubt your sister would want Teo. He isn't her type."

Alisha had privately confided that she did not want to be with anyone at all, not until Avani was older.

She didn't want to be a bad influence on her sister.

Or worse, have a fleet of men teaching Avani that heartbreak was normal. It was commendable, and I couldn't argue with that.

"Your sister wants to wait for the right person," I murmured. "For both you and her."

"Me..." She looked confused.

I nodded, smiling at the soft look in her eyes. "Alisha wants to make sure he's good to you as well. Nothing would hurt her more than being with someone who didn't take care of you or want you in their life."

Avani listened to me with wide eyes as I discreetly explained Alisha's perspective.

Avani wiped her eyes. "Lish doesn't want me to be around bad men?"

"Or someone who might use your sister and leave, setting a bad example for you."

"Like Teo?"

"No," I shook my head. "I think Teo being the son of the CEO your sister works for makes her a bit apprehensive. Also, I don't think he's her type. Something about him, I don't know. He isn't Alisha's type, though." I smiled at her. "But he's yours."

Avani blushed beet red. *"He kissed my fingers the other day—"*

I grinned unable to hold back my laughter now. *"Ma petite romantique.* And you died."

"I *died.*" She slumped back into the couch. "His lips were so soft and dreamy. And he smells like a God."

"C'est trop mignon." Too cute!

I laughed out loud now at her description of Teo and at her flustered embarrassment.

In her soft pastel pink pajamas she looked her age.

And it was *adorable*.

I was watching Avani grow up. And maybe if she ever fell in love I could protect her. Especially if she ever ended up with anyone like Teo DuPont.

My grin was wide, but I realized dimly Avani also felt insecure about herself at her age.

"Have you talked to Alisha…" I didn't know how to approach the subject as she looked at me a little lost and shy. "Your sister would love to take you shopping…"

I drifted off letting her catch my drift.

She was mature and smart for her age. Her crush on Teo DuPont non-standing.

Avani bit her lip, considering, then nodded slowly as she hugged a pillow tighter to her. "Okay. And you won't tell Lish about Teo?"

Her eyes were wide on me with concern.

"I don't want her to think she can't bring me to set. I like being on set."

"And Teo."

She fell back embarrassed and making a noise. My laughter filled the room.

"I won't tell Alisha anything," I mimed zipping my mouth shut. "Just remember he's just a man and much older than you and having a crush is normal."

"You're the best, Gemma." She was in my arms a second later.

"Now then, show me those photos of him you were looking at it. I know one of them was shirtless…"

Avani peered up at me in my arms. "I didn't know you liked him too…"

"I don't," I blushed a little embarrassed. "But I do let myself admire good looking men. Come on, show me your secrets, *mon amor.*"

"Okay, but you have to pinky promise you won't tell a soul."

"I pinky promise."

THIRTY-FIVE
NATE

"Next time we get shot at, you will be the shield."

"Next time we get shot, you can take it."

"Maybe I will."

"I'm flattered." I grinned as Lena grumbled, tossing her brunette locks over her shoulder as we boarded the jet, courtesy of some sheikh with a crush on her, holding her arm to her chest. "Besides, I'm always the shield, *muneca*."

"You were not the shield a moment ago."

I bit back my laughter sensing Lena might kill me on the ride home. She'd sprained her wrist on our last assignment. And I'd gone after the idiot who'd done it with a vengence.

An injured Selena Tavares was crabby.

"I am your shield either way," I teased, following her up the steps. "You'd use me and my body any day. Even now on the plane. Just say the word and I can tongue that—"

"Ahhh!" She made a disgusted noise, green eyes flashing angrily. *"Why do you make everything sound dirty?"*

"Do I?"

"Yes."

"I wasn't trying to—"

"You are a liar."

"I'm telling the truth, you just gotta believe me, baby."

"Do not baby me. I am not your baby."

I grinned wider at riling her up.

I fucking loved fucking with Lena. And then I caught the flight attendant eyeing me as I stepped into the cabin. Blonde. Curvy.

"On second thought. I might need a minute."

Lena glanced over my shoulder, clocking the woman's interest. She rolled her eyes, muttering what I'm sure were colorful insults under her breath.

"You spent the night with those women," Lena muttered. "And now her too?"

"I'm hungry, *muneca*."

She grimaced at my laughter. I was always hungry now.

I spent a lot of nights with a lot of women. It was my thing now. Empty sex. Nameless faces.

A constantly rotating cast of warm bodies to fill the cold space in my bed. In my chest.

The flight attendant sauntered over, all professional smile and knowing eyes. "Can I get you anything, sir?"

I caught Lena's eye-roll as I stood. "You guys got any drinks on board?" I eyed her top unbuttoned now that I'd sat down. Women came to me easily.

She smiled, a hint of mischief in her eyes. "Sure, if you'll follow me..."

I winked at Lena, ignoring the disapproval radiating off her.

Fuck it. I needed this. Needed to feel something, anything other than my last assignment. I was itching for anything other than alcohol.

I didn't even make it to the back before she was on me. I swore a little as she straddled me and I shook my head. "I don't like that."

I had her bent over in seconds. Screaming into the damn pillows.

Afterwards, I splashed some water on my face, trying to wash away the shame that clung to me like a second skin. It didn't work. It never did.

Back in my seat, Lena didn't even look up from her book.

"You disgust me, animal."

I snorted, shrugging, the adrenaline already fading, leaving me craving the next high. "I disgust me, Lena." Join the fucking club.

I was running. Always fucking running.

Even now, years later, her name was a knife in my gut.

There'd been others.

Each one riskier than the last.

A fucking parade of forbidden fruit and potential catastrophes Reed always got me out of.

If Titan needed a job done, I was the one who moved in where they saw fit. And Reed didn't give a shit about bailing me out so long as I did my job.

The senator's wife in D.C. I had her in my pocket feeding me all the information I needed for Gabriel.

The Russian oligarch's daughter to get Lena out of trouble. Reed cut the deal with him he needed to advance Titan.

Gabriel needed a job done in Monaco, and I got a socialite.

Paparazzi drones buzzed over us and Reed deleted all those fucking photos. And now, this. Just some flight attendant that did nothing for me.

Another tick on my box.

I was turning into someone else I didn't recognize.

But I fucking got off on all of it.

I'd become addicted to the risk, the threat of exposure, of violence, of ruination.

It was the only thing that made me feel alive anymore. Because every single time I got away with it? I felt powerful. I felt like I won something.

The higher the stakes, the better the rush. No risk too great, no line I wouldn't cross.

"You act like me being a whore hasn't made you happy, Lena." I muttered when she grimaced.

"I did not tell you to sleep with the models at the show."

"You suggested I distract them—"

"Not with your—" She blushed.

For a woman who looked like Lena, everyone thought she was a man-eater. Nah. I knew Lena. She was a softie.

Underneath the razor sharp designer heels and smirks—Lena was my girl too.

"You can't even say it."

"That's not true—"

"Oh, come on, Lena—"

"Leave me alone."

"Just once." I grinned at her hiding behind her book. "I bet that book is porn—"

She threw it at me instead and I spent the plane ride ribbing her and flirting with the flight attendant.

But in the quiet moments, in the dark of night when the adrenaline wore off, I'd find myself reaching for someone who wasn't there.

Lena fell asleep on the flight and used me for warmth since the plane was set to a temperature closer to the arctic than normal. She stole my jacket at one point and cuddled up to me in her sleep like always and I held her for the majority of the flight.

And my mind drifted as I held her.

I found myself wondering about the one person I would always think about whenever my head would get quiet.

Because I wanted her.

Still.

Years later.

I could have any woman in the world.

Except for the one I wanted the most.

Sometimes I wondered if she would like Lena. Lena was her polar opposite in all ways. But she would find a way to get along with Lena.

Maybe I was trying to prove I was good enough, that I could play in the big leagues, in her world of wealth and power.

Either way, I knew I was fucked.

No matter how high the risk, how great the danger, nothing could fill the Gemma-shaped hole in my life. And deep down, I knew it never would.

You are not good enough for Gemma Marchand.

No, but I was damn good for the world.

I tried to tell myself I wasn't bitter. It had nothing to do with losing Gemma.

That my obsession with my trophies was just that.

And even I knew I was lying.

THIRTY-SIX
GEMMA

THE BASS OF JAZZ MUSIC AT TEASERS REVERBERATED AROUND ME AS I sat with Alisha taking back another drink.

Months ago, a young woman named Lara Ford had messaged Alisha on social media inviting her to this burlesque haven.

Now? Alisha had become a regular at Teasers.

A few other influencers joined us, but it was Alisha who held Lara's attention, and Lara stayed with us all night her eyes on Alisha like she adored her.

The air was filled with the scent of white sage and the plants overhead gave it an otherworldly vibe.

"Hey, *chicas*." She was five foot nothing with hair darker than Alisha's, her eyes bright on us. "How are you ladies doing tonight?"

I had scanned the club's dimly lit interior, as gorgeous as the 1920's decor was, the world seemed to come to a screeching halt when amidst the swirling crowd and flashing lights, stood a ghost from my past.

I was three lavender lemonade martinis in and I didn't even think I'd ever see him in this environment.

After years. For the first time.

Nathan Wyatt. *My Nathan Wyatt.*

I'm hallucinating.

That isn't my Nathan.

But no—there was no mistaking that signature grin, the way he threw his head back with a laugh at something a man beside him had said.

Almost *five* years had passed since I last saw him, since that night in Capri when my world had *shattered*.

And now, here he was, as if he had stepped directly out of my memories and into this New York club. Laughing.

Like…he was having a ball next to a man with darker hair and eerie silvery eyes who grinned wide at him.

"Such a fucking asshole" I heard his lips mouth to Nate. *Their friends…*

The room spun around me, and the music became a distant, muffled roar. And my vision tunneled, years of emotions roaring through me.

Instinctively, I ducked my head, letting my bangs fall to shield my face.

I forced myself to nod and smile at whatever Lara was saying, but my mind was in turmoil.

What was he doing here? In New York?

In this club? Had he been in New York this entire time? No. Nathan didn't stay in one place.

I tried to remind myself that I wasn't the same naive nineteen-year-old he'd left behind.

I was twenty-three now, stronger and more independent.

But seeing his face made me want to cry. I wanted to run to him, slap him, or collapse against his chest and beg for him back.

Something akin to shame swept through me and I didn't understand why. I'd built a life for myself here, apart from the Marchand name and everything it represented.

But as I stole another glance at Nathan, I realized with a sinking heart that none of it mattered.

The moment I saw him, I was that heartbroken girl all over again.

The pain of everything crashed into me.

The baby. Camilla. My life. Or lack of.

It was like being shot in the chest several times and feeling the pain of my heart ripping out.

The weeks after having my miscarriage I wasn't the same girl.

I didn't know if it was the loss of the baby, or the idea of losing a part of Nathan that ripped through me the most.

It felt like the universe had conspired against me in the worst ways possible to destroy me.

And it had worked.

I caught wind of Lara and Alisha's conversation.

"Oh, hey! I didn't know he was going to be here," Lara suddenly said, her voice cutting through the fog of panic surrounding me. She turned to us. "Sorry guys, let me go talk to Reed, he runs security for the place, and I'll be right back."

I barely registered Alisha nudging me.

"Are you all right?" Her accent, thickened by two mojitos, cut through my panic.

I looked down at my apple martini, my hands trembling slightly. Alisha didn't know. "You don't look very well."

She can't know.

Not that I was worried Alisha might judge me. But because I didn't think everyone needed to hear about the worst moments of my life replayed over and over again.

"Perfect," I lied, forcing a smile that felt more like a grimace. "Just one drink too many."

"Don't overindulge; we said we'd get dinner after," Alisha smiled, her eyes brightening with the effects of alcohol, the light shitting them to appear ethereally beautiful. "There's this new Italian place I think you'd love. They make this amazing mushroom pasta, I really want to take Avani…"

As Alisha talked about Italian food, my head swam with memories of Nathan—sitting on his lap, sharing meals.

I blinked back tears and swallowed my emotions as Alisha's smile faltered. "Darling, what's wrong?"

"Nothing, I just…" I shook my head. "Just got a lot on my mind."

"Please let it be food," she snuggled closer to me. "Gemmaaaa. Don't be sad. We don't even get to enjoy things between our schedules. And we're celebrating you finally being out of school!"

I had to manage a genuine smile at her enthusiasm. Alisha liked to celebrate everything. She kept the front of her fridge tacked with all of Avani's accomplishments.

"Aliisshaaa. I am trying." I looked around at one the girls dancing on the floor trying to distract my thoughts at the fact that Nate was in the same room as me.

"Do you ever think about just getting up there yourself?"

Alisha got giggly after her third drink and it was contagious.

"Oh my goodness. Can you imagine? With the feather boa? I do love the navy feathers—" She mimed shimmying and I burst into giggles. Maybe everything was funnier with alcohol.

"Don't do that, you won't even make it to the Italian place—" I batted her away.

"Please, I will always have room for Italian..." she giggled as I wrapped my arms around her. "We should get on the bar forget the stage —too much pressure..."

"Hey guys!" Lara was back though as Alisha laughed into my shoulder.

Both of us turned to her and a man at her side. She grinned at Alisha's laughter slowly died at the man who stood there.

He was right next to Nate moments ago.

"Hey, Lish, Gemma, this is Reed..." I felt my smile dip as Lara introduced him to us. "He runs security for Teasers with Nate over there..." I heard nothing she said.

Because Nate...that was my Nate...or he was. And he was right there. And this man—Reed—worked with him? Nearly impossibly tall and strapping handsome, his eyes were a piercing shade of grey that looked eerily attractive and intense at the same time.

And his eyes locked on Alisha who was blinking slowly a little confused.

"Reed here was just dropping by..." Lara explained trailing off a little as he watched Alisha.

The moment he held out his hand to her, Lara grinned like a cat that got the canary, and I understood *immediately*—her friend Reed was interested in Alisha.

Nate's friend was interested in my best friend.

And I felt *more* than protective of her. I knew her secrets and I knew everything about her. She was my best friend. And I knew how she felt about opening her heart up to men.

Alisha smiled politely, standing to shake his hand. "How do you do, Mr—"

"Reed," he interrupted, his eyes widening a little on her, holding her hand a beat longer than necessary. "It's just Reed."

"Right," Alisha blushed. "Very well—"

"And I work security. I'm with Nate over there..." Reed's casual mention of Nate sent my stomach plummeting.

"Reed doesn't work with Nate, he owns Titan Security," Lara rolled her eyes at him. "He's just being modest. He's the CEO."

Mon. Dieu. This is Nate's boss.

Nate's boss was hitting on my best friend.

Reed looked a little uncomfortable as Lara clearly listed his accomplishments to Alisha clearly shoving it in her face. And I watched Alisha smile up at Reed with warmth.

She giggled at Lara saying. "...he doesn't come out here often but he did tonight..."

"That's wonderful," Alisha said. "Lovely to meet you. You've done such a good job with the place. And it's good to see you."

His lips quirked as he watched her, eyes widening a bit on her like he didn't believe she was real.

"You've got a few fans lingering outside for you, do you want us to let them come in?"

Alisha turned pink. "Oh, it's not a problem..."

"I can, but if they bother you, you can just let me know."

"Thank you," Alisha looked a little flustered as he watched her. Reed was intense looking. If one looked their man dark and brooding.

But he might just be Lish's type.

In all the years I'd known her, I'd never seen her show such interest in anyone.

She'd always prioritized Avani above all else.

"I gotta go," he watched Alisha with softer eyes. He turned to Lara. "Remind Killian if you need to..."

Lara mock saluted him as he shook his head with resignation at her giggles. She bounced after him as he bid us goodbye lingering on Alisha.

"You like him," I leaned into Alisha as Lara followed Reed out.

"No," Alisha whispered, but it was the most unconvincing denial I'd ever heard. Except her eyes followed Reed out. I smiled at her. "Not at all."

"Liar, back to the Italian food then?" I suggested casually.

"What?" Alisha's eyes met mine confused. And I didn't stop myself from laughing.

Someone had a crush. And this time, he was definitely her type.

WE HAD SAT AT TEASERS LONG ENOUGH FOR ALISHA TO DECIDE IT WAS time to head home. She didn't make it a habit of leaving Avani alone often.

Or at all.

But every so often she needed a breather and Avani was fourteen turning fifteen now, so Alisha let her stay home alone promising not to open the door for anybody.

It also gave Avani a chance to be alone curling up with her books.

Both sisters needed their time and this was how they got it.

At Tony's we'd called ahead and gotten everything delivered and found Avani in her little reading nook on the couch with a bowl of pasta.

"Didi!" She had called out to both of us. "I helped myself."

Alisha grinned. "I got your message, if you don't mind Gemma and I will be in the kitchen if you need us."

Avani went back to her food and reading while Alisha and I had made ourselves comfortable on the island.

Now I twirled my linguine onto my fork. *God, I missed carbs.*

"Have you ever met Teo's brother?" I asked Alisha while we split plates at her kitchen island. "Andrei, he's the oldest?"

"He is, but I haven't met him."

She sipped her wine with the deep red lipstick mark on the side. "I have not. Teo mentioned his family is private and he says Andrei keeps to himself really. A bit of a recluse if you will."

"Hm." Seeing Nate tonight stirred up a lot of my old memories from years ago. Over the course of the last few years, I hadn't done anything but make polite conversation with my family. Camilla, excluded, I rarely spoke to my father.

"Why do you ask?" Alisha's question cut me out of my thoughts. "Are you interested in him? I thought he was with someone."

"He's married?"

She shook her head. "Teo just said he has someone in his life. But he wouldn't say anything else. I didn't press. It's not my business."

Right. But something about seeing Nate tonight brought up a ton of memories from my past. Some of Camilla.

Natasha...

I didn't know who she was. But I knew Malcolm Nash and Camilla were friend. And then there was someone she was on the phone with Marcus...

There was so much I had left behind, seeing Nathan again brought it all up. And I didn't know how to start telling Alisha...

"But do you want me to ask Teo about Andrei?" Alisha's eyes seemed concerned. "I do speak to him and if you needed something I'm sure he'd be great to talk to."

That's because part of me wondered if Teo was in love with Alisha too.

"Not at all," I changed the subject not willing to dig into my past any further. "Do you think if Reed asks you out you might say yes?"

Her smile dipped a little and she peered over my shoulder to make sure Avani was still in her book. She was. When she read she was in her own world. Absorbed in it and lost.

Alisha looked relieved when she glanced back at me. "I don't know. I don't want to bring him into my life and he has a problem with Avani...or..." she drifted and I kind of got the feeling Alisha might've been using Avani as projection for her own fear of...well...life.

"What were your parents like?"

Alisha didn't really talk about them to me, but as someone who had one psycho step-mother who'd tried to destroy me, a father who was an enabler, and an absent mother? I got that I couldn't exactly talk about it.

Alisha's smile was soft. "Mum and Dad were the best people in the world."

Avani had told me her parents had been professors. But they'd passed away a few years ago when they'd been back home in England.

Both of them had been hit and killed on impact by a drunk driver.

And I'd met Alisha a year after and she'd been a little emotional whenever she spoke about them.

"I feel so much pressure to do right by Avani." Her eyes drifted to her sister again. "I can't let anyone get in the way of what my parents dreamed of for her, for me…" Bright hazel eyes met mine. "Even if he's handsome."

I grinned but I felt the most respect for Alisha wash over me then. She wasn't the kind of woman to let a man deter her from anything. And in a way meeting her had been a huge push for me to get my life sorted. In the few years I'd known her, I'd grown up so much with her.

After a few hours of eating through our Italian food I finally yawned. Alisha had been cleaning up around me as I finished my gelato.

"It's been forever since we had one of these," I murmured. "We should catch Lara on her day off and ask her to come."

Alisha agreed as I put on my shoes and coat and we both found Avani now fast asleep with her e-reader. Alisha grinned her eyes warm and sleepy on her sister.

"Call me when you're home safe," she said. Despite knowing I had Bonnie waiting for me.

I made my way back home in a blur of a cab ride and I shook off the feeling of unease that grew. Thoughts of Nate swirled in my mind as all the memories came back.

The summer sun, the way he held me, our shared laughter—and my eyes blurred at Camilla. The conversations. The crazy.

All of it began to bubble up inside of me so much I didn't notice anything out of the ordinary. Not as I picked up mail in my letterbox.

Not as I stepped inside and shut the door.

"Bonnie, I'm home." I frowned down at the letters in my hand noticing one of them looked a little more raggedy than the others. Larger.

I opened it while toeing off my heels almost forgetting to text Alisha I had made it home safely.

But the moment I opened the letter all my previous thoughts were forgotten. Inside was a photograph of me. Leaving my publicists office.

My blood ran cold, ice filling it faster than I could breathe as the panic ensued. Someone was watching me.

"Miss Gemma," Bonnie looked comfortable in her robe as she walked towards me and at the look on my face her smile dipped. "What's the matter?"

I handed her the picture. And she frowned down at it.

"Was this left in the mail?"

I nodded slowly sinking down to the steps leading to the second floor.

"Who do you think would follow you? Or have you—" Bonnie broke off. "No. Not her."

I nodded. "Only one person would stoop to this point." Camilla.

The question was—why?

Nate wasn't the only blast from the past tonight.

No, it seemed like the past was intent on reminding me it wasn't truly gone. Nor had it ever left.

THIRTY-SEVEN
NATE

WITHOUT EVIE?

Gabriel was awful.

He was *already* difficult to be around.

The resident grump was even more horrendous to be around. Snipping at everything. Avoiding people and everyone for days.

He would retreat to his side of the house, the basement or upstairs for hours at a time.

I almost regretted fighting for her to leave since he was a piece of shit now when he did come out.

I didn't know how Reed tolerated him. And while Gabriel was being distant, Reed began crushing hard on the influencer he'd met a few months ago.

Alisha.

She had a little sister in high school and it was just the two of them. I had caught a glimpse of her that night at Teaser's with a blonde next to her. But I hadn't caught a good glimpse at her face too busy corralling a bunch of drunk frat boys.

Considering Reed had ditched his ex-whatever for her? I'd say he liked her.

I didn't know what the fuck was happening with them though since it didn't seem like Alisha *wanted* to date him. Which was kinda rare. Everyone threw themselves at him.

Reed wasn't ugly by any means, but he was a mean motherfucker. Sure, he was nicer than Gabriel. But Gabriel was frosty as fuck. An ice-cube was nicer than him.

Nah, Reed was the kind of guy that held back. He didn't let people. He dated women with little to no personality and he never got close to anyone.

So Reed liking anyone was a big fucking deal.

During the years Evie was gone and just visiting, Titan expanded rapidly.

So when Evie came back? It was a fully functional behemoth of a company. With Reed as the face which made me wonder why Alisha didn't want him.

Even with that in the back of my mind?

I threw myself into building our high-profile security division, managing everything from celebrities and models to government officials and executives.

Lena did the international contracts with Gabriel behind her.

Training new recruits became my focus, shaping them into the security professionals Titan was known for.

We handled major events, personal protection details, and developed comprehensive security protocols.

Gabriel, ever the enigma, dealt with the shadowy side of our business, including a prominent operation called Teasers.

That was the murkier part of our work, not discussed in polite company.

Through Teasers, I discovered the darker aspects of Titan's finances and Gabriel's fortune. That's where I learned exactly where the money in Titan was coming from.

Fucking Gabriel negotiated it all.

His wealth, I learned, was linked to Aidan O'Hara, head of the Irish mafia from New York and Chicago.

It was a closely guarded secret—even Reed didn't know the full extent of it. I didn't understand, I just worked with what Gabriel wanted.

Over the years, Gabriel kept our interactions strictly business, but I worked closely with Aidan's younger brother, Killian O'Hara.

Killian, six-three with intense, mismatched amber and blue eyes, oversaw Teasers with an iron fist.

His eerie gaze, menacing presence, combined with a personality of a hellhound, accentuated by his black suit and tattoos, commanded respect from everyone. Nobody fucked with Killian.

Not unless they wanted to die.

I got the feeling he was a shoot first, ask questions later kinda guy.

"This isn't a fucking whorehouse," he'd growl at the security team. "This is Lara's place. If you have any problems with her, you've got problems with me. Do you *copy*?"

As he said it, I caught his canines and combined with his presence? He wasn't someone anyone wanted on their bad side.

There was a chorus of fearful 'yes sirs'.

One guy looked a little concerned.

Killian's presence never failed to make people uncomfortable, something about him stirring the edge on everyone. Even me.

Never mind the half naked women with huge tits everywhere.

No. Killian wanted them to be left alone. I got it. I did.

But then Gianna May, Lara's understudy, a blonde bombshell threw herself at me. Even I wasn't that fucking stupid. I didn't want to shit where I ate.

Unless it was in private.

Under Killian's watchful eye and Lara's management, it flourished into a thriving business over the years.

Killian, I discovered, had a dry sense of humor and he was surprisingly chill as long as nobody touched him. And the ladies *loved* him.

Something about Lara explaining, his whole prince of darkness vibe he had going on had them going crazy. But it was Killian who talked to me about starting my own business ventures.

Auto hobby shops across the country, venturing into the whiskey business, and even dabbled in real estate, thanks to Reed's connections.

Before I knew it, I'd made millions.

Lara, Killian, and I formed a tight-knit team. I met the baby of the O'Hara family Kieran, who had these too bright amber eyes and was somehow always fucked up. Drugs. Sex. Alcohol. *Everything.*

More than one night, I dragged Kieran to his brother or had Killian come get him.

Lara's brilliant idea to bring in influencers to promote Teasers paid off in spades. With Alisha Malhotra. Reed's crush.

Alisha was a vision—raven-haired, bright-eyed, and warm. She was a bit taller than Evie, but with a presence that filled the room. Reed's reaction to her was something I'd never seen before.

Gone were his usual icy...dates? Reed didn't really date.

He had casual relationships that were frigid as fuck. And now he looked at Alisha like he wanted to devour her whole.

One night at the club, I couldn't resist teasing him.

"Careful now," I quipped. "Keep coming here and the girls might think you're a regular."

Reed shot me a glare that could freeze hell. "Fuck off, Wyatt."

But we both knew the truth—he didn't need to be here for work. He could do all his upgrades from home.

As Reed's gaze drifted back to Alisha, who was laughing with Lara at the bar, I saw his lips curl into a genuine smile.

Shit. He had it so bad.

And Alisha became a welcome distraction for Reed.

The world was moving on for everyone around me.

But me.

"I'm gonna go talk to Lara."

Right. *Just* Lara.

Like I didn't see Alisha perched on the fucking barstool on the night he conveniently happened to be here by some stroke of luck.

THIRTY-EIGHT
GEMMA

THERAPY PROVIDED THE MOST HEALING FOR ME.

Dr. Khan's my therapist's office became my sanctuary.

She was a tiny Indian woman with short cropped hair greying at the top and in her tiny blouse and skirt—she looked all too much like a grandmother in her cozy office.

"I think Camilla is trying to get under my skin," I told her about feeling like I was being followed. I didn't have a guard anymore and I was too paranoid in my life.

On the way to Dr. Khan's I felt watched. More anxious.

I told Dr. Khan all this and she frowned.

"Have you a plan of action to potentially combat Camilla's doing?" She asked me her pencil in her hand twirling as she thought hard about what I said.

"I feel frozen." I admitted it after years. "Everything feels overwhelming and I don't entirely understand why this is happening. Even after years of growing into my own person, at the mere mention of Camilla I feel like a nineteen-year old again. Helpless. Lost..." I drifted off feeling the bitter sting of tears in my eyes.

Dr. Khan's face was contemplative. "What if you didn't have to understand why something happened? What if you understood it just wasn't your fault?"

"What do you mean?" If it wasn't my fault?

"Your stepmother is what we call a narcissist, Gemma. She doesn't think about other people's feelings or needs."

"Then why did she work so hard to ruin things between me and Nate? Why does she seem to hate me so much?" I felt the spark of anger in me. "She did everything she could and I left that life and she still can't leave me alone."

Camilla was heinous and I didn't even understand *why*.

"Because she doesn't truly love your father, Gemma. Your relationship with Nathan likely triggered her." Dr. Khan's voice was soft but the steel to it was there. "Narcissists can't stand to see others have something they lack. It didn't matter if it was Nathan or any other man. If she perceived your happiness as a threat to her superiority, she'd try to destroy it."

"So, she sees me as constant competition?" I asked. "But that's *ridiculous*. She's so much older than me. She's married to my father—"

"Camilla doesn't see age, Gemma. She only sees threats to her perceived perfection." Dr. Khan paused, considering her next words carefully. "Tell me, does Camilla have any children of her own?"

I shook my head. A lump had formed in my throat at that. "No. I think she hurt someone named Natasha when I was living with her, but I can't be sure who that is to Camilla."

Dr. Khan nodded solemnly. "Probably another woman she did hurt. If she did have a daughter, she'd likely treat her the same way she treats you. It's not about you personally, Gemma. It's about her inability to celebrate anyone else's happiness or success."

"So me stepping away from Capri..." I began.

"Was everything she wanted," Dr. Khan finished, her words landing like lead in my stomach. "It cleared the space for her to play the role of doting wife and your father's sole support system."

She sighed leaning back. "Women like Camilla, they know you don't think this way. In fact, you being genuinely you poses more of a threat to her because she has to put on a mask around everyone."

I had told her about the night with Cecily. With Nate. I told Dr. Khan about how it had driven me insane.

"They do that," she replied. "They make you doubt your reality. They take every single thing you say the wrong way..."

"And it drives you crazy."

She nodded. "Have you tried reaching out to your father recently?" Dr. Khan asked gently, her kind eyes searched my face.

I nodded, wiping at my eyes, feeling childish and small.

"Every time I call, he's always 'in a meeting,'" I replied, my fingers curling into air quotes. "It's like there's this wall between us now. And I don't know how to break through it. Do you think Camilla is manipulating him?"

"She's going to build a wall between you and him. Cast doubts in his mind. Manipulate him. She's his wife. After what happened with your mother? Your father might be growing older realizing he needs a security net. He can't be alone forever." She adjusted in her seat as she spoke.

"And even if he knows...that—" I started.

"She's abusive—"

"He would..." it hurt to say it out loud. "He will choose her over me." Dr. Khan's eyes were kind but empathetic as I wiped my blurry vision.

"In order to make it," Dr. Khan said. "You have to build up your network. Your friends and support system. I know you mentioned Alisha..."

"I can do that," I told her. "But I don't want to be a part of my family anymore. My entire life, I never wanted to be this."

She completely understood.

"Then you have to be a new Gemma outside of being a Marchand. And you've done a great job building her up. Maybe as you turn twenty-five the final step for you is walking away completely."

And suddenly that idea that blossomed was becoming stronger and stronger.

Because it was coming closer.

Dr. Khan believed before it did though, I needed to have a support system and slowly build it up.

In the meantime, I sorted out my affairs sitting down with Bonnie and talking to her.

As a member of the Marchand family I had every right to retain Bonnie in my house. But I also didn't want her anywhere near me when it did blow up.

"I refuse to leave you," Bonnie seemed almost upset I would even suggest it. "I cannot."

"Bon," I started. She had been my longest companion. "If Camilla were to come after me—"

"Then I should be here with you—"

I didn't even fight her seeing the stubborn look in her eyes. There was no use.

Bonnie wasn't leaving me.

And so I made sure she knew—I was planning on leaving my family and that moment was drawing closer.

But that was the thing—you couldn't leave an abusive home cold turkey as Dr. Khan would say. You had to do it under the radar. Planning. Plotting. Gathering information.

Waiting until the perfect moment for you to run.

And while I had grown up wealthier than most people—Dr. Khan had informed me abuse didn't have a zip code or a dollar sign attached to it—it could happen to anyone, anywhere, for any reason.

Abuse didn't have a rhyme or reason. Most of the time, the abuse had nothing to do with you.

If Camilla had another target to focus on—she would. She probably already had since I had been gone.

"You're not being abused because you are Gemma Marchand. You're being targeted and attacked because you are an empathetic person capable of great things—and sometimes some people will not allow that," Dr. Khan said. "Have you expanded your circle and found good friends?"

I took a deep breath. "I have." I worked with women's shelters I helped with and used my name and wealth to support.

After what I had been through?

I didn't want to ever see a woman go through anything like I had alone. I would be hosting another gala raising money for survivors education programs. And there was always Poppy.

Even with everything going on to distract me from my problems?

I didn't feel good at all.

～

I ATTENDED ANOTHER CHARITY GALA THAT NIGHT AND FOUND IT ABOUT as dull as dishwater. A distant friend of mine, a family acquaintance Caroline Kennedy was hosting it.

Underneath the crystal chandeliers among diamonds and gowns, I found myself out of place again.

Not because I doubted if I belonged, but because I realized even if I did, there was always gonna be a reason why people did not like me here.

Maybe there was something to be said about growing up, because as you did, you realize you didn't really care about all the things that you used to.

I used to care so much about how it was perceived at any of these events.

The right dress, in a shade not offensive, and the right words, the right smiles, the appropriate handbag—and now? In my violet gown I realized I couldn't care at all.

Now, the farther I got away from my family, the more I realized the less I did care? The better I felt.

This was the same life that tore *Maman* away from me. And that tore apart my family. Why would I ever want any part of it?

"Gemma," Caroline swept in with a wide genuine smile, her hair in wisps around her face, her headset in her left ear.

Among the stuffy folks around me and snobs, she was a burst of sunshine.

I caught the flash of silver on her curvaceous and buxom body, that was her gown before she kissed my cheek.

"I'm glad you came, thank you for helping me with this."

"Not a problem, I loved it." I genuinely liked Caroline. She was warmer and bubbly where some of the upper-class weren't.

She was the only daughter in the Kennedy family, and they managed international retail empires.

Or at least, her older brother Callum did. Caroline was trying to be an event planner like her mother.

Which made me see the concern in her eyes.

My smile dipped at the look on her face. "Don't tell me your mother hates it."

"She hates everything I do, but I swear this one was going better than the last." Caroline rolled her eyes tucking an errant blonde curl behind her hair. "I swear if anything else happens in this gala, I will never be in charge of another one again."

"What did she not like about this one?"

I made sure it was perfect.

"I don't know," Caroline's eyes were enormous. At twenty she looked exhausted already of her responsibilities. "I swear she plucks things out of thin air, she said the champagne wasn't the right color or something else—" she shook her head as I felt my stomach tighten. "And she said my dress fit off, and I mean, it's a little tight around my breasts but—"

"Your breasts look amazing. I could walk around naked with your body."

"She said it's too pin-up, and she says women are chattering and my ass will be in the Sunday gossip rag for being too flashy—"

I made an errant noise with my teeth. "Bitch."

Caroline turned red. "I just have to get this right." I felt for her but even I knew what her mother sounded like.

She sounds like Camilla.

"I would vent, but Callum is out in a meeting, and Ollie couldn't make it tonight," she twisted a strand of her curls nervously.

I took it Ollie was her boyfriend by the slump of her shoulders.

"I just need tonight to go smoothly—"

A loud commotion cut through the air then, and Caroline's blue eyes widened.

Towering over everyone by the entrance was a man with inky black hair, and bright green eyes who smirked our way locking eyes with her.

"That motherfucker," Caroline growled.

"He's not in dress code is he?"

"No."

"And he's clearly violating it?"

"Yes," it was a growl from Caroline. "And throwing a fucking middle finger to the crowd. Excuse me I have to go and kill him."

"Who is he?" I frowned over the stranger who was walking over to us.

Caroline's cheeks turned a violent shade of red. "That is the bane of my ever loving existence. Roman."

And Roman pulling a stunt like that would definitely cause Suzanne to rain hell down on her.

"Where's your…" I trailed off smelling a familiar cloud of expensive perfume and judgment rolling my way. "Caroline Aisling Kennedy."

The ice in Suzanne Kennedy's voice could be heard from a mile away and I straightened my own posture.

Caroline's blue eyes closed like she was praying.

At the exact same time Roman descended on us, all six feet plus of him. "Sup, Queen Kennedy."

"Caroline, what is the meaning of this?" Suzanne's hard eyes cut into her daughter. "Roman, did you not get the invite from my daughter?"

Think fast. What would Alisha do?

"Of course he did," I thought fast and despite Roman being handsome, I wasn't letting him get away with it. I quickly linked my arm through his. "He just wanted to let you know that he loved the fall collection of your favorite brand, Davina&Co, is it? That coat looks dapper on him wouldn't you say?"

I eyed Roman and shot him a universal look of, 'I will kill you slowly and painfully if you do not play along' right this instant.

His green eyes went wide with surprise. "Uh—yeah. Yeah. Love it. Davina and who?"

"Silly," I slapped his arm playfully and harder watching him wince a little and Caroline's big blues go wide. "I know how much he *loved* the last collection and we talked about how it was a favorite of yours and so Roman here decided to be funny tonight and wear it. Isn't. That. Right?"

"Yeah," he laughed. I eyed Mrs. Kennedy who was known for being shrewd. My smile was plastered and frozen on my face hoping to convince her and now she bought it.

"Well, Roman darling you could've been a bit more subtle but I do love the Davina&Co shows. They never miss." *No, they did not.*

Mrs. Kennedy practically pounced on Roman who looked wide-eyed and a little cornered.

"Thank you," Caroline whispered, her wide eyes grateful on me. "That was close."

"Don't mention it."

She nodded looking almost tearful at how Roman now accosted by her mother shot us a look. And I saw how Caroline skewered him with one of pure anger.

"If he thought he was going to piss me off, it worked—I see why Ollie hates him so much."

"Who is Ollie?"

Caroline turned pink. "Oliver…Hart? I'll fill you in later."

"You can fill me in now." I tucked my hand in hers. "Come on, let's get some air and let Roman be attacked by your mother. Better him than us."

I led us away. "Now, tell me about your Oliver. Is he handsome?"

"He's not my Oliver…" But he was.

"Au contraire, you call him Ollie," I teased. "Is he nice? Is he cute?"

Caroline's eyes sparkled in delight as she turned pink.

"The most. Unlike Roman back there, Ollie is fantastic…"

THIRTY-NINE
GEMMA

IN AN EFFORT TO MOVE ON FROM THE OLD GEMMA I WAS, ONE NIGHT, I had found myself on a date with a man named Lucas Devereaux, who happened to be a distant cousin of Caroline's.

The Kennedy family and the Devereaux family were distantly related, but close enough to keep good ties. I didn't think Lucas spoke to them much, but Caroline had said he was single.

An extremely wealthy real estate tycoon who'd inherited his family's company a few years back.

Lucas was tall, blonde, and blue eyed with an easy smile—he was exactly my type standing in at six-two in a clean cut suit and tie. But I got the feeling I wasn't his. At all.

He spent the entire night staring at the exit like he wanted to run away from me.

I was trying not to be insulted but it was getting hard when he didn't even order any real food and closed his eyes like he was in pain.

"Am I keeping you from something?" I dared to ask him. It was impolite but he hadn't exactly been the most polite to me. "I can't help but notice you look rather dreadfully embarrassed to be with me."

Lucas's eyes went wide with embarrassment. "No," he shook his head. "I'm sorry, I'm uncomfortable as fuck right now. Can we step outside for some air?"

I agreed and held onto him as we walked out to the balcony and Lucas looked relaxed now.

"I should've asked the fucking waiter for a seat outside. I hated being in there..." he looked shaken up by something and I knew he had been in the military.

Does he have...

"Do you have PTSD?"

He looked surprised and nodded. "I don't usually get out much. I try to avoid it but like you said, people suggested it and I thought why not —" he broke off looking uncomfortable.

I was right. I didn't think I was his type at all.

He rarely looked at me and his mind seemed distracted.

"Why don't we call it pax?" I held out my hand. "We can just be friends instead?"

But it was after my date with Lucas that headlines buzzed about us. Lucas who was patient and kind despite us not being romantically involved simply waved it off getting his team of lawyers on it to have the articles removed.

"I'm not a stranger to drama, Gemma."

"And if Camilla comes after you?"

"She can try," Lucas was quiet, his blue eyes cold. "She won't get anything."

Later with Dr. Khan she reiterated that I was building my life up with stronger people.

"You need to regain control of the narrative of your life," she urged. "It's not my place to tell you what you should do, but it may be worth seeking out an attorney who might be able to combat Camilla should she escalate..."

When I told Dr. Khan my decision to step away from my family for good, she insisted I work with my lawyers ensuring every 't' was crossed and every 'i' dotted.

And Lucas introduced me to a friend of his he felt I might want to meet.

Sonya Amin, a former Turkish diamond heiress who was going through a divorce from Lucas's other cousin.

Only this one nobody liked.

Michael Devereaux was a monster by the sound of how he treated his soon-to-be ex-wife. And Sonya was delightful.

The sable haired woman with bright green eyes and a frail figure was not the kind of woman I expected to be an heiress. But she was.

Sonya answered in her pajamas holding a cup of tea and I was sold.

We talked for a bit since I came vetted by Lucas she trusted me a bit more.

I found I had a world in common with Sonya.

She was a former classically trained dancer who had gone from ballet to ballroom.

"Lucas mentioned you were going through a lot." I didn't know how to approach the subject. "Should you need anytime, I am here. Lucas also mentioned you didn't have much family…I don't live too far away should you ever want to come over."

"Thank you, I no longer speak to my family." Sonya said softly her eyes on her teacup. "I stopped speaking to them a long time ago and thankfully it saved my life to cut them off. I do have a meeting with an attorney later this month, would you like to be there?"

"I'd love to be there for you. But I don't understand…" and my heart was beating faster. She had gotten away from her life?

How?

"What do you mean, you don't speak to your family? How?"

Her smile held no humor. "My mother was the ones that kept me married to Michael longer than necessary. For the longest time my head was filled with…notions of a reality that weren't mine."

Her eyes met mine. "When I cut them off, it was like cutting off a tumor. Painful but necessary. And now I couldn't be better. Even though I'm going through everything I'm still free."

I smiled even as my heart raced being around her. "Free…"

She nodded. "Free. And nothing—no amount of money in the world —ever compared to being free from all the chains that had been in my life. Lucas helped. But he and I both knew I couldn't get out until I chose to leave."

And Sonya explained that by cutting off her family when she did, she had effectively saved her own life with the help of her friends.

"In Turkish, in my culture, we have this saying, that freedom and what lies beyond it is stronger than your fear of staying the same,"

Sonya murmured to me. "I was scared the entire time and since the divorce my social circle has been lacking."

"I could introduce you to my girlfriends," I said softly. "There's this place we all hang out at..." I told her about Teasers and her eyes brightened.

As the night wore on, Sonya and I talked about everything under the sun. She was remarkably easy to get along with.

"In French we say, *Mais la liberté vaut toutes les peurs du monde.* Which mean freedom is worth all the fears in the world. Sometimes I think we are all afraid of the inevitable. But the inevitable is coming whether we are afraid or not."

She leaned her back on her couch reminding me a little of Avani even if her eyes held sadness.

"I had to set myself free and not be bound to anything anymore. I don't want to be any man's doormat. I want to be someone's equal. Someone's everything. In Turkish we say *Kendi hayatımın efendisi oldum,* which means master of your life. Rough translation," she smiled."

I nodded. Master of my life.

Gemma. No Marchand.

What I always wanted.

I loved Sonya so much.

My heart was beating wildly in my chest at everything she said and how it resonated with me.

Even if Sonya had an accent that was lovey and she spoke in a mixture of Turkish and English to convey some deeper emotions, she translated it for me.

I found myself absolutely hooked on her.

I saw a lot of myself in her.

It was a week after meeting Sonya—I took the plunge.

I announced I was leaving my family for good.

FORTY

NATE

After a mission in Belarus, I whisked Lena away to Capri since both of us were burnt out.

I took her to Sorrento, Positano, the Amalfi Coast.

I ended in Capri. And I hadn't been back in years. I was twenty-seven now but even in four years I felt every memory.

Every bit of Gemma and me walking down the paths and living the summer of my dreams here.

Lena and I needed a break and Reed gave us the go-ahead.

May in Italy was perfect—warm sun, cool breeze. I told myself it was for her, a well-deserved break.

But deep down, I knew the truth: I was trying to rewrite my own memories of the place. The moment we landed, my past came roaring back. All of it.

Lena loved it.

I took her to the beach where she was wearing another scrap of nothing bikini that made guys lose their shit when they saw her.

Lena's wardrobe left little to the imagination and usually being her partner meant being her shield—which I didn't mind at all.

I'd do anything for Lena. Her dark hair down to her waist now, made her look like some mermaid out of the ocean.

Over the years, Lena and I had forged something I'd never known before.

It wasn't love in the romantic sense, but it was deep and profound. We'd faced hell together and somehow emerged stronger.

With Lena, I could be my true self.

She saw my darkest parts and never flinched.

During long stakeouts, we'd share stories from our pasts, laughing at the absurdity of our lives. On exhausting flights, Lena would fall asleep on my shoulder, and I'd find comfort in her steady breathing. It became our ritual.

I'd bring her favorite milkshakes, and she'd surprise me with new tools for my growing collection.

And it was strictly platonic. I tried.

I fucking tried to fall in love with Lena. It wasn't hard. Ideally, Lena would be perfect for me.

But I couldn't.

On this last op, I'd had to make out with her at some casino. It was my first time kissing her and I gotta admit, for the first time since I met her, I saw Lena a little differently.

Most of the time I riled her up. Most of the time. But when I kissed her I waited to feel anything. Anything at all.

Nada. And Lena just acted like it hadn't even phased her. She didn't even let it register in my mind.

The truth was, the man I used to be—the one who had loved and lost Gemma—had died in Capri. Maybe it was time to let him rest.

"Do you ever think about getting married?" I asked Lena.

I turned to face her, my expression serious as I asked. "Would you ever consider if neither one of us ended up with anyone by the time we were thirty, you'd want to be with me?" I quickly added. "You don't have to say yes. Ever. And it's okay if you try and stab my balls with the knife in your beach bag."

She didn't laugh. Instead, her eyes filled with confusion. "What do you mean, if I don't find a man to have kids with, you want me to have your babies? What about your Gemma?"

"Gemma isn't mine," I said gently. I had talked to her about Gemma for a bit. "She'll never be. And they'd be our kids, not just mine." I ignored Gemma's voice in my head.

I think you have a lot to your name...plenty.

Oh yeah?

Plenty. I think any woman would be lucky to have you.

"But you don't love me like you love Gemma." The words tumbled out of her mouth, and I could see the hesitation in her eyes. "You and I are only just work partners."

I tried to lighten the mood. "Don't they say best friends make the best partners?"

I injected sincerity into my voice, hoping she'd understand.

"I know you've been hurt, but—" I extended my hand towards her, a gesture of understanding. Lena was my girl too. "If you still want kids, and you don't have any, I'd like to have them too. A partnership in that sense. But you don't have to say yes right now. It's your choice."

Then she asked bluntly because she was Lena. "You want to have sex with me?"

I almost choked.

"I won't sleep with you," I said, looking out to the sea, my hand still outstretched. "There's ways, clinics, places to go to have kids. I'd be there for you through the whole way. I don't see myself ending up with anyone else. I just want to be a father."

"Me too," she replied softly, taking my hand.

I kissed the spot right above her knuckles, sealing our pact. "You wanna be a father?"

I stopped laughing when I knew she was reaching for her knife.

I grinned as I sat back in my lounge chair, glaring at another mother-fucker who tried to stare at her.

In our world, I was her muscle, she was my brains.

The marriage pact I proposed wasn't about romance.

Lena didn't want to have sex with me which was fine with me. I couldn't do that to her.

It was about building a life with someone who truly understood me, someone I trusted completely. *Someone my equal.*

And maybe that was the problem with Gemma. I was never her equal.

Through everything, Lena had been my constant. She challenged me, grounded me. With her, I could simply be Nate.

She knew me for who I was now, not who I used to be. A nobody. Lena didn't care.

It was a straightforward arrangement. Just like all my arrangements with the women in my life.

And as I looked at her, I told myself that I would find *contentment* in this arrangement. Whatever that fucking word even meant.

I'd get the life I wanted, with someone who might not love me in the way I once loved.

Love me for the one bedroom apartment I had.

Despite all my millions, unlike Reed I never upgraded my life. What did it matter?

And when I sat back on the beach Gemma's words from this very beach drifted back into my head.

I can't buy her diamonds—
She might not want them—
Or a villa—
She might not need that—
And why would she ever want any of that?
Because all she might want is you.

Lena wanted me. Not romantically. But enough to say yes.

And right after I made my pact with Lena to marry her? Right after I swore to forget about Gemma completely?

I saw Gemma. In New York. At Teasers, of all places one night when Reed came back to visit Alisha. I didn't know how he knew she was there, but I assumed Lara had something to do with it.

The moment Reed approached Alisha, I spotted her.

The raven black hair, the graceful way she carried herself—it was unmistakable.

My body remembered hers—every curve, every freckle.

And the side profile. I stopped what I was doing.

Including breathing.

Because no fucking way, my Gemma Marchand was here.

At a fucking burlesque club.

Teasers was the last place I'd expect to find Gemma.

This wasn't her scene, not the Gemma I knew.

But then again, the Gemma I knew was barely nineteen. The woman before me was a stranger, yet achingly familiar.

She must be twenty-three, maybe twenty-four now.

Over the years, I'd kept tabs on her, lying to myself that it was just harmless curiosity.

But deep down, I knew the truth—it was a persistent ache, a longing that refused to fade no matter how hard I tried to bury it.

Late at night, I'd find myself poring over her social media, heart racing as I searched for any hint that she might still think of me.

Her posts were sparse, mostly about charity work.

Each time her name appeared in connection with some high-society function, my gut would twist. I'd study those photos, trying to read between the lines of her smile.

Was she happy?

Had she moved on?

She was *stunning*, more beautiful than ever.

But it was the sadness in her eyes that made me pause. What was going on with her? How was she *really* doing?

I watched her that night, aware my entire world had tilted on its axis and I was staring at the woman I had dreamed of. I never forgot she was going to school in New York, but I never thought I'd bump into her. Ever. It was a huge city.

It shouldn't have mattered.

It couldn't.

Because I gave Lena my word. I swore to her I would love her.

And no matter what I kept my word.

Then the news hit.

Gemma was no longer a Marchand. She'd done what I couldn't— she'd broken free.

"MARCHAND HEIRESS RENOUNCES FAMILY NAME"

"GEMMA Marchand? MARCHAND NO MORE.

I almost dropped my coffee cup.

Wait.

What?

What the fuck did I just read?

Gemma...*left* her family? I was *floored*.

Gemma actually did it…Walked away from the Marchand's?

From Camilla. My brain supplied that as it reeled.

One revelation after another slammed into me.

But the whole point of leaving her alone was to protect her and she had done it herself?

And didn't I feel fucking stupid. I'd been an idiot. Tore myself away for nothing? I wanted to run to her and find her and ask her what the fuck happened? What did Camilla do?

Why did she leave?

I found myself obsessively checking Alisha's social media posts, knowing Gemma frequented Teasers with her.

Couldn't help myself. Each photo, a glimpse of her life now.

Without me. She looked…different. Lighter. Still beautiful as hell.

Alisha was her best friend. She would know. And Reed?

Reed would definitely know since Reed stalked Alisha like his life depended on it. My boss was obsessed with this woman.

He wouldn't let an inch of information slide.

I thought about asking Reed, but I couldn't bring myself to. I didn't know how.

And so while Evie dragged and dropped photos of Alisha into a little presentation for Reed I was paying attention to a photo he had up with her and Gemma next to her.

No matter how much time passed, no matter how far I ran or how deeply I buried myself in work, a part of me would always belong to her.

FORTY-ONE
GEMMA

A FEW THINGS HAPPENED AFTER I LEFT MY FAMILY.

I honestly thought they thought I was joking or having a "difficult moment." I wasn't. I was walking away.

And Nigel left my father.

The soft chime of my doorbell echoed through the townhouse, a sound I was still getting used to. When I opened the door, my heart nearly stopped.

There stood Nigel, looking older and more worn than I remembered, with Bonnie at his side, both clutching luggage. It had been years since I spent time with him.

The man that had raised me now watched me with remorseful eyes.

He wiped his clear blue eyes. "I too have left the family, Miss Gemma."

"Why did you leave?" I shook my head in disbelief. "Come in."

Even I admit I felt a little betrayed now looking back he'd chosen to stay, but all these years he'd fed Bonnie information.

"I realized the lengths Camilla would go to had I left with her and I couldn't let that happen," he murmured. "I stayed for your father, truly. He has been in my life for ages. But, I do not think your father is a place to listen to anyone."

Nigel began detailing how my father's health and business had been in decline.

225

Over the last few years, things had fallen apart.

Investors had left, and my father had lost several properties to rumors and ill-timed investments.

Even with all the money he had, amassed over decades of careful stewardship, his life was not what it used to be.

It seemed that our family's once-unassailable position was crumbling before my eyes.

His life was not what it used to be.

"Your father was in business with Malcolm Nash," Nigel said softly. "Or rather Camilla was."

I frowned. Talia's father. By the way Nigel said it, it sounded like after Malcolm died, he took many things with him.

"Camilla used to work with him during her years at art auctions," Nigel said. "It seems her luck and Mr. Nashs' ran out."

"He had a heart attack," I murmured. Our family maintained their wealth through careful management of our strategic investments. Preservation rather than procurement.

Nigel nodded. "And after your father discovered a lot of the investment she had made with his money, as well as all the assets he owned? We're in decline."

Camilla's risky dealings and questionable investments had jeopardized everything our family had built. Nigel painted a picture for me. And I felt for my father. My heart broke for him. He shook his head.

"I left because Camilla was threatening to sack everyone she could to buy herself time. But when you left—" he broke off. "She seemed to have lost it."

"Because she can't control me anymore." I wrapped my arms around myself. "She has nothing."

Nigel nodded. "And it's often then that people do their worst."

It sank into my stomach as awareness blossomed.

Bonnie was the one who said. "Miss Gemma, I know it's not appropriate of me—" I waved it off.

"We'd past appropriate now, Bon."

"But you might consider getting someone to help you. Maybe another bodyguard?"

I considered it. After a few I had? Once I renounced the Marchand name? I didn't want or need one. I just wanted to feel normal.

And as much as it pained me? Since I had renounced my family name?

My father hadn't spoken to me.

Wiping my eyes I listened to Nigel tell us all about Camilla.

Her escapades. How she isolated my father. How she spread rumors about the staff. How she hired people and fired them on a whim. It sounded like a scandal brewing on the horizon.

One I did not wish to be a part of.

"Be careful, Miss Gemma," Nigel's voice was quiet, he looked much more haggard now that he ever had. "I'm afraid of what Camilla will do without her prospects in line with what she wished."

I was afraid of that. But I had years to prepare.

If I had to face Camilla again? I'd be ready this time. I could do it.

It wasn't until that summer, after I turned twenty-six, that life threw me another—surprise *inattendue. An unexpected surprise.*

"Lucas tells me you're staying with friends right now?" I asked Sonya a few dates in.

"Yes," she nodded. "His friend from school Andrei helped me." I stilled.

"Andrei...DuPont?" I dared to ask.

Sonya nodded. "Do you know him?"

"No," I said it quickly recovering from my shock. "My friend Lish, she works with Teo sometimes...his younger brother."

"Andrei's lovely, he and his wife, they're very private people but he helped me and once he did Lucas and Andrei backed me the entire time. They were the ones who witnessed Michael..." she drifted off her smile dipping as she explained the story to me.

Lucas and Andrei had caught Michael red-handed hurting Sonya at a gala. Andrei had almost broken his arm and Lucas had called the police before both of them had stepped in for Sonya.

"Lucas never mentioned it." I was stunned. "He made it sound like he didn't even know."

Her eyes softened. "He's humble and he keeps to himself, he doesn't like unnecessary attention or bragging about anything. So that's probably why."

But my heart was racing for another reason.

Andrei DuPont's *wife.*

227

"Are you close to the DuPont's?"

Sonya thought about it. "Not close, but Andrei is very much adept at helping women in need. He's passionate about it and Talia, his wife, she's the same."

I swallowed. *That's Malcolm Nash's daughter. Talia Nash.*

She's with Andrei again? The last I heard about her, her father wasn't happy they were together.

"And Talia is friendly?" I said carefully.

Sonya's eyes warmed. "The best. I think her own experiences helped her make better..." her eyes went wide. "I think you'd love her if you met her. She struggles with her family as well. Would you like that? It may help having another ally since Talia is no stranger to rifts?"

I couldn't breathe around my emotions.

Meet Talia?

"I'd love to meet her."

∽

I DID MEET TALIA.

Eventually that summer after years of hearing about her every so often, the smaller dark-haired woman about Alisha's height was not who I was expecting.

Her eyes were a bright green compared to Sonya's.

Her features a mixture of her heritage that Sonya explained was mixed with Japanese and Dutch and something else in there. Except Sonya neglected to mention one tiny thing.

Talia was heavily *pregnant.*

And her smile dipped the moment she saw me.

Oh no. Does she know who I am?

But it quickly returned. "Sonya, you brought a friend."

She had an accent I couldn't identify telling me while she had schooling in the States, she'd spent some time abroad.

"Lovely to meet you," I handed her the flowers I'd brought for her. Her eyes tracked all my movements as she led us into the living room. "Andrei's not home?"

"He's at work." Her tone was quiet as she led us in. "He's been

228

busier lately." Her hand drifted to her abdomen. "You're Gemma Marchand. How is your current situation faring?"

I blinked. She was straight to the point.

Did she know…about Camilla?

"Better now that I don't have to deal with my family."

A lie. But I hoped my smile didn't give it away that I was distraught in some ways because turns out cutting the tumor off still ached.

"How is your pregnancy going? I'm sorry, I didn't know otherwise, I would've brought snacks."

She smiled warmly at me then, brighter and looking younger. She couldn't have been much older than Alisha. I didn't know how to ask.

"Better now that I know what my diet should be here," her smile didn't reach her eyes as she rubbed her stomach.

Talia DuPont was beautiful in a way that defied reason and logic. Her nose wrinkled adorably as she said.

"I'm not used to eating American food. Even in school I struggled. My mother raised me in Hong Kong and the diet is really different," she told me about how being pregnant in the States was different for her, but she was adapting. "I am trying. Not succeeding but trying."

Sonya took out some coconut water from the fridge and passed it to us, clearly comfortable unlike me in the space.

"All Talia wants is fried cheese and hot soup," Sonya quipped.

"And in that order," Talia grumbled teasing herself.

I had to laugh. She wasn't what I was expecting.

All I knew was years ago, her father hadn't approved of her being with Andrei.

And now here she was defying the odds and still married to him. I seemed to have met women in my life who had broken free just like me.

I wondered if I could ask her about Malcolm Nash and Camilla if at all. If ever.

"Gemma has been great to me since Lucas introduced us…" Sonya said. "I thought you two might have a lot in common." She handed me a bottle of water as I sipped gratefully.

It gave my hands something to do as I looked around the relatively masculine environment. It was a little cold and all decked out in shades of navy and grey. Some black and white.

It didn't look like a woman like Talia's style at all.

"Do you happen to know Natasha?" Talia murmured to me a look in her eyes I didn't recognize. A glint of something unfamiliar in there.

"Is Natasha your sister?"

As I asked her mouth turned up a little. "She is. Just curious if you know anything about."

Sonya was gathering snacks in the fridge. "Natasha is Talia's younger sister, she currently runs Nash Group."

"Does she?" I said. "That's really impressive."

"It is," Talia smiled again. "You should meet Natasha one day, I think you'd like her. Thank you for coming to my home and with the lilacs. They are beautiful. Do you have any plans for today? I hope I'm not holding you up."

Her voice was a little mesmerizing like one of those sirens in the sea you heard about in stories of pirates and mermaids.

"I don't have any plans, no."

Her smile grew and I saw her canines were sharper on either side of her mouth a bit more than normal. Bright green eyes twinkled as she grinned.

"I have to thank Sonya for bringing more company for me then. What do you like to do on your free time..."

FORTY-TWO
NATE

"It's raining!"

Evie's excited voice echoed through the French-styled kitchen of Titan Manor. "Reed! Are you ready! Are you ready!"

"I'm ready, kid." Reed caught Evie flying into his arms, all wild auburn hair bouncing around her, after she burst through the ornate doors, her bright eyes sparkling with childlike enthusiasm.

Out of all of us, Evie was the nicest part of Titan.

Reed and I were leaning against the gleaming marble countertops, surrounded by lush green plants. Terrariums lined up the center of the island. Or we were.

Now, Reed was holding her with a grin on his face as she chattered openly about her plans.

We'd been discussing plans for the new hires, but Evie's entrance shattered our focus.

"It's raining, come on, we have to do something—"

"I know, kid. We can do whatever you want."

"Another picnic?"

"Sure. Let me order some food for us," Reed brushed her hair back as I grinned down at her.

"I'll go get Gabriel," Evie chirped, giving me a quick hug before darting back out.

Reed looked at me. "You can train Watts and Fuller?"

"Easy. And the other guy?"

Reed was trying to keep it quiet but there was a third hire. He wasn't saying shit about him.

"I got him."

I didn't even know his name.

Reed was keeping it tight lipped for some reason and I wondered if it had anything to do with Reed's six foot five ice shadow in Gabriel.

Before I could press further, Evie reappeared with Gabriel and Lena in tow.

Gabriel, all six-foot-five of wheat-blonde hair and perpetual scowl, entered the kitchen. His ice-blue eyes softened imperceptibly as they landed on Evie, betraying his usual stoic demeanor. The guy was a fortress of emotionless ice, but for his family? He'd melt. A little.

Maybe for Lena too. Me? He tolerated. On a good day.

And Reed? The only one Gabriel actually listened to.

At least until shit hit the fan.

It wasn't easy, but the five of us sat around the kitchen table while Evie and Lena grabbed everything they could. Board games. Movies. Snacks.

Pizza was ordered—which was a nightmare juggling it since we all wanted different toppings. Reed always got enough to feed an army.

Reed and Gabriel and I got the same thing all the time. Lena switched it up from time to time. And Evie got the vegetarian option which was just a smaller pie for her.

And then the five of us picked games first and then maybe a movie.

"No mysteries," I cut in as we debated movies. Reed's frown could've curdled milk.

"What else do we watch?" Lena frowned over at me. "I do not mind the mysteries—"

Evie started. "How about a romantic comedy about—"

"*No.*"

I wasn't about to do that.

Now it was Gabriel's turn to scowl.

Besides the college incident, he never said no to his *princessa* as Lena called it.

Lena smirked at me as Gabriel vetoed me. "We can watch whatever you want, shortcake." But he didn't look too thrilled about the romantic comedy.

"I can pick?" Evie grinned at her brother with her big eyes cuddling closer to him. Lena laughed at my expression as Reed shook his head biting his pizza.

"Evie," Reed said covering his mouth. "Just put it into Oracle and let her pick. She'll randomize it."

"Okay, I can do that."

And we waited until Evie's little AI in her phone picked.

It landed on the mystery series Reed liked and he grinned.

"She loves me."

Gabriel smirked over at Reed as he said it and Evie looked delighted either way.

We all settled for another mystery movie after Evie 'beat' Reed with Gabriel sitting right behind her peeking at Reed's cards.

I smirked at the three of them. This was my downtime. With my new family.

Lena was next to me watching me carefully as she at her pizza.

"You are upset about the movie?"

Even years later her accent was thick and I liked teasing her about it.

"Nah," I drank my beer watching Reed smirk at Evie's cards as Gabriel adjusted them. "Just got a lot going on. You know we got new folks coming?"

"Si, you are taking them?" She usually didn't do training, too busy running around with Gabriel.

"Hopefully." I looked at her. "You don't look too good yourself."

"Just busy." Her eyes were on Gabriel. "He is busier than us."

His pale icy eyes flickered up to Lena warming a little before returning to Evie who snuggled into him.

Thank fuck, she was back. Reed had called her in college to give her a choice and she'd of course taken her brother.

I got that. I also knew how deep he was in the shadows so I figured he would be. Aidan O'Hara's brothers were a handful and when it wasn't them, there was always something Gabriel was a part of.

He knew we were talking based on his expression. It was blank but I knew Gabriel was listening. He had hearing like I did except I knew he wasn't a sniper.

233

Which meant he was just a good enough hunter to know. Former CIA and all that shit.

"Aw, Reed that's not fair—" Evie's voice cut me out of my thoughts. "You didn't even give me a chance—"

"Fair?" Reed grinned motioning to her cards. "You had *seven* bonus cards in hand—"

"The Goddess card doesn't count Reed, you had the Magician this entire time—"

"I had one. You have three."

Evie giggled at his expression.

Reed was bantering back and forth with her which happened more often than not and Gabriel sat back watching her with a smile on his face.

Lena's eyes sparkled when they landed on Gabriel.

I didn't think Lena loved him like *that*. But I didn't know.

She never looked at anyone the way she watched Gabriel. Then again, I knew he'd saved her ass out of Havana once, so I didn't know how deep her relationship with him ran.

Their relationship was like mine and Reed.

If Lena slept with anyone I knew it was never near us. Like that one time in Prague when I knew she hooked up with the brother of one of our charges.

I watched them all, laughing and arguing over a stupid board game.

For a split second, I let myself imagine Gemma here.

Her laugh mixing with Evie's, her wit matching Lena's. She'd get along with Reed since he had a crush on her friend.

The way she'd charm even Gabriel—maybe. How she'd fit so perfectly under my arm. How she fit...all the time.

Gemma had left her family.

Walked away from everything she knew. And here I was, with this makeshift family I never asked for but somehow ended up with.

And I liked them.

For the first time in years, I felt a twinge of something dangerously close to an unfamiliar pang of regret.

What if I'd stayed? What if I'd brought her into this world?

Would she be sitting here now, a part of us?

The person I had become? With the money I had? He could handle Camilla.

But the boy I had been? Would've been taken down. I told myself this. Over and over whenever I thought about Gemma fucking Marchand.

But that was a dangerous road to go down. I shut it down fast. Gemma and I, we were over. Had to be.

Still, the image lingered. Gemma, here. With us. With me.

My phone trilled, snapping me back to reality. Speaking of women...

"I gotta take this."

It was Reed's personal jewel thief on some trip in Morocco. Lucy Devereaux. Former heiress. *World class thief.*

Reed knew or suspected at the minimum I was fuck buddies with her. Reed knew how I was with women in general and that nothing was ever serious. Lucy was feisty and violent in bed.

Just my type.

And she'd be back in the city soon.

Lena rolled her eyes at me stepping out to text Lucy back.

I smirked at Lena. "I've got needs."

"You have too many."

$\sim$

I WAS ABOUT TO TEXT LUCY DEVEREAUX BACK WHEN ANOTHER TEXT popped up on my phone.

Mama.

Nathan, call me.

I did. Immediately.

My mother picked up within the first ring and I knew something was wrong. Deadly wrong.

"Baby...it's your father..."

And I barely heard her. My world tilted a little sideways. I brace myself against the wall as my mother's voice came through and spliced fragments.

Cancer.

235

Dad.

Struggling.

"…he didn't want you to stress—"

"Stress?" I wheezed. Stress? He had been my fucking hero.

"He knew you dealt with a lot," Mama was talking. But I didn't hear her.

Instead, I just jumped into action. I did everything I thought possible was the right thing. I flew down to Texas. Helped her with him. I felt numb the entire time.

The entire fucking time.

His funeral was a blur for me. I felt nothing. Years of killing people had made me numb. I barely felt a thing. Because I had been so busy.

Busy with life.

Busy with Titan.

And when the last guest finally left Mama's house, it felt too quiet.

She was sitting at the kitchen table in her seat.

His seat was empty and I took mine at the other side.

"Listen," I began unsteadily not feeling a thing. Something had happened to me over the years. Something numbing up my soul. "You can't…I don't want you to stay her anymore."

My mom's softer blue eyes met mine. "What?"

"I've got a place you can stay at. Let me take care of you." I couldn't take care of him.

"Nathan—"

"I can't lose you." I cut her off. And then I felt it. The tremor. The way I was breathing. "*I won't.*"

She knew. She knew how I felt. She looked around the kitchen and I felt devastated.

I didn't know how to tell her how I felt.

I didn't snap in half until I got back to New York.

The taste of whiskey burned down my throat. But it wasn't enough. It was never enough. I'd been through bottles and I felt nothing.

"Duchess," I whispered into thin air. In her lilac dress she appeared in my imagination all honey-haired and beautiful, opal eyes blinking at me softly.

Nate?

"You never got to meet him." I whispered. "I wanted you to. I

236

wanted you to get to have that. My family. Now it's just Mama and she's here in the city finally."

She is?

I nodded. "I fucked up, Duchess. I fucked up."

How?

I didn't even know.

It's been my entire life becoming with everyone else needed.

Soldier. Killer. Weapon. Protector. Partner. Son.

"I don't gotta be nothing with you."

When I lost her? I lost something more than a person.

With Gemma—I didn't have to be anything.

When I wasn't her protector? I was just myself.

Calmer. Peaceful. Lighter.

She was everything pure and good and when I lost her? I descended into a circle of hell that was purely for me.

"I think I failed you, Duchess."

I blew out a breath.

"I'm a fucking failure."

FORTY-THREE
GEMMA

TALIA GAVE BIRTH TO ALEXANDRE ANDREI 'DREW' DUPONT.

The night she went into labor?

Andrei had been called internationally to handle a crisis. He thought Drew was going to arrive in three weeks.

The only two people able to help her, was me. And Thierry. The youngest DuPont brother I knew nothing about.

I hadn't known her long. At all.

But I got she didn't exactly have many friends. Now?

Weeks after she'd given birth she was sitting back in Andrei's apartment holding onto the baby who was nursing.

"How is he doing?" I asked, settling into the plush couch across from Talia listening to the hungry sounds of her baby.

Drew was a few weeks old and round as bundle. Talia nursed him so frequently though I tried to come by and take care of her along with the mid-wife and nanny.

"Hungry as ever," she smiled up at me, her dark hair framing her tired, tip-tilted green eyes.

Her features a unique blend of Japanese, Dutch. I knew because Talia was proud of her mixed heritage and it gave her a wilder look.

"He's only a few months old, but I swear he's going to be my height any day now."

"Just like his family."

"Tell me about it, Thierry comes and calls him a little burrito all the time."

"His father is Andrei. Of course he's going to be huge."

At the mention of Andrei, something in Talia's eyes changed, a shadow passing over her face. I bit my lip, drawing my knees up to my chest as I watched them.

"How are you, really?" I ventured.

"As good as I can be," She gently brushed Drew's thick swath of black hair.

One of his chubby fists shot up, grasping her finger, and she let out a soft laugh. "Look at him, Gemma. He's so strong now."

Part of me wondered if I'd ever experience motherhood myself, but I quickly swallowed the sharp ache that accompanied that thought.

Not after what had happened. No, I reminded myself, I kept my relationships quick and fleeting now. Never serious.

I'd been with other men since, but it wasn't the same.

Those encounters usually left me feeling emptier than when I'd started, and it had been a while since I'd been with anyone at all.

"How are you?" Talia asked, her green eyes searching my face. "Your father's been in the news lately. I was worried about you."

I winced, thinking of the latest headlines.

Talia knew a bit about me. Enough, she had said, for her to paint a picture. Her father, Malcolm Nash, had died months ago.

"It's complicated," I replied, knowing Talia didn't have the full picture, but was aware enough to understand I was no longer tied to my family.

She nodded, a knowing look in her eyes. "Camilla was friends with my father," she said, her voice lowered as if sharing a secret. Her eyes searched mine like she knew something. "Did you know that?"

It was her first time asking me. And I felt my body stiffen.

I shook my head lying.

"I didn't. But it seems Camilla's tendrils reach everywhere."

Talia leaned back in the chair as she held Drew tighter almost.

"I think your father is failing," Talia said, her words gentle but direct. "And children do not do well in places where parents fail. Should Camilla try things with you, just let me know."

I was confused. "But you have Drew—"

239

"I still have resources. I still own Nash Group."

Talia's father Malcolm Nash had died of a heart attack a few months ago when she'd come to the city to be with Andrei.

I did know she had a stand in currently.

"Besides, he'll always be my entire world. But that doesn't mean I can't look out for a friend."

But there was a world of sadness in her eyes. A world of it.

Eager to lighten the mood, I kept my voice soft. "Why don't you go shower? I'll hold him. I'm sure he wants to snuggle with Aunty Gemma's bony arms—"

Talia's laughter rang out, a sound I hadn't heard in far too long. "You are not bony, Gemma. You just do not eat right."

I raised an eyebrow, intrigued. "And what's that supposed to mean?"

Her eyes sparkled with mischief. "Drew's nanny is from Hong Kong, and she had me on my confinement diet. It would do you well."

"I am trying to eat as much as I can. But I will take your word on not leaving my house and eating delicious meal-prepped food courtesy of a fantastic chef from Shanghai."

"I'll leave him. But if he starts to cry just give him the elephant binky. He loves that one. " she said, carefully handing Drew to me. His big blue eyes, so reminiscent of the DuPont family's aqua gaze rimmed with black, watched me curiously as he chortled.

"Gosh, he's so cute," I cooed, cradling him against me, his weight familiar in my arms. "Yes, you are so cute, and you know it, don't you?"

Drew laughed, a bubbly sound that made Talia's smile soften.

"He's been on his best behavior lately, after keeping me restless for nine months."

Her movements were slower now, and I understood how challenging it must be for her to essentially raise Drew on her own.

As Talia headed for the shower, she paused, her expression growing serious.

"I'm worried about Thierry," she said softly. "That's the other reason I wanted to talk to you. He's been more restless lately, not acclimating well to his new life."

I nodded, recalling that both Talia and Thierry had worked together in the past, with Talia serving as his instructor in martial arts.

They had worked for a security company employed by Nash Group according to Talia—Thierry had left when she did.

"How is he doing?" I asked, remembering Thierry's intense presence, so similar to Andrei's yet uniquely his own.

Talia made a face. "Probably better if he understood things."

"Is it his..." I began, recalling Thierry's struggle with English.

Talia didn't look happy. "Can you find someone to help him? Between Drew and everything else, I don't have the mental space to help Thierry right now. He doesn't want a stupid tutor like he had in the past, but you would know someone for him."

I agreed without hesitation. "Is he still staying in Andrei's old apartment?"

"He is."

"I'll go check on him this week."

THE FIRST TIME I HAD MET THIERRY HAD BEEN WHILE TALIA HAD BEEN in labor.

Thierry had burst into the penthouse like a force of nature, his presence immediately commanding attention. His black hair fell rakishly over one eye like a pirate. And he was as attractive as Teo.

In the few years I'd known them, it had been my first time meeting Thierry.

His eyes so much like the rest of the family but almost manic in their intensity. His face was grim and cut sharper, way sharper than Teo's.

He was almost pretty had he not been frowning at Talia in labor.

"Why is she in so much pain?" Thierry looked at me concerned for Talia.

"Well, she's giving birth to your brother's enormous off-spring," I spat back. "Have you realized how completely huge the three of you are? What did you think she would have? A normal baby?"

He turned pink.

"What do you need?" It had been the first words out of his mouth as he'd rolled up his black sleeves to reveal tattoo covered arms.

And he'd been helpful. Rushing around doing everything to make Talia comfortable. She had been inconsolably upset during labor.

Thierry had been good for help and Teo had stepped in when we needed a break. I finally met Teo in a setting where he'd snapped into a personality I didn't recognize.

Teo had stepped out to call Andrei again who was rushing back. But we both knew he wouldn't make it in time no matter how fast he ran. I'd been juggling both Drew and Talia and Thierry had gone to do paperwork when I saw him hovering uncertainly.

I guessed something was up when he didn't text. Since I'd met him he spoke in a mixture of French and English, his accent subtle like Teo's but there.

He'd tensed when I'd asked if he struggled with his English.

I didn't judge him. Just needed to know to help Talia who'd been emotional at having Drew.

"It's all right," I said softly. "I don't judge you—"

"I don't care—" he started, his voice sharp, defensive.

"Thierry," I cut him off, my own exhaustion and frustration seeping through. "your sister-in-law just had a baby. I need you to not be an absolute arse right now."

If he was trying to be rude, he'd picked the wrong day. I hadn't left Talia's side for ten grueling hours, all while Teo frantically tried to reach an absent Andrei.

"I'm not stupid," Thierry finally admitted, his voice low, almost a whisper. "I just..." He trailed off, frustration evident in the set of his jaw.

He didn't speak English properly. He was struggling. I had known Thierry spoke a mixture of Canadian French and English, but even then, his English needed assistance. Around me, he'd only ever spoken French.

"I don't think you're stupid, Thierry," I said firmly, meeting his gaze. "Your brain just works differently." I paused, noting his expression. There was more to this, I could tell, but I wasn't sure how to ask. Or if I should. Instead, I squeezed his hand, offering a small smile. "We'll figure it out, okay? For now, let's focus on Talia and the baby. Andrei will be here soon, and we need to be ready."

Thierry looked like he'd rather do anything but face his brother. The tension between them was palpable, even in Andrei's absence.

242

"Je suis bon dans ce que je fais. I'm good with what I do," Thierry said softly, a lock of inky hair falling over his piercing eyes.

Thierry did live in Andrei's old apartment.

When I got there he answered the door in a hoodie with messy hair.

"Gemma."

He looked out of it. Like he wasn't sleeping properly.

"I came because Talia's worried about you," I got straight to the point. No point beating around the bush with someone like Thierry. "She wants you to work with someone to improve your English—"

"Merde, pourquoi elle s'en mêle? She has Drew." Thierry muttered, his brows furrowed. *Why is she getting involved?*

I rounded on him in his pristine penthouse he'd 'borrowed' from Andrei.

At six-foot-three, Thierry towered over me, his inky black hair falling in disheveled waves around his devastatingly handsome face.

If Teo had been *pretty*, Thierry beat him any day.

But Thierry was attractive in a way that defied reality.

Dangerous.

Dark.

Deadly.

Even in his state of frustration, there was a charm about him, but at twenty, he exuded a presence that was hard to ignore.

I sensed from whatever work he'd been involved in with Nash Group. They dealt with securities as well as government contracts.

Traces of Andrei's old life were still here, my eyes catching a gym bag that lay open on the floor with boxing gloves strewn about.

"What will you do?" I asked, tilting my head back to meet his gaze. "Besides mope here all day? I don't know what you plan on doing with your life at twenty, struggling with your English."

Thierry ran a hand through his hair, his long fingers raking through the dark strands. Frustration was evident on his chiseled face, his sharp jawline clenched.

"Ce n'est pas si facile. J'essaie, mais c'est difficile."

It's not that easy. I'm trying, but it's hard.

"Only because you won't allow anyone to help you," I countered, trying to decipher his mixed language.

"Pourquoi je devrais?" He barked, his deep voice resonating through the space. *Why should I?*

And I didn't buy it for a second.

I'd seen him soften with his family, his tough exterior melting away to reveal a gentler side.

"Why did she send you?" He muttered in English, his accent thickening, adding a rough edge to his deep voice.

"Because I know someone who is the perfect person to help you with your studies."

He frowned, his dark brows knitting together. "Who?"

Who. Indeed.

Because I was bluffing.

And just like that, my phone chimed. It was Alisha, texting me a photo of Avani in her graduation cap.

Avani was the most studious person I knew.

She was going to the same university I had attended briefly before dropping out.

I'd even written her a recommendation letter.

And Avani was going to school for *English* Literature.

Avani.

And I knew just who could help Thierry.

FORTY-FOUR
GEMMA

I'm tutoring Thierry this summer 🩶

> And he's okay with it?

> I hope he wasn't too mad about it.

Not at all.

I don't mind either. He's good company.

I was just planning on visiting the library this summer so I guess now? I have a friend to do it with.

He's great.

> I'm so happy.

He's frightening so he should keep all the creeps away.

Hahahaha he already has.

He's not too scary, just enough LOL

> Are you kidding me? THANK. YOU.

> Thierry despises all his tutors so this will be a rarity.

> I'll tell Talia and all is well.

which I was happy to hear.

The season progressed with me attending functions, charity meetings, juggling my life and the only time I saw Alisha was during our late night's at Teasers with Lara.

With the ivy swirling around her she looked like an ethereal fairy in pink chunky heels and vibrant eye makeup.

"Been busy as of late?" I asked her.

She nodded looking ruefully exhausted. "I had no idea university in the States was so expensive."

I felt a twinge of sympathy for her since she was no doubt making more content and posting more gathering more money for Avani to go to school.

Alisha had been doing lots more sponsorships and I could tell it was exhausting.

"Besides," she shrugged. "It's not bad. Avani now has ninety sweater to wear in school."

Even with all the girls money I appreciated them being more frugal than I was. I had learned a lot from both of them.

I stayed the night with her until by some stroke of luck, Reed appeared at the bar with Lara.

"He's always here when you are," I told her as she flushed deeply. "Avani's going away to school soon. Do you think you might date him then?"

Alisha looked down a little nervous. "I don't know."

And in that moment she looked just like her sister. A little nervous. A little anxious. Genuinely out of it. Which I took from her emotional state.

I watched Alisha's eyes follow Reed as he made his way to the bar. His dark chocolate hair rakishly falling over his eyes as he ruffled it brushing off droplets of rain.

In his black jacket and white shirt, women were already staring at him.

Combined with the full force of his eyes? And he was honestly attractive. Not my type.

No, my type was the one I was avoiding. Dirty blonde hair and blue eyes aside, I hadn't seen Nate as of late which I took to be a good thing.

Her usually confident demeanor seemed to waver, revealing a vulnerability I rarely saw. Reed, only had eyes for Alisha.

"You know," I said softly, leaning in closer. "Reed doesn't seem like the other idiots...and you don't look at him like just another man."

No, she looked at Reed like she wanted him.

She smiled ruefully. "That he is not. But I'm just terrified."

She shook her raven locks, tucking a strand behind her ear. "Is it that obvious?"

I smiled knowingly. "Only to someone who knows you well."

"Besides, he's just..." she looked over at him. She sighed a bit like Avani.

I looked over at Reed who cut an impressive figure. I said with no tiny amusement in my voice.

"He's rather plain—"

Alisha frowned at me. "I think he's dashing—"

"That messy hair—"

"It's tousled—"

"Those boring eyes—"

"They're like storm clouds—"

"And those shoulders—"

"Rather large, but I love them—" she broke off looking at me grin. She mock gasped and threw a straw at me. "*Gemma!*"

I giggled. "I got you. I knew you liked him."

"Liking him and being with him are two different things—"

"So you admit your crush is real—"

She covered her face turning a bright red. "I'll take the tab—"

"Oh, I'm just teasing—" I broke off as two girls came to our table giggling as they looked at Alisha.

"We saw your last video and we just wanted to tell you, we love you so much!"

"Can we take a picture with you?"

Alisha was turning red for another reason and I caught the way Reed was watching us now. He was protective of her. Which was rather romantic.

And he did work in private security after all.

I felt the back of my neck prickle as Alisha took selfies with the girls.

But when I turned to see I didn't catch anything. Weird. I must've been imagining it. I usually showed up the nights Nate wasn't here, thankfully.

As they chattered to Alisha happily, more and more people started looking and I caught Alisha looking at me a little overwhelmed. And if he knew, on cue, Reed slowly

"Oh, don't look now," I murmured to Alisha. "Reed's coming."

She bit her lip nervously as Reed handled the growing crowd around Alisha.

"Ladies, we don't allow that," he motioned to one of them as Alisha smiled gratefully at him.

And on cue, Lara sashayed over in her bra and panties and a feather boa she wrapped around one of the girls as Reed corralled them away from Alisha. They were getting the crowd away from Alisha and towards one of the girls at Teasers who was dancing on a table.

Alisha let out a breath. "Intense, always."

"Indeed." I passed her a drink. "Mojito?"

She murmured her thanks as she took it. "Reed's awfully protective you."

She let out a breath and covered her face. "You're never going to let me live it down, hm?" Her eyes turned to me. "What about you?"

And just like that I stopped.

"You never date anyone," she said over the music. "I notice things too, just because I am busy doesn't meant mean I don't."

I shrugged. "Maybe I'm waiting for a man like Reed." I grinned at her expression.

"What about Nate?"

I froze. All rational thought left my brain. Nate.

Who worked under Reed. I struggled to find my composure as Alisha smiled knowingly.

"Do you think he's attractive? In a roguish way?"

I sipped my apple martini. "I haven't found my Reed yet."

"He isn't *my* Reed—"

"But he wants to be—"

"Gemma!"

"He is always here when you're here."

"That's just some stroke of luck!"

WEEKS LATER, IT WAS AT POPPY, ALISHA'S CHARITY PROJECT THAT I received a parcel.

A nondescript box waiting for me at the front desk.

"For me?" I asked one of the teenagers volunteering.

She nodded and I took my mail and parcels to my office. I worked with Alisha at Poppy and today she was upstairs taking a few meetings and parents who wanted to participate in the project as well.

Once I stepped into the office with trembling hands, I opened the box, and my breath caught in my throat.

Inside were pieces of a blonde doll, covered in red splatters. Immediately, I dropped it from my hands shaking a little.

What was this?

Was this Camilla's doing?

Why would she abandon her subtlety now, after all these years?

It seemed too extreme to be her, but who else could it be?

Part of me wondered if this was just an errant scare tactic meant to make me lose my composure.

But *who* would do such a thing?

I couldn't just accuse Camilla because of her vindictive nature; being a horrible person wasn't a crime.

I had caught glimpses of news reports about my father's family struggling, but I had chosen to ignore them all.

The idea of calling the police or hiring security made my stomach churn.

If Camilla was behind this, involving authorities could push her to take even more dangerous actions.

Involving anyone meant opening up parts of my life I'd fought hard to keep private. *Including the baby...*

My fingers hovered over my phone. Lara had mentioned that whenever she needed help, she called Reed.

He *could* help; he ran a security firm. And I didn't really know what else to do.

But the moment I involved him, there would be no going back.

My carefully constructed walls would crumble, and I'd be forced to confront everything I'd been running from.

As I stood there, torn between seeking help and maintaining my isolation, a noise from purse made me jump.

Alisha

I'm just about finished, lunch soon?

Sounds good. Let me gather my things.

Alisha would let me stay at her place if I needed it. I mean I wouldn't want to impose.

And then Bonnie and Nigel...where would they go? I needed to figure out something.

Something about Alisha tickled the back of my head. Why was I— Reed. Reed worked private security. With Nathan.

I could always go to Reed...couldn't I?

Just because I did, didn't mean I'd have to go to Nathan. I could just request a guard temporarily. To accompany me where I needed to go.

I didn't need it at home. Just where I worked.

With a shaky breath, I dialed his number.

It was time to stop running and face whatever—or whoever—was coming for me.

I had to call Reed.

PART II

PRESENT DAY

FORTY-FIVE
NATE

"IF YOU EVER GO NEAR MY GIRL AGAIN? I WILL SLIT YOUR FUCKING throat and let you bleed out in front of your wife."

"Reed," I cut him off. "He's going to die if you keep going."

Reed paused his shoulders stiffening as I said it.

He'd already beaten the motherfucker to a pulp.

The metallic scent of blood filled my nostrils as I scrubbed the basement floor of Titan Midtown.

Just another Monday morning in paradise.

Reed was pissed at Gabriel—*again*. And he even more pissed off at the fucker who hit on Alisha over the weekend. *Suit and Tie.*

Which was the only reason why I cleaning up blood and taking out the body of some passed out finance bro from the Titan Midtown basement.

Reed had also *finally* slept with Alisha. Thank fucking Christ.

But if I thought it would calm him down?

I was wrong.

I knew because now I was cleaning up blood from him, after he threatened her the previous weekend.

I had seen Reed take her home that night knowing full well I had to tie the motherfucker up, get his credentials, and keep him there overnight. I spent my weekend rolling around with an heiress and her sister only to be brought back in the morning to find Reed laying into him.

Most people thought because Reed was the peacekeeper that he wasn't capable of violence. He was.

And ripping things to pieces.

Gabriel wore his close to the surface.

Reed? His violence was a storm. A cold, methodical, and utterly destructive storm baring down on anything in his path.

I'd winced as Reed's first hit slammed into the guys face and his smirk was wiped off. I didn't even blame Reed.

Suit and Tie was lucky he was alive.

"Fifty grand says that bitch in the red dress is mine by the end of the night," Suit and Tie had bragged the night prior, drunk on overpriced scotch and his own inflated ego. *"Fuck her in front of everyone and pass her round to you boys?"*

Reed's eyes did that thing right before he killed someone. His eyes landing on Alisha with precision as he advanced on her that night.

Only unlike Gabriel who would put a bullet in his brain?

Reed would beat him within an inch of his life.

And then ruin his entire livelihood. Ruin his wife's life. Ruin his company. Before he killed him. Reed was a fan of that when he was in a mood.

Which he had.

Reed had lain into him like it was just another day for him. And it was. And then Reed went after his company.

His life. And his money. Done.

I was used to this.

Reed had cleaned his hands and showered after the guy almost died bleeding out on the basement floor of Titan Midtown.

"I need to go meet the new hires," he said quietly as he left without a backwards glance. "His company should be out of the picture by the end of the week."

He motioned to the guy lying in a pool of his own blood.

We all knew why Reed wanted to hire new people.

Hell, we'd known for months.

Gabriel kept fucking it up, scaring away every potential recruit with his intense scrutiny and impossible standards.

But I understood why Gabriel did it, even if I didn't *agree*.

I'd been the point of contact for Kellan Watts and Garrett Fuller, two guys coming in from Kuwait who were pretty capable. Solid operators, both of them.

Reed was handling a third recruit on his own, keeping that guy away from Gabriel's scrutiny for now.

It was a smart move, given Gabriel's track record with new hires. Over the years I'd watch team after team wash out once Gabriel got his claws and fangs into them.

Not a single one stood up to the test and Gabriel had a firm belief I did agree with.

Good enough gets people killed.

Weakness wasn't teachable.

He wasn't wrong. But. We had a tiny problem.

Looking around, I could see the toll our understaffing was taking.

Selena's eyes had dark circles under them, and I felt the weight of exhaustion in my own bones.

We were all stretched thin, trying to keep up with the demands of our growing operation—and well, our leadership here.

Reed was stressed and he desperately needed an outlet which was turning out to be his girl. Or…any potential suitors she attracted.

But he couldn't just murder half the population.

Evie left the manor more and more frequently now. And my mind...drifted to Gemma, as it often did in quiet moments.

I'd caught glimpses of her life in the society pages, seen her name mentioned in passing on social media.

There were rumors about her and Andrei DuPont—nothing concrete, just whispers and speculation.

DuPont wasn't just any CEO; he was the heir to an empire, a global luxury goods empire that made my yearly salary look like pocket change.

His company, Durand, was just the tip of the iceberg.

A photo here and there of Andrei's back at some gala Gemma was attending, or mentions of them being seen at the same events.

Never together, never definitive, but enough to spike my anxiety.

DuPont was exactly the kind of man I'd always imagined Gemma with—wealthy, powerful, part of her world in a way I could never be.

But I had Lena.

That was enough.

And yet, wasn't that exactly why Lena and I had made our pact? To build something stable in our chaotic lives?

The last thing I expected was for Reed to come to me with news that Gemma Marchand needed a guard.

Marchand. Capital M. Gemma. My old girlfriend.

Lena was working with Watts, her new partner, and I was being pushed into guard duty. I wouldn't have cared.

Until he said her name.

"Nate, I sent you a gig as a bodyguard." Those words had come out of Reed's mouth.

"Fuck," I groaned. "Please let it be a sexy young divorcée this time."

"Close, she's important." Reed smirked. "She just needs you whenever she goes to work events, so it shouldn't be bad at all. Enough for you to get back and do what you need with Selena and the lost boys. Gemma is Alisha's best friend. Try not to fuck this one up."

Hang on.

Wait a second.

What the fuck.

My smile fell from my lips

"Gemma Marchand?"

Selena had frowned next to me. "Are you sure you don't want me to do it? Nate will end up on the news."

Yeah. No kidding.

Reed had shot that down. "No, you're with Kellan. He's good for you. Nate, can you overlook your bias to help her or not?"

Bias? Bias had nothing to do with it. Camilla had threatened me years ago to stay away from her. And I had. *Gemma left her family.*

I dipped my head because I didn't say no to Reed who just continued on.

"I need you guys to make sure Evie doesn't do anything that will make Gabriel kill everyone. Selena, I've sent you everything for the new guys. In the event, you guys can't reach me–you're in charge. *Entiendes?"*

"Sí, *entiendes*." Selena bobbed her head looking at Reed with a soft smile.

"Why is she in charge?" I started my concern about Gemma being cut short. "No offense, Selena, you're overqualified for everything you do. What the fuck happened to Gabriel?"

Reed paused. "Gabriel and I are still running everything–"

"You're hiring more than three guys, aren't you?" My brain was working because that meant Reed was looking to expand again. Which meant an insane amount of work for him.

Reed's eyes told me everything I needed to know.

"I'm hiring way more than three guys. The two in there are just a start."

"You're replacing us?" Lena stepped in to ask whipping her knife out from her boot.

"Put the knife away, Selena. I'm not replacing you. We just can't keep pushing like this. I'm trying to find a middle ground." Reed was calm as Lena did just that. "Play nice. I sent you everything you needed going forward. I'm leaving now."

"You are going to your *novia*?" Selena asked.

But Reed just tipped his head and left.

I was left standing there to process the fucking card I just got dealt.

Gemma.

Marchand.

The only two words in the English dictionary guaranteed to make me feel less than.

Nothing haunted me more than the memory of her crying. Then the memory of me turning and leaving that house.

Over the years I'd grown beyond the boy that had left her. Invested in my own business. Had my own brand of whiskey. Real estate. Mechanic shops.

Everything I could think of. Lena was the one who wasn't money savvy so Reed did the job for her. Investing her dollars into *all* our investments because Lena didn't get all the science behind things. Reed took care of her.

Even Gabriel as a ghost had money. Sure, it was tied up with the O'Hara's. But he had it. I thought I had grown past the man I used to be.

I thought a lot of things.

And all of it mattered fuck all when I saw her name.

The email contained all the details that I read over ninety times with Lena over my shoulder with her green eyes wide as she blinked at me. Her eyes were a little alien bright right now and it looked striking on her face.

"You will take this, no."

"I have to." I never said no to Reed.

I read the email again.

> *Miss Marchand requires a guard temporarily during the*
> *duty day for her hours…*

Reed had conducted a discreet interview with her, and she had specifically requested protection. Not me. No. Just a bodyguard. Because she was in danger.

As I pored over the information, my heart raced with each word.

Someone was trying to *attack* Gemma?

And *I* was her new guard.

Again.

Oh. Motherfucker.

∾

"GEMMA'S BACK."

I sat on the back of my truck with Selena who ate her burger like a woman starved. I felt bad because I knew she wasn't taking care of herself properly.

Hopefully her new fucking partner Kellan Watts, golden boy new hire would take care of her. Step up where I couldn't. Where I didn't know how to.

Lena chewed as she ate quietly, her brunette locks blowing a little in the wind. "She's different now. You said it yourself, she left her family. Maybe this is a chance for…"

I couldn't stop myself from cutting her off. "She made it clear she didn't want to see me. Not after everything that happened."

"You are not the same person you were back then. You've made something big for yourself."

259

"I can't say no to Reed. He already asked me for a few favors and I got in touch with his jewel thief so you know he needs shit done," I murmured feeling nauseous at the prospect of seeing Gemma again. "What am I going to do?"

"You can just be her bodyguard," Lena said softly. "You do not have to do anything else for her."

And that was the thing. I didn't fucking know what to do. Or what I wanted. Or what to feel about Gemma. I didn't know. I just knew, I couldn't face her and if I did, I'd lose my composure I barely held together for the last seven years.

I had plans. Goals. A life outside of what I thought I had wanted in my past. I wasn't twenty-three anymore. I had money and income and things going for me.

And I had Lena.

"This doesn't change our deal, does it?"

"No." She ate her burger some more.

We ate in silence for a while; the only sound was the crinkle of the fast food wrappers and us chewing.

"This was my first meal in America. It was the only place still open at the shopping mall," Lena said quietly looking down at her food. It was some generic burger place. "Milkshake."

And just like I remembered why I had become a Titan and why I stayed. Lena was one of those reasons. "I'm going to miss you, *muñeca*."

A faraway look entered her eyes.

"I'll miss you too…I'm just exhausted."

I can see it. Maybe Watts would be good for Lena.

"You need a break. You're not Reed or Gabriel. You can't push like this."

"What about you?" Lena asked my fingers instinctively tangling with mine. "Are you sure you're going to be good for this?"

I squeezed her hand. "Guarding an heiress who has lunch with prime ministers? It'll be a vacation compared to the last few months."

But even as I said it I knew I was lying. I was lying. I was absolutely fucking dying to see her again and now up close. Honey blonde hair. Opal eyes. Pretty face. My old Gemma.

Now…this woman who left her fucking family behind.

Someone was trying to hurt her. How could I not feel something?

"Gemma is not an heiress anymore. She is not her family."

"She's not you. And you're still my wife."

"She may not be the same girl you remember. Not the same Gemma. You are not the same, Nathan."

"Maybe not…But I guess I'll find out."

FORTY-SIX
GEMMA

ALISHA AND REED SLEPT TOGETHER.

Finally.

And while I was prepping all the pastries and tea, Lara was leaping onto Alisha. "*Aliiishaaaaaa!*"

I laughed at their antics. Lara was peppering Alisha with questions about Reed.

"How was he? Is his cock long and thick? Did he destroy your cookie? How's it doing after the beating it got? Oh my God!" I laughed as Lara launched herself at Alisha. "What did I say about Big Dick Energy?"

"Help, Gemma. She's killed me," Alisha called out.

I took that as my cue to emerge from the kitchen where I'd been watching the two of them go at it. Carrying in a tray with snacks for both of them I just moved around to the coffee table while Lara pressed biscuits into Alisha's arm and sides.

"Gemma can't save you from these paws, chica," Lara looked delighted over Reed and Alisha finally getting together.

"It was just one night," Alisha was protesting but Lara was quick.

"It is not! Reed likes you!"

"He does not."

Lara pulled back, eyes wide. "¿Estas loca?" she exclaimed, switching to rapid-fire Spanish. "Por supuesto que le gustas..."

"Let me translate," I interjected. "Lara asked if you were insane because Reed likes you. He stares at you and hovers protectively at the club. She says he's crazy about you and has asked about you before. Hang on—"

I paused, listening as Lara erupted in more Spanish.

"She says she told him you were single, but he said—"

"What did she say?" Alisha asked, her accent thicker now. "You guys can't keep your language a secret from me."

"It's not a secret, Alisha," Lara replied playfully. "You're just bad at learning languages."

"She's not bad," I countered. "She just needs practice."

"Alisha doesn't have a hot motorcycle-riding surfer bro to help her learn Spanish," Lara smiled slyly at me.

I did not in fact regret that little bit I had lived.

"He was a kite surfer," I clarified, turning pink. "And I learned a lot in Miami, but…I learned more from him."

I wanted to hide my face but lucky for me Lara moved on and quickly.

Lara and Alisha talked about Reed and my mind was pondering why someone like him would wait this long. Reed was a patient hunter. He would take his time with Alisha.

"A wolf," I added to Lara's comments about Reed. "He reminds us of a patient wolf."

"Yeaaaahh," Lara agreed, her fingers curling into claws. "Like he was watching you through the club's foliage, waiting to catch you like a bunny. And he went gr—" She mimicked a wolf snatching its prey, her teeth bared in a playful growl. We burst out laughing at Lara. "Now that he has you in his den—or your den—he's not letting his meal go easily. I know men. I am the Dick Whisperer," she said, her voice dropping to a conspiratorial whisper.

"I'll never get used to you," I said through laughter.

"You can loiter with me and be defiled with—what was that word?"

"*Debauchery*," I hid my smile behind my cup.

Lara frowned. "Debu—Deba—*Dabuchery*."

Sometimes I swore Lara had an accent I couldn't place and wondered if she grew up in Mexico. I didn't know, she never talked about her past.

"Good effort," I laughed.

"Thanks, I try," Lara grinned before turning back to Alisha. "Reed and Gabriel never bother coming to a client's place *just* because. And Reed isn't upgrading the security system *that* often when he's admitted he could do it from home."

There was that name. Gabriel. Once, a long time ago, I had seen Lara hugging a man in a gray suit. Considering I'd never seen Lara in a relationship, I knew he might've been important to her. Blonde, too handsome to be real and I thought Lara had been oddly friendly.

Because Lara didn't let in men. Not into her life.

"Have I met Gabriel?" Alisha asked.

I didn't even hesitate to ask Lara. "Is he the gentleman who comes around occasionally?" I could've sworn I saw him every so often but he vanished too quickly for me to tell.

"Yeah, but Alisha hasn't met him, and he isn't a gentleman," Lara's cheeks turned redder as she answered and I knew she was lying. Just a tiny bit. Because I did the same thing when I was lying.

"The point is, Reed's good to *you*." Lara shifted in her seat as she said Gabriel's name too.

Alisha and Lara bantered back and forth about Reed and him being a dominant man. Nate was like that, but not as intense as Reed. Nobody did dark like Reed Whittaker.

Lara motioned for me to fill her cup a bit more.

"It's ten in the morning. I thought we talked about this."

Lara raised a brow. "For you, it's morning. For me, it's almost bedtime. And Mama needs some sleepy juice to pass out."

It was slight, her accent, but it was there. I could ask her later. As the girls and I talked I only found myself half participating and saying things I knew were true. But another part of me couldn't stop thinking about Nate. My secrets. Alisha was dating Reed, inevitably if Reed and Nate were close, which they looked like they were?

I would have to face Nate eventually.

One day. Some day.

Alisha said something about not knowing what she was doing.

I kindly put in my few cents on the matter. "Darling, none of us do. Last year, I was having tea with the prime minister of a foreign country. Now, I'm currently a plain Jane who serves tea to my best friends."

Alisha chewed her lip watching me. I didn't think Reed meant her any harm. I didn't think he'd wait this long to hurt her, but I do think as a man, he was terrible at communicating.

Like Nate.

Lara yawned then. "Love you, *chicas*, but I am exhausted. I need to head back to my...what did you call it?"

"Den of debauchery?" I teased.

"No."

"Hovel of Whoredom."

"No," Lara repeated firmly, though amusement danced in her eyes.

"Sanctum of Sin?" My eyebrows rose.

"Oh, that's a good one," Lara grinned. "I'm gonna catch a cab, I'll see you chicas later."

"Hang on. I'll drive."

"You don't have a license," Alisha looked at me confused.

"No, but just because I'm no longer...doesn't mean I don't have adequate funds to take in a driver..." I shrugged lightly.

"Nigel, here I come," Lara squealed. "Let's stop and get cake!"

Oh boy. And the day was only beginning.

FORTY-SEVEN
GEMMA

"We're getting cake!"

Lara shouted as she ran ahead of me, tipsy and a little out of it. I chased after her, my skirts all around me. We had just spent the last few hours at Alisha's over breakfast.

"I didn't know you knew so much about Reed," Lara asked me, her words slightly slurred as she linked her arm with mine after we'd finished.

"I asked around, Lish is my sister, so I try." It wasn't much of an excuse, but Lara was a little tipsy, so it was all right.

I had met with Reed. I just hadn't told anyone the things I had talked to him about.

Under normal circumstances, I wouldn't have hesitated to confront Reed about his behavior.

However, having met him personally during my client intake interview, I knew firsthand how demanding his schedule could be.

Our meeting had been interrupted no fewer than five times, his phone buzzing incessantly. He'd put it on silent ignoring it.

Reed had taken the time to meet with me because I was Alisha's best friend, just as he had done for Lara when she needed him.

I wouldn't have understood why he couldn't just call her. But that wasn't Reed's style.

Do you need to get that? I had asked him for the fifteenth time. And he shook his head.

No, this is more important.

He was trying to do right by Alisha, I knew that in a heartbeat. Reed had always tried to do right by her.

His crush on Alisha wasn't a secret, but why he waited so long to act on it confused me.

As we sat in his quiet office, Reed's storm cloud eyes met mine.

"You had one of my guys work for you, Nathan Wyatt, about seven years ago. How'd that go for you? I trust he was professional?"

My heart raced at the mention of Nate's name, but I managed to keep my composure, nodding with a smile.

"Yes, he was very professional."

Reed's eyes narrowed slightly, studying my expression. He didn't believe me.

"Anything else you'd like to share about your experience with him?"

Hesitating, I struggled with how much to reveal. *"No, that's all. He did his job well."*

Leaning back in his chair, Reed kept his gaze fixed on me. *"And the tension between you two at Teasers? That's nothing as well?"*

Mon. Dieu.

My eyes widened, and one side of Reed's mouth tipped up.

"I pay attention. I've also worked with Nate for a few years."

Clearly.

Surprised that he had picked up on something I thought I had concealed so well, I tried to shrug it off.

"Oh, that? It's nothing, really. Just a silly crush from when I was younger." I forced a laugh. *"I was nineteen, and he was twenty-three."*

"Just a crush." Did he know I was lying?

I felt my palms grow clammy. Did he know more than he was letting on? Had Nate told him something? But why would Nate even bring it up?

Taking a deep breath, I met Reed's gaze head-on. *"The truth is, I had a crush on Nate when I was a teenager. But that's all in the past now. I've moved on, and I'm sure he has too."*

I didn't like the look in Reed's eyes as he looked down at his phone.

I needed to move on anyway.

Reed had several questions for me, and he asked to see my townhouse.

Having the imposing, intimidating man in the space was something else. He'd checked everywhere he could, suggested a few security improvements, and moved on. Bonnie and Nigel a little wide-eyed as they'd watched him.

And now? Three glasses of wine at ten in the morning had transformed Lara into a whirlwind of energy.

"Do you think Reed will come back for Lish soon?" Lara was prancing down the street, her five-foot-nothing frame belying her speed.

"I hope so, Lush seems worried more than usual." But it could also be because Avani had left for school and for once she had an empty nest.

I hurried after her, my heels clicking on the pavement, skirts swishing around my legs, while Lara ran off in her jean shorts and bedazzled bra on. Her dark hair behind her whipped in the wind.

"Oh Nigeeeeel!" Lara's shout echoed off the nearby buildings.

His eyebrows shot up at the sight of Lara, clearly not expecting her presence. I bit back a laugh, remembering the last time Lara had surprised him—she'd nearly given the poor man a lap dance.

As we approached Nigel, Lara's enthusiasm got the better of her. She launched herself at him and Nigel—being Nigel—didn't know what to do with himself but hug her back.

"Easy there, firecracker," I said, gently prying her off our stunned driver. "Let's not scare Nigel away, shall we?"

"But Gemma," she protested, her words slightly slurred. "Nigel needs some excitement in his life!"

"Trust me, darling, you've given him enough excitement to last a lifetime. Now, let's get you home before you decide to liven up the whole neighborhood."

Lara leaned in close, her breath warm against my ear.

"Why should I call you a filthy slut again?"

I blushed, remembering her previous antics.

"What's going on in that head of yours?" Lara's voice cut through my musings.

I glanced over to see her slouched in her seat, looking adorably cat-like as she fiddled with her seatbelt.

Trying to deflect, I said. "Just thinking about what you were saying—"

"Lies, Duchess!" Lara interrupted, a knowing smirk on her face. "I know when you're not being straight with me."

"Just worried about a few things..." I trailed off, then decided to shift the focus. "Lara, do you think you'll ever be comfortable letting a man into your life again?"

Earlier in Alisha's living room, Lara had admitted she was celibate, something that surprised me.

But now that I thought about it, it made sense.

At my question, Lara's eyes shifted, and I witnessed a rare moment where her showgirl persona faded away.

I caught a glimpse of someone else entirely—a woman beneath Lara Ford's carefully crafted exterior.

This version of her was someone I didn't quite know how to handle, as she reminded me vaguely of myself when I was younger.

Despite being only a year my junior at twenty-five, Lara seemed so much more vulnerable in these moments.

"I don't know," she said softly. "Never met a man like Reed who made me stop and think." A wry twist of her lips accompanied her words. After a brief pause, she turned the question back on me. "What about you?"

Lara knew about Nathan—not everything, but enough to understand why I avoided him and how I felt. She had kept my secrets, never breathing a word to anyone.

"No," I whispered back, matching her tone. "I can't say I've met anyone like Reed either."

Glancing in the rearview mirror, I caught Nigel watching me, his eyes holding a contemplative look.

Quickly averting my gaze, I focused instead on Lara, my eyes falling on the faint mark on her wrist—a four-leaf clover she'd had since the day I met her.

It looked like a burn mark. *Like a brand.*

"Where did you get that?" I looked down at her body. Usually, Lara was in sequins and feather boas or covered in glitter.

I rarely ever saw her actual body.

But now that I did, she paled.

"Just a scar from when I was a kid," she shook her head. "Nothing big."

But her cheeks turned a little pink which I was learning was a thing when she was lying and I heard a hint of an accent in her as she said it. Lara was Mexican, I knew that much.

But I didn't really know too much about her.

It struck me then how little we sometimes know about the people closest to us.

I had only recently learned that Lara had been celibate for years, a fact that surprised me given her flirtatious persona.

Over the years, Lara had been good to me, offering tips and advice, always encouraging me to be myself.

She was a huge reason why I'd developed more of a backbone.

Her latest piece of advice was to channel my inner Latina if my new guard from Reed acted out of line.

Breaking the momentary silence and changing the subject, I admitted.

"To be honest, I'm a little nervous about meeting my new guard."

Privately, I knew it couldn't be Nathan, but the thought of someone new still made me uneasy.

I just hoped it wasn't anyone like him.

Nigel pitched in from the front seat, reminding me that he was still listening. "Mr. Whittaker seems quite competent."

"If only Mr. Whittaker would be the guard," I quipped. "But I doubt Alisha would be happy and not worried all the time. Nigel, please stop by Butterscotch's bakery. They have the best cakes in the city."

"Yes, Miss Gemma."

"Nah, he'd *only* do that for Lish," Lara grinned. "I think Reed messed up the guy who tried to touch her the other night. Heard his friends gossiping about him when they got kicked out again last night."

And that was the other thing.

Reed and Nathan's world was different. Dangerous. I knew interacting with Reed meant exposing myself to another aspect I hadn't considered.

A world where, with a bodyguard, I was aware that

Nigel had met him and Reed had questions about the townhouse, where he'd met again, looking around for security issues, installing

270

cameras outside the doors, and he'd met Bonnie as well—sitting both of them down to ask questions.

Reed had been an intensity neither one of them had been prepared for.

Lara's eyes sparkled with mischief. "If he gets too crazy, throw a shoe at him, chica."

"A shoe?" I had gotten Lara's advice before and even though some of it made sense. Some of it still didn't to me.

She nodded, a hint of nostalgia crossing her face. "It fixes most things. Mi mamá, she would throw a shoe at my Papi all the time when she was angry."

Lara never talked about her family. And I took the opportunity to absorb the information.

Something had shifted in her eyes, and I realized this was one of those rare moments when I was seeing her not as a showgirl, but as a friend—a real person with a past.

"Your parents..." I hesitated, treading carefully. "Where are they?"

A haunted look crossed her eyes, dimming their usual sparkle. "I don't know. I haven't seen them in years. It's just me." She smiled at me with something unfamiliar in her usual bright eyes. "And you and Lish. You're my family now."

"I'm sorry," I said softly, swallowing hard. It hit me then how much Lara knew about me while I knew so little about her past.

The realization that Lara didn't have anyone left me with a mix of sadness and fierce protectiveness. I realized as girls, we'd all banded together in some ways to be close to one another.

And I'd found a family among these women. Lara, Alisha, Avani, they were my sisters.

"We're sisters to you."

She nodded. "I used to have sisters growing up. Not biological ones. But when I lived in Mexico, my parent's neighbors were family friends. They had two daughters. I was friends with both of them until they came to America. I don't know what happened to them. But sometimes when I'm with you and Lish and Avani, it reminds me of my life growing up. Simpler times. Easier times." She leaned back in her seat as Nigel drove. "I'm happy for Lish. It's been forever since he's wanted her."

271

I knew. Reed had been patient with Alisha. Waiting until she'd been ready. But it didn't erase the sadness in Lara's eyes.

And I remembered when we were with Alisha, Lara mentioned she'd been celibate for years now.

"Lara..." I didn't know how to ask this. "How come you haven't been with anyone for years?"

Her smile was sad. "Maybe I'm waiting for my Reed."

Maybe. But something in her eyes told me otherwise.

"I'm exhausted," she whispered, leaning into my arm. I wrapped it around her, pulling her close. "Let me know when we get back to my place."

"What about the cake?" I asked quietly. But Lara was already dozing.

I ended up picking it up myself before dropping her off.

FORTY-EIGHT
GEMMA

THE NEXT MORNING, I WAS JOLTED AWAKE BY A SOUND THAT DIDN'T belong in my quiet New York neighborhood.

It sounded like a loud dying dragon was outside my window. On a train. It was horrendous.

Mon Dieu! What on Earth!

The low rumble grew into a mechanical roar that vibrated through my bedroom walls. I stumbled out of bed, bleary eyed, my silk robe tangling around my legs as I rushed to the window.

There, in my driveway, a motorcycle pulled up. *What on…Earth?*

"This can't be happening," I whispered, my heart pounding in my chest as I threw open the window.

The cool air slapped me in the face, the acrid scent of exhaust burning my nostrils. And my head spun a little at having lurched up so fast.

"Hey!" I shouted at the leather-clad figure on the bike. *"What on Earth is happening?"*

He was almost on my marigolds.

The rider's tinted visor of their helmet fixed on my window, an unnerving and all-too-familiar presence.

My hand groped blindly for something, anything, to hurl at the intruder. My fingers closed around the heel of last night's shoe. Absolutely not. I would not have my morning ruined by the Sons of Anarchy.

273

The rider's shoulders tensed, the broad expanse of their back sending a jolt of recognition through my body. Who was that? Why did he look so familiar?

With agonizing slowness, gloved hands reached up to remove the helmet.

And just like that, my carefully constructed world shattered.

No. No, no, no.

The ground beneath me seemed to tilt, my vision blurring as I stared at the man I had once loved with every fiber of my being. My entire face fell. I felt my body go numb.

His dirty blonde hair, tousled by the wind, gleamed in the early light.

The strong jaw I had once traced with my fingers now sported a rakish stubble that made my heart ache. Why had life made him more handsome?

And those eyes—those deep navy pools that had once promised me forever—now glinted with a hardness that stole the breath from my lungs.

"*Nathan.*"

Impossible. Absurd. Utterly, maddeningly real. He was my body-guard? Courtesy of Reed?

Who does he think he is? Showing up looking so devastatingly handsome this early in the morning?

And Nate. He had grown up.

The young man who had caused women to break their necks to look at him had turned into a heartthrob.

The kind of man women fought over. All rugged charm and biker good looks, long dirty blonde hair, navy blue eyes that watched me from below. That expression in his eyes I recognized.

And in that moment of staring at him from my French windows, in nothing but my pajamas and ratty hair, I felt the seven years of emotions run through me. In one full sweep.

Devastation. Pain. Shock.

Rage.

All the rage of the universe.

I once read, hell hath no fury like a woman scorned and I forgot who had said it but whoever they were—they had no idea just how much fury I felt for Nathan Wyatt.

His eyes didn't look away and I felt the raw aching parts of my wounds from him ripping open. Seven. Years.

Of pent up anger and rage bubbled out of me like an overflowing geyser erupting. He had no right to look that handsome.

And that is when it clicked in my head why out of every single Titan that could've appeared in front of my house—*Nathan fucking Wyatt was here.*

Reed's cryptic text now made sense. My *new* guard.

The cosmic joke of the century.

Chica, if he tries anything, just throw your shoe at him.

Mi Mama did that all the time.

With a growl that would have made my etiquette teacher faint, I launched the stiletto.

"Get that stupid bike off my property!"

FORTY-NINE
NATE

GETTING HIT ON MY BIKE WITH A SHOE WASN'T THE WELCOME I'D envisioned.

But what the fuck did I expect?

A red carpet?

The second shoe came flying at me and I ducked, eyes wide. *Jesus.*

What the hell happened to Gemma?

This Gemma was all fire and fury, her eyes blazing with an intensity that knocked the breath from my lungs.

Seven years stretched between us like an open wound, raw and festering.

What the hell had I expected? A warm welcome?

After I'd walked away without a backwards glance.

But you did look back. Every single day. For seven years.

I did.

But I didn't recognize this Gemma. Not this version.

The girl I knew wouldn't have dreamed of chucking designer heels at anyone, let alone me.

But then again, the guy she knew wouldn't have abandoned her either. Fucking A—Reed couldn't have known *where* he was sending me.

Only that Gemma was Alisha's best friend. Therefore, a priority of Reed's.

The French windows slammed shut with a force that rattled the panes, leaving me standing in the street like some jilted Romeo.

Except in this story, I was the one who'd done the leaving.

Fuck my life.

Her discarded heel lay accusingly on the pavement, a crimson reminder of just how spectacularly I'd fucked up.

Emotions I thought I'd buried years ago bubbled up, threatening to choke me. Guilt, regret, a longing so intense it made my chest hurt. I swallowed hard, trying to keep my shit together.

Some nosy neighbor poked their head out, clearly pissed about the ruckus. I forced down the urge to tell them to mind their own fucking business. Instead, I took a deep breath, pasting on my best "nothing to see here" face.

"It's all good," I called out, smiling like I wasn't dying inside. Jesus fucking Christ. This was going about as well as a lead balloon at a birthday party.

I drove my bike into the side garage, my heart hammering so hard I thought it might burst. What the hell just happened? One thing was crystal clear—Gemma definitely knew I was here now.

No taking that back.

As the garage door groaned shut behind me, a familiar voice cut through my spiral of self-loathing.

"Good day, sir. Can I help you?" *Shitshitshit.*

Why did I forget Nigel was here?

After all these years? I had completely forgotten Gemma had her… family. Because once they'd felt like mine too.

Over the years I talked to my parents, but kept it brief. Didn't really tell them I killed people for a living.

They thought I was Reed's assistant or some shit.

Nigel's crisp accent hit me. Slammed into me. Because it had been years since I heard him asking me if I was okay.

Memories flooding back then. I turned, feeling a smile tug at my lips despite everything.

"Hey Nigel," I managed. Shit. "How's life?"

Was my voice that rough?

I didn't think I'd have to face him again and my stomach turned even as my heart was happy to see him.

For a second, I thought the old guy might have a heart attack. His blue eyes opened so wide as he took me in.

"Mr. Wyatt?" Before I knew it, he'd launched himself at me, wrapping me in a bear hug. *"I daresay! You've grown up!"*

"You don't look like you've aged a day, Nigel." I grinned at his sputtering. He was emotional for fucks sake. I was emotional.

"Dear Lord, Mr. Wyatt, you cut quite a rogue dashing figure in this bike..." As Nigel went on I caught the gasp from the doorway. Dark brown hair and wide eyes looked at me in shock. In delight.

"Mr. Wyatt?"

And cue the hugs.

"Miss Bonnie." And suddenly I had two of them in my arms all emotional and teary eyed. Shiiiitt. Now I was there too.

I thought they'd hate me for what I'd done to the lady of the house.

"We never thought we'd see you again!" They both sobbed.

"So good to see you, Mr. Wyatt," Nigel hugged me tighter.

"I didn't think I'd be back," I admitted, the words scraping my throat. "But I'm...I'm really glad to see you both."

More than they could ever know.

"I take it, Miss Marchand was not aware of Mr. Whittaker assigning you to her until this morning," Nigel's eyes were worried as he looked at me. "We heard the screaming."

"I didn't know until recently."

Another loaded glance passed between them. Nigel cleared his throat. "Miss Gemma is...aware of the reason of your presence?"

"I'm pretty sure she's figured it out."

She'd thrown a fucking shoe at me.

I think she knows.

Bonnie's expression softened as she patted my arm. "Well," she said. "I suppose she's in for quite a surprise."

They exchanged a look again which I took that they were nervous. I was walking into a minefield, and we all knew it.

Part of me wanted to bail, but I'd learned to face my problems head-on over the years.

Even if I didn't like it.

"I'll talk to her," I said, striding away.

I bit back a smile as I caught Nigel and Bonnie eyeing my bike with awe. I walked through Gemma's new place.

The townhouse was all European elegance—high ceilings, artwork worth more than I made in a year.

But Gemma was everywhere: royal purple violets in vases, books piled haphazardly, soft throws tossed over furniture. All her. And it smelled like grapefruit and lemons. Everywhere.

I inhaled it into my lungs willing myself to not break the fuck down.

I scanned the space, taking it in. Beautiful. Expensive. Elegant. Pure Gemma. Then I heard her footsteps on hardwood. I turned, and there she was.

Gemma, storming down the hall like a hurricane in human form.

After seven long years I was within a few feet of her.

And she hated me.

Gemma was *stunning*.

Her blonde hair fell in waves, those opal eyes blazing with intensity.

Twenty-six now, wearing shorts that left little to the imagination and a bra that was barely there. I could see her body had changed and she looked like she was ready to kill me.

Which was hot as fuck.

She had always been gorgeous when she was pissed off.

I knew because I'd pinned her down and fucked her until she cried in my arms and told me what was wrong.

And right now what was wrong—was me.

"You're the new guard?"

I fought a wince, meeting her gaze, forcing myself to stay professional despite wanting to drink in every detail.

"Seems like it, Duchess." The nickname slipped out before I could stop it. Her eyes flashed.

"And if I refuse?" Her eyes flared. "I didn't request you."

I suppressed a wince. Of course she hadn't. "Reed assigned me. If you have an issue, take it up with him. He's my boss."

She knew that. Her eyes narrowed dangerously. "Maybe I will."

On second thought…looking at her dressed in next to nothing?

The idea of someone else guarding her, seeing her daily, sparked an unwelcome surge of possessiveness. Something I should not have felt for Gemma Marchand.

I pushed it down, forcing a smirk.

"That's why you showed up like this?" I asked, my voice rougher than intended. "Is that your way of declining?"

The moment the words left my mouth, I knew I'd crossed a line.

Her cheeks flushed crimson.

She was riled up, and damn if she didn't look beautiful when she was angry.

"If I didn't know any better, Duchess, I'd say it was something else..." I winced internally but outwardly?

I didn't think Gemma understood in seven years I'd become a different man.

I'd changed into a man I didn't recognize and didn't really care to analyze.

"Showing up naked in front of me, to tell me you didn't wanna see me? You couldn't text?"

What the fuck was wrong with me?

I didn't know why I said it. To rile her up?

To get her real reaction? Or to show her she wasn't the only one who'd grown the fuck up.

I didn't know.

"I am not naked," she hissed spitting mad now, those eyes of hers flashing at me. My dick liked Gemma still. "You showed up on my property at an ungodly hour."

"Duchess, those shorts barely qualify as underwear, and that's not even a bra..." My gaze lingered on the curves hugged by thin fabric.

Her nipples are hard. And I knew how sensitive she was.

Keep digging that grave, Wyatt.

"You don't get to comment on how I dress in my own home," she said, her voice sharp as ice. "Or how I dress for *anyone.*"

"Anyone?" I latched onto that, something red hot flaring in me. *Andrei?* I'd been so fucking caught up in her I didn't even think to ask. "You got your man upstairs with you?"

Why did that bother me so much? It shouldn't.

"If I did, it would be none of your business—"

"Actually," I bit back a wild laugh that threatened to emerge. "I'm your new bodyguard, Duchess. Everything about you is my business now. So if you do got a man," I forced the words out. "I suggest you tell him to put his clothes on so I can meet him too."

She didn't like that.

Her eyes went wide. "This is *preposterous*."

Maybe. But if he was I'd fucking meet him now.

"Do you have a man upstairs?"

The idea of Gemma being with Andrei DuPont.

Someone who looked like her polar opposite.

I didn't know much about him and what little information I got was what was available for the public.

She bristled. I saw her. She didn't. *So then why—*

"I can't believe Reed assigned you." Her voice was a growl.

"I'll be down here when you're ready and you decide to put on—" I dropped my eyes to her chest shamelessly noting her nipples were hard. "Real clothes."

I let out a breath as she stormed off turning to find Nigel and Bonnie's wide eyes peering out the door.

Both of them scrambled backwards disappearing from sight.

Well, that had gone about as well as I'd expected.

Which is to say, not well at all.

FIFTY
GEMMA

I was fighting the urge to murder him and fuck him at the same time.

Mon Dieu, when did I become such a walking cliché?

Damn my traitorous body. Little hussy.

You'd think seven years would be enough to forget the feel of his calloused hands on my skin.

With trembling fingers, I meticulously applied my make-up. I couldn't go outside or anywhere without looking the part.

I was still Gemma.

I was still expecting to uphold my image in society. It had been my entire life. And I wasn't about to let Nathan disrupt that.

Did I do my highlight to make myself glow? Yes.

And then I added some SPF.

Anything to create an impenetrable glow that screamed—"I'm totally over you. I am. And I'm going to stand here and glow like a fucking donut while you look like a hot and sexy biker—"

No.

NO.

I would not be going there.

I refused to face Nathan Wyatt looking anything less than flawless. Even if he'd seen every inch of me, pebbled nipples and all.

Even if part of me ached to be that exposed to him again.

I shouldn't have let him impact me the way he did. But he *still* did. Maybe it was because I was exhausted.

Maybe because I hadn't been with a man in forever.

Or maybe...it was just Nathan Wyatt.

My imagination had already wanted him to take me on his bike.

On the balcony. In my bed. In that infernal motorcycle of his.

My thighs clenched together, a telltale sign of my arousal.

Merde.

I needed release before facing him again. Years of solitude had taught me to satisfy my own needs—no man required.

Locking myself in the closet, I reached for my vibrator.

Nate's calloused hands filled my imagination as I worked myself to a shamefully quick orgasm.

He was wrong about me having a man upstairs.

The only man occupying this space was the one in my head, bringing me to climax with the thrill of potentially getting caught.

But even as the waves of pleasure subsided, I felt no relief.

How could I, with the source of my frustration just downstairs?

I styled my hair into an elegant twist, donned my most sophisticated dress, and slipped on my battle heels. Armor, all of it.

The sharp click of my heels announced my arrival in the kitchen. Nigel and Bonnie's eyes widened before they hastily excused themselves. Smart.

They recognized the storm brewing between Nate and me—seven years in the making.

Why is he even more attractive now? The traitorous thought slipped through my defenses.

"Mr. *Wyatt.* A moment of your time." I injected as much ice into my tone as possible.

He followed me into the library, that infuriating smirk on his face. I shut the door, trapping us in this charged space.

My body instantly betrayed me, yearning to erase that smug look with my lips.

His presence was overwhelming—six feet two inches of pure masculinity stealing the very air from the room. Dark. Seductive.

All biker glory in that ridiculous leather jacket, his stupidly perfect dirty blonde hair, and that beard that I knew would feel deliciously rough against my skin when he—*Mon Dieu, Gemma. Get a grip.*

"Do not bring your blasted bike around," I snapped. Nate's eyes raked over me, a flicker of appreciation quickly masked by cool professionalism.

It shouldn't have thrilled me. It did.

"And you need to wear a suit. Something presentable. I can't have you looking like *that* around me."

His smirk never dropped. "Afraid you can't resist me in leather, Duchess?"

"Don't get your hopes up."

His eyes glinted dangerously.

Why did he look so smug? He had changed since I saw him. He'd grown into his looks, his body, and that smirk. Ten-fold. I had grown but Nathan had returned with a vengeance.

I wanted to wipe that look off his face. Preferably with my lips—*Mon Dieu, Gemma, stop it!*

What was wrong with me?

Maybe I was furious at him for shattering my peace after another anxiety-ridden night.

Maybe seeing him again reopened old wounds.

Maybe seven years of bottled anger were finally boiling over.

It didn't matter.

All I knew was that Nate's mere presence ignited a cocktail of fire in my veins, and I was letting him burn.

"Anything else, Miss Marchand?" His tone, once warm honey, now cut like ice. The formal address stung more than I'd ever admit.

I used to be his baby.

And I don't know why that hurt.

"Yes." I laid out his role, each word a deliberate jab. "There will be nothing else I require from you other than accompanying me to work and back. Is that clear?"

"Crystal." His composure never wavered, but a muscle ticked in his jaw. "Now that we have your ground rules, I have a few of my own."

His gaze locked onto mine, dark with unspoken history.

"Someone's trying to kill you. I'd say that warrants a bit more than just work escort. Unless your assassins keep banker's hours." His eyes narrowed. "Is it Camilla?"

"No," I blurted, too quickly to be convincing. "I don't know. I just keep getting threats—"

"In your home." It wasn't a question. He stepped closer, his scent overwhelming my senses. "You're lying to me, Duchess."

"I am not—"

"Someone's trying to hurt you." Nate's voice dropped, laced with a concern that made my traitorous heart skip. "And you're playing with fire by keeping me in the dark."

I inhaled deeply, cursing my decision to hire Reed for external security only.

A live-in bodyguard was the last thing I wanted.

Especially not him.

"I don't know for certain. I asked Reed for help so my *freaking* bodyguard might figure it out for me." The lie rolled off my tongue, well-practiced.

Nate's eyes narrowed, piercing right through my facade.

"Bullshit. You've always been a terrible liar, Gemma."

I stiffened, hating how easily he could still read me. "You don't know me."

"Don't I?"

Mon. Dieu. How did we end up here?

I turned away, desperate for distance. "It doesn't matter what you think. You're here for external security. Nothing more."

"Is that so?" His voice was dangerously soft. "Then why did Reed tell me about the break-in attempts? The threatening notes?"

"That is the only thing you are here for. And it isn't a big deal." I tried to keep my tone businesslike, detached.

"It's a big fucking deal when it's my job to keep you breathing, Duchess."

"Then do your job outside of my house. You didn't have to show up —" And then it hit me. He could've called. He could've texted. *No.*

He had shown up to my home. Leather jacket and motorcycle in tow.

Why?

I took a step forward. And made the mistake of meeting those true blue eyes—the same ones I'd fallen in love with before he shattered my heart.

"Why did you come all the way here?" I held my head up high. "This could've been a simple meeting. You didn't have to do any of this."

Privately, I wondered—dared to wonder—if he wanted to see me. If he missed me. If he cared...

And for a moment Nate's eyes watched me. Soft. I could've sworn he was going to say something soft. He didn't say a word.

"Just doing my job." But his throat worked as he said it. His eyes moved over me again. "You know Duchess, for someone who doesn't care about me, you sure seem pretty angry—"

"Don't get ahead of yourself, you're disrupting my peace—"

"Is that what it's called?"

"Yes. And stop calling me that."

"What?"

"You know what."

"I'm afraid I don't."

I was *seething*. "Don't start with me."

"Don't tempt me."

"I'm not tempting you at all. I'm letting you know what I will and won't tolerate."

"And what's that?" Nate lazily cocked his head looking sexier than a man should. And I swore, for a moment, for a heartbeat, I was back in Capri—lost in lazy mornings and whispered promises.

If he had asked then, I would've run away with him. Been his wife, carried his child...

And just like ice washed through my veins.

My baby...

Gone.

And so was Nate.

This Nathan wasn't real.

Take back control.

"You need to change," I said, giving him a deliberate once-over. "Then we'll discuss your employment terms."

FIFTY-ONE
NATE

I TUGGED AT MY COLLAR, FEELING LIKE A FUCKING CLOWN IN THIS SUIT Gemma wanted me in.

Part of me wondered if it was because she knew how much I fucking hated these things.

How Gabriel wore these things was beyond me.

Reed and I couldn't fucking stand it.

Poppy's conference room buzzed with energy as Gemma stood up front speaking.

Her light accent evident even after years of schooling in the States. Gemma had always been beautiful, but right about now? The way she commanded attention—she'd lived up to all her dreams.

"...I think it would be best to consider what they need in different age groups," Gemma continued, her voice clear and confident. "For our younger teens, we're looking at after-school programs…Keeps them off the streets and gives them a chance to discover their talents. We might want to find a few music instructors…"

My eyes drifted to Alisha, Reed's girl, with Kellan Watts hovering next to her like he belonged there. Watts was Lena's new partner—a golden boy college quarterback looking kid had won the lottery, guarding a civilian who actually cooperated.

I got that if he was her with Alisha? Reed might've taken him under

287

his wing to keep Gabriel from scaring him out. Reed knew we needed the help.

Did Alisha know she and Gemma were in the same boat, threat-wise? I doubted it.

Gemma kept her cards close to her chest, even with her friends. Hell, Reed hadn't known how bad things were until I filled him in.

At least Alisha was honest with Reed. Unlike Gemma.

My jaw clenched as I caught her classic tell—that little shoulder shrug, eyes darting right.

She was lying about something, probably downplaying the danger she was in.

Gemma's gaze skimmed over me, pretending I was invisible.

But I caught every glance, felt the weight of her attention even when she tried to hide it.

I kept my distance, unlike Watts who was practically glued to Alisha's hip. I didn't bother talking to the kid.

Once Gabriel sank his claws in, Watts' days at Titan were numbered. Not my problem. My job was Gemma, end of story. I had Lena waiting for me. That was enough.

Wasn't it?

Watching Gemma work the room, all easy smiles and genuine warmth, something twisted in my gut. She'd done it.

Everything she'd dreamed of on that beach in Capri, she'd achieved. And me?

What the fuck had I accomplished?

Sure, I'd made money, done some high-profile jobs. But had I become the man I wanted to be?

The man who could stand beside her as an equal?

Gemma was in her element, and I was just the hired muscle lurking in the shadows. From where I stood, I was still on the outside looking in. And why was I even thinking about it? She belonged to Andrei DuPont. Not to me. Never to me.

The applause jolted me back to reality.

As Gemma wrapped up, I noticed Alisha slip out, Watts in tow. She looked pale, unsteady.

Gemma's frown told me she'd noticed too.

For a split second, I saw something in Gemma's eyes. But it was gone before I could be sure.

After the meeting, we hit up one of the schools benefiting from the Poppy Project.

Watching Gemma work her magic was…something else.

All smiles and warmth, posing for pictures, greeting everyone like they mattered. This was Gemma 2.0—living her dream.

But something was off.

Her million-dollar smile didn't quite reach her eyes when she thought no one was looking. There was a split-second hesitation before she joined each new group.

It hit me then—Gemma might look like she belonged, but part of her still felt like an outsider. Just like me.

I caught her eye across the room, and for a moment, we were back on that beach in Capri.

Then she looked away, mask firmly back in place, and the moment was gone.

Her, playing the polished philanthropist.

Me, playing the tough guy who didn't give a shit.

Both of us pretending we belonged in worlds that would never truly accept us.

Gemma and I clicked because we were outsiders in the past in our own lives.

But right now? I felt like I was on another planet, watching her from afar. Gemma in her world, me in mine. Even Watts got to sit next to Alisha, part of her inner circle.

I tried to ignore the ache.

Shaking off the thoughts, I refocused. My feelings didn't matter. I had a job to do, and getting lost in what-ifs wouldn't keep Gemma safe. That was my role now—not friend, not equal, just a shadow making sure she could keep living this life she'd built.

We had a packed schedule. Gemma handled it all like a pro, even when Alisha had her moment of panic. Those two were tight, no question.

In recent years, the Marchands had cut Gemma off, treating her like she was Jacqueline.

She'd left, and they'd washed their hands of her.

All except one. I knew in my gut it was Camilla. No doubt about it.

Gemma, though? She was in her element. Handled everything like a pro. I couldn't help but be impressed. People looked to her for answers. Teenagers flocked to her, one even crowning her with some paper thing. She wore it, laughing.

"Miss Gemma, check out my drawing!" "Miss G, see my new bag?" "Hey Miss Gemma, someone left presents for Miss Malhotra—"

She juggled it all with ease, sampling snacks, chatting with everyone.

Someone brought in lunch, thank God, or she might've forgotten to eat. She just kept going, sandwich in hand, never missing a beat. Even passing me food along the way with me trailing next to her as her shadow. I didn't think the kids would hurt her, but I was with her everywhere she went. That honey blonde hair, the scent of grapefruit and lemons.

We finally left as evening set in.

That's when all hell broke loose. Paparazzi swarmed us, vultures looking for their next meal.

"Miss Marchand! Over here!"

"Gemma, is it true that—"

"Who's the new man, Gemma?"

I moved on instinct, shielding her with my body.

My arm went around her shoulders, pulling her close.

Gemma's face was a perfect mask, but I felt her trembling against me. Nigel already waiting behind the wheel of the car and I quickly ushered her in. I was in there next to her shutting the door cursing as Nigel took off.

I turned to ask her if she was all right when I saw her adjusting her clothing. The scuffle had left Gemma's dress askew, revealing a teasing glimpse of blue lace underneath. The slit riding up to give me a glimpse of the edges of her garters. Gemma liked lingerie.

That fucking tattoo.

That night in Capri flashed through my mind...when she'd screamed my name so loud into the carpet.

With her family below.

Maybe it was the tension of being around her all day, her purposefully ignoring me. Maybe I just wanted to get under her skin.

I reached forward and hit the button to raise the privacy divider between us and Nigel. I caught his flicker of interest as I did.

Gemma's eyes flashed. "See something you like, Mr. Wyatt? Or is imagining your clients naked when their most vulnerable part of your job description?"

I couldn't stop the wolfish grin that spread across my face and I saw her eyes widen at it. *Good. Still got it.*

"Trust me, Duchess, I don't need to imagine you naked. I still remember every single inch of you."

Her eyes narrowed, but her cheeks flushed pink. "Really? Must not have been that memorable for me. I don't recall a thing."

Little liar. I caught the way her nipples pebbled through the thin fabric, her breathing quickened. The way she clenched her thighs together.

I saw *everything*.

And fuck me if I didn't want to remind her exactly how memorable I could be.

Leaning in close, my lips barely grazed her ear, but I felt the shiver from her. "Not memorable, huh? Funny, 'cause I remember making you come so hard you nearly passed out."

I pressed closer, my breath hot on her skin. "Sliding my fingers deep inside you," I rasped, my dick straining painfully against my pants. "Bet if I touched you now, you'd be dripping for me."

Gemma's breath hitched, her cheeks flushing crimson. For a second, I thought she might slap me.

Instead, she turned, her lips a whisper from mine. "You're delusional—"

"Am I?" I was right there. I could kiss her. Right over her lips.

"Keep lying to yourself, sweetheart," I murmured over them, lush and pink, my hand sliding up her thigh. "But we both know the truth. You're soaked right now. Imagining my tongue inside you, my fingers, my cock stretching you open wide—"

"You're a bastard—"

"Maybe," I conceded, voice rough as my tongue darted out tasting her skin, and she closed her eyes.

Both of us were breathing heavier now. Both of us turned on. I fucking knew she'd be soaking wet if I slid into her.

But I'm the bastard you're aching for.

"When did you get such a filthy mouth, Duchess? Maybe I should remind you what it's good for. Put that mouth to work the rest of the way back."

What the fuck is wrong with you?

One fucking week with her and you're already an animal?

She scoffed trying to look away but I held her jaw. "I hardly remember our time together."

I caught the way she looked at my dick though.

"Bullshit," I breathed, fingers inching higher.

Her legs parted slightly. *There you fucking go.*

"I bet you think about it every fucking night. About me. Alone in that big, empty bed of yours." I leaned in further, my hand hitching higher. "I bet your man doesn't make you come like me—" I was tugging at her garter.

She gasped and then her eyes turned on me seething mad. Those opal eyes of hers flashing. *"It's none of your business who I take to bed—"*

And yet she's not moving away.

And my restrained snapped when I imagined Gemma. Taking that pompous self-righteous dick Andrei fucking DuPont some trust-fund kid to bed.

I was on her then my lips moving over hers. "Keep lying to yourself, baby. Tell yourself you don't think about me, bending you over this fucking seat right now, driving my dick into that tight little pussy, into that spot that makes you scream my name—"

She was panting as I said it. "You think you're hot—"

"I know I am." I grazed my lips over her ear. "And I know you're hot for me."

Andrei DuPont fucking *who*?

"I know your man doesn't make you scream. Because if he did, you wouldn't be panting on my fucking dick right now—"

Gemma growled a little squirming back. *"Like you aren't obsessed with me?"*

"I am obsessed with you." It was a wild growl leaving me. *"I am so fucking obsessed with you I live and breathe you."* I had been for years. "I know exactly what you need—"

"And what's that—"

"Me." I said it. "You need me."

I had her in a heartbeat close to me nipping her lip until she whimpered.

We were fucking *awful.*

Shiiit. Who was getting turned on now? My dick was so hard it could cut through anything. Into her.

"Did you miss me inside of that little pussy? You could always hop on my lap right now and ride it until we get back to your place? Is that what you needed?" *Shit.* "Need my cock after a long day—"

"You talk to all your clients like this?" She huffed sounding breathless.

Nah. Not all of them.

"Some of them." Her eyes flashed fire at me. "You're not the only one with a life, baby." I lived too.

Still had it though.

I watched her throat work.

She was fighting me verbally, but her body couldn't lie to me. I hitched my fingers so high I could brush her clit. Her chin rose in defiance.

"You know what, Nathan? I did live my life." A haughty look came over her features. "And you know what I know?" Her hands dropped to my pants and I bit back a groan as her slender fingers rubbed over my cock. "I know if I played with you long enough you'd lose your mind."

"Baby, I'm already losing it."

My middle finger dipped into her panties. Might as well stay busy.

"You're not wearing panties." Holy fucking shit. "*Just* the garters?"

Oh. Mother. *Fucker.*

How the fuck was I supposed to stop?

"Spread your legs for me, baby." I had my fingers on her groaning at how wet she was. "You're fucking drenched. Bet you'd come for me, wouldn't you, Duchess? I wouldn't even have to try."

"Just like you," she whispered fiercely, but I saw the effect I had on her. "Did you miss the way I tasted, Nate?"

FUCK. *YES.*

I felt her gripping my thigh. *Tight.* As I dipped lower. My head dipped to her exposed bra.

"Pull that shit down."

She didn't even bat at eyelash yanking at her dress until her pretty little nipples bounced out. I was on them like an animal. My fingers slid lower.

"Tell me you're not with anyone. Tell me you're single. Tell me—"

The car jerked to a stop.

"*Motherfucker*—" I licked the top swell of her breast before pulling back. *"Fucking, Nigel."*

But then my instincts screamed. *Something* was off. Something was —I turned my head behind us.

"*Wait.*" My body coiled, ready to spring.

"I'm not sleeping with you, Nate." She was breathless and unconvincing and I tucked that bit away for later.

"That's not why I stopped, Duchess. Stay here."

A shadow where there shouldn't be one.

In the blink of an eye, the heated tension between Gemma and me evaporated, replaced by a different kind of intensity. The kind that usually ended with blood spilled and bodies on the ground. I reached for my gun, all thoughts of seduction forgotten.

"Shit," I hissed. *"Nigel, stay put. Lock the doors."*

I drew my gun, ignoring Gemma's sharp intake of breath.

Years of training took over as I moved. And I saw the shadow in the moonlight.

The dumbass trying to break in never stood a chance.

"Drop it, motherfucker," I snarled, gun trained on his chest.

The idiot lunged. Two shots cracked through the night. He hit the ground, knife clattering away. He swore and groaned and I had him on his stomach in another stomach.

I called Reed, keeping my voice low and deadly. "Gemma's been holding out on us," I growled, laying out the shitstorm we'd stumbled into.

Next, Killian. His guys, Derek and Sean knew their shit, they would handle cleanup.

Sirens wailed as I sprinted back to the car. Gemma was still inside, thank fuck. She was white as a sheet, trembling.

Fear barely hidden behind that stubborn set of her jaw.

But there was something else in her eyes. Something that said this wasn't new, and she knew it was far from over.

This wasn't some paparazzi bullshit or empty threats.

Someone wanted Gemma, and they were getting bolder. Only guarding her to and from work? Like hell.

I made my decision then and there. She'd hate it, but tough shit.

"I know Camilla's coming for you." And then. "I'm moving in."

FIFTY-TWO
GEMMA

I WAS GOING TO MURDER HIM.

In cold blood.

It had been *weeks* since Nathan Wyatt moved into my townhouse.

And little by little—he was driving me over the wall. Over a cliff. An edge I couldn't return from.

The man who had shattered my heart seven years ago was now a constant presence in my space, stirring up emotions I'd thought long buried.

Nigel and Bonnie tried their best to mediate, but their efforts only highlighted how foreign yet achingly familiar this arrangement was.

It was like muscle memory, having Nate around. And that terrified me.

Especially when he was in the kitchen first thing in the morning, shirtless and sweating after his workout, his abs on display.

> I'm pretending I'm in a relationship with Andrei so my bodyguard is jealous

Your current hot bodyguard?

With the abs?

> Don't remind me.

Want photos?

No. Andrei will lose it.

Don't even get me started on this one's jealousy.

I'll tell him he should be improvising his lines when your guard comes to question him.

Titan you say?

Indeed.

I did send Talia a discreet photo of Nate I had.

Good

Lord.

That's your guard?

Do him. Immediately Gemma.

For the female population do us a favor and fuck him.

Why are you like this?

Brb I am crying.

I might cry.

I just showed his photo to Andrei—I was right.

Jealous.

I didn't even know he would be jealous.

How is Drew?

Talia and I spent the morning texting while I made mental notes to check in on the plans for Haven.

Sonya was indisposed with some family matter and she'd asked me for help with Haven.

Considering I had a brooding biker with his motorcycle parked in my garage distracting me? I took it.

His shirt draped over my couch let me know he was in fact half-naked walking around my house like he owned it—I just stayed busy.

> For the love of God, Gemma.

> Just tell me when you've fucked him.

> Andrei is invested since he's a part of this love triangle too.

> I'm glad Andrei is getting amusement out of my misery

> He's betting you do him in a few weeks.

> He's betting wrong.

> He says. "we shall see."

Little pieces of Nate invaded my carefully constructed life after that.

"Why are you always shirtless?" I hissed one morning, watching a bead of sweat trail down those damn abs.

He smirked, the bastard. "Distracting you, Duchess?"

"In your dreams," I shot back, ignoring the heat pooling in my belly.

I didn't know when Nate had become my enemy, but it was easier to treat him like this than to admit how much it ached to have him so close yet so far.

The distance between us, once measured in miles, now came down to mere feet—and it was unbearable.

My vibrator was getting a workout, the battery drained every night since he'd moved onto my floor.

I could die from the intensity of the orgasms I'd given myself, muffling my screams into my pillow as images of Nate flooded my mind.

His hands, rough and demanding, exploring every inch of my skin. His lips, hot and insistent, trailing fire down my neck.

His body, hard and unyielding, pressing me into the mattress as if he tried hard enough we would become one person.

Shameless. I did think about that limo ride. When neither one of us cared about anything but being on top of each other.

And part of me wished I had just told him I wasn't with anybody. I was single.

I had been for some time.

I imagined Nate moving over me, his muscles flexing under my fingertips, under me, his hands gripping my hips as I rode him to oblivion.

Nate inside me, filling me so completely I could barely breathe.

Each morning, I'd wake up tangled in sweat-soaked sheets, my body humming with unfulfilled desire.

And then I'd see him, casually sipping coffee in my kitchen, shirtless with his stupid abs, and the cycle would begin anew.

I wanted to murder him every single time I saw him.

Or kiss him senseless. Often both at the same time.

The urge to slap that infuriating smirk off his face warred with the desire to trace it with my tongue.

This push and pull, this constant state of wanting and hating, was slowly driving me insane.

And the worst part?

I had a feeling Nate knew *exactly* what he was doing to me.

When he brushed by me on accident.

When he walked around with his abs on display. Bonnie shamelessly admiring him with Nigel in tow blinking.

The constant state of wanting and hating him was dizzying, and slowly it was eating away at my brain cells. I felt like a strange of pearls pulled tight and ready to snap at any moment.

At one frustrating sexy biker in my house.

He grinned at both of them tossing a towel over his shoulder. He did pull ups in the garage for fun.

Not that I *watched*.

Or when he did sometimes ride his bike for fun.

Not that I *knew*.

But my breaking point came when he sat me down, pushing a keychain across the table. With his abs.

"No," I hissed, my voice laced with venom. "I will not be wearing a tracking device. I'm not your prisoner, Nate."

"You either wear this—"

"Or what? You'll manhandle me into submission? I'd love to see you try."

"I bet you fucking would." Nate's eyes darkened dangerously, his gaze dropping to my lips for a fraction of a second. "Don't push me, Duchess. Not when it comes to your safety."

"The only one pushing anything is you."

"Duchess, I'm trying to do my job—"

"And your job is to accompany me to and from where I need—"

"Stop fighting me—"

"Stop tempting me—"

The words slipped out before I could stop them. We both froze, the air between us electric. For a moment, I thought he might kiss me.

Part of me hoped he would, just so I could slap him. Or kiss him back. I wasn't sure which.

Instead, Nate took a step back, his expression unreadable, masking over with something else. Something darker.

"Wear the tracker." He shook his head. "Not here to fight you."

There was something in his eyes. Something dark. He looked exhausted. And some traitorous part of me ached for him.

I snatched the keychain from his hand, our fingers brushing.

Him and his large hands. I wanted to growl.

"But I'm not wearing anything else."

My heels clicked against the hardwood, Nate's heavy footsteps following close behind.

"I already agreed to your stupid tracker—"

"Stop running from me—"

"Aren't you supposed to be training Alisha's guard?" At the mention of Kellan Watts, something came over his eyes. Something else.

"Change of plans. You're my sole focus now." His clenched. Did he not like Kellan? I didn't understand why. Everyone loved Kellan.

"Oh joy," I muttered sarcastically.

"You know, for someone who claims to loathe my presence, you seem awfully...affected, Duchess. If I didn't know any better I'd say you wanted me around more."

"Don't flatter yourself. I'm just overheated from arguing with your big head—"

"You loved my big head—"

"Oh shut up—"

"I'm trying—"

"Go to hell!"

"I'm already there!"

Ahhhhh.

"Stop! I don't want this."

Mon. Dieu, I cannot think with this man.

His eyes raked over me, lingering on the rapid rise and fall of my chest. "Is that so?"

"Yes, that's so. Now if you don't mind, I'd like to change."

He motioned for me to continue. Was he serious?

"You're planning on watching?"

"Wouldn't be the first time, would it?" He moved from his position closer.

"Get out," I whispered, my voice lacking any real conviction.

"Make me," his voice was gravel. "Bet you'd try real hard."

Closer.

Closer.

Nate's thumb brushed my lower lip, his touch electric.

My nipples should not have responded to him. My body should've hated him but here we were, less than a centimeter away from each other. Yet again.

"Is that your grand plan? Keep me locked up in this house until you find who's behind all this?"

His eyes narrowed, something dark flashing in their depths as he got closer.

"You would fucking *love* if I kept you locked up in this house."

And I saw it in his eyes. The desire.

How he planned on keeping me in the house. In the bed. My throat worked and I felt my thighs clench. My panties were done for.

His eyes were pitch black now. And my lips parted. He was so close. So close.

Nothing mattered anymore.

I didn't know who moved first.

His lips crashed onto mine, hard and demanding.

I gasped, and he took advantage, his tongue sweeping into my mouth. My hands fisted in his shirt, torn between pushing him away and pulling him closer.

Nate growled low in his throat, one hand tangling in my hair while the other gripped my hip, fingers digging in. It was explosive. And I loved every second of it.

"Dammit, baby," Nate raked a hand through his hair, frustration radiating off him. "You keep fighting me and—"

"And what?" I kissed him back harder. "You'll leave without another word?"

As soon as it left my lips, I knew I messed up.

Because that was the equivalent of me handing Nate a grenade for him to use against me. *That is what it was always about.*

Me.

Nate.

The baby I lost.

Our life.

His eyes went wide as he looked at me stunned. His hand gripped my chin as he pinned me to the wall.

"Is that what this is about?" he growled, his breath hot on my face. His navy eyes in mine. *"That's* why you've been spitting mad at me? I should've fucking known—"

"Get off me—"

"You're pissed because of your fucked-up family—"

"Don't you dare!" I shoved at his chest, but he was immovable. *"They are not my family—"*

"Then why cling to their name?" Nate's voice was a growl. Our faces were inches apart, both of us panting. His gaze dropped to my lips, lingering. Like he wanted to kiss me again. Like I wanted him too.

"I left my family—"

"You love putting me in my place, don't you, Duchess?"

"How dare you—"

"Just like Camilla did."

I froze, his words a dagger to my heart.

All the pent-up hurt and frustration of years crashed over me at once.

"Just like she did to me."

He was shaking. I saw the fury in Nate's eyes. The aftermath of her rage inside of him. His throat muscles bunched as he looked at me with everything. I saw it in his eyes. The horror. The embarrassment. The words that kept us tied together even now.

He was my guard.

I was his charge.

Like actors forced to play a role in a play we didn't want to be a part of—except I wasn't playing. I knew I would always have feelings for Nate. Years and years of longing drowned me in waves.

My lip trembled traitorously, and I saw the moment Nate realized he'd gone too far. His eyes were molten and raw.

The horror of what he'd said seeped into my skin.

Mon. Dieu. Was I just Camilla now? In my hatred?

That was how she was molded. And I was left horrified the poison of his words spreading through my skin until it sank into my veins.

I couldn't stop from feeling the ice forming underneath the layers of what I knew was my identity.

That hurt more than words could form.

Did I put that look in his eyes? Had I been the one to hurt Nate?

"Gemma—"

"Get out. Now."

Nate stepped back, conflict warring in his eyes.

For a moment, he looked like he might say more, might try to take back the words that hung between us like shards of glass.

Instead, he turned and left taking every inch of the warmth in the room with him.

FIFTY-THREE
NATE

Being full-time for Gemma meant sacrificing everything else.

Garrett Fuller, now under Gabriel's watchful eye, stepped into my shoes. He was thirty—*maybe*—six-six and he kept up with Gabriel from what I knew from Reed.

Gabriel liked the fucker. For once. Which surprised me.

I should've felt relieved. Instead, I felt like I was losing a part of myself. Losing my grip on reality.

Being around Gemma was a special kind of torture.

Gemma in her workout gear, all curves and sweat, making my mouth go dry. Gemma in her kitchen, domestic and alluring, stirring up fantasies of a life I had no right to want.

Gemma in those dresses that clung to her like a second skin, testing every ounce of my self-control.

Alisha's "little stalker" problem had escalated into something far more sinister, and Gemma's safety concerns weren't far behind.

The only silver lining was that the attempts on Gemma seemed to have abated somewhat with me in the picture. Small fucking mercies.

The break-in attempt had given us a lead, but it was a dead end—literally.

The guy I'd caught spilled that someone had paid him to scare Gemma, but before we could dig deeper, the trail went cold.

Reed had Liam, the new guy, trace it back to the source, only to find our lead with a bullet in his head.

And Liam would be working with me in tandem with whatever I needed. Reed had his hands fucking full.

He gave me a quick call to fill me in. "Miss Marchand's got a mean stepmother."

"Tell me about it," I didn't mind. He cut to the chase. I could hear his fingers clicking away and I figured he was the new IT guy since he worked out of Midtown. "What did you get?"

"Small sums of money deposited into both of their accounts from an offshore account. No traces back to Camilla Marchand." Liam paused, sounding a little uneasy and my stomach flipped a little at what he was about to say. "The money came from an associate of Gemma's father."

"What?" My heart would've bottomed out had Liam not continued.

"Yeah, a distant associate of Gemma's father apparently dropped the money into their accounts. Your friend Killian and his guys were on him. They said that he was supposed to scare her. That's it."

"Into what? Why? He had a knife on him."

"My thoughts exactly," Liam said calmly. "I'll look into why this particular person sent the money but it doesn't add up. Especially with what I know about her stepmother."

Because like it or not Gerard was bleeding money.

The last seven years he'd been giving Gemma the silent treatment.

And he didn't sound like the man I remembered. But I hadn't gotten a chance to speak to him.

He was always out. Always busy.

Part of me wondered why a man like that was so beholden to his wife. Reed said it was because he was convinced at his age he needed to turn to something stable. Solid. A woman.

I thanked Liam who was going to dig into the technical side of the house while I handled physical security.

This was calculated. Dangerous.

And I'd bet my last dollar it had Camilla's fingerprints all over it.

I had to tell Gemma.

Fuck, I didn't want to, but she needed to know. I cornered her in the kitchen, laying out the facts as gently as I could.

Her hands wrung together, knuckles white, as she listened.

"What?" Her face fell. I saw the way her eyes watered. I fucking knew.

"*Baby*—"

"My father—" she broke off searching her down to Earth kitchen for answers I knew it didn't have.

"It isn't something Liam's sure of—" I broke off. "He suspects it's all a ruse. He's going to work with me." In the meantime Liam was going to work out a few options for us to potentially test out his theories as to who was trying to come after Gemma.

My money was always on Camilla. Always. But the point was to prove it was her. We couldn't just accuse her.

I explained it all to Gemma.

"I believe you, Duchess. I know it's Camilla. The question, why? And why now? Just trust me to fix this with you." Not to mention I clocked the gossip rags, the photos of Gemma, the way paprarazi hounded her or camped outside her town house.

It was a recipe for something brewing.

When Gemma left, Bonnie stepped in. Her eyes, full of concern, met mine with a depth of understanding that caught me off guard.

We both knew this was far from over, but Bonnie's gaze held something more—a knowledge of Gemma's pain that went beyond the current situation.

"Mr. Wyatt," she said softly, her voice tinged with a maternal warmth. "It's not my place, but…I hope this time you don't break her heart."

I blinked up at Bonnie, a swirl of emotions churning in my gut. "I didn't want to break her heart, Bon. Not then, not now."

She nodded, her eyes soft but knowing. "I think instead of you two being at each other's throats, you need to sit with her and speak to her properly. There's…more to her pain than you know."

"I'm trying—"

"Try harder." Her voice changed, a hint of steel beneath the gentleness. At my widened eyes, she paused. "Sorry. It's just…Gemma's been through more than you realize."

Like what? I felt like since I stepped into this house, nobody was telling me things I needed to know. Fucking Gemma had secrets.

Bonnie and Nigel barely interacted with me. What the fuck was happening?

"I'm doing the best I can, Bon."

A moment of understanding passed between us.

Bonnie's eyes softened again, and I sensed she was carrying a weight—Gemma's secret—that she couldn't share. Which rankled me. Since I was supposed to know but what right did I have anymore.

Eager to lighten the mood, I changed the subject. "How's you and Nigel?"

Her smile turned shy, a blush creeping up her cheeks. "We have lunch more often. It's a bit slow for us."

"Try harder," I echoed, a smirk tugging at my lips.

THAT NIGHT, WE HAD AN EVENT TO ATTEND. GEMMA HAD SOME BEAUTY thing she went to for Alisha's sake.

I cleaned myself up, trading up my suits to borrow something from Reed's closet.

He had a line up of clothes and hadn't given a shit to send me something I could wear, despite having two inches on me, we were both broad and it fit.

It looked better than my usual suits but it also cost as much as a house.

I looked decent enough. Cleaned up nice.

Standing outside her bedroom door, I hesitated before knocking.

"Duchess, you good?" I called out, realizing I hadn't heard from her in a while. The silence that greeted me was unsettling. My hand tightened on the doorknob, every instinct on high alert. "Gemma?"

I pushed the door open and froze.

Gemma stood by her vanity, dress hiked up to her thighs, fumbling with her stockings. Those…bits of nothing. The scent of alcohol hung in the air, explaining her unsteady movements. *She's tipsy.*

The news of Gemma's father potentially being involved in scaring her, I knew, hit her hard.

Gemma had been decent with her father, despite her mother abandoning her at such a young age.

307

But now? All semblance of niceties were out the window. And Gemma was coping.

heart ached watching her like this.

The Gemma I knew…she wasn't…this woman.

But I didn't recognize her as much myself. I'd been lost for a while. But now she was lost too.

"I'm fine," she slurred, struggling with the delicate lace. "Just… peachy." But it wasn't. She was fumbling.

Against my better judgment, my heart racing in my chest, I approached. "Here, let me help."

I knelt before her gently batting her hands. "Hands on my shoulders, Duchess." She placed them there and I pretended like this was fine.

This was normal. I wasn't skirting boundaries.

Or that it didn't burn through my fucking suit when she touched me.

I gripped her stockings, adjusting them, lifting them, as her legs parted.

I could almost imagine that little pink butterfly on her…*nope. Nope. Nope. I'm not going there.*

My breath hitched as memories of that night in Capri flooded back —licking that spot. Her moans. Her need to get that tattoo.

Part of me. Part you.

She has never stopped being a part of me.

"See something you like, Mr. Wyatt?" Gemma's voice was husky. "Never took you for the type to take advantage—"

"Duchess, you'd love it if I took advantage of you."

I straightened to find her mouth opening and closing like a fish.

"Alisha's going to be there tonight and we both know you're excited to see her."

Ever since she'd been with Reed, Alisha had been pretty busy in her own life, with Gemma seeing her less frequently.

But then again, Gemma wasn't being honest with anyone. Part of it I knew was her being alone in her life, but another part of it?

Alisha was like her family. She wouldn't want to stress out her family.

I tucked her hair behind her ear, my touch lingering. "Does Alisha know about your situation?"

Her eyes softened as I held her face in my hands.

"Or are you keeping your secrets from everyone?"

As soon as I asked that, a shadow passed over her eyes. It was something familiar I recognized.

"I don't want to bother Alisha," Gemma said softly. "This is the first time she hasn't had anyone to worry about. I don't need her to be worried when she's been…bothered with her own issues."

I made a mental note to check in with Reed.

If anything happened to Alisha, it would devastate Gemma, who considered her family. But even then, Gemma wasn't telling Alisha anything. Stubborn as always.

"You need anything else?" I asked, still acutely aware of our proximity. Aware she'd had a drink. Or two. Already.

She shook her head, looking adorably disoriented with me so close to her.

Her cheeks were flushed, whether from the alcohol or our nearness, I couldn't tell. But she looked so fucking beautiful, I wanted to kiss her.

I did.

But she belonged to someone else.

Andrei DuPont.

When has that ever stopped you before?

A part of me held doubt over it since he'd never called and I never saw him around her.

If Gemma was my girl, I wouldn't—*she's not your girl.*

And that sobering thought led me to speak.

"Good," I said, stepping back with a smirk. "Because I'm pretty sure your panties are inside out."

FIFTY-FOUR
NATE

IF I THOUGHT THE CURVEBALLS FOR THE NIGHT WERE OVER.

I was wrong.

Because the second curveball of the night hit me straight in the face. Watts had come to the event with Alisha.

And Lena on his fucking arm.

I knew with one fucking look at them, Watts was fucking her.

Lena. Who had never been with anyone I knew. Was sleeping with Kellan fucking Watts, the golden boy at Titan.

The fact that he was Reed's now shouldn't have irked me. I held my seat as one of the originals.

I shouldn't have felt threatened.

But I did. Because I saw the way he eyed Lena up and down.

The way he bit his lip as her eyes glanced at him. All shy and shit. Since when did Lena look at anyone like that?

I waited until Alisha left with him to go to the restroom to approach her.

"Don't look at me like that," Lena whispered, her voice strained. She knew why I was coming up to her.

From the moment I'd shown up to this fucking beauty influencer event, Gemma had been tipsy, off her rocker, talking to her girlfriends in the background. And Lena.

Lena had shown up out of all people.

310

"I kept my half," I said quietly, desperation creeping into my tone. "I just turned—"

"*The deal's off,*" she cut me off. Those words sliced through me. *What the fuck?*

"I cannot do it. I'm so sorry." As she stumbled through her confession—being with Kellan, liking him too much—I felt like I was drowning. Each word was another weight dragging me down. Lena was ending our marriage pact.

Because she was fucking Kellan Watts.

"I see the way you look at Gemma," Selena said softly. "She is yours. She has never stopped being yours—"

"*She's with someone else—*" *Even if I thought she was lying. It didn't matter.* Lena couldn't be serious right now. Because of Watts. *She just met him.*

Lena's eyes welled up with tears, and I hated myself for putting them there. But anger and hurt were coursing through me, a toxic cocktail that made me lash out despite myself.

The last thing I wanted to do was hurt Lena. Out of all people? Not her. But I was angry.

I was pissed.

"*You'd throw it all away because you're fucking Quarterback—*"

"Don't talk about him like that," Lena hissed, her own anger flaring. "He has a name—" *Oh.*

She wasn't *just* fucking him.

Lena wouldn't defend him if she didn't like him.

She liked him. But it was just a fucking fling.

"*You call it off because you want to have a fling?*" The words came out harsher than I intended, but I couldn't stop.

My heart was pounding, each beat a reminder of what I stood to lose. "*Lena, what are you doing?*"

"*He is not a fling.*" I could see the conflict in her eyes, the fear warring with something else—something I'd *never* seen on her face before. "I don't know. I just want to *try*—"

The invisible word was right between us. *Love.* It echoed, a concept so foreign to what we'd built together.

Because when I asked Lena to marry me years ago? I asked her as her friend.

Not as anything more than that.

There was no love there. But Lena had been my lifeline.

She'd been what I was holding onto.

She was everything.

And now I felt that hold snapping like a rubber band out of the freezer. Gone. Shattered within seconds.

"For him," she continued. "I will never be yours. I never have been. Not like her." I struggled to breathe, to think. "You want me because you are afraid—"

"Afraid?"

"Yes! Of being with someone who might love you.". I could see the raw honesty in her eyes, so close I could count her lashes. "Nathan. You don't love me."

"Of course I love you, Lena," I insisted, disbelief coloring my tone. "You and me, Lena. That's all it's ever been."

That's all it ever was. Without Gemma.

"Not the way you love her," Lena pressed, her eyes boring into mine. "I see your eyes. I see you. This is not that love."

"You love him." Oh fuck, but I knew the fucking answer. I did.

Lena's hands shook as she nodded, ducking her head. I watched her fight back tears, and something in me broke. I'd never seen her like this, so vulnerable, so...in love.

"Does he love you?" I asked, dreading the answer but needing to know.

"Yes." Lena's green eyes met mine. And because I knew Lena, I knew she wasn't lying. Watts did love her.

I took a deep breath. *Fuck.* Lena looked devastated by what she was doing. Shaking her head. Telling me no.

Blinking back tears in her dark eyes as she wrung her hands together.

I closed my eyes, letting the finality of the moment wash over me. This was it. The end of our pact, of our safety net. Of mine. *What the fuck was I going to do?*

I didn't even know how to say the words out loud.

Sonya, Gemma's friend, came over to pull Lena away for something about nail polish.

I extended my hand to Lena. Like I had all those years ago.

Without hesitation, she placed her hand in mine letting me kiss her knuckles the same spot I had years ago.

"I'm sorry," Lena whispered.

"I'm sorry." Because I was. And I didn't know how to let it go.

I turned, scanning the room for Gemma. My eyes found her instantly, drawn to her like a magnet.

She was laughing with Lara, her head thrown back, eyes sparkling.

I had no idea what I was going to do next, but one thing was clear— I needed a drink.

FIFTY-FIVE
GEMMA

THE WORLD TILTED AND SWAYED AS NATE GUIDED ME OUT OF THE party.

My thoughts were as fuzzy as cotton candy, dissolving the moment I tried to grasp them.

Flashes of light burst around us—*paparazzi*—my brain supplied. His arm tightened around my waist, solid and warm.

"Just keep walking, Duchess," he murmured, his breath tickling my ear.

I wanted to tell him not to call me that, but the words wouldn't come.

Instead, I leaned into him, drawing comfort from his familiar scent. I caught him watching me, a slight furrow in his brow. I wanted to smooth away his concern, to tell him I was fine, but my tongue felt tied up in thoughts of him.

Wanting him. Craving him. God, why did he still affect me like this?

Lara and the girls had been a fun break for me.

But right now? The stairs were my next problem.

"Careful there," he said, his voice low and husky, and his voice was always what undid me. Making my lady parts clench down.

In my room, Nate's hands were gentle as he helped me undress. A distant part of me knew I should feel embarrassed, but I couldn't summon the emotion.

Instead, I watched his face, fascinated by the clench of his jaw, the dark flash in his eyes.

"You've done this before." That's what I meant to say. It came out a mumbled mess of *mmmmhmffmhhm*.

Nate paused, his hand on my zipper. "Yeah, I have. Come here, I gotta clean you up…Why do women fucking wear this shit?"

"Makes me look pretty," I murmured, teetering on the edge of consciousness.

"You're always pretty, Duchess," I thought I heard him. But I couldn't be sure.

I was passing out.

Morning arrived with all the subtlety of a sledgehammer. My head pounded, my mouth tasted like I'd licked a sandbox.

I groaned, burrowing deeper into my pillow.

A pillow that…*moved*?

My eyes flew open to a white shirt-covered chest.

I blinked, willing my hangover-addled brain to make sense of what I was seeing.

Wearing only a white t-shirt and boxer briefs, looking unfairly handsome in his sleep was Nate. Right next to me.

Last night, I had felt him a little more distant. No snarky comments. Nothing rude coming off him.

And had met his former work partner.

Selena Tavares, the most gorgeous Cuban woman with a thick lush accent that made everything she said sound poetic.

And Kellan Watts, Alisha's bodyguard had been all over her.

For a moment I thought Nate had been her partner, I had assumed he'd had something romantic with her.

But I'd seen the way Kellan kissed her over and over when he thought none of us were paying attention.

Selena had all but melted into his arms.

Kellan had been *jealous* of Nate.

Well, of any man around Selena.

He didn't take his eyes off her or Alisha, doing his job for both of them. And I didn't know how Nate felt about Selena last night but she'd insisted they weren't romantically a thing ever. Given how Kellan had been all on her?

I knew they were together.

Kellan who was was adorably sweet.

Until last night when I saw him glaring down Nate for even remotely trying to flirt with Selena.

I closed my eyes again, breathing through my emotions. All of them bubbling up to the surface when it came to this man. I couldn't focus.

Nate wasn't mine. I shouldn't have been jealous. *He probably thinks you're with Andrei.*

No, for a moment around a woman as gorgeous as Selena, I felt nothing but intimidated.

Because she had spent the last few years with Nathan. He'd mentioned her once or twice in passing, but I never imagined meeting her in person.

She didn't react to me or engage with me in any way that let me think she knew who I was to Nate.

In fact, she'd been so kind.

I got the feeling she wasn't used to a gaggle of women around her and she loved it so much, I found myself liking her.

And then there had been Lara.

Who was actually dating someone. *Liam.* Out of all people.

It took my brain a second to put it together.

Lara dashed off to a blacked out car. Liam had been driving and I didn't see his face. He didn't get out but the way Lara had quickly bounded over she didn't give him a chance. I saw her entire face light up though.

Alisha was with Reed. Sonya was going through her divorce. And happily so. Lara was with someone. Selena and Kellan made out whenever they could.

And me...I felt stuck. In my past. Unable to move on. I watched Nate sleeping in my bed like he belonged there.

A long time ago…it was you and me against the world.

What happened?

I had left Sonya's place. And now...I woke up to him. Every woman in my life was living their lives.

I was in bed with a man who I should've hated.

But I didn't.

I didn't truly hate Nate. *No.*

I felt angry with him for abandoning me. The baby. My life. I had wanted him to take me with him so much that I had never considered how that young man might've taken care of me.

Now? I knew a little about him. He had a few successful ventures he had his fingers in.

I took in his weary eyes, dark circles under them and I felt a pang of guilt.

Was I being hard on him? Camilla had been cruel to him. Was I being cruel to him? The little boy from the middle of nowhere just hustling to make it as he'd said?

My eyes welled as I watched him.

I missed you, Nate.

I was mad at...my life. Being a Marchand. Former and present. Carrying the name around like my weight. While every other woman in my life was moving on—I was the only outsider.

The one paralyzed with my past. Obsessed with it to the point where my past controlled every inch of my present. The threads of it holding me so tight I couldn't breathe.

I didn't know what to think.

I couldn't let the girl I was go. The ghost I was.

Maybe the ghost was all I had for so long if I let her go? I would feel like I was betraying her. If I didn't hold onto my hurt forever—what would I become if I let it go?

I didn't know how to. Was I letting that girl ruin me from becoming someone better?

I don't want to let Camilla ruin my future.

My path was my own.

And right now my path was in bed with me.

FIFTY-SIX
NATE

"Nate...wake up."

I was imagining her voice in my sleep. It happened so fucking often I almost gave into it. In my dreams she wore a lilac silk slip.

She was ethereal. Opal eyes. Soft skin. All purple and wonderful.

Usually, though my dreams transformed into Lena waking me up by punching my arm. All hot pink and sass.

Not Gemma.

But this was the realest I ever got to Gemma's grapefruit, lemon scent. The realest it had ever felt to me at least.

"Wake up...it's almost noon."

"Duchess..." I mumbled something I couldn't figure out. "Tired..."

"I know...but maybe Bonnie's made breakfast."

Hm. That was funny. That's what she said in my dreams.

I could have her for breakfast and it would be the same thing.

I didn't know if I said it out loud though. I had spent years building these walls around my heart, I couldn't just let them down after her ending up in bed with me.

Dream Gemma smelled really good though. It was tempting.

"*Nate.*"

But the *real* Gemma hated my guts. She was probably lying about having a man I never saw, but she wasn't mine. She didn't want me. Not anymore. Not like the past.

When she had been mine and mine alone. Not anyone else's.

If I could be hers again, I'd go back in time and keep her close to my heart. Bury myself so deep inside of her, she wouldn't know how to shake me.

I wanted to take every moment I could with her and savor it now.

I had fucked up so bad with her in the past. Sneaking out like a ghost. After the fucking condom broke.

Gemma clearly hadn't had a kid.

But damned if I didn't wish I had taken her with me. Had the baby. Had a little life. Sooner. And my chest ached again.

I kept my eyes closed as that scent ghosted over me calming me down.

This wasn't real. So maybe I could enjoy it.

I let myself sink into the fantasy, knowing it would hurt like hell when I truly woke up.

Gemma didn't like me. Lena didn't want me.

Nobody wants me. Because I'm not good enough.

I was right back to that piece of shit scum.

I didn't want to let anyone too close to me sometimes. But Gemma was the only woman in the world who could crack me open. See me for who I was.

None of the money in the world mattered if I didn't have my life. Or her.

Reed was dating Alisha. Watts was fucking Lena to the point where she was calling off what she had wanted her entire life for him.

I didn't know who I was again. But then again, I hadn't known for the longest time.

"Nate, wake up." I felt her lips ghosting over my cheeks, my brows. My temples.

That felt too real.

Except Gemma…she was in her room.

And I was in mine. Her lips ghosted over me, leaving trails of fire on my skin.

"Baby," I could barely speak. "Tired." I shouldn't have had anything last night.

"I know, darling." She brushed my hair back with her nails and I sighed as she threaded her fingers into it. "Did you want cuddles?"

Gemma loved that in the past. I sighed and mumbled something about needing her as she cuddled me to her.

"Need you too."

And then Dream Gemma kissed me. Slowly. Softly. And she moaned. And then she was all over me. Hot. Soft.

Lush. Gemma.

"Baby—" I rolled her over easily loving the way she softened, her legs spreading open for me, pliant and soft. Kissing down her throat. "Fuck, I love you."

I still did. Somewhere deep down my obsession with her had never ebbed.

Beneath me Gemma moaned softly as I kissed my way lower.

"Nate, not like this...no...come here."

I obeyed.

Because she was my girl. She always had been. Drowsily, I moved up to her kissing her again.

"Nate...come on, wake up."

What? Wake up from what?

This?

And then I drowsily blinked to find tanned skin, lush pink tipped tits in my face as Gemma fucking Marchand rubbed my scalp, my neck, her lips moving over my forehead.

What the fuck?

"Nate, I—" her voice was hesitant, almost shy. "You're...awake."

I was now.

What the fuck was I—*I went to sleep next to Gemma last night.*

And Gemma...Gemma was...under me.

Blinking up with soft eyes on me. Looking sweeter than I had ever seen. Oh. Fuck. She was gorgeous.

She has a man.

That never stopped you before.

Yes, but this is Gemma.

So where the fuck was he?

Where was Andrei fucking DuPont?

And so did Lena. She had Kellan fucking Watts.

I pushed back a little. "What are you doing?"

She blinked shyly up at me like she didn't understand. "What?"

"What are you doing?" I sleepily asked. "Don't you have Andrei?"

Her eyes went wide. And I saw it all over her face.

Wait...did she not...what...

And before I could process any of it? *Any* of it.

The shrill ring of my phone cut through the moment like a knife. I groaned, torn between the urge to ignore it.

But I couldn't. It could be important. It could be work.

"I gotta get it. That's Reed," I muttered, reaching for the phone buried somewhere in my pants on the floor. *Shitshitshit, Gemma just kissed me. In my sleep.*

And I'm pretty sure I was right about her not dating Andrei.

It went to text and it pinged.

Gemma's face fell slightly, but she nodded. I answered, my eyes still locked on her.

I looked down at the message frowning at it. And then I swore.

"Fucking..." I shook my head.

This was bad. And Gemma...she wouldn't like this one bit.

I watched her slowly sit up, wrapping the sheet around herself. It was like she could sense the bad news coming.

As I ended the call, I took a deep breath.

"You might wanna go to Alisha..." I started, my voice rough with the weight of what I had to say. "Her apartment was broken into last night."

FIFTY-SEVEN
GEMMA

K2 WAS A FORTRESS.

That was what Nate said. Compared to other buildings, there were several doors before I got to Reed's apartment.

Alisha had moved in with Reed.

And she wasn't happy.

I knew Alisha well, had seen her tackle life with a fierce independence that both inspired and intimidated me. She valued her space, her freedom.

That apartment she'd shared with Avani was more than just walls and furniture—it was their home, filled with laughter and the comfort of chosen family. Her family. Me. Lara. Avani.

Now, I held her while she cried in the guest room while Nate was moving around the kitchen.

He had mumbled something about coffee. It didn't surprise me he knew Reed's apartment.

When he'd brought me here, Reed wasn't home. Working, was all Nate had told me.

I had texted Avani to make sure she was all right before coming to Alisha's.

I held her as I said. "I think whoever hurt you wants to get under your skin."

Just like Camilla wanted to get under mine. Make me aware she had her eyes on me. It made my skin prickle.

"Nate also thinks that it has nothing to do with you specifically, but you might be the target of someone who gets off on doing this to other women too."

"How did he know?"

"You didn't hear it from me, but I think Reed and Kellan are working on it. I overheard Nate on the phone with them."

I had. It was one time.

"Nate…he caught me outside the door," I admitted feeling my face heating up. "But that's beside the point. He told me that it's just a hunch, but Reed will be gone tonight. I offered to come visit you and stay with you tonight if that's all right."

It was.

"Is there something going on with you two?"

I felt bad for lying to Alisha. "Nothing at all."

On cue, a knock came twice, and Nate stepped carrying two cups of tea. I blinked as he took me in.

His eyes focusing on me under the covers. Where we'd been a mere hours ago. And then I saw his jaw tense.

I looked away as he spoke. "I have dinner on the way, Reed said he wants to make sure you're eating."

I felt his hand on my back. Lower. "Let me know if you need anything else, Duchess."

I resisted the urge to growl.

"Lish, will you excuse us for just a moment?"

I slowly got out of the bed not wanting to do this with him at Reed's penthouse out of all things. But I had to.

NATE LED ME INTO WHAT APPEARED TO BE A STUDY.

The space was all navy and dark, mirroring Reed's entire penthouse —designed to emulate a high-end hotel.

Halls branched off in different directions, adorned with pieces of high-end art. Luxurious, but with a cold edge.

He shut the door, and suddenly, those navy eyes locked onto mine.

"You kissed me," Nate said, his tone unreadable. "Why did you do that this morning?"

I had. Words failed me.

"You kissed me back," I managed to reply, aiming for haughty but landing on breathless. So much for my dignity.

He exhaled sharply, raking a hand through his hair. "*Andrei—*"

"I'm not with Andrei." The words tumbled out faster than I thought possible.

His brows drew together. "What do you mean you're not with Andrei?" He looked so lost, I might've laughed if I'd had my wits about me.

We were in Reed's home. Alisha was crying. We couldn't do this here.

"I'm not with Andrei," I repeated, my gaze sweeping the lavish study. The opulence was staggering—some of these items must've cost a small fortune. "I never was. We just get photographed together, but it doesn't mean anything—"

"Like fuck it doesn't. Why would you—"

"Because you!"

We both fell silent. Our eyes locked, and for a moment, I forgot who I was. Forgot everything. Like I always did around him. The breath left my lungs as I realized what an idiot I'd been. I had loved Nate so deeply.

"Because of me." He looked away, uncomfortable. "Why?"

"I don't know," I said quickly. "I thought maybe I could protect myself from my emotions. From—"

"From me?" His eyes met mine as he took a breath.

"Listen, as much as I want to have this conversation, now isn't the time or place. Alisha's right there, and Reed's trusting me to take care of my best friend—"

"This isn't a conversation." He stepped closer. "You lied to me. You held back. You kissed me this morning for what?" His brows furrowed. "For what, Gemma?"

His eyes searched mine, and I saw something unfamiliar in them.

Something completely foreign in Nathan. I couldn't identify the fear or where it was coming from.

"Are you all right?" I had to ask.

"No. I'm not fucking all right, Gemma." He turned away. "The only thing I've learned is that *you aren't with DuPont. Which I fucking figured—"*

"Nate—"

"I can't do this right now either—" he cut me off. A muscle ticked in his jaw as it clenched. I didn't understand what was happening. He seemed off. Just...off in general.

Nate's hand was on the doorknob when I found my voice again.

"So that's it? You're just going to walk away?" I don't know why I said it. "Is that all you ever do? Run from your bloody problems—"

He turned to look at me over his shoulder, eyes flashing. *"Are you fucking—"*

"That's all you've ever done!"

I couldn't help it. I didn't know what I wanted or why I was frustrated. I just knew I was trying to let him in and failing miserably, and I didn't know how to shut up once I started.

The words ripped out of my chest like a stone damn breaking into pieces. Shattering at the slightest provocation. I couldn't stop it.

It took Nate two long strides that I didn't even process as he closed the distance between us.

When his lips stamped down on mine, my entire body sighed. I realized I needed him. Just him. Always.

The kiss was fierce, desperate, full of pent-up emotions we'd both been holding back. My hands fisted in his shirt, pulling him closer, while his cupped my face, thumbs brushing my cheeks.

"Fuckkk," he swore. "Only you do this shit to me." He licked his lips as his eyes burned through me. "Only you."

It shouldn't have felt good to hear him say that. But it did.

"We're messed up, Nate." I don't know why my eyes stung. "We really messed up. *Nous sommes tellement brisés."* We are broken.

He looked at me like he knew we were both guilty. In our own ways. "We can't do this here…"

"Then when?"

The abrupt loss of his lips left me reeling. Cold. Exposed.

Unwanted.

I felt desperate and I didn't even know why.

He'd done this to me for years. I was grasping at his arms unsure of why.

Nate looked at me for a second like he didn't recognize me as he brought me closer to him. "*Je suis perdue. Je ne peux pas penser quand tu es près de moi.*"

I am lost. I cannot think when you are near me.

He didn't understand me but his mouth turned down like he did. "I don't know, but let me go figure out who Reed is trying not to kill. He's out tonight with Watts. No more eavesdropping on me, Duchess—"

I turned pink at the mention of the one time I'd done that.

"We can sort this out after I grab you two some food."

I let out a shaking breath. "After."

He tipped his head and held me tight to him as we left Reed's office.

FIFTY-EIGHT
GEMMA

THAT NIGHT I SLEPT BY ALISHA WITH REED GONE.

All night. And I was beginning to lose it a little at him. Nate reassured me Reed's disappearances were normal.

They often didn't speak about their work. But Reed in particular was tracking a lead on who was taunting Alisha by breaking into her home.

The next morning the moment we stepped into my townhouse—Bonnie and Nigel were rushing to us.

While we were gone, someone had attempted a break-in, though neither of them had realized it at the time.

Nate's demeanor shifted instantly from the man I'd kissed hours ago to the consummate professional.

He checked the security footage to find what we'd come to expect—another faceless perpetrator in a mask and ball cap, operating under the cover of night.

They'd thrown a rock, shattered the glass in the basement, and vanished without a trace.

And then I had to juggle my never-ending list of responsibilities.

My phone buzzed incessantly with reminders and messages.

First up, a last-minute crisis with the annual Lennox Gala.

Our headline performer had caught bronchitis, and we needed to source a replacement ASAP.

Nothing like corralling A-list talent on short notice to get the blood pumping.

Then there was the dinner parties later on this week.

To top it off, I had a site visit scheduled at the women's shelter Poppy had been working with for victims of domestic violence.

I glanced at Nate, still engrossed in the security footage.

We lived together, breathed the same air, and yet sometimes it felt like we were worlds apart—like I couldn't get to him fast enough.

But it seemed once I admitted I wasn't with Andrei, something in him changed.

It was like he saw right through me.

Like he knew.

I set down a cup of coffee for him as he worked at the kitchen island. And when I sat down next to him, he pulled my chair closer. He turned his head to look at me, his eyes deep navy and dark.

"You look exhausted."

"I am pretty exhausted."

And I felt almost shy reaching over understanding I wanted to kiss him.

"Do you want to talk about it?" I kept my voice low. Nate turned to me, his arm out and I didn't even hesitate to scoot closer into his lap.

"Nah, I got it." His entire expression was one of exhaustion. "I got it, baby." But something was bothering Nate. I could see it on his face.

And I didn't know how to ask him.

"Are you worried about Alisha's case or something else?"

"A little bit of everything."

That's what I was worried about.

"I need to get some air," I brushed his hair back. "Want to step out with me? I wanted to go see Avani. Maybe get some coffee." He looked like he was fighting a grin as he looked down at his full cup of coffee.

"Sure, let's go."

~

"Gemma!" Avani floated up to me for a tight hug, our feet crunching the leaves and Avani's bright mocha eyes beaming as I handed her chai. "Oh, that smells so good."

Avani's own honey scent smelled like something else. A faint hint of masculine cologne to them. It was familiar but I couldn't pinpoint it.

As we walked, leaves crunching beneath our feet, Avani chatted animatedly about her classes and, surprisingly, about Reed.

"He's really sweet. He's helping me move into my own apartment on campus."

"That's wonderful, darling," I replied, noting the excitement in her voice.

But there was something else there too—a nervousness that piqued my curiosity.

"And your sister is moving in with Reed now. Did you visit him in K2 yet?"

She shook her head, eyes downcast. "Reed said he wants her to get settled and move all our stuff in." A pause. "I know about her stalker. Rather uncomfortable if you ask me. But Reed said he's going to make sure he takes care of all of our things."

Despite my reservations about Reed. He was doing his best with the girls.

Nate held the door open to our destination—a cozy lounge-cum-coffee shop. Her eyes drifted to him curiously. "Is he your guard?"

"Just a precaution for me in public," I confirmed. "but it's all right. He won't say a word." I shot Nate a pointed look, and he nodded politely.

I tried to suppress a smile at the softness in his eyes as he watched Avani. Since Nate wasn't exactly soft and cuddly on the eyes.

He looked more like someone who fought for a living.

And he had. That always tugged at my heart strings.

We settled onto a plush couch, Nate taking up position behind me, close enough that I could feel his presence.

"Reed has been wonderful. I think Alisha's just nervous. We had dinner together a few weeks ago when he treated us to Japanese food..." Avani trailed off, glancing at Nate, who was doing his best to appear disinterested.

I lowered my voice reassuringly. "It's fine. Nate won't say a word. Will you?" I called over my shoulder.

Nate shook his head, miming zipped lips.

Mocha eyes returned back to me as Avani bit her lip, hesitating.

"Remember when we talked about...me and Lish?" The look in her eyes spoke volumes. "Do you think she's afraid that if anything happens with her and Reed...I might think less of her?"

"Not at all," I rushed to reassure her, my protective instincts flaring at her vulnerability. "I think she just doesn't want you to develop a negative view of men in general."

"But I don't think that way at all."

"Sometimes, the wrong people enter our lives and hurt us. I believe your sister wants to shield you from thinking that any potential problems between her and Reed are the norm in relationships."

Avani's eyes, wide with curiosity, met mine. "Did she tell you that?"

"In a way. Lish is primarily concerned about protecting you, about not giving you the impression that it's normal for a man to love you and then leave."

I felt Nate stiffen behind me, the weight of my words hitting us both. *Right.*

Because one of us had already been burned, and even if Alisha didn't know Nate had hurt me, I knew she suspected something.

She didn't want her little sister hurt the way I had been.

I didn't want Avani to be hurt either.

But I knew Thierry never would.

"I don't think Reed is like that at all," Avani said softly, her gaze shy. "He actually reminds me of Thierry."

Her cheeks flushed pink as she continued. "I haven't told Lish yet... I was worried she might be upset if she knew."

It shouldn't have surprised me that Thierry DuPont was dating her. It really shouldn't have.

"I mean, I'm not completely shocked, but I am surprised—" I stammered, my mind racing to catch up. "How is he..."

Avani's eyes lit up and she gushed about him. How he took care of her. Spent all his time with her. They'd gone from tutoring to dating and now they were going steady. She turned rapidly pink as she grinned at me.

"I just don't want Lish to be upset," Avani rushed to explain. "She stayed single for so long because of me. I didn't want her to think I started dating the moment I left home—"

She'd gotten herself a boyfriend with the temperament of a Doberman. Somehow it felt impossible to see the two of them together but it also made sense to me. Polar opposites. One of them dark and prickly and the other light and squishy.

I grinned at Avani telling me he stayed with her now all the time.

I cut in gently, trying to ease her worries. "I don't think she'd see it that way at all. She would be happy for you, Avani. I'm certain she'll be supportive once she sees how happy you are."

She beamed at me.

"Thierry mentioned that his friends might be coming to the city soon. He wants me to meet them." Avani added, her excitement palpable. "I thought it would be lovely for them to meet Lish. Maybe have a big girl's brunch. She would love that. After I met Reed, I wanted to introduce him to Reed too. I think they'd get along well..."

They might. Now that I thought about it, they really might.

"I think you and Lish might have a type," I teased gently, trying to lighten the mood. "Tall, dark and brooding."

I felt comfortable enough to lean against Nate who was drinking my coffee silently. With his hearing he didn't even have to try.

"Although I think Thierry definitely takes the cake for being a little more brooding than Reed. I think you're right. They'd love him."

Avani's cheeks flushed deeper, confirming my suspicions. "I love him, Gemma." Her eyes were wide and lit up and I had to force myself to keep smiling because I knew that look. I knew it from the bottom of my heart. I saw it in the mirror whenever I talked about Nate in the past.

I saw it now sometimes when I watched him look at me.

And just like that, my heart cracked open for her. The raw emotion in her voice, the vulnerability in her eyes—it all hit me at once.

She's me.

He's Nate.

Falling in love over the summer, a little too fast, maybe careening into something she shouldn't.

But...Avani wasn't me.

Her situation was different, wasn't it?

Her sister would love him.

Alisha wouldn't force them apart.

Alisha would love Thierry.

"Until Reed moved me out of my dorm, I was staying with Thierry sometimes," Avani admitted softly. "His place is much bigger, and my roommate was awful. Lish didn't know..." She shook her head.

"I didn't want to tell Alisha how bad things were at the dorm. But Thierry came and got me one day after days of not sleeping. I never keep secrets from her but now I have too many."

She looked at her hands like a guilty child.

"I feel so bad. I usually tell Alisha everything. Now I have all these things I can't say."

"There's no pressure for the world to know," I meant it as I said it. "Sometimes it's okay to bask in what you have among the two of you. Reed and Alisha don't need to know right now. And maybe it's best you and Thierry explore your relationship and see where it goes without the pressure?"

I shrugged lightly and gave her what I hoped was a winning smile.

She beamed. "That's true. I can tell Lish when it's the right time for me...and for now, Thierry and I can just be—"

"Together." I nodded. "I know you want him to meet everyone but maybe he's happy with keeping you to himself for the time being."

I was happy with keeping Nate to myself. I always had.

She blushed at that, turning an adorable shade of pink. "He is."

"I wouldn't have guessed you two—"

"Erm...me either...but it just kind of happened..." Avani blushed harder. "He stays with me all the time or I stay with him and since you introduced us...I don't think I've spent a day without him."

And Alisha didn't know?

Why?

I watched Avani's eyes and I realized why. I had spent years with her. Years of understanding her insecurities. Her world. Her living in her head. She was living. She didn't want to be a burden to Alisha.

"If you tell Alisha about Thierry," I whispered knowing full well Nate could hear me as I was pressed into his back. "She won't hate you, Avani."

Her eyes softened. "But what if she does? She waited years to be with Reed...and I couldn't wait a week? Alisha doesn't know I've been seeing him all summer...I feel like a horrible sister."

I held her hand tightly. "You are not a horrible sister. It's okay to want your happiness. Alisha made a choice. She never once thought ill of you for those choices. Do you understand? You don't have to feel guilty for falling in love with Thierry."

Ever.

Her eyes watered and her bottom lip trembled as she nodded.

"How is he doing?" I asked softer. "Better, I hope. His English was something else."

"Better..." she laughed. "You have no idea. He's such a quick learner, ever since he found out I love to read..." She turned a deeper shade of red as she fanned herself.

And I saw so much of me in her. I always had.

I won't let anything happen to the two of you.

Avani's face brightened. "Maybe I can ask Reed if he'd be okay with me bringing Thierry to a lunch date sometimes, maybe Reed can meet him and it will soften the blow to Alisha..."

"I'm sure Reed would be delighted."

Behind me Nate snorted and I smacked his thigh as Avani giggled at him.

FIFTY-NINE
NATE

Lena and Watts were both on Alisha's stalker case.

Lena had reached out to me for assistance, given that she and Watts were now living together.

Gemma was always there when she did and I wanted to let her know it was fine if she listened.

At this point, I doubt I could keep shit from Gemma.

Gemma finally admitted she hadn't told me about Andrei because of me, everything clicked into place.

I should've known.

She was my girl.

I'd always been able to read her, to understand her motivations.

And I should've fucking known she was lying when he never turned up. Where the fuck was Andrei this entire time?

For a second I thought Gemma might've been with Teo, the younger one, and I remembered he had a crush on Alisha.

And it wasn't like I wasn't keeping my own secrets as well. I was. I wasn't devastated about losing Lena as my potential wife. More so the future of promise and possibility than anything else.

"…We've been doing well…" Avani was saying.

I found myself drawn out of these thoughts by Gemma's laughter as she chatted with Avani about her boyfriend. That was Alisha's little sister.

From what I got—Avani didn't want to tell her sister she was dating an older guy who, from what I could gather, sounded decent. But I knew Reed had waited three years to fucking date Alisha who hadn't wanted anyone.

Our coffee shop meeting came to an abrupt end when a blacked-out Roadster pulled up outside.

I noticed it first, the license plates obscured by the frosted glass at the bottom of the shop windows. Avani's face lit up at the sight.

"He's here. Thank you, Gemma," she exclaimed, hugging Gemma tightly. The scent of honey and roses enveloped us as Avani gathered her books.

"Who's she with?" I asked Gemma quietly as Avani rushed off to the car. I couldn't make out the driver, but Avani's wide smile told me all I needed to know about her feelings.

"Thierry," Gemma replied. "He's Andrei's youngest brother."

Before I could process this new information, my phone rang. "Never-ending chaos," I muttered, answering the call. "Liam?"

"I've got a lead on Camilla," Liam's voice came through, immediately capturing my full attention.

I was all ears, stepping closer to Gemma who stood up and moved, eyes wide on me. I listened to what Liam said. As he spoke I blinked. "Hang on, Liam."

"I turned to Gemma. "Duchess. Get to the car. Come on, we need to find a private place to talk to Liam."

She nodded, her eyes wide as Liam continued to list off what he'd found. Besides the obvious money trail.

"That lead about Gerard's associate? It's a dead end. Literally. The guy doesn't exist. I dug deeper and found out it's a fabricated identity, created about six months ago. The paper trail is impeccable, but it's all fake."

I ushered Gemma into the car, putting the phone on speaker as Liam continued once the door closed.

"I traced the offshore account on that guy, back to a holding company in the Cayman Islands. Guess who's the beneficiary? Camilla. The company was set up using Gerard's lawyer. The same one who's been handling his declining health."

"Declining?" Gemma whispered confusion etched into her face. "My father is fine—"

"He was," Liam interrupted gently. "But according to the medical records I've accessed, he's had a few serious issues recently."

I watched as Gemma's face paled, her hand gripping the car seat.

Liam continued, his voice somber. "In the past six months, there have been multiple hospital visits. First, it was for severe migraines and dizzy spells. Then, about three months ago, he was admitted for what they initially thought was a minor stroke. The latest records show he's been experiencing rapid cognitive decline, memory issues, and extreme fatigue."

Gemma's breath hitched, her eyes filling with tears.

"His blood work has shown some anomalies. Elevated levels of certain compounds that don't match his prescribed medications. It's subtle, but it's there. Given what we know about Camilla, she might be fucking him over. And he's isolated. So he wouldn't know."

"Come here, Duchess." I was holding onto Gemma as Liam talked in the car.

"There are records of calls and emails to you, Gemma. Quite a few of them. But they never went through. It looks like Camilla has been intercepting his attempts to contact you. And has been for some time…"

She turned to me, her lips trembling, tears threatening to spill. In that moment, I saw the little girl she must have been once. It didn't matter that Gerard had let us both down in his own ways. Camilla was the one brain washing him.

"Camilla isn't known for having good connections. She used to work for people in the art industry that were put away by Interpol. You're not wrong to assume it could be her. But we need concrete proof. I need to come up with a takedown plan for Reed with the information I do have. When we escalate this—"

"What?" Gemma cut Liam off, pulling back slightly, her tear-stained face a mixture of confusion. I could see the wheels turning in her head.

"Escalate—"

"Because we have to for our client," Liam sighed a little. "Camilla might come after you two. Reed and I wanted to wait to tell you but we think she would come after everything around you as well. When she does? Tell me. I am lead on this. Do you copy?"

"Yes, sir." I didn't know why I was saying that to Liam but in that moment he was leading.

And I was just making sure nothing happened to Gemma.

"I'll get back to you guys if anything happens. I think Camilla hired some idiotic hacker to try and fuck with me, but it isn't working…I'll be busy over the next few days but just text me if anything happens."

SIXTY
NATE

Gemma and I rushed to the Primrose the morning we got a call from Alisha.

"He's done something to Alisha. We have to hurry."

We were out the door in minutes, racing to the Primrose Hotel.

Apparently, Reed and Alisha had broken up after some incident with Lucy *Devereaux* showing up at his place.

The details were fuzzy, but I knew Lucy wasn't involved with Reed romantically.

That's because she was involved with me. But I wasn't some moron to say that out loud.

She was just another woman in my life I didn't need to talk to Gemma about. I knew Alisha didn't have anything to worry about.

But Gemma didn't know that.

The Primrose was a fancy joint, all marble floors and pink crystal chandeliers. It screamed money and class—Gemma's world, not mine. She fit right in, while I felt like a bull in a china shop. Gemma was everything I wasn't. But it was the only time I felt like I was home. Safe.

Wanted.

Loved.

Accepted.

Gemma was visibly anxious, and the moment we knocked on the door, I understood why.

338

Alisha, was usually the picture of composure, crumbled into Gemma's arms. Her usually appearance was in disarray, her eyes red and swollen from crying.

Gemma's eyes widened as she held her friend, silently passing me her bag.

As they retreated to the bedroom, Alisha's hysterical sobs echoed through the suite.

My mind raced, recalling the incident a few weeks ago when Watts and I had to deal with a body outside Poppy.

That had shaken Gemma, but this seemed worse.

Watts' absence was worrying enough. I texted Reed as soon as I saw her alone.

I was doing some digging into Alisha's case and whoever her stalker was, wasn't exactly a cake-walk to catch.

The guy was good. Which meant it was someone familiar with us.

Within the hour, Reed arrived with an exhausted Watts in tow. We moved outside the room as Reed went in to talk to Alisha.

"I can hear her crying," I said to Reed. I felt my duty to protect Alisha as Gemma's best friend. I knew how Gemma felt about her. I knew how much she loved Avani.

"What did you do this time?"

"I need to see her," Reed was six-foot four inches of a human tank and he was going to shove me the fuck out of his way if he had to.

Too bad I was still capable of taking him.

I was one of the few Titans who could take him and Gabriel. Which was no fucking feat.

"She doesn't want to see you."

"Since when are you so fucking protective of my girl? Get Gemma out of here. I'm going to see her, if I have to break that door down."

Gemma appeared a moment later no doubt having heard this shit with Reed immediately. Her bearing was regal and the way she looked at Reed was one that told me if she could fight him—she would. That was my girl.

"Absolutely not," she all but spat. *"You cannot see her."*

She positioned herself in front of the door like he would have to go through her to get to Alisha. Over my dead body.

"Step aside, Duchess—"

"I am no longer a part of my family," Gemma hissed. *"And I will not let you tear apart what little family I have now."*

She crossed her arms over her periwinkle blue cardigan.

"Gemma, I swear to God, let me see her—" Reed began.

"Not bloody likely. I won't let you hurt her anymore..."

"One way or another, I will see her. Did you forget who's in the room right now?"

"She isn't yours. She stopped being yours the moment you decided lying to her and going behind her back—"

"It wasn't about her—"

"You keep hurting her—"

"I would never hurt her."

The moment the words left Reed's lips, I moved.

I moved so fast I blocked Reed from talking to her.

"I will take anything for you," my voice was steady. Strong. "But not a word against her. You hear me? You got something to prove, you'll go through me."

"I'm going to explain everything to her," Reed's storm-cloud eyes met mine.

"When were you going to do that? What was Reed's master plan?"

I whirled around to see Gemma's best friend and sister staring at Reed like he broke her. Because he did.

I had heard her crying. And I suspected I knew why.

Reed had asked me before I got the job for Lena, to contact Lucy Devereaux. His personal jewel thief.

She was sent to steal something from Dakar, Senegal months ago.

And now Reed had her visiting his apartment in K2 and Alisha thought he was having an affair with her.

I knew for a fact—Reed wasn't sleeping with Lucy. I was. Or I had been.

Being fuck buddies with someone who liked violent sex was usually right up my alley.

But Lucy liked the kind of sex that was intense even for me. Lucy liked the kind of stuff that had me worried about her. Not that she'd listen to me.

The girl was free falling into danger but he did ask me to talk to her.

And I sent her a message to go look for the necklace. Last I heard? She had.

It would take one fucking hell of a man to wrangle Lucy.

"Lish," Reed sounded gutted. "Please let me in."

Whatever passed between the two of them? Even I couldn't deny that Reed loved her. He did. But then why did he keep being an absolute idiot?

As Alisha moved aside the door to let him in, Gemma went to protest either way. She was her family. I got it.

But now was not the time.

Reed had a lot of secrets to explain and considering before Alisha?

He basically dated women who were absolutely fucking meaner than Gabriel—it explained why he had a harder time talking to Alisha.

I stopped Gemma from going after her friend, my hand around her waist tucking her into my side. I shook my head at her.

Not now, baby.

"Thank you, both," Alisha murmured. "If it's alright with you, I'd like to speak to him alone."

"We'll be outside," my eyes locked with Reed's.

Don't you fucking hurt her again.

Reed tipped his head as he followed Alisha into her room.

Beside me Gemma stiffened.

"It's okay, Duchess. I got it. I promise." I tucked her into my side aware that similar to how Reed and Gabriel kept secrets? So did I.

I needed to tell her everything—about Camilla, about Lena, about why I left.

I swore once I figured out whatever the fuck was going on here, I would tell Gemma. *Everything.*

Because some part of me knew it was wrong to keep it from her.

And the other part of me knew, I had wasted enough time.

I felt Gemma in my arms resting her head against my heart where she had held space for a long time.

I took a deep breath when I heard the shouting stop inside. My eyes opened.

Alisha was done reaming Reed out.

Because there were too many things I'd kept from her and now?

I could feel it bubbling over the surface.

Especially with Watts lingering in the hall looking less than pleased.

It didn't matter to me.

I knew he had Lena. I should've let her go. But some part of me would always love her.

Not like Gemma.

Nobody was Gemma.

Nobody would ever take up that space and I knew I had to tell her the truth.

SIXTY-ONE
GEMMA

"Who is Lucy?" I asked Nate. "Do you know her?"

We had barely gotten in through the door before I pounced on him.

"Reed hired Lucy years ago," Nate murmured closing the door and locking it behind him. "She's your friend Lucas's baby sister. She also happens to be part of Titan."

What?

Nate explained how Reed had hired Lucy to work directly under him. Like all the Titans, Lucy had her place, and it was collecting things for Reed and doing work.

Lucy had appeared at Reed's apartment and Alisha assumed he was cheating on her.

"Can't she just tell Alisha why?"

Nate shook his head. "I wouldn't tell a soul what I do for Reed." His expression went blank and I realized the rumors were true.

"Because he's dangerous."

"Because we all are. You think Selena's gorgeous? Selena can kill you with her heels."

I blinked as he said it with caution. "Lucy works for Reed, she isn't allowed to talk about what she does. I don't even know what Reed sends her to do."

"What did he send her for?"

Nate paused as though he was thinking it over. "The last job Reed had for Lucy was in Senegal, Africa. It was for a necklace. She must've showed up to Reed's to give it to him. I don't know for certain. I just know—"

"You guys don't speak about anything you do."

"Correct." His throat worked. "But Reed would never cheat on Alisha. Promise you that. He isn't the type."

The house was dark and quiet when Nate and I entered putting our things away as he turned on some of the low lights. Warmth filled the air and lit us both up. He looked dashingly handsome with his tie slightly askew and his dress shirt on.

"I don't like leaving Alisha," I murmured. "It feels wrong."

"Yeah, but Watts has her and if he's tired or some shit, he'll know better to ask us to cover. I don't mind taking you out to see her."

"We can go see her often?"

"Whenever you want, Duchess." But even as he said it, I detected a wariness to him. Since we had left, the Primrose, Nate had been contemplative.

Reed had left without saying a word to anyone save for Kellan. He had done something but it looked like Nate understood what it was.

Nate looked tense. His jaw was tight, the muscle ticking on the side visibly as he shook his head.

"That's got nothing to do with Reed and Alisha. That's all Gabriel. Reed's just doing what he normally does. But now it's complicated as fu—"

"Why?"

"Because Alisha isn't a Titan. And she's wants answers to things Reed's never answered to."

I frowned, completely confused.

I had a quick run in with Gabriel at Poppy for once. During the time Nate was covering a crime scene with Kellan.

He *was* in fact the same man I had seen at Teaser's with Lara.

I knew I recognized him. I just didn't know what his relationship was with Lara. She had denied knowing him outright but I knew Gabriel visited Teaser's.

I didn't ask anything as I had silently tolerated his rude company while Nate and Kellan had gone to handle a body. But now? I got the intertwined webs at Titan felt more like a chokehold.

"What does Alisha and Reed's relationship have to do with Gabriel?"

He shook his head looking a little grim. "It doesn't. That's one half of their problem. I doubt Reed would let Alisha go far. Watt's is gonna stay with her at the Primrose. I don't know what the fuck Reed is thinking about anything. It's not even the stalker, he's keeping too many secrets like he always does. It's something I learned when I worked alongside him. Titan has a lot of things they don't say outright."

"Like what kind of work this woman does for Reed—"

"You know her brother—I'm guessing the family ain't horrible."

"No, Lucas is…" I bit my tongue as Nate watched me. "What? You can't possibly be jealous."

"You dated him?"

I narrowed my eyes. "Did you date Lucy? I can see you're quite familiar with her."

He made a noise looking away almost embarrassed. "Duchess."

A hot flash of jealousy ran through me. "Did you?"

"Baby—"

"Don't baby me, Nathan."

"Oh, it's back to Nathan now? Not your Nate anymore—"

"You *did* sleep with her! If you didn't you'd have told me—"

"I didn't assume you slept with Lucas Devereaux because you didn't confirm it—"

"I didn't sleep with Lucas," I don't know why he got under my skin like this. "I *wouldn't*."

His throat worked and I saw those navy eyes widen on me as he took me in.

"You didn't sleep with Lucas Devereaux."

"No. But you slept with Lucy—" I broke off biting back my next comment.

You can't get mad at him, can you?

Not when you're keeping the worst secret of them all.

I didn't know how to process the burning jealousy in my gut. Nate. With another woman.

Nate with her. I didn't even know Lucy Devereaux but I bet she was pretty.

I for one knew a thing or two about keeping secrets and even if I

345

despised Reed for hurting Alisha—I knew why he kept his secrets. I kept mine.

And by the looks of it? Nate kept his.

Standing in the foyer, my stomach twisted. Nate had that look on his face, like he was about to say something I didn't want to hear.

"Duchess—"

"*Don't.*"

"It wasn't like that—"

"I also doubt you just went on a simple date—"

"Duchess—"

"No. I don't want to do this. It's late."

And I was jealous.

Of Lucy Devereaux having any part of my man. Even though it wasn't her fault and it wasn't right. I could just imagine them together.

A beat passed. Another.

"Did you love her?"

"What?" He looked stunned. "Duchess, it wasn't like that."

"Then what was it—"

"A quick fuck and even quicker goodbye. It was never serious with Lucy—Duchess. Tell me what's wrong?"

"You stopped me from protecting Lish—"

"Your friend was already in trouble three years ago when Reed saw her—he's not gonna let her go."

"That doesn't mean I had to walk away!"

And I didn't know who moved but in another second Nate was closing the distance between us sealing his mouth over mine. Hot, steadying, commanding every inch of me to him. His tongue tasting like mint and something just Nate thrust into my mouth with no grace. No permission.

He just came and he took what he wanted.

Like some Viking conquerer. And I would let him.

I moaned a little as he rubbed my back. Over and over Nate's mouth worked over mine. Until a soft noise left me.

"It's all good, baby," he whispered over my lips. "Happens to the best of us. Lena get's like that on assignments too. Adrenaline. Fear. Anxiety. I still gotta talk to you about something but if you're not up for it tonight, just tell me. We don't gotta do nothing you don't wanna."

I didn't know what he did or how he managed to calm me down. But every single softer kiss after that eased my anxiety and fears. Until I finally felt like I could breathe.

"Tell me you don't kiss Lena after every assignment like this to calm her down."

He was fighting his laughter. "Nah, she'd kill me if I did. I think Gabriel hugs her lots and she's better after. And no I don't think they fuck."

I swallowed my anxiety down again. "Should we go upstairs?"

"Living room's fine if you're down."

I puffed out a breath realizing I'd have to just face tonight head on.

Nate stripped down to his undershirt, his tattoos showing. I caught a glimpse of myself in the mirror and hardly recognized the woman staring back. My hair was a mess. I'd put it up hours ago, but now it was falling all over the place. I gave up and let it down as we walked into the living room.

My eyes were too bright, like I was running a fever or something.

My shaking hands felt like props as I tried to light one of the lavender candles in my living room. I led the way into my space.

One I usually found comforting with its blend of white and violet, plush sofa, and soft lighting. But now?

Now with Nate there, the atmosphere shifted completely.

Maybe the smell would slow down my heartbeat. But I knew I was lying to myself. I had been since the day Nate showed up into my life.

"Is everything okay? You said we would talk when we came home about something."

I ignored that I just called it his home and mine. I ignored everything but the look on his face.

"Camilla threatened me. My family too. She said if I stayed with you, you'd end up like your mom. I left because I was scared. What if you ended up hating me? I had nothing to give you back then. I was...empty. A nobody."

He was not.

I wanted to tell him to stop.

That he didn't need to explain. My chest hurt. *Nate, you idiot. You were always enough.*

"These past few months, watching you—" he paused. Had it really been months of us dancing around each other? "I had to tell you."

He looked right at me, and I knew whatever he said next was gonna hurt. "I asked Lena to marry me. Years ago."

The words were the equivalent of a physical blow to my stomach.

If I could've I would've bent over on the couch sitting there with him, as a part of me crumbled. Broken. And completely shattered.

I had to look away my eyes trying to find anything other than my anxiety.

Trying not to let him see the tears in my eyes while he kept talking, not knowing he was tearing me apart.

"But you…you never kissed her…"

"Not like that, Duchess. I swear."

"Not like Lucy—"

"It's not like that, I promise. I fucking promise to you, Gemma. There is no woman—"

"I need a second."

Because if there was anyone in the world who could do this to me, it was him—a one Nathan Wyatt who knew exactly how to push all my buttons. I wiped my eyes unable to breathe.

I don't know why I was so sensitive to him.

Instead of feeling like a twenty-six year old who was mature and stable and eloquent—I became a nineteen-year old girl around Nate. One who felt vulnerable. Cracked open.

And I felt like he didn't choose me.

He chose so many other girls.

But me.

"It ain't like that," Nate said, his voice far away. "We were partners at work. We even talked about having kids through a clinic. I never loved Lena like I loved you. I never once thought about her like—"

"But you asked her to marry you—"

"It was a pact. It was only if we didn't settle—"

"Does Kellan know this?" I turned to him. "Kellan's going to be devastated if he hears this." Because I had seen the hungry way he'd been all over Selena at a party we'd all gone to. He hadn't stopped kissing her.

Kellan was just as obsessed with Selena and Reed was with Alisha.

348

"I don't know," Nate's navy eyes held a quiet forlorn look to them. "I just know I didn't love Lena or Lucy or any woman the way I loved you."

"Then why didn't you choose me?" I whispered. I felt like my chest was shattering into a million tiny pieces. "Why didn't you stay? Why didn't you take me with you?"

His mouth fell open. *"I would've ruined your life."*

"What?"

"Camilla said she would tell everyone I brainwashed you and raped you under duress. Camilla was going to make sure I never worked anywhere again. That my face would be plastered on every news article known to man. Duchess, what the fuck was I supposed to do?"

Nate's words hit me like a tidal wave, threatening to drown me. Along with the rage I felt for my step-mother.

They were friends. They made a promise.

Even if I tried to tell myself it wasn't romantic?

It didn't soothe anything in me as it felt like he had stabbed me with his words.

How could I tell him?

I had carried his child, felt it growing inside me, only to lose it.

The pain of that loss still echoed through me, a hollow ache that never quite went away.

I covered my mouth, trying to hold back a sob.

I gripped the couch cushions, my knuckles turning white as I fought to keep myself from falling apart.

They had shared the same beach in Capri where I had fallen so helplessly in love with him.

It was as if he had taken my memories and rewritten them with someone else. If Kellan hadn't come along, Selena would be Nathan's wife right now.

"I just wanted what I always dreamed of," Nate said, his voice thick with emotion. "A simple life. Kids. A wife."

The tears came harder now, and I had to turn away. The pain was unbearable. *Lena.*

He had chosen Lena.

Not me.

And I knew why. I knew why. It didn't change the fact that it still hurt. Did I know Camilla was evil?

Yes.

But did it ache imagining Lena with Nate?

Yes.

"You loved her," I finally managed, my voice was a croak. If that. "You chose Lena."

"I never chose Lena romantically. I love Lena so much, but...not like—"

"Not like..."

"You."

And in that one word alone I broke again.

"I only told you that I was with Andrei to protect my heart..."I blurted out, the words rushing out before I could second-guess myself. I don't know why I said it.

"I'm sorry," Nate said softly. "I didn't think I helped from the moment I showed up."

"I'm sorry too."

We both had so many regrets.

"I deserved it," he whispered. "I snuck out that night... but I never really left you. I just didn't want you to see on the news that you were married to a rapist. Who conned you for money."

"Me neither," I admitted, my voice breaking at what Camilla had done to him. "I've been stuck in that moment for seven years. Like I couldn't move."

The weight of all that time felt like it was crushing me.

"Do you feel—"

"Like you can't move on?" I finished for him. "Like you're frozen in time?"

Like both of us had been obsessed with that singular moment that left us shattered because of my family?

That's how I felt. Like it took Nathan in my life for things to start moving again.

Otherwise, I'd existed in purgatory of my own making.

We both went quiet. I looked up at him, my heart racing.

His eyes were red-rimmed, full of all the same pain and regret I felt.

"*Duchess.*"

That one word, and I was in his arms.

All the guilt, the hurt, the years we'd lost - it all came flooding out. I wanted to tell him about the baby so badly.

My body ached with the need to share that secret. But I couldn't. It would hurt him too much. And I couldn't open my mouth to say it.

Nate. I hated you because I thought you abandoned me and the baby.

The ache in me—it doesn't go away.

Sometimes I dream we had a little girl. And she had your eyes. And I can't stop thinking about her.

But the words? They were trapped in my throat, lodged there unable to leave.

Because it was everything Nate wanted.

And I had taken it away.

I couldn't break him anymore. And I stayed hugging him tighter as the emotions rolled through me, wiping my eyes as I cried and grieved for the loss of my past.

The old me.

The old Nate.

But those two people were trapped within ourselves. Maybe we'd come together to get them out?

"Do you think we can start over?" He murmured. "Ever?"

I sniffled pulling back and I felt so greedy for him I nodded. My hands shook harder as he took them in his.

"You're not upset about me and Lena?"

"I thought she was with Kellan..." As I said his name, I saw the emotion in Nate's eyes. "I thought she loved him very much when I saw them."

"She is." He didn't like Kellan. I didn't need to ask I knew Nate. "She does."

"You don't think he's good for her?"

Nate was quiet for a second. "I think he's immature. He's younger. He doesn't understand her. I don't know if he will."

"You're protective of her?" I don't know, I still felt jealous but in a different way.

Selena had been around Nate for years longer than I had. I felt jealous for the time she had him, but I understood even still—there was nothing romantic in it for her or for him.

It had been a pact. It burned, but logically I knew.

"I am." His smirk was back but it didn't reach his eyes. "Good news is, if he hurts her, Gabriel's already got a cabin upstate we can use to bury his body—"

"I will never get used to how blood thirsty you are." I shook my head in disbelief at the man he was.

"You like me bloodthirsty, Duchess."

"I like you better when you're kissing me."

His eyes met mine. "Oh yeah?"

"Yes."

He dipped his head to mine. "Lena and I...we never—"

"I know."

I remembered my girls night with Selena when I'd gotten drunk with her, progressively drinking more at her presence as Alisha's second guard. Kellen had brought her.

But I saw the way she looked at Kellan.

She didn't have feelings for Nate.

"Did you ever..." I whispered. "Like her?"

"Not like you," he admitted. "I never liked anyone the way I liked you. Lena's a good friend."

Silence. A beat passed.

Another.

"Is there anyone else I should know that you've been with?"

"Uhhh. Still want me to kiss you?"

"I'd be pretty upset after that conversation if you didn't."

His chuckle was dark. "Come here, Duchess. You don't gotta worry about nobody. Nobody's got me like you."

And that was true for me too.

SIXTY-TWO
GEMMA

The next few days were quiet.

We were getting to know each other again, figuring out this new honesty between us. Trying to start over with each other.

But there was something else holding me back. If Nate and I did get together what if I lost the baby again? What if I couldn't be a mother?

What if I let Nate down?

And the spiral began anew.

I couldn't stop myself as the thoughts took over.

Bonnie and Nigel seemed happier about us getting along. They had realized at some point we made peace since we weren't at each other's throats.

The four of us had dinner together, and it almost felt like no time had passed at all.

"I dare say, Mr. Wyatt," Nigel said, his eyes twinkling. "I might have to try riding motorcycles myself."

Nate grinned over his wine glass as Bonnie's cheeks flushed ten shades of red. "You planning on taking Bonnie out with you?"

They both sputtered in response, and I couldn't help but laugh, feeling all of nineteen again.

"You two really need a break," I laughed at their expression.

"Yeah, Gemma and I can run the household." Nate winked at my laughter.

"Oh no—" Bonnie said.

"I couldn't, sir." Nigel started.

And I laughed harder at Nate teasing them like he always had.

I felt like my family was back. And the thoughts of being a failure as a mother ebbed a little as I watched Nate tease Nigel across the dinner table, his eyes crinkling with laughter, a familiar ache settled in my chest.

The doctor had said it wasn't my fault.

But it felt like it was.

I wasn't ready to be that vulnerable, not yet. The wound of losing our child was still raw, even after all these years.

Telling Nate meant facing that pain head-on, and I wasn't sure I had the strength for that.

Not when I knew...being a father was all Nate wanted.

In the days that followed though my own jealousy was put on the back burner when Lena called Nate asking for help with a case. Because he was her old partner.

He didn't even look at me as I sidled closer when she had called and I began speaking to her comfortably as well.

At one point Nate hauled me into his lap and the two of us began working on Selena's case with her.

The casual intimacy of the moment didn't escape me even as we teased each other several times.

After Lena, Liam called us.

He updated us on his discreet challenge to Camilla, mentioning he'd delivered information to my father about Camilla's years of conning him. Which broke my heart.

When the night was said and done Nate looked at me exhausted holding his fist out. "Go team. You're technically a detective now."

I giggled bumping him back. "I'm basically a Titan now." I felt the warmth rush through me at even being a part of his world. A world I wanted to be in.

"Oh yeah? What's your nickname?" I tried to ignore the way Nate's eyes sparkled with amusement.

I pretended to think about. "There's no space for Duchess?"He grinned wider. "Hang on, what's yours? Do all you have like nicknames?"

"They're call signs. Yeah. Everyone gets one. Easier to communicate when something happens to us."

"What's yours?"

He chewed his lip. "Neptune."

"Why?" I didn't know anything about the god of the sea.

"He lives at the beach." Nate's eyes softened on me and my heart flipped as I realized what he was saying.

The beach.

The sea.

Our island.

"And for the last few years I haven't left that part of me behind. It felt like the only thought in my head."

I didn't know what to say.

The lump that formed in my throat stayed there at Nate's honesty about where his head had been.

"When I'm in danger, or when the team needed me, my call sign reminded me that I needed to focus. I couldn't lose anyone else, the way I lost you," his eyes met mine. "I promised myself I'd never let it happen again. And I never did."

I felt the tension between us then as his words left me speechless. What could I say?

"And Selena?" I whispered.

He smirked aware of me trying to diffuse my emotions unsucccesfully. "Venus. She's definitely the bombshell, seduce and destroy is her thing."

I laughed outright as he shook his head. "I can't imagine the Selena I met killing people." He nodded his expression amused. "Reed is Jupiter, the King…Evie is…I think she's Mercury…she's the closest to the sun, the intellectual she says. And the sun in her case, happens to be Gabriel. He's Apollo…"

Nate explained to me then how every single thing at Titan was rooted in deeper subtext. All of it. The way they spoke, the messages they passed.

"Nothing happens for no reason," Nate explained. "Even this case with Alisha's stalker, too many variables in the air—none of this is a coincidence and I know that's why it's bothering Reed and Lena more."

I frowned sensing something was deeply wrong. "You think someone is taunting Titan?"

He nodded his eyes grim. "I think someone out there is watching our every move. And they think they're ahead—"

"Which means we have to get ahead of them?"

He tipped his head. "Exactly."

I DIDN'T NEED TO WONDER WHY NATE USED CALL SIGNS FOR VERY LONG.

The very next day—everything was turned upside down in our lives.

"What the fuck did you just say?" Nate's voice, sharp and panicked, cut through the air. Something was deeply wrong.

Kellan had called him out of all people.

Bonnie and Nigel froze in the kitchen, their eyes wide with concern.

Nate's shirt stretched across his chest as he stood abruptly, his entire body tense. *"What the fuck is wrong with you, Watts?"*

My first thought was that Kellan and Selena had broken up. But the growing dread in Nate's eyes told me it was much worse.

"Duchess...grab my phone, text Evie..." Nate rattled off orders, his words clipped and urgent. And he began rattling off code to type into his cell phone to Evie. I understand he was signaling for help from her.

Nate spoke in rapid, terse sentences, before reaching out to Gabriel. And that was when I knew Selena was in danger.

"I can't get a hold of Lena," Nate told Gabriel, his voice tight with worry. "I called Evie...yeah, I'm with Gemma—"

And in the middle of it all, I received a call from my father.

"ARE YOU OUT OF YOUR MIND, YOUNG LADY?"

My father's voice, sharp and unfamiliar, cut through the line. After years of silence, these were his first words to me.

I tried not to let it hurt, but the pain sliced through me anyway.

Nate made a frantic cutting motion, silently urging me to hang up. But I couldn't. This was my father. After all this time, I needed to hear what he had to say, even if it broke me.

"Hello to you too, Papa," I managed, my voice steadier than the trembling in my chest. "It's been a while."

"Don't you 'Papa' me," he hissed, sounding like a stranger. "What do you think you're doing, digging into our family affairs?"

I caught Nate's worried gaze and put the phone on speaker. My heart raced as I replied. "You mean Camilla's affairs, not ours. Or have you forgotten why I left?"

"Gemma, you don't understand. You're meddling in things—" His voice rose, frantic and defensive. "You're making wild accusations about a woman who's done nothing but support this family. Camilla would never—"

"She would and she has!" The words erupted from me, years of pent-up frustration boiling over. I saw Nate's face fall, but I couldn't stop. "How can you be so blind?"

"You left us, Gemma. You chose to walk away."

His accusation ignited a fire in my veins. "Are you kidding me? I've been trying to reach you for years!"

"I never received a single call or message."

"Because she deleted them all!" I was screaming now, tears streaming down my face. I felt Nate behind me. "She's been controlling your entire life and you're too blind to see it!"

How could he not understand?

"That's enough!" he roared and for a moment I stared at the phone like it was a stranger. "I will not stand here and listen to you slander my wife. You're just jealous, Gemma. You've always been jealous of Camilla."

Was he out of his mind?

Out of all the things my father could have called me about, he chose his wife?

He never checked on *Maman*, and he never checked on me. But now he wanted to play this role? Of doting husband?

Why?

Was he so blind?

And years and years of pent up rage burst into something lethal and volatile inside of me. I had been waiting for this moment. I was prepared for this moment.

I couldn't throw a shoe at him.

No.

I did however always have a tongue on me.

I laughed bitterly. "Jealous? Of what? Of a woman who's systematically destroyed our family? Who's isolated you from everyone—"

"Camilla is the only one who's stood by me. Where were you when I needed you?"

"I was right here!" I shouted, my voice breaking. "I've always been right here, Papa. You're the one who pushed me away. You're the one who chose her over your own daughter. Was it for me when you missed my graduation to go off on your honeymoon! Nigel, bloody Nigel has been here longer than you!"

"After everything I've done, provided for you—"

"*Provided*?" I cut him off, my voice rising to a shriek. "I didn't need your money, Papa! I needed my father when some vapid bitch decided to take over my family to ruins!"

Just then, the doorbell rang, its chime piercing through our heated exchange.

Nate, who had been silently watching with a mixture of concern and frustration, threw his hands up in exasperation.

"For fuck's sake," he muttered, moving towards the door. "Who the hell is it now?"

But I barely heard him.

"Camilla has tried to isolate me and ruin your life all in one. She's a vapid bitch. And frankly, so are you!" I shrieked into the phone. "*I am done with this conversation. From this moment on, I am not your daughter. I stopped being it the day I left Capri and you let me go over a woman you barely know.*"

I was on a bloody roll. Because I had my entire heart living with me. Nothing was worth losing that freedom.

"Now I understand why *Maman* hates you." I couldn't stop it. "Why she never came back! Because she had the worst husband in the world. A man who couldn't protect her from anything in the world. You destroyed Maman. Your wife tried to destroy me. *And we both left you. You're a horrible man.*"

"Gemma—"

"No! The last thing I have ever wanted to be in this world *was a fucking Marchand! You took my life away from me. You let that vile woman into your life. I am done being a Marchand."*

And then I hung up.

SIXTY-THREE
GEMMA

A TEXT MESSAGE LIT UP NATE'S PHONE, AND I SAW THE COLOR DRAIN from his face.

Evie, a young woman we'd been in contact with, called moments later.

"Gabriel found Lena," Nate's voice shook. "But... it's not just her."

My heart stopped as I felt myself sitting up straighter. "What do you mean?"

"Alisha and Avani are with her too."

The world tilted on its axis.

Not just Selena, but Alisha and Avani—my family. I felt my knees give way, a sob building in my throat. Nate's strong arm around my waist was the only thing keeping me upright.

We rushed to the hospital together.

But Nate was gone the moment he saw Kellan Watts. Selena's partner.

"Nate!" I scrambled after him as he stormed through the hospital halls. The moment he learned of Selena's brutal injuries, his entire demeanor changed.

I knew Nate, and I'd never seen him like this.

The car was barely in park before he was rushing to her.

My heart pounded in my chest as I raced after him, my fingers desperately clutching at his arm.

I had never seen him like this before—his usual composed demeanor shattered, replaced by a raw, uncontrolled fury that terrified me.

"Nate! Stop!"

I watched in horror as he stormed towards *Kellan Watts*—the one person he blamed for what happened to Lena. I knew because I had seen his face. I knew Nate. With all my heart.

He's going to kill Kellan.

Selena was like family to Nate. I saw how much he loved her. I didn't feel jealous when I saw his relationship with her, with me, on his lap talking to her as well.

The hospital corridor seemed to part before him, nurses scattering, Adam pushing Nisha to safety, Garrett moving aside.

"*You*," Nate's voice dripped with a venom I had never heard from him before. This was not my Nathan.

Not my Nathan.

I stumbled to a halt as Nate reached for his gun, the world around me seeming to slow down.

Suddenly, I was wrenched to the side by someone—I thought it was Reed for a moment, but this man was in scrubs with blonde hair.

From my position behind the desk, I watched in horror as the scene unfolded before me. Nate was going after Kellan.

And Selena who was lying there in the hospital bed.

"*What did you say to her?*" Nate demanded, his gun pressed against Watts' forehead. "I know her, she would *never* do something stupid. *She had nothing to prove.*"

My heart raced, tears blurring my vision. *Nate, please. Do not kill Kellan.*

"Nate, do not hurt him," I pleaded, my voice breaking. "*It's not his fault.*"

"*It is!*" Nate roared, his voice reverberating through the corridor. "It fucking is. *She chose him.* I gave her to him. *She was my girl.*"

What happened next was a blur.

Kellan somehow took Nate's gun out of his hands, and I watched as the usual charming man, the golden-haired softer bodyguard Alisha had by her side, vanished. In his place stood someone else entirely.

"She's *my* girl. She *always* has been," Kellan growled. "You were her partner for five years. I was her partner for *five minutes*. And she let me in."

As he advanced on Nate, gun steady in his grip, I felt my breath catch in my throat. *This can't be happening. Not here, not now.*

"Wanna know why?" Kellan's words cut through the air, each syllable dripping with venom that made me flinch. "Because I make her better. She's safe with me—"

I saw Nate's lips move, his voice reaching me like a distant echo. "She wasn't safe days ago—"

The muzzle of the gun pressed harder against Nate's forehead, and I had to stifle a cry. My heart was pounding so hard I could feel it in my throat.

"You don't love her. You like the idea of her. I. Love. Her."

As Kellan continued to speak, I saw something shift in Nate's eyes.

"I love her so much, I scare the shit out of her. Because for fucking years, she had a partner who kept her at arm's length, too much of a coward to admit he trapped her in a fucking pact that her bleeding heart kept. Until me." Kellan's words were like daggers, each one striking deep. "She chose me."

My world narrowed to a single point—Nate, with a gun pressed to his forehead. My Nate. The father of my unborn child. My love. My only love in the entire world.

Nathan. Don't. Please, God, no.

And then, Kellan's finger moved.

The safety clicked on, loud in the sudden silence.

He handed Nate's gun back, the gesture almost casual, as if he hadn't just held my world in his hands.

As Kellan turned to leave, his eyes met mine. I couldn't hide my reaction—the utter shock at almost losing Nathan.

"My apologies, Miss Gemma," he muttered, his voice rough with emotion I couldn't decipher.

The adrenaline that had kept me upright suddenly drained away, leaving me weak and shaking.

My knees buckled, and I would have fallen if not for the doctor's strong arms catching me, holding me steady.

A sob built in my throat as the reality of what had just happened crashed over me. Everything had changed in the span of a few heartbeats.

Voices swirled around me—the doctor who had pushed me to safety, a dark-haired man I didn't recognize—but I couldn't focus on their words.

All I could think was that I had almost watched Nathan die. The father of my child. My partner. My future.

Almost.

～

I couldn't bring myself to look at Nate, let alone *speak*.

I had gone to see Alisha, but Reed had left with her and Avani hours before.

Right now, my mind was a broken record, replaying the same horrifying scene over and over.

A nightmare I couldn't escape.

A gun pressed to Nate's forehead.

Nate, dead. Nate, gone.

The moment the door closed behind us, something within me snapped.

The house was eerily quiet, and I saw him start to speak, his lips parting.

But I didn't care what he had to say.

The pent-up energy from the hospital surged through me like a live wire. Everything crashed into me. The moment I was alone—I snapped.

I almost lost Nate. I almost lost Nate. I almost lost Nate.

And in that moment, one truth blazed through the chaos of my mind with *blinding* clarity. The most honest I had ever been with myself.

I. Love. Him.

Before he could utter a word, I crashed into him.

My lips found his with an urgency, pouring every ounce of my fear, my relief, and my love into the kiss. My hands fisted in his shirt, tugging him closer.

I needed to feel him, to reassure myself that he was here, alive and *whole.*

We stumbled backwards, a tangle of limbs and gasping breaths, until my back hit the wall. Needed him. Needed this.

"*Get inside me.*"

If Nate felt what was coursing through me he didn't argue.

I needed to sink my teeth into him and keep him there.

His mouth moving over mine as he tore my dress apart, the length of him, pressing into the entrance of my body.

I gasped at how soaked I was.

"*Fuck, Gemma.*" Nate's voice was guttural. "Hold onto me."

I obeyed lifting up into his arms as he lifted me up and I bit back a wild cry as he sank me down onto his length.

I screamed into his throat at the sensations of the broad head of him stretching me open. And nothing felt better in that moment.

"*Nate…*"

"Shh, I gotcha."

"Please," I whimpered, not even sure what I was begging for. For him to fill me, to claim me, to make me forget everything but the feel of him inside me.

Nate surged forward, burying himself to the hilt in one powerful thrust.

The sensation was overwhelming, bordering on too much. I felt every inch of him stretching me, filling me so completely that it stole the breath from my lungs.

"I missed this, missed *you*," it fell from my lips as I clung to him, feeling my eyes blurring. "Fuck me. Nate. *Fuck me, please.*"

He held me tight to him as he pressed me into the door.

Setting a punishing pace with his hips as he slammed me down onto him over and over again, my screams animal and muffled into his mouth.

I clung to him like I was drowning letting him take me. Rougher. Harder. Wilder.

Not caring if anyone knew or saw. I didn't care anymore.

For so long I had cared. I had listened to the world. I didn't want to listen to the world anymore—it had no clue what it was talking about.

Relentlessly pounding into me, Nate's mouth groaned into mine as the door rattled.

"*Harder.*" I kissed him harder. Each drive was powerful, pushing me higher, stoking the fire in me. Feral.

Vicious.

"I love you." I cried out. "*I love you so much.*"

His eyes were low as he kissed me.

"I love you," his voice was guttural as I felt the tears streaming down my eyes. "I'm sorry, baby."

I couldn't stop crying as I felt our love making change into something else.

Nate's mouth found my neck, his teeth grazing the sensitive skin. I shuddered, tilting my head to give him better access.

He alternated between biting and soothing with his tongue, marking me, branding me as his.

"*Needed you for so long.*"

"*I know.*"

I was lost in sensation, drowning in the overwhelming onslaught of pleasure. Because I did know.

I had known for years. I had known Nate the way the planets knew their orbit. He was mine. He always had been. His love.

The kind that came without barriers, conditions, rules, and defied expectations.

The kind that came with acceptance, happiness, and a joy that belied logic.

Every nerve ending was alight, my body thrumming with an energy that bordered on painful in its intensity as he took me. And nothing in the world felt more familiar to me than him.

I held onto him so tightly I wanted to fuse us together into one person.

I craved it. I loved it. *Loved* him.

Nate shifted slightly, changing the angle of his thrusts, and suddenly he was hitting that perfect spot inside me with every stroke.

"That's it, baby," he growled against my ear, his voice rough and strained. "Take it. Take all of me."

I could feel my orgasm building, coiling tighter and tighter in my core.

"Nate, please," I panted, not even sure what I was pleading for.

More, harder, faster.

As if sensing my need, Nate redoubled his efforts.

His hips snapped against mine with a force that should have been brutal but instead only ratcheted my pleasure higher.

The coil inside me wound tighter, tighter, until I thought I might shatter from the tension.

And then, with a particularly hard, deep thrust, I did.

My orgasm crashed over me like a tidal wave, taking out everything in its wake. All my emotions came crashing down.

I convulsed around his cock, my inner muscles clamping down on him like a vice. I muffled my screams into his neck, whimpering, crying out, sobbing his name.

Through the haze, I felt Nate's rhythm falter.

With a low, guttural groan, he buried himself to the hilt one final time, his cock pulsing as he emptied himself deep inside me.

Dimly, I was aware we hadn't used anything. I wasn't on anything.

And I didn't care. I had always been Nate's. *Always.*

There would never be anyone else.

With Nate—I was just a woman. His woman.

And I had never wanted anything else more.

Slowly, gradually, we came back down to earth. Nate's hold on me gentled, his hands smoothing over my skin with a reverence that made my heart ache.

"Take me upstairs." I whispered, sniffling a little as I felt myself breaking. I held him close to my heart. Always.

My hands wrapped around him, holding him tight.

The first sob left me as he did.

Like I would shatter to pieces if he didn't hold me back.

"I love you," I whispered it across his skin. "I love you. I love you. I love you…" I couldn't stop crying as I kissed him all over.

SIXTY-FOUR
NATE

IT STARTED TO FEEL A LITTLE SURREAL AS GEMMA FINALLY SLEPT IN MY arms.

After rounds and rounds of wild sex that made me reconsider just what I knew about Gemma.

I think we'd been here all night and all day today.

The sun was setting outside and my stomach was grumbling painfully.

I needed to eat. But neither one of us had wanted to leave each other.

Every time Gemma reached for me, I felt that reckless abandon.

I felt that need from years ago bubbling over into something dangerously dark as I took her. I didn't even try to resist this woman.

None of the consequences had ever phased me. And after almost dying the night prior? I didn't want to let her go.

She rode me like she was trying to prove something to both of us, her kisses desperate and needy as her hips snapped and bucked.

It was as if she thought I might disappear if she stopped.

And fuck, maybe I felt the same way.

The hospital scene flashed through my mind—Lena lying there, broken. The rage that consumed me when I saw Watts.

His eyes a stark deep blue now and darker. Everything about him had changed. I fucking knew he loved Lena. More than I ever could. I wasn't angry at him about her. I was angry he was dumb enough to fight with her.

I could see it all over his expression.

But now, looking back, I saw something else in his eyes.

He knew what he'd done, the weight of it crushing him. Lena wasn't a confrontational woman—unless she got pushed into a corner. Then she reacted like a terrified wild animal.

But it was Gemma's eyes that haunted me after more than anything else.

The look she gave me at the hospital, full of fear and something else —something I was too afraid to name.

And now, as she moved above me, tears streaming down her face, I saw that same look.

Her quiet moans as she came undone, working herself on me like she was trying to claim every part of me.

"You're not on anything," I whispered, the words escaping before I could stop them. "I fucking know it."

I knew she wasn't taken anything the night prior. And it didn't matter. Not anymore.

"I don't care anymore," she breathed, wiping her eyes.

I rolled us over, my eyes searching hers. *"Gemma—"*

"Stop talking." Her kiss was fierce, demanding, her cheeks wet from crying so much. When I stopped moving inside her, she let out a frustrated growl. "Why?"

That single word held so much. Confusion. Hurt. Her need for me. And I didn't have an answer.

Not one that made sense, anyway.

How could I explain that I wanted this—wanted her—so badly it scared the shit out of me?

That I was terrified of fucking up again, of losing her, of not being enough?

So I didn't say anything.

I just kissed her back, pouring everything I couldn't say into that kiss. I brushed her hair back her eyes filled with emotion.

"Don't stop, Nate."

I felt it there. Somewhere deep. Tears leaked out of her eyes.

"Gemma."

"I almost lost you," she cried. *"Don't stop."*

So that's what this was. I felt my lips stamp on hers and I moved my hips.

I knew we were crossing a line we couldn't come back from. But maybe, just maybe, that was exactly what we both needed.

Gemma and I were determined to make up for lost time.

In one marathon session of sex and emotion, I took her every way I could. Holding her down, filling her with me.

"Is that what you needed?" I growled into her mouth.

"Yes."

Fucking Gemma returned it.

"Need me to pump you full of my cum."

A wild noise left her as she came. I groaned, filling her for what felt like the ninetieth time.

Hours blurred together.

The room filled with the sounds of our lovemaking—skin against skin, breathless moans, whispered promises.

By the time the first rays of sun crept through the windows, Gemma lay passed out in my arms. And that's where I stayed for hours my mind swirling.

My thoughts absolutely everywhere despite holding my fucking girl in my arms. It had been years of running from her. My nightmares. Camilla. And now I was right back to the moment I ran in the past. My girl in bed with me. And I had decisions to make.

I could never run from her again. The way she understood me?

Gemma defied reason and logic for me. She always had. It wasn't just that Gemma was pretty—no, that would be too easy—no, Gemma made me feel like my past, my identity, who I was? Never mattered.

I wasn't the son of a mechanic and a stay at home Mom. I wasn't someone who dropped out of college to join the military and make my ends meet scraping by. My smaller apartment. My life. My entire past was obliterated with her love—because Gemma didn't care who I was.

I healed.

And nothing else mattered to me more than feeling like I was something to someone. I told myself initially it was because I couldn't have her. That didn't exist anymore. And she was under my skin. In every thing I did.

I brushed a strand of hair from her face, marveling at how peaceful she looked. The fear and desperation from earlier had melted away. Now, both of us lay here like survivors of some storm.

If I was her freedom from society. She represented a life I never thought I could have.

We'd both spent almost a decade obsessed with each other.

Now that I had her? Every thought in my head went quiet.

And then my stomach growled again.

Better fix that before she wakes up.

Realizing we hadn't eaten in hours or left the room—I carefully extracted myself from Gemma, pausing to not stop looking at her.

Goddamn, she was pretty.

The sight of her there, tangled in the sheets, her skin marked by me, made my chest tighten with an emotion I couldn't quite name.

It had started years ago. And it never stopped. With Gemma there was contentment. And every single time she told me she loved me last night? Something more solidified in place.

Something that I knew was rightfully mine. She had never stopped being mine.

Gemma was my girl.

And right now my girl looked content. Compared to the desperation from hours ago.

Even if my mind was swirling with the relief of having her back in my arms, to everything that had happened—I knew she'd reacted because she thought Watts was going to kill me.

The night prior? I thought he might. I honestly was a dead man and in that moment I barely heard him. I only heard of what I didn't have. My only girl. Gemma.

Her eyes flashed in my face instead of Watt's brighter blue ones.

I pulled on a pair of sweatpants, not bothering with a shirt, and made my way downstairs to grab some food.

The house was quiet, and I prayed I wouldn't run into Bonnie or Nigel.

I was almost in the clear, arms full of sandwiches, milk, and Gemma's grapefruit juice that tasted like shit to me but she loved.

On the way out, I bumped into Bonnie. I stumbled back a little damn near dropping something.

"*Shit*, Bon. You scared me."

Her eyes went wide, taking in my shirtless form. They grew even wider as she noticed the lipstick stains on my neck, the nail marks scoring my chest and arms.

Her gaze darted away, a blush creeping up her cheeks.

"Did you need anything, Mr. Wyatt?"

I couldn't hold back my smile. "No, I think I got everything I need, Bon." For once. I had my whole world. Part of me lingered over worry with Lena, but I'd seen the way Gabriel watched me. He would handle it all. I knew that much.

She nodded then hesitated. "I assume you've talked?" Her eyes searched mine.

We did more than that. Gemma was currently passed out from how I fucked her. I kept that to myself. "We did. About everything."

Her eyes widened as she sighed. "Thank Christ. Nigel and I were worried about the two of you moving on from everything."

"Yeah, well, I'm still sorting through Camilla's shit." I muttered. That was a nightmare Liam was untucking. "But we talked."

Bonnie nodded. "I was worried, I didn't think she'd ever be the same again with losing you and the baby. But I'm so—Mr. Wyatt. Are you all right?"

I could feel my brows drawing together. "What…"

I felt like I heard Bonnie underwater. Like I heard her, but I didn't actually hear her words.

Losing you and the baby…

"What are you talking about? What baby?"

"Mr. Wyatt." Bonnie's kind brown eyes went wide on me. "Oh…"

"Oh what?" I rounded on her then. "What are you talking about?" I shook my head, trying to clear the fog. "Gemma was never—"

Everything inside me turned to ice.

Bonnie's face went white. My eyes widened as the milk slipped from my hand crashing to the floor. Bonnie looked down at the spill as I looked at her.

"What baby, Bonnie?"

Bonnie's eyes got all watery. "Mr. Wyatt—"

Gemma had been pregnant.

Gemma.

Lost the baby.

"Gemma was pregnant when I left?" Suddenly everything in me stopped working.

My single-minded focus was on the thought of my girl upstairs keeping a secret from me. This one. The one that had the power to shatter me.

"*That's* why she hates me." The realization slammed into me like a *fucking* train. "*That's what it is.*"

My vision went blurry as I squeezed my eyes shut, reeling.

The shock morphed into a rage so hot it nearly blinded me. She wasn't going to tell me. Was she?

I dropped the food and bolted out of the kitchen.

"*Mr. Wyatt—*"

I slammed the door in Bonnie's face as I took the stairs two at a time up to Gemma's room.

Gemma had been pregnant.

Gemma lost the baby.

I'd fucking left her.

And she never planned on telling me.

SIXTY-FIVE
GEMMA

I WOKE UP TO FEATHERLIGHT KISSES.

Nate often did this to me in the past.

The tickle of his beard as he pressed his mouth all over my neck sent shivers racing down my spine.

"Baby, you awake?" His voice was a low rumble against my skin.

"Mmmm." I was slowly coming to, the cobwebs of sleep gradually clearing from my mind. Last night had been a dream.

A feverish dream I hadn't wanted to wake up from.

Every inch of me was deliciously sore. I felt exhausted, yet more alive than I had been in years. It was all I had ever wanted.

"You know," he murmured. "You were so good last night." I clenched internally even if it hurt, as he said it. "Such a good girl for me. Did you like that?"

I nodded dreamily, melting into the bed further as he spoke.

"You were so wonderful. I came so much in you, you made a mess all over the sheets. All over me."

"Nate, I'm sore…"

He made a soft noise through his lips that made him irresistible.

"I *know*. Don't worry. I won't do anything you don't want. Don't beg me for." His tongue darted out drawing circles on my pulse. "You know, I had this thought all night…"

Nate drew me into his arms and I sighed in contentment. The strength of him seeped into me.

"All night," he whispered. "I just wanted you...full of me...In every way possible." I felt him kiss me softly as he said the words. "Do you want me to do that again?"

"I do." He had no idea.

He hummed low in his throat. "You want my babies?" And just like that an ache bloomed and a shuddering breath left me. It was a whisper but I felt my eyes water on command.

"I do."

"You wanna be mine." A statement. Not a question.

"I do." Nothing had ever made more sense to me.

"And you'll be my girl, won't you?" He growled low. "Mine in every way. Full of my seed. My cum. My life. I own this little body of yours don't I?"

"Yes." I felt my eyes water as I opened them but he was behind me, his face buried in the crook of my neck. "I have always been yours."

"You belong to me?" He didn't move as he pressed...his face was wet. "All of you, hm?"

"I do." I held him tight to me.

"And if anything happens to what's mine, you'd tell me?"

My breath caught.

"Because you don't have secrets anymore do you?"

And just like that, a sickening sensation went through me. My blood turned to ice as it hit me. It flowed through me.

All of the traces of drowsiness vanished from me.

"Nate–"

He made a noise with his lips as his teeth raked over my pulse.

"Because as far as I'm aware, I came deep in you so many times last night, you might be pregnant right now. I wanna know if anything touches my girl and my kid."

And just like that. I was caught. Trapped. I knew what he was doing. I knew. And I ached.

"Nate."

The tears in my eyes spilled over and when he pulled back enough I saw his face. His eyes rimmed red. The answer all over it.

"You know."

His mouth turned down as he looked away from me, agony written all over his expression and I reached for him.

Neither one of us said a word as I felt my eyes streaming then. "*H-h-how?*"

He shook his head swiping at his face. "Why...why didn't you..."

"*You left.*" And my voice shattered.

"Not by choice." He whispered it. "I would've never left you…" his entire face crumpled and for a moment, I didn't know what to do but I wanted to scream. "For the longest time I hated being your secret, hated not being brave enough to be your man in public. You have no idea how much I wanted you. I fucking craved you every single fucking day of my life."

My throat worked as Nate gruffly said the words into my skin.

"Every single fucking day I wondered if I went back and took you, if our lives would've been different. I spent years building up walls around that piece of my heart that I gave to you so nothing would hurt me. Seven years drowning in the misery of my own fucking making." He let out a shuddering breath. "But if I had known—Gemma, I would've fucking done anything. I would've told Reed. I would've moved heaven and hell to see you."

I wiped my eyes feeling my sob erupt out of my mouth. "You left me...you left us. I know it wasn't you…but it felt like it."

Nate looked shattered as I said it. "And you didn't...I...I let you in...I told you my truth. Why didn't you tell me? It was mine too. It was *my kid.*"

"*I didn't know how!*" My chest clenched and the grief that I had clung to for years washed over me. Was I losing him? Was he leaving me?

He shook his head turning to me, his expression making me cry harder.

"I woke up one night…and I was bleeding…"

I told Nate about that night. All of it. Breaking down as I did and Nate covered his eyes as he laid back, one arm over his face.

His breath shuddered as I got to the part about the hospital and finding out the moment I lost the baby.

"I thought it was *my* fault—"

"It was my fault." He uncovered his eyes, his gaze piercing me. "My fault. I dropped the ball. I left you. I should've fucking taken you with me."

At that his expression broke. "I should've taken you with me. Reed would've known...he would've helped..." He covered his face. "You kept this from me for *years. I fucking saw you with Lish at Teasers. I should've said something.*"

"No..." I had seen him too. "I saw you. I didn't either."

And we'd both let our misconceptions our misunderstandings eat us alive.

"It's not your fault—" I wiped my eyes. "But I wish you *had* taken me with you." I shook my head. "*Nothing*. Nothing would stop me from being with you had you asked. I would have left with you. I would've stayed."

Had the baby.

I cried harder at the turmoil in his eyes as he tipped his head back. Nate just laid there staring at the ceiling and I saw nothing but raw pain etched into the lines of his face.

The words I'd held back for seven years finally spilled out.

"I would've lived in that one bedroom with you, making pasta with our..." I broke off, unable to finish feeling my heart aching as I wiped my eyes. Our baby.

"I would've taken that chance with you. And I hated you for so long for not taking me with you. I wanted to be with you. Always. I know why we fell apart. Maybe I'm broken knowing it took us seven years to fall together."

Nate's expression crumbled as I said it.

"I know everything happens for a reason, I know I have everything I could ever want—but I *never* wanted all these things—I just wanted you. You are the only space I ever fit into. The only one I truly felt home with," I wiped my eyes more. "I felt like I wanted that family with you. That home."

But something else had occurred to me in the time he'd been with me. The younger Nate and the younger Gemma wouldn't have been able to face Camilla.

"But I don't think we would've been happy."

"What?" Nate's eyes were furrowed.

The two kids we had been? We didn't have resources or anything to their name. Titan had been starting out as a company. What if Camilla leveled them? She would. She would've came after us both.

I told Nate this.

I had been thinking about the girl I was. And how much I despised her for tolerating everything she had.

And then I had to remind myself she had made me who I was now. She had been as strong as she could be.

"I didn't want to be strong. I wanted to be yours. But because I became strong...I was *ready* to be *yours*."

I whispered the words I held back.

"I am only me when I am with you. And every single day that you were gone, I thought about you. I thought about who you'd be. I thought about us and what kind of woman would stand by your side. I grew up, Nate. We both did. And I felt like we came back together now to be better together." I felt it then, the way my throat tightened, the way my eyes stung.

"But for years I wondered why you left. And it wasn't until you came into my life that I realized why."

Nate had money now, power, control, a team—things Camilla didn't. It had taken us both time to get it together, but once we had?

We had our support system. We were a team. We came back together —better.

I took a shaky breath. "Losing the baby was the worst thing in the world. Because it made me wonder if I could be a mom."

My voice broke as I said and my lips wobbled as I clutched the comforter in my fists.

"I didn't think I could..."

I looked away at my hands then.

"And I know you just wa—want to be a d-dad..." And I broke then. *"What if I let you down..."*

I was in his arms another moment later feeling the last seven years of grief wash over me.

The sob that tore from my throat shattered something deep inside me. One after another, they kept coming.

"I thought I had no right to say this to you," his voice was dark and gruff as he held me tight to him. "Leaving you was the biggest mistake I could've made. Every single day that passed for seven fucking years I thought about you. You have been my single obsession. My only one consuming thought, Gemma. Nothing else has me in this chokehold the way your name did. But I couldn't protect you. I can protect you now. And I will."

I absorbed those words like a lifeline as he went on.

"Every single time I wanted to quit I remembered you. I never left that island. I never left the beach. I felt like I've been frozen in the moment I lost you. Before it all went to hell. And then Bonnie tells me you lost our fucking kid. Do you know how I felt? I fucking...I did that."

"No—Nate—"

"I did that. I left you. You were at your lowest—"

"Nate—"

"I did that to you—I failed you both."

"But—I didn't care anymore," I choked out. "B-because I had you *now*."

Nate pulled back to look at me with red rimmed eyes. He let out a shuddering breath.

"I have you now," I whispered. "I'm sorry I didn't say it. I was too hurt to say it. I feel like life brought me back to you for a second chance. Another opportunity at love. And I felt so stupid squandering it. Even when you weren't here in my life? You took up everything I did. Every thought that consumed me. And I couldn't let you go."

"I don't want to let you go—" he broke off.

"Then don't." That's the truth isn't it? "Don't." I held onto him. "Don't let me go."

SIXTY-SIX
NATE

SOMETIMES I WANTED TO BELIEVE I WOULD FIND MY WAY BACK TO MY girl, that our love had just taken a scenic route.

And that maybe like rivers that split apart we would find our way back to each other.

I had measured all my success and milestones against what I lost with her.

I built myself up thinking maybe one day—someday—I would feel worthy of her.

Finding out Gemma lost our kid after I left gutted me.

"You being a Mom, ever, is not your entire identity," I held her tight to me wanting to protect her forever. "I might want kids, but there's other ways to get them."

She was shaking in my arms, her frame rocked with tremors from telling me and no fucking doubt—feeling that loss all over again.

"Duchess, you act like having kids is the only reason why I would want you." Which broke my heart.

"B-b-but you want them so much—"

"Not as much as I want you." I pulled back to look into her eyes. *"Not as much as I have ever wanted you.* You were the only reason I worked the way I did. The way I built myself up. Do you have any idea how hard I busted my ass to make sure I'd never struggle again?"

Maybe I'd worked to make sure I could become the kind of man who'd protect Gemma.

I didn't know. But it made sense looking back.

I wiped her eyes. "Whether we have kids or not, I'd rather have you alive and healthy in my arms any day. We can figure out the rest later."

And as I said it? Something else clicked into place.

Maybe I wasn't chasing the perfect life.

Maybe I'd been chasing the one woman I'd walked away from. The one woman I didn't want to walk away from. And this entire time, I did want the life with the house, the wife, the kids—but none of it mattered without Gemma.

Now I saw why Watts came after me.

Because that's what he was for Lena. Her life. I'd seen it all over his eyes. Lena had given up the potential for the reality with me. And I had to do the same.

The reality of Gemma.

"I love you." I held her face with both hands as she sniffled. "I have loved you forever. I've held onto your memory for the last seven years, *you* have been my only obsession. I would've turned back time to go back to the moment I walked away to get you. To take you with me." My heart was breaking.

"Keep you by my side forever. I'm sorry I wasn't the man you needed me to be then, but I fucking promise I'm going to be the man you need now."

Fuck. Now I was emotional as fuck.

"I'm sorry I failed you. When I took the job, it was the only thing that brought me to your doorstep this time around—to never let you down. I'm sorry. I have never stopped being yours. It's always been you. And I fucking promise, I will never leave you ever again if you give me the chance to. I'm sticking by your side. I'm taking Camilla down with you. And after it's all said and done—" I felt my lips tip up. "I'm marrying you, woman."

Her laughter mingled with mine. "About time, Nathan Wyatt. Took you forever."

"I was waiting for the right moment." I kissed her steadily, this time pouring everything I could into it. My girl. I rolled her over easily. Kissing her face. Her eyes. Everywhere I could until she giggled.

I felt like I was twenty-three again. Loving her for the first time.

"You sure you're not too sore?" I murmured, searching her face.

She shook her head, pulling me in for a kiss that set my blood on fire. "Not too sore for you. I need you, Nate."

I held her after feeding her and kissing her everywhere I could. Lingering over the space over her womb.

And I tried my fucking best and failed to not break down.

So I kissed her. Steadily. Softly.

Until I felt nothing but heat running through me with the urge to possess her in every way shape and form I could.

Nothing had ever felt like Gemma.

No one would ever come close to how she made me feel and after years and years of living without her I knew I needed her the way my heart beat. I knew I needed her with a desperation that defied all reality.

"I love you, Duchess."

"Love you, Nate," she breathed against my lips.

I sank into her, slow and deep, catching her wince. "Too much?"

A growl rumbled from her throat as she nipped my lip. "Don't you dare stop."

I stilled, buried to the hilt, needing to feel every inch of her. "Feel me, baby." Gemma nodded, her lips steady on mine.

"I do."

"You love me." It wasn't a question.

"I do."

"You want to be with me." My voice roughened.

"Oh, God. I do."

"You want to be mine?" My heart was oddly calm as I said it, pulling back to lock eyes with her. "Be my wife, Gemma."

Tears streamed down her face, her eyes full of a love that knocked the wind out of me. "I do," she whispered.

"I promise to protect you," I repeated my words from years ago as Gemma wiped my eyes. "I'll cherish every moment with you. I'll be faithful to you, only you. I'll stand by you, no matter what comes our way." I almost choked as I said the words. "I fucking love you. I'm sorry it took me this long." I kissed her hungrily as I ground down into her, aware she was sore. "Don't wanna hurt you."

Gemma dug her fingers, her nails into my ass cheeks. "I want to feel you, Nate. I don't care." I groaned as I began to move in her.

"Take what's mine?"

She nodded, her expression one of pure pleasure as I ground deep in her. "I am yours."

Fucking. Finally.

I FELT LIKE GEMMA AND I NEEDED A SANDBLAST AND A HALF TO HEAL from the last few years.

But every single time I met her head on as we made love.

I didn't know how much time had passed.

I just knew she called out sick from her duties, and I stayed in bed with her. Feeding her. Taking care of my girl.

Making sure nothing ever hurt a hair on her fucking head anymore.

I'd found Bonnie in another trip around the house and talked to her. Gemma and I both needed to clear that air so Bonnie didn't think she'd fucked us both over.

She hadn't. If anything, the final piece of the puzzle finally solidified, nothing felt more real to me.

And I kept Gemma in bed with me, loving her, playing with her. Teasing her from the years I missed out on her.

She lay facing me her leg wrapped around my waist, me buried deep in her. Gemma, I was learning, didn't mind a little pain.

Or a little soreness. She didn't let that stop her.

Which was wild. And because she didn't I thought I might try something out on her.

I'd found her stash of toys she had and fit her into a pink butterfly clit vibrator before sliding deep in her pussy.

"Duchess," I whispered against her lips, as I reached for her ass cheeks. "Take a deep breath for me."

She did as her eyes widened. "Nate—"

"Trust me?"

She nodded trembling in my arms as I pressed into her ass with one of the many toys she had.

This one curved just enough. I slowly worked it in her with enough lube. Gemma gasped and winced as I reassured her to breathe. Slowly. Ever so slowly.

It took ages but I didn't care. I had all the time in the world in her. As I toyed with her, I turned on the vibrator at her clit.

A low moan left Gemma as she clung to me, letting my fingers play. Working the other toy deeper in her ass. Deeper. Until it was fully seated.

"Hurts?" I kissed her softly loving the way she rocked her hips onto me.

"A little," she whispered. "I just feel full."

I knew. I could feel how tight she was.

"Hm," I was still holding onto the vibrator. "Wait for it." Her eyes went wide for a nanosecond, before I turned it on. We both groaned.

Clutching at me, her hips working on my dick more. I growled finding her lips. "How's that?"

She said something unintelligible and I bit back a grin rocking my dick in her feeling it through her walls. I wasn't going to make it. And that was the point.

"Baby—"

"Nate—" Gemma made an adorable noise as she came just like that and I stopped holding back, letting myself go in her. "Oh God…stop it…too much."

I reached and turned it off. Both of them. Gemma sighed.

"I think I'm gonna pass out."

"I'll be here when you're up." I planned on staying forever now.

SIXTY-SEVEN
GEMMA

I needed to go see Alisha. And Avani.

After everything that had happened to everyone in the last few days, with nobody being allowed to see Selena, I needed to see my family again.

The found family I had in the girls was something nothing in the world could foster.

And so I went to go see them with Lara on her way.

When Nate and I got there, it was a much crisper Autumn morning, the air hitting at the approaching winter ahead.

I burrowed into my coat as we stepped inside the heated massive lobby of K2.

It wasn't until we got into Reed's penthouse that I had to double blink.

"I feel like I'm in an entirely new world," I murmured to Nate who hung up my coat and his.

None of the stark, navy masculine colors remained anymore.

Instead, hues of whites and pinks, combined with brighter colors—for a moment I thought I was in Alisha's apartment.

"What happened to this place?"

"Probably Alisha," Nate said just as Reed came into the hall.

His face was grimmer than usual. I could see the weight on his shoulders and how upset he looked. Even after bringing Alisha home. Nate and I looked at each other as Reed looked at me.

"Lish and Avani are in the bedroom," he said to me, his voice tight. Then, his eyes shifted to Nate. "I need a word with you, Wyatt."

I glanced at Nate, noting how he paled slightly.

A knot formed in my stomach—I had a feeling this was about his actions at the hospital.

I held out my hand in worry, not wanting to leave him for a second. Not another second without this man in my life. But I moved like my feet were in sand as he shook his head at me.

"'S all good, Duchess." And he moved away with Reed as I made my way down the hallway. I could hear Lara's voice chipper as usual.

I found myself in front of a bright, airy bedroom that looked nothing like the K2 I remembered.

Inside, I saw Alisha and Avani, both safe, both alive.

The moment the door opened and they saw me, Avani rushed at me and Alisha beamed ear to ear.

"Gemma!"

Avani was in my arms a second later and I held her tight feeling overcome with emotion. *Finally.*

Lara was already there, perched on the edge of the bed.

She offered me a small smile as I entered, but my focus was on the sisters. Alisha looked exhausted in one of Reed's t-shirts.

I settled onto the bed, pulling Avani close.

"I'd ask how you're all doing, but judging by the mochi donuts and pizza boxes, I'd say Lara's been taking good care of you."

Lara, uncharacteristically subdued, offered a small smile.

Her outfit, usually a riot of sparkles, was noticeably toned down. "I do what I can," she said softly.

As I curled up with Avani and Alisha, Lara on Alisha's other side. We were family, had been for a while now. My last name didn't matter; these girls were my world.

The thought that I'd almost lost them to some stalker made my throat tight.

"I'm so glad you're all okay," I managed, blinking back tears.

Alisha let out a soft laugh, though it didn't quite reach her eyes. "Me too. I seem to have a slight case of memory loss which I think I should be grateful for considering I cannot remember *anything*."

"And maybe that's for the best," Lara interjected, propping herself up on one elbow. With her dark eyes and high bun, she looked impossibly young. "Some things are better left forgotten, Lish."

I caught the worried look Lara shot Alisha, filing it away for later.

Turning to Avani, I noticed her wiping her eyes. I held her tighter as she spoke. "Honestly, I wish I didn't remember. Any of it."

Something in Avani's eyes caught me off guard—a pleading look that made my heart clench. What wasn't she saying?

What was that?

"I'm so glad to see you both safe," I said, glancing between Alisha and Avani. Then, noticing Avani's restless fidgeting, I added softly. "Avani, did you want to show me something?"

Relief flooded Avani's eyes as she nodded.

I turned to Alisha. "Mind if I steal your sister for a bit?"

"Go ahead," Alisha smiled, waving us off. "I need to interrogate Lara about Liam anyway."

Lara groaned dramatically, flopping back onto the bed. "There is nothing to interrogate."

"Lies," Alisha whispered. "Pure lies…"

"Didi," Avani said softly. "I'm just going to show Gemma what Reed got for me."

Alisha's smile turned teasing. "Don't let them gang up on me, Gemma. Those two are always conspiring."

I grinned, recognizing the deflection for what it was. "Probably for your own good. We both know you're terrible at taking breaks."

As Avani took my hand and walked me into her bedroom, the guest room at K2, I marveled a little at Reed's ability to turn the space into an upscaled version of her former bedroom.

But the moment the door closed on us Avani turned to me.

She burst into tears and held onto me. *"Please don't tell Alisha."*

For a moment I was stunned. "Darling…who are you talking about?"

"T-T-Thierry…" she stammered. "He hasn't—he didn't—I didn't—" she was sobbing so hard into my chest I felt my chest expand painfully and contract at the sound of them. "He d-d-d-oesn't care."

"Sweetheart, please tell me what happened?" I held her face in my hands as she sniffled and hiccuped.

Brokenly Avani explained that since she'd been injured and at K2, he hadn't spoken to her, hadn't reached out to her, and his number was disconnected.

At those words my blood ran cold.

"His number was…disconnected?" It was a whisper from my lips. Because it was all so familiar.

The way she was crying. The way she was breaking down. I knew it. Because that had been me years ago.

And Avani was *younger*.

Avani's face crumpled and I held her tight to me. "I'm sorry, I'm so sorry—"

"Nonono, don't apologize, tell me what happened?" I held her face as she hiccuped and told me what she could.

Because she'd been at K2 injured and she wanted her person. He had been her person.

"He…he…he hasn't—" she couldn't even form the words and I held her to me. Only one thought went through me.

"Did he…what happened before you…" *How did I even start?*

"He-he-he was coming to get me that night…and then he said he was running l-late. I was w-w-w-waiting—" she sobbed as she told me after she'd been brought to K2 after the hospital Reed had given her a new phone. "I was waiting for him…when it happened…"

She broke down as she explained how she hadn't heard from Thierry since and when she called him the line was disconnected and he wasn't speaking to her.

A flare of anger coursed through me as she cried harder into my arms.

I wanted to cry for her. My heart broke. I needed to go see him. *Why was he doing this?*

This wasn't like Thierry at all—

Unless something happened.

Unless someone made him.

Unless someone else was the reason why he was in this position in the first place.

But who? Who would ever stand to gain from tearing someone like Avani down?

Privately, I had always seen Avani's relationship with Thierry as similar to mine and Nathan's.

Now, watching her break made my heart ache.

Sharp thorns of regret and disbelief dug into the space where I had trusted Thierry not to hurt her.

It didn't make sense to me.

But there was another question niggling in the back of my mind.

"Did you and Thierry..." How could I ask this without coming across as insensitive? "Did he ever...?"

I looked into her wide, tearful eyes. "Did you two...were you romantically involved? Physically that is?"

She shook her head turning several shades of pink. "Not...not like that...he said he wanted to wait...but we—"

"It's all right. I just—" I broke off running my hands over her reassuring myself she was safe as I hugged her. Avani didn't stop crying harder.

"I don't know what I did wrong—"

"You did nothing wrong—"

"He won't talk to me—"

"I know, darling—"

"I don't know where he is—"

"I'll find out, I promise. I'll talk to Talia." I held her tighter my only concern in the back of my mind still there.

"No," she shook her head. "Nobody can know. Nobody knew about us. I was staying with him."

I don't want you to be pregnant and alone.

Not that she would be. But I would personally shoot Thierry myself if he did *anything* to her.

I didn't take him for the type, but at least there wouldn't be the same kind of loss. Heartaches weren't all the same.

"Alisha doesn't know," her eyes were haunted as she looked at me, red rimmed and swollen from crying. "I can't tell her."

"It's okay I won't say anything."

"And Reed... I know Reed would be angry...I know he's protective..."

"I know," I held onto her. "It's okay. It's okay."

It wasn't okay.

Avani sobbed into my chest like a wounded animal.

That was an understatement considering the lengths he went to keep both of them safe—I broke off—the lengths Reed went to.

Reed.

My mind was spinning.

No. Reed wouldn't gain anything by hurting Avani. No, he would want to protect her.

Especially if he felt she was being manipulated by an older man.

But even if Reed knew about Thierry, why would he ever tell him to stay away?

As protective as Reed was, Thierry wasn't a problem or a threat to anyone. Even if he was older, Avani and he had been closer for a long time.

What on Earth was going on? I held Avani who was crying tighter and tighter.

"P-p-p-lease don't tell Alisha…she has e-e-enough going on now… and she has a h-h-head injury…"

"I know, darling. Shhh. I have you."

I wiped my own eyes remembering what this felt like.

Heartbreak was different when you genuinely loved someone.

"…I hate him so much."

I closed my eyes.

Because Avani didn't know but I was reliving my worst moments.

And I prayed to everything Avani was telling me the truth—and that she *hadn't* slept with Thierry.

Because if she turned up pregnant in a few weeks I'd kill him myself.

SIXTY-EIGHT
NATE

THE MOMENT THE DOOR SHUT IN REED'S PERSONAL GYM, I GOT A VIEW of the Hudson river.

And then I got Reed's fist in my face.

The impact was a burn I should've seen coming after years of him kicking my ass.

Nobody fought like Reed and Gabriel.

Those two might as well have been Siamese twins with the way they moved.

I should've fucking known he was going to kick my ass. Should've seen it coming.

I groaned as I felt it hit my cheek and I stumbled back. "What the—"

"A fucking marriage pact!" He shoved me into the mats. *"That's what you had with her!"*

Oh shit. Everyone knew.

And they were *pissed.*

Reed was on me straddling me then bearing me to the ground with his arm on my neck. His storm cloud eyes were vicious and lethal as he looked into my own.

"Watts didn't fight her about an assignment. He fought her about you."

And then his fist got into my face. Right into it. I groaned. Shoving

390

him off was like pushing a tank off me. Reed was one of the few people who could fight Gabriel. And taking him on was another beast.

"We broke it off—"

"Did you?" He asked me. *"Did you let her go the moment you fucking knew you didn't love her like Gemma?"*

Shit. I *hadn't*. But it didn't matter.

"Lena is an adult—"

"So are you," Reed growled, slamming me against the wall. I groaned at the impact. "You knew better. You fucking knew what Lena went through in Havana. All Gabriel and I wanted was for her to have a better life—"

"By what?" I spat back, getting in his face. "By killing people and being a spy?"

"Gabriel never planned on keeping her in this life forever!"

I fell silent, stunned by Reed's words. He dropped me, his face livid.

"I'm done with you right now," he snarled. "Lena came from nothing. She didn't need you or your stupidity. That pact? It was never about her. It was all about you. You think I don't see that?"

His words hit me like successive punches to the gut.

"I saw her with Watts. Alisha says she's happy—truly happy. Something she never was with you." Reed's voice was cutting. "The moment you realized you didn't love her, you should have let her go. Instead, you kept her tied to your idiotic pact!"

Reed's imposing figure seemed to fill the room.

I could see how much he was holding back, knowing his girlfriend had been a target. Reed loved Alisha fiercely.

"I've been cleaning up your messes for so long," Reed continued, his voice rising. "But I never thought you'd go after Lena. Not her. Out of all the women in your life." He took a deep breath. "Watts and Lena fought. She went out alone, doing God knows what, for whatever reason. *And she almost died!"*

Reed was shouting now, something he rarely did.

He'd worked tirelessly to shape the team, and losing Lena in any capacity was a devastating blow. If anything happened to her, I knew Watts would follow her without hesitation.

But my heart ached for a different reason. Because I was right. Lena was an adult. And she had made a choice too. When she ended it, it ended for me.

She hadn't told Watts until the night they fought. I didn't think that was on me.

"Yeah, that's what I fucking thought!" Reed snarled, his eyes blazing. "What the hell am I supposed to do now?"

His composure, held together for so long, was finally cracking. Because I was Reed's right hand. He trusted me to not fuck up with the team. Everything else was fair game. But not the team. We had rules about that.

But I wasn't about to take this lying down. My own anger flared.

"I've done everything you've ever asked of me," I spat back. "Don't I deserve to be happy too? You and Alisha—"

Before I could finish, Reed was on me again.

He slammed me against the wall, his forearm pressing into my throat.

"Keep her name out of your mouth," he growled, his voice low and dangerous. "Alisha and I are *nothing* like you and Gemma. I didn't spend *seven* years avoiding her, *hurting her, lying to her and to myself."*

My heart sank at how much information he had.

"Liam informed me of Gemma's ties to you. Old security camera footage aside, you thought you'd lie to me?" He leaned in closer, his eyes hard as steel. "About Camilla threatening you? About everything?"

His arm suffocating me even still.

"Who—" I gasped.

Reed's voice was a growl. "I didn't tell Alisha about a black ops assignments, or any of the things we keep buried. It's my job. She thought I was with someone else, but I *wasn't.* I would never play games with her."

His gaze bore into me, those storm-cloud eyes maddeningly bright.

"But you? You kept Lena on one side of your life and Gemma on the other. Did you really think it wouldn't all blow up in your face the moment Watts got involved?"

Reed had always been level-headed. Always.

But right now, he wasn't.

I got that. He'd finally lost it on me.

Reed, who had been patient. But even with all that said. I got why he was angry with me. I did.

But it didn't excuse the fact that I'd been fucked over too.

"Camilla came after me—"

"I fucking know she did! And I would take that bitch out in a fucking heartbeat the moment she stepped on American soil—" Reed was *pissed.* And it took a lot for him to get to this point. "I would take her out if it meant not bothering either one of you! *But you should've came to me!"*

I had never seen Reed this livid. His voice echoed off the walls.

I took in air as he let me go finally. Gasping and trying to catch my breath as my lungs struggled.

"You need to get your shit together—"

And I would.

"I'm out."

He stopped. Just straight paused. Reed was my oldest friend. But I had to say the words.

The words left my mouth before I could even stop them. But as they hung in the space between us? It felt more right than it ever had. I watched storm-cloud eyes widen on me. He was stunned. I was stunned.

Especially once Gemma and I had decided what we had.

A family. A life.

I could support my kid with her. I had the money.

"I'm out. I don't wanna do this anymore. I never wanted it. I only did it to be someone."

But I wasn't anybody now. I looked at Reed clearing my throat the long overdue confession trapped in it.

"I didn't want this. I took the job right after Camilla threatened me the first time. And I did everything for the team. Everything I could. I did work my ass off. I told the truth. Most of the time. Lena was my girl. But she doesn't want me the same way. I was just her safety net to get her through the shit moments."

I knew Reed knew Lena would never settle for me.

And I always figured she would make the right choices.

Because she always did.

I shook my head.

"But I don't wanna do this anymore."

Reed's throat worked. "You're out."

It was a statement.

Like he'd seen it coming.

But of course he had.

"I'm done at Titan after Gemma. When she says she's done. And her contract ends—I'm done. I've given everything to Titan. I have. Built it right up with you since day one. It has a piece of my soul in it just like you and the team. But I have never wanted anymore than what I've got right now. Gemma? It's always been her. And you fucking knew it, didn't you?"

I breathed out.

"I'm not trying to fuck you over. I'm trying to choose me for once. A future. A life. A partner." I shook my head.

"I'm sorry about Lena. I swear to fuck all it was just a simple promise. And we did end it. But Gemma? She's it for me. And you know if this was Lish? You'd walk the fuck away from Titan in a heartbeat for her."

Something dark crossed Reed's expression at the mention of that.

He knew just as well as I did—he would do anything for Alisha.

And for me? Walking away from Titan hurt? But the moment I said the words?

Peace filtered through my heart. This life we lived? Was short-lived. It wasn't normal. It wasn't easy.

But it was good for me for what I needed when I needed it.

Now? I'd outgrown Titan. My body, my back and my motives were all fucked. I wanted something different. I'd outgrown the man I used to be. I was in denial if I thought otherwise.

Reed was quiet as he took me in. And he tipped his head at me. "Fine." I saw it all over his eyes

What do you want more than anything else in the world?

I wanna be a husband. A father. A lover.

Just a man.

Just Nate.

What would she want in someone like me?

The answer was always right there.

I had always been enough for her.

Just me.

SIXTY-NINE
GEMMA

"WE REALLY SHOULD STOP SNEAKING OUT."

I panted into Nathan's mouth as he lifted me up and down on his cock.

"Why?" He grinned pounding into my body somewhere so sweet I cried into his mouth. "I thought we were doing great just like this."

A laugh bubbled up from my throat as I giggled into his kisses. Before long they were turning into moans.

We were hiding in the closet out of all places. The freaking closet.

"You had meetings all day," he whispered hungrily. "When was I supposed to get you?"

I moaned into his kisses as I felt my body give in exploding with the force of my orgasm.

Nate groaned louder as he went harder prolonging the sensations.

"There you go, baby. Let me have it."

"Nate!'

He quickly fixed up my clothes after and carried me up to my room both of us hurrying and laughing as we did.

It felt so good to have him back in my life.

And just like anything in life—it wasn't without struggles.

Within days of finding out Nate wasn't going to be in Titan any longer.

I got a wake up call from the publicist I had hired months prior.

"Miss Marchand," Pauline sounded worried. "There is a tiny matter at hand that might require your attention…" As she explained my brows were at my hairline when she finished.

"Camilla blasted photos of me and Nate…"

Nate's head whipped around to me as he took his phone out. At the same time his phone began going off.

"Liam," Nate whispered.

Pauline began explaining how the paparazzi stalking me had caught photos of myself and Nathan. And that the headlines were buzzing.

"They're painting you as a flight heiress having an illicit affair with her guard," Pauline said calmly. "But don't worry, we are shutting it down as we speak. We have a rep from Titan Security, working with us in their cybersecurity department."

It was endless.

I wanted the floor to open up and swallow me whole, but I recognized this as another tactic from one vindictive bitch.

And I was tired of playing nice.

"What are you thinking, Duchess?"

I took a deep breath. "It's time to fight fire with fire. Camilla wants a war? I'll give her one. I am tired of being a prisoner to my name. I no longer want it. I want to stand on my own." And the other thing. "Our love isn't anything to be ashamed of. I refuse to let her soil anything to do with us over what? My bloody image? I don't care. My past, our past dictates nothing—we do from now on."

His eyes lit up watching me. I huffed out a breath. "Don't start—"

"You're so hot like this, baby."

I felt laughter bubble up as he kissed me. "I'm here for you the whole way. I promise."

Over the next few days, I set my plan in motion. A restraining order was filed against the paparazzi and Camilla.

My attorneys prepared a defamation lawsuit against her with the evidence we did have.

I prayed it all worked out but I also knew besides that? I needed to fight back. In every way I could.

Camilla was a narcissist. This was her game. To get a reaction out of me and I couldn't allow for that to happen.

I didn't feel bad about my father regardless of his situation.

"He's an adult," Nate explained. "He made his bed. Now he can lie in it."

And so when I sat once again with the same journalist to state my point of view I knew I couldn't balk.

I sat with her in a quiet room, Nate ever-present at my side. Now more than ever.

Alisha and Avani and Lara knew what was happening, but Alisha had warned me something else was happening right now. Something with Reed and he was busy.

But he trusted Liam to do right by him to report it all to him.

My publicist suggested I go through with an article that she coordinated to be released as a statement from me.

She'd found a journalist she'd frequently worked with, approved by Titan, who greeted me with a warmer disposition than most. Nate was in the room with me and she sat down to ask me a series of questions.

Eventually, we got to the most pressing one.

"And you've been with Mr. Wyatt for some time?" she asked me.

"I don't think it's appropriate to even discuss my relationship with him. He does his job. And I do mine. Independent of our relationship. But yes, I have—" I broke off to look at Nate.

My heartbeat ratcheted up.

"I have loved Nate forever. He's my first love. And the only thing I ever wanted in life. I would do anything for him. But I didn't leave my family for him. I left for me. I chose myself. And my sanity…"

And then I went and spoke candidly about what Camilla had done to me over the years.

What she had done in Capri. And all the things I had lost.

And then she said. "The effects of these machinations must be devastating on your body."

I smiled not feeling a thing.

"It has been. As a matter of fact Nate and I just dealt with one of the worst things I could deal with."

And then it was out of my mouth.

"I miscarried my child years ago because of Camilla."

And I didn't think my voice would break but it did.

I swallowed as she stopped writing to look at me with empathy.

"I lost my baby and Nate's. And I felt like such a failure as a mother

397

for a long time. I felt the world shaking underneath my feet like nothing would ever be the same again. I was separated from Nate for a long time holding things back thinking if I kept all my secrets to myself the world would somehow leave me alone. That Camilla would leave me alone. But the truth is, Camilla is one of the reasons why my life is where it is and her constant hounding created the most unsafe environment for me to exist in." I paused. "And my baby."

I didn't look at Nate to know how he felt.

This was enormous. I was leveraging everything against her.

I had to. I needed to. Because this was bigger than me. I wanted this to be known.

Camilla wasn't special. She wasn't even unique.

There were a million other women out there just like her—vindictive bitches who lived off their daughters suffering.

And I wasn't even her *real* child.

Distantly I remember a name I had a hard time piecing together over the years. Natasha? Nadya? I couldn't remember.

"I am utterly devoted to my life with Nate. To my life with my friends. Whom Camilla has gone after." I continued finding my voice wavering but I kept going. "Countless times, I have been threatened, belittled, berated, and I am done with it. While this may not clear the air and everyone is unfortunately entitled to their opinions, this one is mine —I am done letting Camilla dictate how I live my life."

As she spoke, I wiped my eyes and I realized for once in my life? I felt more powerful than I could've felt.

Ever.

Nate by my side. He wouldn't be a part of Titan if I cut him free on his contract. And make him *my* husband.

Potentially pregnant since I had missed my period.

And now? Standing up to Camilla?

Seven. Years. Later. I was finally doing it right.

Except when I finished the interview and everything was done I went over to a pale looking Nate. He looked unwell.

"Darling—"

"Gemma," he said, his voice tight. "It's your father."

And just like that, everything came to a crashing halt.

My father was dead.

SEVENTY
NATE

In a matter of seconds everything shattered.

Nigel and Bonnie were devastated regardless of their personal stances.

The two of them had gotten together watching Gemma and me—and both of them were devastated.

Including Gemma who looked like she'd been punched.

I didn't know how to console her but hold her as I got the news.

Her mouth opening in horror. One moment, we'd been against Camilla.

And the next?

Gerard Marchand was dead.

And the kicker?

He had left *every single thing* in his will to Gemma.

I didn't know who was more stumped. Me. Or Liam who delivered the news to us courtesy of him hacking into everything.

"...and to my daughter, Gemma Aurelia Valois Marchand, I leave the entirety of my estate, holdings, and assets."

Gemma was pale on the couch as she cried her eyes out as Liam was on speaker.

"Miss Marchand, I believe that brings your current net worth to..." As he said the amount my eyes went wide as she didn't even look phased.

Gemma's a fucking billionaire.
Several billions...that's several billions.

As an heiress to a fortune, Liam listed off Gemma's portfolio of assets. My head was swimming and I couldn't imagine what Gemma was feeling as she numbly nodded.

"The Herondale Estate—"

"Yes," she murmured. "That's his favorite—"

"That's yours in full..." Liam went on listing every single fucking property they owned it sounded like. Until he said. "...there's twenty-six more on the list you need to approve..." And he kept going.

I swore internally as he rattled off Gemma's investments, business interests, and everything she needed to do now that the entire Marchand fortune...was hers.

Gemma was now the steward of her family's wealth and legacy. And she was now working with a team of financial advisors, accountants, a fleet of lawyers and her publicist was scrambling overtime.

On top of it all?

Even with the death of Gerard, it seemed like Gemma—who had no idea—had no time to even grieve.

"I'm sorry," Liam apologized. "I know it's sudden. But I think you need to know now. Camilla might be coming after you. She hasn't landed on American soil yet. When she does, we plan on holding her in custody."

Gemma's face had paled beyond belief. "Do you think this is why Camilla was trying so hard to tear me down?"

"I think so," Liam said. "Reed and I didn't see this curveball coming. But I guess it worked."

"But why?" Her voice was a croak. A whimper. "Why? None of this makes any sense."

"It doesn't have to." Liam said. "You have a meeting in a week with the folks invested in this. You are now in control of everything. Every. Single. Thing. And Camilla—"

"Is going to be livid." I finished watching my girl realize the extent of what just happened.

To say the next few days were a storm was an understatement.

I didn't understand half of it.

400

All I saw was my girlfriend, soon to be wife hopefully, now become…what she had never wanted.

Even I saw it all over her face. She had grace. She did.

But I also saw the extent of who she was written all over her face. The way she adjusted in her heels. The way she took everything in like it was foreign to her.

"I don't know how to do this, Nate."

"You're already doing it, baby."

"And you…" her eyes searched mine. "This isn't your quiet life…"

I held onto her face. "What did I say?"

Her smile was watery. "You're not going anywhere."

I looked at her. "I'm not going anywhere, baby. I've spent my entire life waiting for you. You will never go through anything alone anymore. As long as I'm around. I swear it. We've already been through everything. I won't ever let you go again. I thought by leaving you in the past, I could protect you. In all reality? I was always meant to be by your side. I'm not going anywhere, Gemma."

The look in her eyes was all I needed to know I had stunned her. And rightfully so. I couldn't imagine a life without Gemma. Not anymore. I had for the last six years and it had taught me enough.

And because privately as I held her, I knew regardless of what happened—if Gemma was in fact the sole owner of *all* things Marchand —Camilla wasn't done with her.

Not by a long shot.

Something told me something worse was on the horizon.

And I had to be there for my girl.

"I'm not going anywhere."

THE DAYS BEGAN BLURRING FOR US INTO ONE DAY AFTER ANOTHER UNTIL two weeks passed with Gemma poring over finances, Haven expansions for Sonya and putting up a domestic violence shelter and home while Sonya recovered from an accident she had.

Gemma grew frustrating muttering in French as she took over Marchand Holdings International.

Now she wasn't an heiress. She was a fucking billionaire.

From private banks, art collections, real estate developments, and philanthropic foundations—I didn't even know how much power Gerard had.

The connections, the callers, the flowers being delivered, and the food. It was insanity.

It was completely over my head even after years of being a guard for the wealthy—the Marchand wealth was like nothing else. And it made everyone else pale in comparison.

But something in me had changed with Gemma's love.

I no longer felt like I was running from her.

For the longest time I had built chains and iron walls around my heart thinking I could protect myself, not realizing Gemma had taken my heart with her all those years ago.

Now I felt whole.

And I was willing to be whatever she needed from me in her journey. Her safe haven. Her partner. Her protector.

No longer running away but towards her.

A future, the light, and a new life.

One where Camilla wasn't going to take anything away from me.

SEVENTY-ONE
NATE

SOMETHING WAS WRONG.

Spooky.

Off about the house when we got home.

Gemma and I got back from meeting with Adam Whittaker at Haven, when I felt the back of my neck prickle.

Something is deeply wrong.

"Nate?" Gemma reached for me in the dark, dim sunlight still seeping into the house. The space felt colder, dead, and empty.

Like a ghost town. In the house that usually smelled of lilacs. One lamp lit on for us from Bonnie who was…not here.

I tried one of the light switches and it didn't turn on. At all.

And I felt the spooky sensation crawl up my spine.

The silence was more than deafening without the hum of all the electronics in the room.

"What just happened?"

"Breathe, baby."

I was already reaching for my gun and my phone. "At least I have service. I'm going to check the circuit breaker. Is it in the basement?"

She shook her head. "Upstairs near my room."

"Stay here." I hadn't heard from Bonnie. I knew Nigel had stepped out but it wasn't like Bonnie to be quiet.

"On second thought, do me a favor, baby." I motioned for her to follow me and I not to gently manhandled her into the coat closet. "Stay here."

Her eyes were wide with understanding and fear. "Nate."

"I mean it. Stay here. Do not under any circumstances leave. Text Liam if I don't show back up in ten. Do you copy?"

Gemma's nod was shaky and I quickly kissed her before shutting the door. She'd lock it from the inside out.

I quickly and silently made my way up the stairs. I cleared the hall and everything looked fine.

Nothing looked out of the ordinary as I cleared Gemma's room. Pausing in front of mine. Where the door was open. And suddenly the back of my neck prickled.

I had closed it earlier. I remembered that. Gemma and I had the habit of closing the door of the rooms we weren't using.

The security system hadn't triggered anything. The cameras hadn't gone off. Was Bonnie in there? I didn't want to trip the lights anymore.

I was fine with operating in the semi-dark—it was my ally at this moment. I slowly approached the room, gun drawn.

Before I even swept into the room, I knew—I fucking knew—something was off.

Every instinct in my body was screaming. I registered the body on the floor as being Bonnie's before my head snapped to find Camilla holding a gun to me. Except she looked wild and off. Composure completely gone and her outfit wrinkled, eyes wilder than ever before.

A kind of madness in them that made psychopaths look sane.

"Don't move," I growled. *"How the fuck did you get in?"*

I saw Bonnie unconscious and I hoped to fucking God she wasn't dead. Because she had to have let Camilla in. But why?

"You've got nerve speaking to me like that, boy." Camilla sounded different. Her eyes were wild and unhinged. "Considering I let you live this long."

"You didn't let me do anything you psycho bitch—"

She waved her gun. *"That's enough! I let you live."*

She's insane.

She's losing her mind.

Gerard left her nothing.

And now she's come to collect.

404

My anger was overriding my caution to stay calm.

"I've spent years running from your bullshit. Your evil. I'm not running anymore. Gemma is my life now. Not my past. She's my future. And you aren't taking anything away from me."

I hadn't seen her face to face in years.

She'd hurt Bonnie. And now she was in my house threatening me. My vision turned into a tunnel of red hazed fury.

She was threatening my world again. And this time she wasn't walking out of here alone.

"You got some nerve—"

She threw something at me. "Get Gemma to sign this. Hand over everything to me." She pointed her gun at Bonnie. "And she lives."

I barked out a laugh. *"Are you fucking kidding me right now? I've got a gun on you, bitch. I'm not doing shit. If you so much as shoot Bonnie, I'll put a bullet in your brain. Easy. I've been itching to do that for years."*

My fingers tightened on my gun, years of training at war with the urge to just end it right here—right now.

Gemma was downstairs. Sage. Bonnie was unconscious. And I couldn't risk Nigel coming back to this shit.

"I'm not signing shit. You move. You die."

Camilla took a step forward to me and I held the gun to her.

"Don't you fucking move."

I didn't get another word in. I couldn't. I saw the dot appear quicker than I thought possible. Over Camilla's head and my eyes widened in shock.

Sniper.

I fucking know that dot.

I was the one behind it years ago.

No fucking way.

And then in another second Camilla's head snapped back as the shot fired and I hit the floor, sparks going off in my vision.

I heard someone screaming my name.

"NATHAN!"

Gemma.

Ohfuckingshit.

I was crawling out the room to find Gemma rushing towards me horrified. Fuck, she was supposed to stay in the closet.

I moved lightening fast hauling myself up and dragging her into a room and onto the floor, tackling her faster than I thought I could.

Another shot went off again.

"GET DOWN."

I didn't know what the fuck just happened.

I held Gemma tight to me waiting for another shot. A sniper.

Holy. Fucking. Shit.

Camilla got taken down by a sniper...

Not taken down.

Executed.

I covered my body with Gemma's waiting. Looking around to make sure we weren't visible. I quickly explained to Gemma what was happening.

"Stay down. Stay down. We need to stay out of sight. Someone just shot Camilla. I don't know if they're out to get us as well."

"*What*?" Gemma sounded as panicked as I felt but my training kept me composed. I covered her from top to bottom.

I was waiting for another shot.

The silence was deafening and spookier than anything I had ever felt. Someone was out there.

And I didn't know who had it worse for Camilla than Titan.

Unless there was someone else involved this entire time.

SEVENTY-TWO
GEMMA

Liam had Titan operatives rush to the house in under an hour.

Nate hovered with me nearby trembling at the idea of Camilla attacking Bonnie.

Nate held me tightly, his lips over my forehead.

The first thing I had done the moment I heard the shot go off, was ignore everything I could think of. I heard the sound of breaking glass. And I screamed running to Nate.

I kept seeing him hurt. Injured.

Almost losing him over and over again had conditioned me to go after him. I hadn't stopped crying the moment I'd been in his arms.

Even with the operatives, I kissed him solidly for so long as he explained it all to me.

We'd checked on Bonnie who woke up with a head injury from Camilla.

Nigel had been distraught as he'd come home to find us in pandemonium.

Eventually Bonnie had tearfully explained to me that Camilla had held a gun to her demanding to be let into the house.

Bonnie knew the security code to the door and entered and once she had, Camilla had her take her upstairs to the breaker panel with the gun held to her head.

"We were on the other side of the house," I whispered. "She was trying to protect us…" I had almost lost my family. I couldn't stop breaking down in Nate's arms.

Bonnie had cried when Nigel had finally come back to find complete chaos as they'd carried and cleaned up Camilla's body.

One of the darker haired operatives with dark eyes and a muscular build—Landon—came up to Nate and filled him in on a few things with me listening.

As they spoke my eyes drifted to the windows and the curtains.

I couldn't shake the sensation of being watched even still. Nate recounted how he'd caught a sniper shooting at Camilla.

"I have to report that to Mr. Whittaker. Unfortunately, he's unavailable to make it. But I can track it."

"Where's Killian? He's usually with you guys," Nate asked.

Landon looked a little embarrassed. "I'm covering for Killian…he's about to be a dad."

Nate's face fell. "*What*?"

For some reason Landon grinned, his face splitting into a handsome grin as he adjusted his beanie turning a little red. "His wife's having a baby and he needed a break."

"His *wife*? *When* the fuck did Killian get fucking married?" Nate's face split into a smile even if his expression looked like Landon had grown two heads. *"You're shitting me."*

"I wish I was." Landon looked amused at Nate's reaction. "Nisha and Killian have been dating for fucking ever. But I wasn't expecting him to be a dad."

"I take it Killian is not a likely candidate for settling down?" I whispered.

Nate shot me a look. "Baby, you ever meet him? You'll see why."

Landon grinned wider. "Reed's giving him a few months off for fucking paternity leave while he figures this out with Nisha, so you'll be seeing me and Derek a lot more."

Nate blinked a little bemused. "Killian…go fucking figure."

I didn't know who Killian was but judging by the look on Nate's face that was the last person he expected to become a father.

Or a husband.

He swore softly as Landon looked back at Nigel and Bonnie.

"Those two are shaken up. But otherwise, the place checks out. Bonnie said she let Camilla in under duress."

Nate's nod was curt. "She was scared."

"Good thing for the fucking sniper..." Although Landon looked far from pleased and his eyes landed on me. He held out a black card to me with gold claw marks. "Have you ever seen this card, Miss Marchand?"

I frowned down at the card studying it. "No. What is it?"

"Mr. Whittaker said you were connected to the Nash family. Are you sure you've never seen this?"

I shook my head. "No. I don't know what it is. Is that a business card?"

Landon looked at me and Nate. "No. Just routine questions. If you guys are good, I think my guys are done."

Nate pulled me into his side. "It's gonna be fine, Duchess."

I nodded shaking feeling the events of the last few days catch up to me. Tucking my face into his body I stayed there for long moments as the people moved around me.

ADAMANTLY, NATE REFUSED TO LET ANY OF US RETURNED TO THE townhouse after the dead body. He insisted we move on and because he knew I was particular to the Primrose? He had everyone moved in there that night.

Nigel and Bonnie got their own space, Nigel unable to keep his hands off her. The two of the were emotional and I thought this experience might've jarred him as much as her.

Nathan insisted on paying for everything handling it for us and for once I was reminded he had his own money.

Nate ordered enough room service to feed an army and insisted we both just relax.

"I think Nigel's gotten tired of pretending he's fine with being friends with Bonnie," Nate said eating with me. "Thank fuck."

I felt a light laugh bubble up despite the events of the night. "I was so worried about you when I heard that shot go off," I kept saying it. Kept kissing him to reassure myself he was there.

Navy eyes landed on me full of emotion and something softer there.

"I wasn't gonna let that bitch take me out anymore. I was going to make sure I walked out of there right to you."

I felt my eyes watering for the ninetieth time that night.

"Eat, Duchess," he murmured. "You'll need the fuel." He motioned to my plate of food I'd been picking at.

"Alisha says they serve great brunch here," I murmured. "She comes here all the time. You haven't heard about Avani?"

Nate shook his head looking out of it as I felt. "Reed's probably got that one. I am worried about the kid though, we should check on her."

And my heart warmed at hearing him say that.

We both had been through a lot.

Liam had checked in with us and let us know that a minor oversight on his part had led him to slipping when alerting us about Camilla's last minute trip.

But it hadn't mattered. Camilla was gone.

Nate ate dinner and went to shower and it was when the sound of rushing water filled the room that I heard the knock at the door.

I froze after all the events of that night as I heard the paper sliding through the bottom of the door. I stilled as I looked down.

Nate had told me Bonnie and Nigel had instructions to not come into our room tonight. So it wasn't hotel staff.

After what happened with Camilla I was extra cautious.

I looked down at the white paper as it was offensive to my existence catching the feminine script on it.

Come to the dining room.

Don't bring Wyatt.

SEVENTY-THREE
GEMMA

I FROZE MY MIND SPINNING.

What was this? That feeling from my townhouse came back, the back of my neck hairs prickling. *What*? Leave Nate?

Everything in me screamed something wrong about this. The shower was still running, giving me a moment to breathe.

It was a woman's handwriting.

Who was this? I didn't want to sneak out around Nate.

He was my team. I needed to tell him.

I didn't want to do anything without him anymore.

I folded the note into fours. Eighths. My heart racing. Whoever it was. She knew...*she knows his name.*

Which meant...she knew...

I looked at the shower door.

The curiosity was going to kill me. It was. Or she was.

I grabbed Nate's gun remembering he'd shown me a long time to shoot.

He talked enough about it for me to know how to use it.

I tucked it into my purse and slipped into my jacket as I put my hotel slippers on.

The elevator ride felt ominous like I was descending into danger and I don't know why—I had never been a coward and I wasn't about to start now.

Only a few guests remained in the dining room, at this late of an hour it turned into a space where it just felt like twilight. Somewhere between evening and midnight.

My eyes were sweeping over the female diners until they landed on a singular one and my heart raced.

It's her.

It's her.

She called me here.

I just knew it.

I slowly began walking towards her. Some of the guests shifted a little bit and I wondered if they knew how terrified I was.

I wondered if they knew that I was carrying a gun. I wonder if they knew that Camilla had died in my house tonight. I wonder if they knew that I would be moving out of the townhouse as soon as humanly possible.

But they didn't know any of that.

When I rounded the corner, though, the scream that was trapped in my throat stayed there.

Mon. Dieu.

The eyes that looked up at me were the spitting image of Camilla's. That face. Her entire disposition. My jaw dropped as I saw her.

"Camilla…"

Her eyes widened in recognition her voice soft. "No. Not quite. Gemma. It's nice to finally meet you."

Who….

She even sounded like Camilla. My heart was going to explode.

She slowly stood and I saw her reach to balance herself on the table. She was shorter than me, platinum blonde hair, bright eerie blue eyes as she smiled.

Innocent and youthful with how she watched me.

"Who—who are you?"

Her smile turned mischievous with full dimples at my expression almost shy as her eyes met mine. *How old was she?*

"My name's Natasha. Natasha Nash. Camilla was my—"

"Your *mother*." My hand moved over my mouth. "Your Camilla's daughter…"

412

I never thought Camilla had kids. But looking at her, it was unmistakable. I couldn't breathe.

"*Yikes*. That obvious huh?"

I needed to sit down.

"How is that possible?" I whispered. "She doesn't have any kids. How are you—"

Hang on.

Natasha.

Nash.

Natasha.

The girl from years ago. *Camilla...Talia...*

"You're Malcolm Nash's daughter?"

That makes her Talia's sister...and mine.

Technically. Camilla is my stepmother.

If my eyes grew any wider I would've collapsed in shock, my heart was racing. Camilla had an affair with Malcolm Nash.

"I'm related to Talia too?"

She grinned wide at me looking amused.

"Not exactly. Just me. And I'm not related to Talia. I just took the Nash name because of her father. He was kind enough to let me use it once Camila didn't want me."

Her eyes looked almost sad and it was weird. Because I kept seeing a young Camilla—once when she'd been beautiful and not a harpy.

"Why didn't you want me to bring Nate? He would've wanted to meet you."

Her eyes softened on me as though she were sympathetic of me.

"Why would he want to meet me? I killed Camilla."

And just like that my stomach dropped into my body.

"Figured it out yet?" she asked quietly tipping her head to the side holding a glint to them I didn't recognize but I also knew looked awfully familiar. *Talia looks the same.*

"It took me a second to come to you..."

"How do you know about me? Why didn't I know about you?"

"You might want to have a seat."

"Nate, he's going to freak out—"

"I don't think the Titan's are fond of us—"

"*What*? Nate isn't a Titan—"

"Yes, he is. He always will be." She leaned back watching me and I realized how much smaller she was compared to me.

"How old are you?"

"I just turned twenty-one," she shrugged lightly. "You grow up fast as a Nash. Talia's still getting used to me even now."

She didn't sound like Camilla, but the resemblance was striking, her features much sharper and in a way I realized had it not been for Camilla's personality she might have been pretty.

"How—why? Why did you kill…" I couldn't even breathe at finding out I had a stepsister…let alone…one that was a Nash.

"She took my legs, I took her life," Natasha murmured sipping her drink. "Do you know why Malcolm Nash adopted me, Gem?"

"No," I whispered confused and thrown by her.

"Because Camilla didn't want me."

Natasha stated everything as a matter of fact.

And it was even more eerie knowing she looked like Camilla as she said it.

"Malcolm was kind," Natasha shrugged. "I was nine when I got into an accident with her in the car. She was complaining about me wanting a candy bar at the grocery store. She said only evil fat girls wanted food. I still remember the truck that hit us. I remember everything."

I blinked as Natasha told me her story.

"I needed surgery. I had it. Camilla felt forced to pay for it. When I was in bed unable to move, Camilla told me she would starve me post surgery to lose weight."

She held up her wrists which were skinny enough to begin with. As I listened—horrified.

"Now, you can lose that baby fat, she said," Natasha murmured with a smile that didn't meet her eyes. "Did she tell you that too?"

"The pancakes…" I whispered it realizing my nightmare had been Natasha's. "But…"

I looked at her legs and realized then I'd missed her cane. Long and silver and elegant.

Natasha was…disabled? Handicapped? I didn't know.

"Camilla never let me get physical therapy and said that I hadn't earned it enough. She said that I was defective and so why would she

414

waste any more money that she had on me? She said me being a girl was a drain on her financial resources."

I felt my hands shaking in rage.

By that account I had gotten off easy. Because the most horrific thing was—I believed every single thing Natasha said. I did.

"Did she tell everyone you were faking it for attention?" I whispered knowing where this was going.

I knew because Camilla was a narcissistic mother.

If I thought that she treated me badly, Natasha was her biological daughter, and this is how she treated her.

"Camilla once told Malcolm, a long time, that a lame horse needs to be put down. And if she had known what I was, she would've had me put down when I was a baby. And that was my mother on a good day."

"I'm sorry. You didn't deserve any of that."

"No."

Natasha shook her head pouting a little and I realized...she couldn't be older than Avani.

My vision blurred at how calmly Natasha relayed this to me.

"Malcolm stole from your father for years," she swallowed as she continued looking uncomfortable now. "I'm here to give you your cut. I've been tracking Camilla for a while, waiting. One of my girls tonight Renata, told me she was in the city. I just moved a little slower tonight." She motioned to her cane. "Feet hurt."

My head was spinning with the information, but at the horror.

Camilla had done worse to her blood than me.

"You shot Camilla?"

"No," she smiled. "Renata did. But I was there giggling in the background eating snacks. Perks of being Talon."

Talon?

Her smile was maniacal and I wondered what years and years of Camilla would do to someone's brain.

What mental torture did to a human being.

I saw the look in Natasha's eyes. Someone haunted and drained. Someone abused for years and brought out into the reality of her world.

"Did...Talia ever help you?"

"She's the only reason I can walk," Natasha murmured. "I'm here because I wanted to meet my step-sister after Talia realized we might be related."

I blinked. "What?"

"Talia thought about it when she first met you and did some digging. She said it made sense since I looked like Camilla."

I didn't even know how to speak as Natasha just hit me with what felt like multiple bombshells.

"Thank you, you saved Nate's life..." And mine.

"I also dropped a few billion into your bank account for Haven. Thought you and your friend might like that."

"You didn't have to do that. I don't need the money—"

"No, but everyone else in Haven might," she leaned back. "Those women are just like me. It's the least I could do."

I didn't understand why she was saying all this so easily.

I shook my head. "Malcolm Nash was stealing from the Marchand's...how?"

Now she looked uncomfortable.

"Camilla siphoned money from your father for seven years to fund Talon, the security group that grew under my father. Malcolm. I didn't know until I came into control of his business when he passed away. Talia gave me control over Nash Group."

Something else was in her eyes as she said it. Like she knew why he died.

"Talon?"

"Nash Group's security company. I oversee it. But I have someone else running it in New York. Nobody knows. I'm returning your money. And I wanted to meet another sister."

"You're visiting *her* in the city?"

"I am."

"Talia...she knew...you were my—"

"Yes." Natasha answered. "But my sister likes to keep everyone's secrets. Dead bodies. Ghosts. *Missing* wives." She winked. "Talia usually knows everything you're searching for. She just won't tell."

I felt like Natasha was hinting at something.

Missing people. Ghosts. Nate's world. Not mine.

I didn't understand what she was saying.

I was sitting there feeling like I had been hit with too much.

"This feels like a weird dream."

"It probably is," she laughed lightly and her face was so eerily like Camilla's I couldn't stop trembling.

"You look so much like your mother," I whispered.

"I know." She tipped her head to the side looking sad. "I wanted to let you in a little so you knew who I was. Go back to Wyatt, Gemma. Before he thinks I'm killing you." She stood slowly. "I'll be in touch. I sit in Nash Group if you need me. It's not too far from Titan Midtown. And if you ever need our help—"

"Our—"

"Talon."

Her cane was in her hand and as she stood, everyone else in the room did too.

"If you ever need our help, we'll come." She smiled politely. "Talon is where Malcolm funneled the money into. Technically, it belongs to you as well since it was your money that built it."

I didn't understand what she was saying. I just knew every single woman in the room that stood was with Natasha. Every single one.

"I'm leaving now. Let me know if you ever need me, sis."

At those words my chest tightened.

"Mon Dieu, they are all with you."

"I'm disabled, *not* an idiot. What if Wyatt got curious?"

"Why don't you want—"

"Another time, sis?" She smiled. "I have to go."

I sat there breathing hard for a moment as Natasha giggled like a kid and left me there stumped.

And then I knew I needed to run to Nate before he began breaking down doors.

As I made it to the elevator the doors opened, and Nate stood there his towel around his waist, abs gloriously glistening, messy blonde hair.

I met hard navy eyes head on as he looked frantic at me.

SEVENTY-FOUR
NATE

"Duchess—"

"I'm all right." I was in his arms a second later. "I promise I'm all right, but you are not going to believe this…"

"Don't scare me like that—"

"Were you planning on frightening the women to death?" I wrapped myself around him. "Please tell me you know what Talon is—"

"Never heard of it."

"That's what I was thinking…"

What?

Free?

I never wanted to be free of her.

She smiled. "You are no longer my guard. Your contract is over. Now that Camilla isn't around—I have no more threats—"

"That you know of, Duchess. What happens when someone tries to hurt you at an event or—" I broke off imagining the horror of ever losing Gemma.

"Well…I was actually hiring full time—"

"For a new guard?"

"Perhaps."

"Perhaps?"

My blood boiled at the thought of another man's hands on Gemma ever. Let alone her finding a new guard after almost losing her several times.

Her eyes twinkled. "Well, I was thinking the position was already filled."

And then it dawned on me. "Damn, baby."

Her laughter was musical. "You looked so offended."

"I was." Gemma's laughter mingled with mine. "What you got in mind after making me have a heart attack?"

"I can think of a few things."

"Like?"

Her hands strayed lower to my towel where my dick was very aware he was in bed with Gemma.

"I don't know," she shrugged playfully. "I'm sure we'll think of something." Gemma kissed her way down my chest lightly.

"Still thinking about it?" I wheezed.

"Mhm."

I held my breath as Gemma's tongue darted out over my stomach.

Lower.

"Duchess…"

"Let me…"

And so I did.

STROKE OF TEMPTATION

Titans Book 6
Stroke of Temptation

Avani Malhotra & Thierry "Reaper" DuPont

Pre-Order Avani's Book Here

INTRODUCING 'UNDERWORLD KINGS'

~

<u>Book I</u>
Legacy

Killian O'Hara and Nisha Graham

Book II

Aidan O'Hara & Sonya Amin

STROKE OF LUCK: BOOK I

He's the the last man I ever saw coming…

Sexy. Seductive. Sinful.

I had no room in my carefully planned life for romance.

Especially not one dangerous man hellbent on proving he's the right man for me.

But Reed Whittaker has always had a way of tearing down every wall I built with precision.

So when I find myself trapped with nowhere to turn, he becomes my only hope for survival. The only man who can protect me. The one man who would burn the world down to keep me safe.

He's a man known for being ruthless and dangerous.

Now? He's mine.
Except I don't know if his luck will run out before he can save me.

Or if the secrets of his world will consume us both.

425

But I know one thing.

Reed will stop at nothing to make me his.

His woman.
His life.
His love.

And I'm helpless to resist.

Get Reed and Alisha's Story

AUTHOR'S NOTE

Thank you so much for all the love and support you've given The Titan Series.

I cannot thank you guys enough for everything. If you like this book please leave a review, it helps an author so much!

Love,

Lilah

ABOUT THE AUTHOR

Lilah Lance has been writing for about twenty-two years now.

When Lilah isn't writing she likes to travel and spend her downtime on the beach.

For more info, check out www.lilahlance.com where you can subscribe to her newsletter for all things exclusively Titan.